M

M:

CW00348908

Murder
on the
Marshes

CLARE CHASE

Bookouture

Published by Bookouture in 2018

An imprint of StoryFire Ltd.

Carmelite House
50 Victoria Embankment
London EC4Y 0DZ

www.bookouture.com

ISBN: 978-1-78681-431-9
eBook ISBN: 978-1-78681-430-2

For Charlie, George and Ros – and new beginnings

PROLOGUE

The house had been clean. Even now, the smell of bleach brought flashbacks with it.

But almost all the details of that day were still clear. It was as though shock had fixed them – like a permanent negative print in the brain.

There was the silence. An emptiness that was wholly unusual and unnerving. Going from room to room revealed an almost clinical atmosphere; the place was so bare.

The kitchen taps had gleamed. That came back clearly.

And then a feeling of time slowing down at the sight of each vacant room, until there was just one door left unopened. Memories of looking at the unturned handle were suffused with a feeling of dread. 'A cold sweat' wasn't just an expression.

And then the sound of the door creaking, and the scene inside. She was in there, of course, hanging. Her face was in shadow; the curtains were drawn. It was just her outline, her feet dangling, her hair long and as limp as she was. A shell.

It was impossible to move, forward or back. The horror extended from seconds into minutes. And then the voice came from behind.

'Come on, it's the end she deserved.' It was said in a matter-of-fact tone. 'You must have known this was coming. It's better this way in the long run.'

CHAPTER ONE

Twenty years later

It was the hooded figure that shocked Tara out of her alcohol-induced haze that night. She'd travelled the length of Riverside without noticing her surroundings – too bound up with the events of the day, its edges blurred by several shots of vodka. The sight of the person, standing perfectly still ahead of her, brought her back to reality. It was just a silhouette in the distance, almost invisible in the shadows of Stourbridge Common. She stared, but it was impossible to resolve the dark shape into anything more detailed. Someone from one of the houseboats? Or heading back towards Fen Ditton after an evening out in Cambridge? Perhaps they'd stopped for a pee or something. Behind them the open ground stretched on, empty and fading into blackness.

Tara glanced at her watch. Just past eleven thirty. To her left the river Cam looked inky black in the moonless night. A couple of sleeping swans floated motionless on the water, their heads tucked under their wings. To her right, the few houses in the terrace just before the gate that led onto the common were already in darkness, their windows blank. Her own home was still ahead of her – a tiny Victorian cottage, built on no-man's-land, surrounded by the meadows – across a dark expanse of open space. Closer to the figure.

Pretty much everyone had warned her against buying the place, but too much good advice could be annoying. It had been years since she'd had any trouble, and all things being equal, she liked her own space.

Not taking her eyes off the figure, she pushed the rusty swing gate open to make her way onto the common. Its creak was loud and jarring in the hot, silent night.

She ploughed on towards home, waiting for the person to move off.

They didn't. They were beyond her house still, not so far off now.

What on earth were they up to? Was this someone playing games? Wanting to scare her?

They stood there, absolutely still, facing dead in her direction. Then suddenly she was dazzled by a beam of light. There were no lamps on the side path where the figure waited, so the glare from their torch stood out, strong and startling. They adjusted the beam slightly – down onto her T-shirt – and then straight back into her eyes.

And then they did it again.

Gut instinct took over. The taste of fear was all too familiar, despite the passing of time. Her breathing turned quick and shallow. She swallowed as a shiver overtook her. Fight or flight.

She glanced to her house, then to the figure, then over her shoulder to Riverside. Her house was nearest. Better to get there and lock herself in than run back the way she'd come and risk being outpaced. She could knock on a door for help, but the houses that were in darkness might be empty. And in the time it took to check, the figure would get closer still. In a second the beam of the torch dropped – fully this time. All she could see was the long grass in front of where they stood.

She strode forward, towards her home. It was sectioned off from the rest of the common at the back by a half-rotten wooden fence, and at the front by nothing more than a knee-high brick wall. She was ready to run if the stranger did. As it was she kept to a fast pace, up on her toes, primed – watching, always watching. She was damned if she was going to let them see she was scared. Unless she had to…

As she propelled herself on, she felt for the personal alarm in her jeans pocket. *Useless.* Who would hear it, out there on the common? And didn't people always assume alarms had been triggered by accident, anyway? She did. With her right hand she fished her keys out of her other pocket, ready.

She kept her eyes on the figure as she approached the house. They'd started walking and she upped her pace. They were getting closer. But she was almost there now. She took a gulp of air as she rushed through her front gate and shifted her focus to the door's Yale lock. She pushed the key home and turned it. In the last second before she disappeared inside she looked over her shoulder. The hooded figure had moved quietly and rapidly forward.

She pushed the door shut behind her and leant against it, listening. For a moment all she could hear was her own ragged breathing. After she'd controlled it, she listened again. Nothing.

If she went to the sitting room she'd be able to see them – whichever way they were heading.

As she stepped forward she realised there must have been something on the edge of the doormat. She heard it slide off onto the wooden floorboards just after she'd kicked it. But she didn't stop to pick it up or turn on the light.

From the bay window in the sitting room she was able to peek at the figure from behind one of the inherited chintz curtains. It was still on the move. They'd gone beyond her house now, towards Riverside and town. They'd be off the common in seconds, ready to disappear down any one of the many side streets and into a rabbit warren of Victorian terraces. Pointless to call the police. They'd never be able to identify the right person, even if they could make it in time. And besides, shining a torch into someone's face wasn't exactly an arrestable offence. Maybe the figure had never been following her in the first place? Maybe they'd always been intent on making their way through to Riverside, and she'd given *them* a fright.

But then they paused at the common's gateway and turned once more in her direction. The beam of their torch swung towards her window. They knew she'd be watching.

She felt her heart rate ramp up again. It wasn't fear now, but anger – anger that they'd had such an effect on her. She'd had enough of being played to last her a lifetime.

She went back to the hall, switched on the light and pushed off her Converse without bothering with the laces. It was only then that she remembered the thing she'd kicked off the doormat. It was a packet – an A4-size Jiffy bag with her name and address printed on the label. She thought again of the figure and goosebumps rose on her arms. Had they left her a present? It was hardly usual to get something hand delivered on a Tuesday night. Her fingers trembled as she picked it up, making her grit her teeth.

She carried it through to the kitchen by one of its corners. First things first. She needed to clear her head. She put it down on the table and went to fetch a glass from the dresser. She'd probably been dehydrated when she'd started her pub session with Matt – another hack on the publication she worked for. *Shit.* She should have stopped about three drinks before she had. Not that she ever got crazy drunk; that would be too reckless. She'd let down her guard that evening after a testing meeting earlier with Giles, her editor. If it weren't for him she would be sober – or at least more sober – and she wouldn't be getting so freaked out over some stranger in the dark.

She went to the freezer and half-filled a tumbler with the contents of her ice tray before topping the glass up with chilled water from the fridge. She drank it down straight before she went back to the table to look at the packet. It had been years, but still the standard checklist came back to her. No sign of any grease or powder on the outside of the envelope. No strange smells. The advice that a ticking sound, protruding wires or exposed foil were bad signs had always struck her as supremely unnecessary... This package had none of those things, but it was lopsided. That had been on the checklist. She risked feeling the shape gently. It was soft, but firm; rounded, and bulkier at one end than the other.

She sat down and carefully peeled back the sticky seal of the envelope. Looking inside, she frowned.

It was a doll.

She put her hand in to pull it out. The moment she saw the thing clearly she dropped it on the table.

The doll was made from cloth, neatly hand-sewn, with black wool hair reaching down to its waist. It was dressed in a nondescript white top and blue skirt, but that was the only normal thing about it.

Around its neck was a noose – pulled tight – and its white cotton face had been dusted with some kind of blue powder. It ought to have looked ridiculous – the details the sender had added, coupled with the doll's bright, fixed smile and her big blue eyes, both of which had been stitched in satin. But the combination made it all the more nightmarish.

On its feet were embroidered blue shoes that matched the skirt.

The shivers were starting up again. She couldn't stop them. She gripped the sides of the chair she was sitting on and tried to focus on controlling her body's reaction. Breathe in for four, count four, out for four. The combat breathing Kemp had taught her. But already she was feeling light-headed and a little sick.

It took a minute before Tara was ready to go back to the packet. At last she picked it up again and looked inside for any other enclosure. She found one single sheet of paper with a typed message.

It was a warning. This is a warning.

CHAPTER TWO

Tara considered getting the hell out. She could try to find a cheap hotel. She didn't want to. Didn't want someone controlling what she did. Though if she ignored the most sensible options just out of bloody-mindedness that was still letting them win. But heading out would mean crossing the common again, even if she called a cab to pick her up. There was no vehicular access to her house. She could use her bike, but that would involve fiddling about in the dark outside, which could put her in danger. And if she went for her own car she'd have to enter that same network of streets that the figure was probably walking that very moment. Parking in the Riverside area was a free-for-all. Her Fiat was halfway up Garlic Row. It was better to shore up her defences where she was. Shame she hadn't got as far as doing any maintenance on the house since she'd moved in.

She focused hard on practicalities, moving from door to window, checking each lock and catch, making sure they were all as secure as their state of repair would allow. Once she knew she'd done all she could she called the police.

The operator sounded calm. She supposed that to him someone posting a rag doll with a threatening note through a letterbox sounded more like an unpleasant prank than something serious. And of course, he could be right. But when she told him about her past he seemed to warm up a bit.

The guy asked if she lived alone, and then if she could call someone. (She could, but no one who could help.) Then he asked her to check that the figure with the torch hadn't come back. She walked to the sitting room window and tweaked the curtain marginally to look out. The lamps that ran next to the Cam gave the pathway below an eerie glow. All around, everything was still. A few of the swans from the river were standing up on the bank, asleep, like the ones on the water. But away from the path and between the pools of sickly light there were shadows. She went back to the kitchen to look towards Fen Ditton. There, the night had an even greater hold.

'I can't see anyone,' she said, but that wasn't saying much.

He promised that an officer would be round to talk to her about the 'incident' the following day and told her to call again if she was worried. Then he mentioned the idea of going to stay with friends. She didn't bother explaining the practical considerations.

Instead, she went to the kitchen drawer and took out all the cooking knives. She wasn't planning on using them herself – she of all people knew run-ins could lead to trouble – but equally she didn't fancy leaving a Sabatier around for an intruder's convenience. She carried them upstairs carefully, watching their blades as they glinted in the pale landing light. For a second she looked around, thinking, but then she remembered the lockable suitcase she'd got in her bedroom cupboard. She stowed the knives away and put the key in her bedside drawer.

Then she walked around the house, looking for anything that might be useful. The wedge she used for the kitchen door. Hairspray. Some unopened scented body powder. Marbles from an elegant solitaire set she'd succumbed to at an antique fair. A selection of tin cans. Foil. She put the marbles on the bottom two steps of the stairs once she was beyond them. After that she set about bunching up the foil in pleats and spreading it over the small landing before turning out the light. If anyone trod on it, it ought to be enough to alert her. The cans, hairspray and powder went by her bed. Bombarding an intruder with a combination of the three should buy her some time. Finally, she shut herself into her bedroom and jammed the wedge under her door to make it hard to open from the outside.

At last, she slumped down onto a chair she'd pulled up close to the window.

Why me? Why me again? She blinked hard and pushed the thought away. Self-pity was a waste of time.

She'd sit up until the first dog walkers, rowers and joggers appeared outside. After that she'd sleep.

If she could.

As she waited, her eyes wide and dry, she thought of the precautions she'd taken. The marbles, the talcum powder. Kids' stuff. At last, she got up stiffly and went back to her bedside drawer, took out her suitcase key and went to the cupboard.

Moments later, she was seated again, gripping one of the kitchen knives tightly in her right hand. As she stared ahead into the night, she felt a tic start up in her cheek.

CHAPTER THREE

At seven in the morning, DI Garstin Blake was standing in the fellows' garden of St Bede's College, Cambridge, looking at a dead woman.

The heat that had oppressed the city for weeks now was already building. Blake felt a wave of it wash over him. For a second, instead of the stranger's body, he saw his wife's. Two months earlier he'd imagined killing her and the vision still haunted him. It had been short-lived – a split-second image of a blow packed with the force of all his feelings. In an instant it had gone – his rage doused by despair – but he'd still had it. That could never be undone. How much distance was there between him and a killer? Did you just have to be standing opposite the person who'd driven you to the brink when that feeling of rage took over? What if you were holding the right weapon and added drugs or alcohol to the mix?

But there had to be more to it than that. Even the idea of his spontaneous vision filled him with horror. He closed his eyes tight for a second. He wished to God he could wipe it from his memory.

The scene in front of him didn't look like the result of uncontrolled anger. In fact, it reminded him of a canvas, its composition carefully thought out. That was his mother's doing. Being brought up by a professor of art history had left its mark. He didn't mention his family background much at work and his mother didn't tell her chums about his job either. They didn't see eye to eye on the best way to spend a working day, but they'd learnt to live with it.

Thanks to her, the scene made Blake think of Millais's *Ophelia*. It was partly the intense greens in front of him and the water that did it – not a river in this case but a fountain in the centre of the garden. But most especially it was the sense of regret. Ophelia in Millais's painting was singing just before she drowned whereas the woman in front of him, slumped over the edge of the fountain, the bottom half of her body still quite dry, was very definitely dead already. But with both there was that aching feeling of a tragedy that might have been averted. The woman here in the garden, struggling alone, slipping from having a future to being beyond help… the idea gave him a sharp pain that stuck in his chest.

One of her arms dangled in the fountain too. The other was bent at the elbow and rested on its stone edging. Unlike Ophelia, she hadn't been driven to self-destruction; some bastard had made that call for her.

Moving all over the picture in front of him were CSIs, operating efficiently, going about their work, all dressed head to toe in their white protective gear, just as he was.

One stood photographing the woman's body. The guy shifted position frequently, getting her from all angles. A second was videoing the woman and her surroundings. The garden was still caught in the shadows of early morning but there was enough light for their work.

Blake was after every detail too; the only useful thing he could do now was to catch the person who'd done this. Cut off emotion and zone-in on the job in hand. He could already feel a hundred questions jostling in his mind.

For a start, what kind of killer would choose this setting? The garden had a feeling of being totally separate: a high-walled haven for a very select few. The russet bricks kept the idyll hidden from the hoi polloi; luxurious for those who had access, distancing and hierarchical for those who didn't. Blake had always thought that allowing such privileges for fellows whilst denying them to other hard-working staff was stupidly divisive. Cambridge was full of little rules and traditions that set people apart. He ought to know; he'd been brought up in the thick of it. But did that have any bearing on what had happened here?

The choice of crime scene was certainly going to get the killer plenty of attention. The press wouldn't bother disguising their satisfaction at its staginess. All around, the colours were intense: the deep greens of the late-summer foliage on the trees and shrubs, the hot pinks and intense blues of rock roses and cornflowers. The fragrant smell of grass and flowers filled the air. And then in the middle of it all the deathly pale skin of a drowned woman. As for the college fellows – well, they'd be asking each other questions. High table at formal hall would be a strained affair for a while to come. He wished he could be a fly on the wall. Who knew what might be revealed amongst the whispered sniping?

The fellows each had a key to the gate. Ornate iron ones would have matched the garden's style, but even in this rarefied place the twenty-first century had made its mark. It had been Professor Ernest Haverstock who'd found the murdered woman and he'd used an electronic key card to get in at – so he'd said – six that morning. And because of that modern digital arrangement, they'd been able to check.

Blake walked over to the garden's gateway, which was currently open, to view an area of lawn beyond. The aforementioned professor was sitting on a bench there, in the middle of the grass, being comforted by Jill, one of the PCs who'd been first on the scene. He was a frail-looking man with wispy white hair. He still clutched the copy of the *Times Literary Supplement* he'd been intending to read in what he'd probably imagined would be early morning tranquillity. Blake hadn't been surprised when the St Bede's security team had confirmed his time of entry. The guy didn't have the air of a hardened killer.

Both the garden and the grassland were college property, and the CCTV coverage wasn't extensive. Still, it might yield something, and the location had at least made it easier to get the area locked down. The outside world rumbled on in the distance. Beyond the grass, Blake could see the rush-hour traffic queueing along Queen's Road.

That was Cambridge for you. He wouldn't live anywhere else, but it was an odd city. Everything collided inside its compact boundaries: the ancient and the modern, the rare and the humdrum, the haves and the have-nots. And now, back in the garden, one of the most intensely beautiful scenes he'd ever witnessed was a backdrop to one of the most chilling.

At that moment, the pathologist, Agneta Larsson, appeared in the garden's gateway. She held up a gloved hand in greeting and raised her eyebrows from over the top of the face mask she wore. 'So, Blake,' she said, 'when I saw the man sitting out there on the bench I thought for a moment I'd found my corpse. Then he opened his eyes. Gave me the fright of my life.'

Blake managed a flicker of a smile. 'He doesn't look too chipper, does he? Jill's called his doctor.'

Agneta nodded. 'Just as well.' She turned towards the dead woman and Blake heard her sigh. He went to crouch by the body too. The smell of pond weed hit him as he got closer to the water.

The victim was clothed all in black: a long-sleeved top, leggings of some kind and curious-looking shoes. She looked young – thirties at most.

'You're not going to breathe down my neck, are you?' Agneta said, giving him a look.

'That's just exactly what I had in mind.' He'd known her a long time. Been out with her, in fact, before he'd met his wife. He was glad they were still good friends at least.

She was saved by one of the CSIs who came over to have a word. He stood to talk to them.

'The zip pocket of her leggings contained a wallet with a couple of business cards in it,' the woman said. 'They show her to be Samantha Seabrook, Professor of Childhood Inequality at the Cambridge Institute for Social Studies. The name matches the University ID card that was also on her, and that's got her photo on it.'

Professor? She didn't look anywhere near old enough. 'Thanks. Any indication she was attached to St Bede's?'

The CSI shook her head. 'None that we've found. She wasn't carrying a key card for this place. She hadn't got a phone on her, by the way. Maybe the killer took it.'

Blake turned towards his detective sergeant, Emma Marshall, who had been talking to another of the CSIs. 'Emma? Find out which college Professor Samantha Seabrook was attached to, would you?'

'Boss.' She walked over to the garden gateway and spoke to someone outside.

If someone else had let the professor in, it hadn't happened overnight. The security team at the college had already confirmed that no one had used a key card to enter the gardens between five thirty the previous evening and when Professor Haverstock had arrived. Other members of Blake's team were checking out the seven fellows who'd visited the previous day. He was impatient to hear the results, but only so he could officially rule those visitors out.

On the face of it, the last one could have let Samantha Seabrook in as a guest, either killing her or leaving her inside alive for whatever reason. But Blake had already abandoned that idea. At five thirty the previous day the heat had still been intense. The dead woman would have sweltered in the clothes she was wearing. He was putting his money on an illicit night-time visit. And if she hadn't got in using a card…

'Blake?' Agneta's voice brought him back to the here and now. She looked up at him from where she was kneeling, next to

Samantha Seabrook's body, her head cocked. 'So you can probably guess what I'm going to say,' she said. 'First impression, asphyxia brought about by drowning. I hope you're impressed.'

'Overawed.'

Her eyes gave away her smile. 'Thank you. I'll be able to confirm everything later, but I would guess that if she'd been drinking – or had taken anything – it hadn't affected her much.' She pointed to Samantha Seabrook's hands. 'She struggled hard to push herself up out of the water. Her palms are heavily abraded. I would say her attacker got her in just the position he or she wanted.'

'I wonder how they achieved that?' Blake said.

Agneta's eyes told him she had a theory. 'Look here.'

He moved so that he could see where she pointed, under the water. There, on the fountain's base, he saw a pile of coins; maybe six or so – enough to have made the dead woman curious, if her killer had pointed them out to her.

'It would fit if she'd crouched down to look,' Agneta said. 'My guess is her attacker was able to hold her from behind, in such a way that all she could do was try to shove her way up by bracing her hands on the fountain's base. I don't think she'd have been able to reach any part of the person who killed her.'

Such careful planning.

'Did you notice the pendant?' Agneta asked.

He bent closer to look. It was a crucifix, wound tightly round the woman's throat. He watched the pathologist's eyes. 'What's on your mind?'

'The marking under the chain makes me think it was twisted to and fro.'

He could see where it had cut into her skin. He turned away for just a second, but then forced himself to face the scene again. The pendant would certainly carry Samantha Seabrook's DNA, and maybe the killer's too.

As one, they glanced at the surface of the fountain. It was covered in floating hair. The perpetrator must have yanked at the professor's scalp to control her movements and force her head under the water. 'What about time of death?' Blake asked.

Agneta gave him a look. 'Two thirty-seven and twenty seconds this morning.'

'Blimey.'

Once again, the ghost of a smile showed in the pathologist's eyes. 'Her watch ended up in the fountain and I guess it wasn't waterproof. Of course, it might not have stopped instantly if the water took a while to seep in, so it could have been a little earlier. But the general estimate fits roughly with rigor too.'

'She's quite petite,' Blake said.

Agneta nodded. 'It would have made her more vulnerable. And if the attack was from behind and entirely unexpected...'

'The killer wouldn't have had to be very strong?'

Agneta nodded. 'As you say. I should have more detail for you by late morning.'

'Thanks.'

A team was gathering now, ready to move the body. They looked like strangely clad aliens in that traditional place. Nearby, a blackbird sang. Blake's phone rang. He glanced at the screen. DS Patrick Wilkins. Mr Smooth himself. 'Blake.'

'Boss, I wanted to let you know we've spoken to the person who entered the garden at five thirty yesterday: the last official visitor we've got down before Professor Haverstock this morning.'

'Good. What's the news?'

'It was a Dr Jenny Devlin. She came with two other members of the college's academic staff. I've got their names. She says they closed the gate after them, both on the way in and on the way out. And they all left together without noticing anything unusual. I've managed to track down one of the other two as well, a Dr Harry Field, and his story matches hers. I'll get on to the third, but—'

'But it looks watertight.' An unfortunate expression under the circumstances. 'Thanks, Patrick.' He rang off. It was as he'd thought. Leaving aside some kind of larger conspiracy, Samantha Seabrook couldn't have come into the garden with the last group of legitimate visitors. No – it had to have been an illicit night-time visit. He walked over to DS Emma Marshall.

'Professor Seabrook was a fellow of St Francis's College,' she said when he got closer.

'Thanks.' He stared up at the garden's high brick walls and she followed his gaze. They were worn, with mortar missing in several places. 'Not an easy climb,' Blake said, 'but not impossible. Besides, there's no other way in, assuming Samantha Seabrook and her killer weren't winched down by helicopter.'

Emma nodded. 'And apropos of that, one of the CSIs has just found a pair of thought-provoking gloves.'

Blake raised an eyebrow. Emma nodded towards a white-suited woman holding an evidence bag and he went over to her.

'Fingerless climbing gloves with grips on the palms,' she said when he asked, opening the bag for him to see.

'They look small enough to have been the victim's.'

She nodded. 'I'd say so. We can do more checks on them.'

Blake turned back to Emma. 'Let's go and look at the outside walls.'

But as they turned towards the garden's exit, they had to pause. Two men blocked the way. They were carrying Samantha Seabrook's body on a stretcher, under a white cover. He could see from their posture how light she was. What were her family doing now? They'd probably be waking up, going to get themselves a coffee perhaps, fetching the post from their doormat. They'd have no idea that their lives were about to be shattered forever by the worst possible news. Unless of course one of them had been involved...

He shook himself. The exit was clear now and, after catching Emma's eye, they followed the stretcher bearers out.

Blake made sure he and his DS stood a short distance away from the garden walls, but the dry grass around the perimeter didn't look as though it would yield any footprints. The CSIs had also had news of the gloves and were skirting the walls too. Like Blake, they focused on the areas where the mortar was most damaged. The small resulting gaps between the bricks would have made the climb slightly easier – all the same, Blake guessed Samantha Seabrook and whoever had been with her must have had practice. The walls had to be fifteen feet high.

And even then, in the ordinary way, it would be nigh on impossible not to scrape yourself as you scaled such an obstacle. Except if you were dressed from head to toe in durable sports gear, of course. Samantha might still have grazed her fingertips as she'd climbed over but he was willing to bet her killer would have chosen a different style of glove: one that covered his or her whole hand. If they'd been wearing kit that otherwise mirrored Samantha Seabrook's they could have cut the risk of leaving DNA evidence behind to a minimum – and all without making their victim suspicious… Blake shivered in spite of the warm morning air.

Their perpetrator was clever; they probably thought they were quite secure. The chilly unease Blake had felt was replaced by a hot determination. *We're coming to get you*, he made the mental vow. *You might think you're safe, but I'm damned if you'll get away with this. You'd better watch your back.*

CHAPTER FOUR

Tara watched the dawn creep in. She'd spent the first part of the night sitting rigid in her chair, straining to hear any unfamiliar sounds. She'd sat in the dark with the curtains drawn back so that she could see the common. Occasionally a late passer-by had crossed her view: a lone cyclist with a broken back light, and much later someone shuffling along, carrying a bag – a bent shadow. Probably a down and out. It took a while for thoughts that didn't directly relate to self-preservation to crystallise. When they did, Tara focused on the note that had come with the doll.

It was a warning. This is a warning.

'*This is a warning*' was clear enough. The doll sure as hell looked like one. But what about the other part of the message? Was the sender someone from her past, telling her they were back – referring to warnings they'd given her previously? But the gap after last time was huge, and the style and approach were different.

No – more likely this was someone new. But the question remained: what did '*It was a warning*' refer to? Had she missed something? Did the sender mean they'd made a previous attempt to intimidate her and she'd ignored it? And if so, was she running out of time to react in the way they wanted? Whatever that might be.

She sat there, staring out at the dark, her mind working. She'd had to toughen up in her life – it was that or go under. But privately she had to admit she hadn't achieved blasé yet. Surely she'd have picked up on any earlier message, even if it had been oblique?

Maybe the note and the doll were the random act of someone who was totally irrational. That would make it worse. At least someone driven by logic ought eventually to become predictable.

Her mind turned to who might be responsible. What could she tell about the figure on the common? Precious little. They were agile – probably somewhere between their late teens and middle age. Medium height, medium build and as far as she was concerned, faceless. *Great.*

As a journalist she'd upset the occasional person – it went with the territory. And some people felt the publication she worked for, *Not Now* magazine, was edgy; it liked to irk people. Even she knew it was a bit obnoxious – but work was work and it was nice to eat. Besides, her career had had the odd hiccough; she was pretty glad she had any sort of employment. She tried to mitigate *Not Now*'s lower-quality content by doing a professional job. All the same, she didn't mince her words. And then there'd been occasional tensions between her and other people in the profession. But it was four years since the only serious run-in she'd had. She couldn't imagine the guy she'd crossed then would wait until now to get his own back. In any case, this threat was way beyond anything she could imagine resulting from her role.

The thoughts hadn't made her plan to sleep during daylight any more realistic. She lay down on the bed, her eyes dry and wide open, every muscle tensed and ready.

But at last she must have dropped off – at least for a short time. Her mobile ringing jolted her back to consciousness, sending her heart thudding. She grabbed the phone from the bedside table and registered the time as she picked up. Ten fifteen. And the caller was her editor, and the owner of *Not Now* magazine. Perfect...

'*I emailed, asking you to ring me.*' Nice to speak to you too, Giles. On the upside, his economical approach cut down the time she had to spend talking to him. *'I heard you and Matt were out on the tiles last night,'* he went on, *'so I'm guessing that's the reason for your late start.'*

Telling him about the doll would shut him up, but that wasn't going to happen. He'd want to put it up as breaking news on *Not Now*'s website. The publication was a monthly, and still sold unusually well in print, but Giles was making a nice lot from online advertising too. He needed to keep the website's hit-rate high, so he'd leap at the chance to draw in the punters. The news of a death threat against Tara would work well as clickbait. *But no, thank you very much.*

'I had a doctor's appointment,' she said. 'I told you about it yesterday at the editorial meeting. I had a feeling at the time that you weren't listening.' She loved lying to Giles. He so deserved it.

There was a pause. *'I'm a busy man – these things escape me. Someone was probably telling me something important at the same time. Email me next time if you've got an appointment.'*

He was bound to forget he'd asked her to do that too. It was one Giles's more positive traits.

'Anyway,' Tara said. 'What's up? I was just opening my laptop.' Well, she would be, once she'd got downstairs. She slid out of bed and went out onto the landing, lifting the bunched-up foil as quietly as she could.

'Interesting subject for you – only just come in,' Giles said. *'The word is, a body's been found in the fellows' garden at St Bede's.'*

Giles loved a whiff of drama. Tara suspected the fact that this person was dead was far more interesting to him than who they'd been. She stepped round the marbles on the bottom two stairs and went into the kitchen.

'So it was one of their staff then?' she said.

'Puzzlingly not, from what I can gather. Apparently the dead woman is a Samantha Seabrook, Professor of Childhood Inequality.

She was attached to the Cambridge Institute for Social Studies and St Francis's College.'

Okay – so Professor Seabrook did sound like a fascinating person to write about. Maybe Giles's motives were more genuine than usual. But then he added: *'And there's no question of natural causes. She was found drowned in the fountain, apparently. They've no idea who attacked her.'*

Tara's legs felt as though they'd turned liquid. Cambridge wasn't a big place. How likely was it to be coincidence that she'd received a death threat on the very same night as a murder? She was dimly conscious of the relish in Giles's voice as she reached for the kettle. Tucking the phone between her ear and shoulder, she went to add enough water for a coffee.

It wasn't the first time Giles had asked her to write about a murder victim. She was well aware that the articles had led to a spike in sales and she was helping him make money off the back of someone else's misery. But she also felt she was fighting the victim's corner; she made it her mission to ensure they were remembered for themselves, not just for the way they'd been wiped out. All the same, it tended to feel like a compromise.

'How horrible,' she said after a moment. Her words sounded mechanical; her mouth felt dry. 'Was she elderly?'

'Thirty-five.'

Very young for a professor – and far too young to die, whatever the cause.

'She'd still packed a lot in,' Giles said, as though reading her mind. *'Her work would be enough for us to feature her, even if she'd died at home in her bed.'*

Tara took that with a pinch of salt. She spooned coffee into a one-cup cafetière.

'And she's got an interesting background too,' he added. *'Her father, Brian Seabrook, was given a knighthood last year. He's a*

multimillionaire – made his money in publishing. And her mother's dead, but she was an actress – Bella Seabrook – so your mother might have the low-down on her.'

Tara was tempted to say that was a bit like assuming two people from Wales would know each other, but in truth, he was probably right. Acting was something of a small world, and her mother might well have useful background – acquired on the grapevine if not in person. Whether Tara wanted to go asking her for it was another matter. Their history still weighed heavy at times, but at least her mother had insisted on hanging on to her when her father had wanted her to have an abortion. They'd both been teenagers at the time, so Tara was supposed to make allowances.

'And how certain is all this?' she said. 'Where did you get your information from?' She didn't want to go calling the institute where Samantha had worked unless she was sure of her facts.

'Oh, it's certain all right,' Giles said. She could tell he was enjoying his privileged knowledge. *'Matt's already putting it up as breaking news on the website, but I want the full feature and in-depth stuff from you.'*

Matt. He was her one good friend on *Not Now*'s staff. His wry comments about their colleagues were all that kept her going sometimes.

'Okay. And who filled you in on the details so quickly?'

He gave a light laugh. *'I've got contacts everywhere. You know that. Ask me no questions and I'll tell you no lies.'*

God, he was annoying.

'You're safe to call the institute,' he went on. *'You might want to take your lead from them as to when it's appropriate to contact the family though.'*

She was amazed he'd managed to think of that all on his own.

After she'd rung off she finished making her coffee. It was no wonder the police hadn't got back to her about the doll then. They'd be stretched with a murder on their hands. But when they came, they'd probably take it away. Steeling herself, she took it from its packet for a moment and photographed it using her phone. She wanted a record. Realistically, she'd need to investigate it too. It was no use assuming someone else would do a proper job.

Once she'd finished her coffee she went to shower. She'd been wearing the same clothes for over twenty-four hours and it was good to shed them. But time in the bathroom meant time to think...

She stared at the cracked green tiles through the fragmented jets of water. This woman, Samantha Seabrook, ought to have had everything ahead of her. And she'd been researching social injustice – her findings would have made a real a difference. How dare someone take her life away? And who were these bastards who lived in the shadows and went around terrorising people? Tara reached for the shampoo bottle. As she rubbed soap suds hard into her scalp she took herself in hand. She'd won an award for the second article she'd written on a murder victim. She rinsed her hair clean. The fact was, she was more than capable of doing a decent job. Now she was going to do her damnedest to represent Samantha Seabrook's life properly.

And besides, she desperately needed something unrelated to focus on, alongside trying to work out who wanted to do her harm. All the same, it was pretty bloody ironic to use reporting on a murdered woman as therapy.

Dressed and dry, she was just going to her laptop when there was a rap at the door. She went to the sitting room window to check on the caller. A man, somewhere in his thirties, Tara guessed – medium-height, in a well-cut suit. It contrasted with his dishevelled brown hair, stubbly chin and his tie, which looked as though it had been put on in a hurry. Possibly in the dark, in fact. She'd kept herself mostly hidden behind one of the curtains but he spotted her in a fraction of a second. He raised a hand and smiled – accentuating a collection of laughter lines – and dug in his pocket.

It was four years since she'd seen a warrant card. The one he pressed up against the window looked all right. Beyond him she could see a mother walking her kids out on the common, urging a toddler along whilst she tried to steer a pushchair round a group of truculent-looking swans. Just beyond them, the poll cattle that grazed the meadows looked on as they chewed lazily on the grass. All of life went past her window – from carefree people to those who were down on their luck. People who'd seen the worst of life, and perhaps those who'd been sent way off course because of it.

The man on the doorstep stood well back when she went to open the door. 'Detective Inspector Blake,' he said. 'I'm here about your call last night. You reported that you'd been followed, and that you'd received a hand-delivered package when you got home: a doll with a threatening note. If you want to close the door and call the station to check, I'll understand.'

'There's no need,' she said, stepping back.

'Thanks.' DI Blake walked into the hallway. 'I'd like to take a look at the doll please.'

'Sure.' She led him through to the kitchen. Her breath shortened as she indicated the packet and its contents, which were still on the table. She hoped he hadn't noticed. 'Can I get you a coffee?' She turned her back on him and her delivery before he replied.

'Yes – fantastic – thank you. Black. No sugar.' He sounded as though he'd be prepared to wrestle her for it. She put the kettle on again.

He'd be examining the doll now.

She shook out the old grounds from the cafetière and gave it a rinse, managing to keep her every move controlled. The days of dropping stuff and spilling things out of nerves were over. She'd learnt a long time ago that you couldn't always eliminate what threatened you, yet somehow you had to find a way to carry on. That meant learning to cope – both practically and emotionally. You got power from knowing you hadn't been beaten. And from learning how to protect yourself.

She made the fresh pot of coffee and took it over to the table with a clean mug for him. The doll was there to his left, next to the note and the envelope. But she focused on his face instead. His expression had changed. His jaw was taut.

'We always take something like this seriously,' he said, as she pushed the cafetière's plunger down, 'but in this case there's an extra dimension to what's happened.' He paused for a moment. 'I don't know if you've seen it yet – it's already hitting some of the online news sites. A body was discovered this morning. That of an academic, Samantha Seabrook. She'd been drowned.'

What was he about to say? She needed to prepare for it; news out of the blue was harder. She dropped into the seat opposite him.

'Professor Seabrook was sent a doll, just like the one you received – we think a few days before she died.' His brown eyes met hers. 'There was a note with it. It said "This is a warning". It looks as though it was the precursor to yours.'

Tara felt her skin prickle. For just a second, tiny sparks of light flickered in her peripheral vision.

DI Blake was watching her – well, of course he was. She sat up straight. She'd got no intention of buckling in front of a stranger – or anyone else for that matter. At least he'd told her outright; he must think she could take it. 'I understand.' Her voice was steady. 'I'm a journalist – I'm going to be writing about Professor Seabrook. I guess I might find out more about what links us first-hand.'

DI Blake's eyes were on hers. He looked curious. 'I guess you might. We'll need to talk more about that. But first, I have some questions.'

CHAPTER FIVE

Blake headed straight back to the station for a briefing after he'd left Tara Thorpe, his mind full of their meeting. She wasn't quite like anyone else he'd ever met. He'd looked up her background before he'd gone to see her. It made him wonder what on earth she was doing, living out on the common with only cattle for company. He'd imagined she'd want the comfort of crowds, but he'd been way off the mark there. Understanding her might help him keep one step ahead of her would-be killer. Maybe he'd need to keep one step ahead of her too, if he could.

Now he was sitting between his sergeants, Patrick Wilkins and Emma Marshall, listening to his boss, Detective Chief Inspector Karen Fleming. He was finding it difficult to focus. Operating as a team was essential, of course. It was just that it was hard to switch off the private information sifting he was doing in his head. He shifted in his seat and made a conscious effort to tune in. At least the briefing would be short and to the point; Fleming was on a mission to run the tightest ship in policing history, with half an eye on the victims and half on her own career. Her focus meant she spent most of her time behind a desk or schmoozing the management at drinks parties. Blake was in two minds about whether he wanted to take the next step and fill her shoes when she was inevitably promoted. He often wished he could control the investigations he worked on, but Fleming was welcome to the rest of it.

Unfortunately, the DCI's desire to curry favour with those in power meant she watched her team like a hawk too. He'd seen her glance at his hair and tie as he'd taken his seat. She'd given him a look and raised an eyebrow. Wilkins next to him was smart as a politician on polling day, which didn't help. It wasn't that Blake couldn't comb his hair; he just didn't feel like it. Seeing Fleming's face confirmed his opposition to the idea.

Karen Fleming's own hair was perfectly in place, though the black dye and the spiky style she wore it in were a bit unconventional for the chief super's tastes. As for her designer clothes, Blake occasionally wondered if she had some sort of private income. His own suits were the real deal too, but only because his sister worked in fashion design. He wore them to please her.

'Sir Brian Seabrook, the professor's father, has been informed of his daughter's death,' Fleming was saying. 'Samantha Seabrook's mother died some years ago. Sir Brian is based up the road, north of Ely. The local police are with him at the moment. Going forward, I've assigned Kirsty Crowther as family liaison officer.' She put her shoulders back. 'We don't have much information from Sir Brian as yet – he's completely flattened by all this as you can imagine – but we do have the name of a boyfriend. Apparently Samantha Seabrook had been seeing a man called Dieter Gartner on and off for the last couple of years. Sir Brian says he's a university lecturer based in Germany and believes that's where he is now. He's not sure when they saw each other last, and he doesn't know which institution Dr Gartner is based at. It turns out that there's more than one academic with that name.'

Blake turned to Wilkins. 'Do some digging please, Patrick.'

He nodded. 'Will do, boss.'

'So let's turn our attention to Tara Thorpe – the journalist who was sent a doll, just as Professor Seabrook was.' Fleming met Blake's eye. 'What's the story there?'

Blake explained the events Tara Thorpe had relayed to him. 'It's not the first time she's had anonymous mail,' he said. 'Her mother's the actress, Lydia Thorpe. When Tara was a teenager someone with an interest in the mother started stalking her instead. They look a bit alike and Tara was easier to get at. She was followed and sent a series of packages containing substances that looked ominous but turned out to be harmless.' If you ignored the emotional impact, anyway. 'Some of them were pretty sick though; one contained hundreds of dead bees. On top of that they killed her cat, then wrote to tell her where to find its body. All in all they made her life a misery for a year and a half. Much longer probably; they were never caught.' She must have been waiting for the next incident for months before she finally decided they'd given up. It sounded like a particularly cruel campaign. Blake wondered again what kind of person it had turned Tara Thorpe into.

'D'you think there's any connection between her previous stalker and the current case?'

'No, I don't.' According to the notes he'd read, the investigating officer on the old case was convinced he'd identified the perpetrator; he just didn't have enough evidence to make anything stick. Blake had done some digging and found that if he'd been right the person responsible was now dead. Right or wrong, it didn't alter his conclusion. 'The impetus behind the approaches appears quite different and it's ten years between the two. All the same, I'll ask for one of the psychologists' take on it. But either way I'm still not sure it's entirely a coincidence. Perhaps Samantha Seabrook's killer knows Tara Thorpe's background and picked her thinking she'd be all the more vulnerable to their intimidation?'

Fleming nodded. 'It sounds possible.'

'But if so I think they miscalculated.'

She raised an eyebrow.

'Four years ago, Tara Thorpe gave a guy who was following her a black eye and broke one of his fingers. Turned out he was another journalist, trying to pinch a story she was after. He dropped the assault charges – officially when he heard about her background. Made himself out to be a humane man who understood why she'd lashed out – I think he gave up when he realised the publicity would do him more harm than good. His tactics were pretty low. Anyway, it seems Tara Thorpe took steps to get some control back in her life after she was first stalked, self-defence classes included.'

The rumour was that an ex-cop had taught her. Some guy called Paul Kemp. From asking around, Blake had the impression he'd resigned from the force before he was pushed.

'D'you think she gets tooled up before she goes out?' someone at the back said, and there was a ripple of laughter.

Fleming's eyes were fiery. 'There's nothing to joke about here.'

The room was instantly quiet again.

'She might need reining in,' Fleming went on. 'We all know fighting back often puts you in more danger. If she lashes out then our killer probably will too. And we certainly can't be seen to encourage vigilantism.'

All fine, textbook stuff. Blake wondered how Fleming would react if *she* received a death threat. But he was worried too. Tara Thorpe might take risks. And what if she suspected the wrong person again?

'I'll ask Pam to talk to her,' Fleming said. 'She can warn her about the consequences of carrying anything that could be seen as an improvised weapon. We don't want her taking matters into her own hands.'

Pam was the crime reduction officer and she'd be awful at it. She had a patronising tone ('We wouldn't want to cause extra trouble, now would we?') that she'd couple with a soupy smile. He suspected Tara Thorpe might prefer to be treated as an adult. 'I understand that Pam will need to talk to her about general security,' he said, 'but I'll speak to her about her past, and the dangers of lashing out.'

Fleming looked as though she was about to object, and their eyes locked. At last, she nodded. 'All right. Now, how about the person Tara Thorpe saw on the common? Will her description help us?'

'No.'

There was a pause and Blake saw Patrick Wilkins roll his eyes. 'Was it an "average height, average build" job?'

So easy for him to say, sitting there in his comfy chair. 'It was. Being frightened might have had an effect on how much she took in, but she also said she'd had a few drinks.'

'Refreshingly honest of her,' said Fleming, drily.

But Blake was already clear that Tara Thorpe would rather be thought drunk than stupid.

'Have you found any connection between her and the professor?' Fleming went on.

'Not socially, ma'am. Tara Thorpe says she never met Samantha Seabrook and so far we haven't been able to trace any link between the circles they moved in.' Except they both lived in Cambridge, where everyone knew someone who knew someone.

Fleming's blue eyes were on his. 'But?'

'But Tara Thorpe's a staff writer on *Not Now* magazine.' He saw the DCI roll her eyes. *Not Now* was consciously trendy – a bit 'read us if you think you're cool enough'. It had a massive, national following. 'In recent months, her editor has asked her for articles on a couple of murder victims; one from London and one up north. She won an award for the second feature.'

'So you think the killer in this case was anticipating a connection between Tara Thorpe and Samantha Seabrook which would be triggered by the latter's death?'

'It seems like a possibility. By the time I arrived to talk to Ms Thorpe about the doll she was already aware that Samantha Seabrook had died. Her editor had called, given her the news and asked her to write about the professor's life. No doubt he'll want all the gory details about her murder too.' He looked around the room. 'So we're all going to have to watch what we say in her hearing. We need every scrap of evidence she gleans as she does her job, but the information can only flow one way.'

Fleming nodded. 'That's true enough. So, back to the killer. We're looking for someone who's highly organised and capable of planning a complex series of arrangements in advance, paying a lot of attention to detail. And who had the skill to sew two near-identical rag dolls and the clothes they wore. As well as the singlemindedness.'

Blake nodded. It hinted at an obsessive, and it was another thing he wanted to run past the psychologists. They might be able to tell them the sort of qualities such a person would display, day to day. 'And it has to be someone with plenty of nerve too,' he said. 'If they were the figure on the common they waited around the Riverside area, ready to put the frighteners on Tara Thorpe when she came home. And yet they were up against a deadline, assuming the meeting with the professor had already been arranged.' And how could it not have been?

'One hell of a cool customer.' Karen Fleming's eyes were on the middle distance for a moment, but then she was back with him. 'So what about the killer's motive for introducing Tara Thorpe to the mix?'

'Given her job, I wonder if they want her to unearth something about Samantha Seabrook and splash it all over the press.'

Fleming looked at him. 'If so, then what's stopping them publicising whatever it is themselves? They could send Tara an anonymous tip-off easily enough.'

Blake frowned. He'd wondered the same thing and still wasn't happy with his answer. 'Maybe it's something they know but can't prove, so they're looking to Tara Thorpe to dig up the evidence. But if that's the case it's still odd. They haven't given her anything to go on.' It was almost as though it was some kind of test. 'Either way,' he went on, 'I think Tara Thorpe's working to a deadline that's in the killer's head.'

Fleming nodded. 'I agree.' Her expression was grim. 'And I don't think we can bank on them being the patient type. We need to solve this one fast. And you mentioned that Ms Thorpe has opted to stay in her house in spite of the threat. Is that because she can't stay with family, or won't?'

He paused for a moment. 'Won't,' he said at last. 'But she has her reasons.'

The DCI pulled a face. 'Of course she has. And what about the man who told you the professor had received a doll?'

Guilty as hell, case closed. But then again, maybe not... 'His name's Jim Cooper. Works at the Institute for Social Studies, just as the professor did. He's the building supervisor – responsible for all the practical day-to-day running of the place, from making sure there's enough loo paper to checking security.'

'And his story?'

'It's pretty shaky on the face of it. Emma took the call.' He looked at his DS.

'That's right, ma'am,' she said. 'Jim Cooper says Professor Seabrook told him she'd been sent the doll around ten days ago. He says she was quite open about it and laughed it off, even though he encouraged her to report it to someone. Then this morning when he heard the news of her death, he claims he went into the professor's office to see if the doll was still there.'

Blake heard a snort from somewhere behind him that mirrored the one he'd given himself when Emma had passed on the explanation. But of course it could be true. On the other hand, he could have gone in there to take the doll away having sent it himself. Jim Cooper had given Emma his details – which included a home address in Chesterton. That meant – assuming he biked to work (and who didn't, in Cambridge?) that he would cycle past Tara Thorpe's house twice a day.

'Good of him to call and let us know,' Karen Fleming said. 'Shame he didn't do anything more proactive earlier on if he's telling the truth.'

'Reading between the lines,' Emma said, 'I'm not even sure he'd have called us today if someone hadn't forced his hand. He told me he'd "bumped into" the institute administrator in Professor Seabrook's office and that she'd "advised" him to call us.'

'It's disappointing that he got in there before us.' Karen Fleming's eyes had turned dark.

Blake didn't bother to reply. They'd been through all this already. They'd asked for the door to be kept locked and one of his detective constables had picked up what he thought was the only key. Unfortunately he'd forgotten to ask if there were others and it turned out Jim Cooper had copies for every door, drawer and cupboard in the place. The DC shouldn't have been given the job. He wasn't firing on all cylinders at the moment. It had been Karen Fleming herself who'd sent him out there, and Blake wondered if she'd done it as a test. She saw him as a weak link.

Still, luck had been on their side. Jim Cooper hadn't managed to complete his mission in secret, and they'd got information that might prove useful. The office was secure now and the professor's doll had been bagged and brought to the station. Both it and the one sent to Tara Thorpe were being examined to see if the fabric used provided any clues. They were too rough to yield any prints, of course.

One way or another, Blake was looking forward to meeting Cooper. He'd have to be patient though. He and Emma were due at Addenbrooke's Hospital mortuary to talk to Sir Brian Seabrook after they'd finished at the station. Blake was more than keen to get that out of the way. And then they'd catch up with Agneta to find out more about how Samantha Seabrook had died. Only after both those appointments would they go to the institute. Jim Cooper was top of his list of people to see.

Fleming's beady eyes glinted. 'Keep me informed. But before you go, is there anything else you want to highlight?'

Blake explained about the crucifix that had sawn its way into Samantha Seabrook's neck. 'I got word through to officers at the institute to ask her colleagues about it. None of them recall ever seeing her wear that sort of necklace or anything with any religious connotations.'

'So you think the killer might have brought it with them? Or that she wore it last night for some particular reason, associated with the rendezvous she'd planned?'

Blake nodded. 'We're checking with local and online shops to see if any of them sell the item. If it was worn especially for the occasion – at the killer's instigation – then I can't believe it was a random choice. They plan too carefully for that. It might hint at the murderer's identity or their motivation.' He'd learnt not to use the expression 'religious nutter' after a previous case, but Emma Marshall was probably remembering it. He could see a slight smile playing over her lips.

'How do you think the killer managed to take Samantha Seabrook by surprise in the garden?' Fleming asked.

Blake told the assembled group about the coins in the fountain. 'It's possible the killer slipped them in there in advance, or last night when the professor wasn't looking. They might have used them to lure her into a vulnerable position when the time came. If they'd pointed them out, and she'd crouched down to look, it would have enabled them to come at her from above and behind.' He visualised the scene. 'Her head would have been in just the right place for them to force it under the water.'

There was a moment's silence before the DCI spoke. 'That thought's enough to spur us all on, as if we needed it. Let's get going, everyone.'

Blake was just about to leave the room with the rest of the team when Karen Fleming called him back. 'What have you got Max Dimity working on next?' she asked.

Max was the DC who'd failed to ensure Samantha Seabrook's office was secure. 'Trying to track down suppliers of the necklace.'

She paused for a moment, then nodded. 'Good call. But we can't carry him, Blake.' He went to speak but she held up a hand. 'I know. I understand he's going through hell, but we suggested more leave. If he wants to come in and carry on working that's fine by me, but only if he remains operationally effective. Keep an eye on him. I want updates immediately if he's putting this case in jeopardy – even in a small way. Understood?'

'Yes, ma'am.' He was going to do his damnedest to find Max jobs he could manage. Though identifying the right tasks might be a challenge when the guy was still reeling from his wife's death in a car accident. She'd only been twenty-five, and Max wasn't much older.

'Oh, and Blake,' Fleming said, just as he was on the brink of freedom.

'Ma'am?'

'Sort that bloody tie out.'

He didn't somehow think tidy dressing would be a consideration for Brian Seabrook when he arrived to identify his daughter's body.

When he caught DS Marshall up she was heading straight for the car park. Blake shook his head. 'Vending machine first, Emma. My brain feels like something the cat spat out. I need sugar. And more caffeine.'

She grinned. 'You have a point, boss. I had a chocolate bar just before the briefing but I'll join you in a coffee. It might work a minor miracle.'

'In my case it'll need to.' He went over to the drinks machine first. He was still feeling the effects of a late phone call with his wife, Babette, the night before. They'd talked until two – a fruitless conversation that had gone round and round. It was she who'd walked out, and now it was she who wanted to get back together.

But for him the sorrow that had replaced his initial rage towards her had dulled. He was back to feeling angry. Angry, but in control. That was all the more important for Kitty's sake. Having a two-year-old innocent bystander was the hardest part of all this. His urge to make things better for her was strong, but there were some lengths he couldn't go to, and at the moment that included allowing Babette back into his life.

That didn't stop Kitty's image filling his head each night as he tried to sleep; he missed their bedtime story sessions so much that it hurt. But things were better than they had been. A few short weeks ago, his wife had made secret plans which would have cut him off from Kitty for good. At least she was back in Cambridge now. He rubbed his chin. How could he square this circle? He wanted the family life he'd thought he'd had so badly, and on the face of it, that's what Babette was offering. But in reality, it had never existed; it had been built on a foundation of lies.

He shook the thoughts away. They were too painful, and he needed to focus. This wasn't a case he could work on with only half his attention.

After he'd got his coffee he selected the most solid-looking chocolate from the options on offer: a large Galaxy bar. When Emma had sorted out her own drink he offered her some but she shook her head.

'I can't have any more. I don't want to turn into a lard-arse.'

'Eloquently put.'

'Thank you. I don't know how you manage to avoid it.'

He didn't either. But the eating was justified. He'd learnt that – to some extent – sleep could be replaced by food.

He topped up his coffee with water from the cooler to bring it down to a drinkable temperature and they started the walk towards his car. They paused outside on the wall to finish their drinks before they got in.

'I wonder why Samantha Seabrook was sent a doll with a noose around its neck,' Emma said, 'given that she was drowned.'

'To be fair, conveying death by drowning would have been a lot more challenging. Especially by post.' She gave him a look, but he knew she understood. They all used flippancy as a way of getting by. 'Maybe the important point was to let her know generally what was coming,' he added.

She shivered. 'Quite possibly. God. Whoever's responsible certainly made good their promise.' She drained her drink and crumpled the paper cup.

He'd finished his too. 'Here,' he reached out for her empty, 'I'll chuck them in the car. We can get rid of them later.'

After a moment they were on their way. Parkside was crowded with traffic: coaches offloading hordes of tourists, cyclists making kamikaze moves and pedestrians dashing through concertinaing gaps between the queuing cars.

'So, I'm guessing choosing St Bede's as a setting was significant?' Emma said.

'I think so. Using a locked, walled garden for a murder certainly increased the effort involved for the killer.' He inched his vehicle forward. 'The more complex a murderer makes their job, the more chance they have of getting found out. It was a risk they didn't have to take.' He paused. 'It gave them isolation and privacy of course, but they could have found that elsewhere.'

Emma glanced sideways at him. 'So, what's your thinking?'

'The killer might have used climbing into a walled garden as a lure. If the professor liked adventure it could have tempted her into going along with the plan. Those climbing gloves the CSIs found at the scene weren't new. I'm guessing it was a passion of hers. But I think the fountain was important too. After all, once they were in there, why go for drowning? If the killer really did put the coins on the fountain's base to lure the professor into position, it was all very calculated. They'd have to have known the water was shallow and clear enough to see the bottom by torch or moonlight.'

'So,' Emma said, 'supposing drowning was a deliberate choice, then why?'

Blake stared ahead as a bus moved off at last and allowed them to drive on. 'It would have given the killer a way of drawing out Samantha Seabrook's death. She'd have known she couldn't escape, but her murderer could have kept her going like that for some time. Allowing her up for air for long enough to deliver a message and then plunging her under again.'

It might not have been that way, but now he'd imagined it, he couldn't get it out of his head. And then his thoughts turned to Tara Thorpe.

CHAPTER SIX

There were police all over Tara's house – or that's what it felt like. She hadn't got a clue who most of them were, though the man with them, DS Patrick Wilkins, had introduced them all by name when they'd arrived. He'd also told her he worked for DI Blake.

Preparing to write about Samantha Seabrook ought to have been a distraction but it wasn't working. The hubbub was too much, and every so often one of the team would come to check she really wasn't going to have second thoughts about moving out.

She'd already explained to DI Blake why it wasn't practical. The main contenders for the provision of temporary accommodation were all unsuitable. Her mother would have her, of course. Tara would explain to her about the doll and she probably wouldn't take it in, because she'd be busy with other things. But she'd get someone to make up a bed and Tara would be installed without much fuss. She'd have to have stilted conversations with her thirteen-year-old half-brother, Harry, who would be around all day, every day, thanks to the school holidays. He was the 'wanted child', in stark contrast to her. Even though her mother had opted against an abortion, Tara had always been superfluous, whereas Harry was prized. Now, she found interacting with him difficult. And her stepfather, Benedict, would wonder how long they'd be saddled with her. He'd be extra polite to try to disguise what he was thinking, and she'd see right through him but have to pretend that she hadn't. She wouldn't be able to keep that up for long.

But all that aside, her mother lived deep in the Fens. It was the land of 180-degree skies – they were said to send people mad. It was the feeling of endless space and loneliness. The peat soil all around was black, and the landscape trapped you, just as surely as any mountainous terrain. Instead of being hemmed in by rock, you were cut off by flooded land. The area was criss-crossed with vast drains – channels of deep, dark water, dug by the Dutch centuries earlier to make it possible to farm the land. Each winter you heard of drivers who had drowned after taking a turn too quickly and running off one of the narrow byways. And although you could always see if someone was on your tail – the land was so flat – you could also be sure that *you* would be seen – and from miles around.

Tara would have to travel into Cambridge each day through all of that to quiz Samantha Seabrook's contacts. If anyone wanted to get rid of her, running her off the road there would be a perfect way to achieve closure. She'd die under water, just as the professor had. She shuddered. She loved the stark beauty of the Fens, but she'd always felt their menace too.

So not her mother's house then.

The other options were her father and stepmother's place or Bea's. Leaving aside what her stepmother would say about giving her house-space, there was no way she'd approach them. They had three children (yet more favoured half-siblings) still living at home. The youngest was only six. What if they got caught up in something because of her? No one deserved to run that risk.

Which left Bea – her mother's cousin. She'd been the one to step into the breach most often when Tara had been farmed out as a child. Tara felt just as protective towards her as she did towards any six-year-old. And besides, Bea ran an old-style Cambridge boarding house and the place was crammed to the gunwales at the moment. Tara couldn't defend herself there without putting the other residents at risk. And then there was the worry she'd cause.

No. There was no way she was even going to tell Bea about the doll, let alone descend on her.

DS Wilkins appeared by her side. She'd scream if he brought up the subject all over again.

'My apologies for the interruption,' he said. He must have read her look. 'I just wanted to let you know what's going on. My colleagues are fitting cameras so that if anyone comes near we can get a good look at them. They're also installing an alarm that'll send an alert straight to the station if you have to trigger it. It's silent, so any intruder won't know we're on our way.'

She took a deep breath. That sounded practical at least. 'Thanks.'

'I'm off now,' the DS went on, 'but our crime reduction officer will talk to you before the team leaves. As well as the alarm here she'll give you a standard, personal one to carry with you when you're out and about. It could come in handy if you need to make a racket.'

It was probably just like the one she already had. She'd have to get hold of something more meaty.

The DS smiled for a moment. Tara suspected it was meant to be encouraging. He looked the sort to enjoy his role as protector and it made her skin crawl. 'And I've just had a message from DI Blake. He'd like to talk to you again later in the day. Will you be heading over to the Institute for Social Studies to speak to the staff?'

She nodded. 'I made an appointment earlier to interview the head, Professor da Souza, and then another colleague of Professor Seabrook's in town after that. I gather they're fitting me round the interviews the police want to conduct.'

The DS nodded. 'Would you call DI Blake on his mobile when you've finished? He'll probably still be over there too.' He gave her a card with the inspector's contact details on it.

'I'll do that.' She got up to see him out.

After he'd left she entered DI Blake's number into her mobile and then tried to block the rest of the team out of her mind. She needed to get on with researching Samantha Seabrook. It was no longer a distraction from her own problems but a potential way of solving them. Working intensely would get her through this. Hopefully.

Her first list of Google hits took her to a mix of dry academic sites showing Samantha Seabrook's impressive CV, as well as some more glossy media ones. She'd been on television once. The production company's website still had the related press release with a large photo of her attached.

She'd been beautiful, but not in a cool, model-like way. There was something red-blooded about her, from her shining chestnut hair to the mischievous light in her eyes. She looked as though she'd been trying not to laugh.

Tara found a short clip from the TV programme on YouTube. The professor's delivery had been charismatic, which made her hard-hitting message all the more stark. She'd estimated that childhood deprivation led to 1400 deaths each year in the UK. Then she'd gone on to list the many effects of being born into poverty, from making it more likely that a child would die in the first year of its life, to having a higher risk of death in adulthood across almost all conditions that had been studied. The camera zoomed in on her face as she pointed out that most people were totally unaware of how hard life was for some of their fellow citizens.

Tara glanced at the comments under the video. The professor seemed to have attracted the standard ratio of positive to troll-like responses. Had the person who'd killed her viewed this clip? Were they one of the people who'd written a comment that referred to her anatomy, rather than what she'd wanted to achieve? The world was so full of creeps and dysfunctionals. How was anyone to know which might cross that final line and kill?

It got her thinking about her own social media accounts. She called up Twitter. Four new followers that day, none of whom she recognised, either by their names or photos. And of course, those names and photos could be false.

This wasn't getting her anywhere. She went back to the tab of search results, where she found a reference to Samantha Seabrook's doctorate. Her thesis had been on the effects of cash-rich, time-poor parents on their offspring. Tara could guess where that topic had sprung from. With a multimillionaire businessman for a dad and an actor mother it seemed likely Samantha had been inspired by her own experiences. Relatable.

The professor's Wikipedia page had already been updated to show when she'd died. Today's date. The door had been shut on her life and she'd passed into history. What would people write about Tara if she or the police slipped up and her story ended too? She hadn't done anything as worthwhile as Samantha Seabrook, but she hoped someone would remember she'd been a fighter.

Tara glanced over the record of the professor's academic achievements: a first in her degree from Oxford, then a PhD from Cambridge, followed by time spent lecturing at London School of Economics. After that she'd taken up her role at the university as a senior lecturer. Just two years later – a year ago now – she'd got her professorship. Further down the page there were details of her early life. Her mother had 'died in an accident' when Samantha was just fifteen. There were no further details. What kind of an explanation was that?

Tara searched for the mother's obituary on the web but drew a blank; 1997 was well before newspapers had established their online operations. At last she found an 'On This Day' feature in a Wisbech newspaper. A write-up of Samantha Seabrook's mother's life had been revived just a couple of months earlier to mark the twentieth anniversary of her death. Bella Seabrook (her acting name had been Bella Dempsey) had had various small parts in big-name films. The article made much of her local roots and – irritatingly – her marriage to the great Brian Seabrook. Tara wouldn't have written the article like that. Again, Bella's early demise was explained away in that one liner: 'died in an accident'. Well, whatever had happened to her, Tara intended to find out; it couldn't be that difficult. Her death must have sent a crack through Samantha's childhood.

Tara was just about to follow another link when a woman appeared in the doorway.

'Sorry to interrupt,' she said, smiling. 'I just need to run through a few things before we head off.'

Tara stood up slowly and dragged her gaze from the computer screen. 'Sure.'

The woman showed her the silent alarm they'd installed on the upstairs landing that would summon the police to her house. It had a wireless activator she could take with her from room to room. 'I really would advise you to use the chain on your front door too,' she said.

No kidding.

'And, if you can run to it, a new back door wouldn't be a bad idea.' She glanced over her shoulder down the stairs. 'I don't want to alarm you but it is just a little on the flimsy side.'

You could kick it in wearing flip-flops.

'And, well, the fence round your garden isn't all that robust, is it?'

'I booked to have the back door replaced just after I saw DI Blake this morning.'

'He suggested it too, did he?' She smiled again. 'Well done you for getting it sorted out so quickly.'

Explaining that DI Blake hadn't suggested it would have involved ungritting her teeth, so Tara didn't bother. She'd been well aware of her house's inadequacies for a while now. And funnily enough the events of the previous night had focused her mind.

'For when you're out and about,' the woman went on, 'a lot of what we advise is just common sense. I've got a personal alarm for you here.'

Tara had been right. It was just like the one she'd already got.

'But on top of that,' the woman said, 'make sure you keep to well-populated places. Don't come home after dark and avoid situations where you could get cornered.' She counted the points off on the fingers of one hand. 'Check who's at the door before you answer. All the kind of things you'd probably do anyway.' Her tone was cosy, but then her eyes met Tara's. 'We'll ask patrolling officers to keep an eye out when they can, and to treat any related call-outs as an emergency.'

The officer started to descend the stairs and Tara followed. Down below she could see the other members of the team had gathered in the hallway. Just as she reached the ground floor the woman turned to look at her again. 'One more thing I should have said. It might be an idea to put your hair up. It sounds so silly, I know, but it really can make a difference. Long hair like yours makes it that little bit harder to see who's around you, doesn't it? And for an attacker it is just one more thing to snatch at.'

Tara thought of Samantha Seabrook's photograph and her elbow-length glossy hair. 'Did that happen in the professor's case?' she asked.

'It's just advice we give as a matter of course,' the woman said.

But that didn't answer her question, and Tara noticed the woman didn't meet her eye.

The team left, but the feeling of their presence still hung about the house. There was a small pile of dust just inside the front door, where they'd been drilling to fix the security camera. It had been installed outside, but the walls were thin; the hole they'd made must have come right through. And the plastic packaging the wireless panic button had come in lay on top of the bookcase on her landing. Even the air still seemed to be swirling after their fevered activity.

She went to make herself another mug of coffee and then made up her mind. She was going to tell Kemp what was going on. He'd been the one who'd taught her self-defence after the last time. He'd had lots of tips then; he was ex-police turned security – tough, practical and a renegade. It had been his training that had stopped her feeling like a sitting duck. Besides, with their past, holding out on him felt wrong. Especially if anything did happen. Other than him, she'd keep the whole thing secret. She didn't want people worrying, or treating her differently because of the threat she was under.

She sat down to drop her old mentor an email.

CHAPTER SEVEN

The visit to Addenbrooke's mortuary was just about as much fun as Blake had anticipated. Sir Brian Seabrook was a big, powerful, bear of a man, but he looked as though someone had sucked all the air out of him. It was as if he was collapsing in on himself. Blake did his best but he knew he had no words that would give any comfort. He focused on the action they were taking; it was all he could think of.

After the formal identification had taken place, Kirsty Crowther, the family liaison officer, shepherded Sir Brian back to her car and Blake and Emma paused to speak to Agneta.

The pathologist hadn't added much to the conclusions she'd detailed in the fellows' garden that morning at St Bede's. As she'd thought, the professor had had no drugs in her system and only a small amount of alcohol.

'She had several tattoos,' Agneta had said, passing over an envelope of photographs. 'None of them look recent, so I don't know if they are relevant.'

He'd had a quick look before he'd begun the drive back into town. One of them – in the small of her back – read: 'No Tomorrow'. Whatever its significance had been when she'd had it done it was painfully apt that day.

Now Blake and Emma were up on the second floor of the Institute for Social Studies, standing in what had been Professor Seabrook's office. The room was stuffy. It faced west, but much of the afternoon light was blocked by Gonville and Caius, the tall college opposite. Already the room had that strange air of having been permanently vacated. The professor's belongings lay around as she'd last left them, frozen in time like the hands of a stopped clock. The CSI team had already been in to do their work. Photographs had been taken; the scene recorded. Through the window, Blake could see Caius's upper storeys. The carved stone heads on its façade looked back at him, their eyes blank. Shame they couldn't see and talk. Someone had made that arrangement to meet Samantha Seabrook at St Bede's. Had they done it in person? The application had been made to access the professor's mobile records via the phone company. The mobile itself still hadn't been found.

Jim Cooper was with them. Blake shared a look with his DS as the building supervisor bent his buzz-cut head over one of the desk drawers. The man had the build of a rugby player and made the furniture in the room look tiny.

'The doll was just in there,' he said. 'Like I said it was. Only your people have got it now of course.' The note that had been with it had also been bagged and removed.

'And Professor Seabrook told you about it when?' Blake asked.

'About a week and a half ago, just like I said.' There was an edge to his voice and Blake saw him shoot an accusatory glance at Emma. He probably imagined she hadn't passed on his message, but Blake had just been hoping to catch him out. They already knew he, and most of his colleagues, had no alibi for the time of Professor Seabrook's death. Still, he hadn't really expected the man's story to change. Either he was on the level or lying through his teeth with well-rehearsed words. Blake still wasn't sure which, but there was something about the guy he didn't quite like. For one thing, Cooper was sweating. It might just be the weather, but he didn't think so.

Blake leant back against a filing cabinet. 'And where was the professor when she told you about the doll?'

'Right here,' Cooper said. 'That's how I knew where it was. She pulled open the drawer and showed me.' He sighed. 'She didn't take it seriously. It wasn't in her nature. She was more focused than any of them when it came to her work, but everything else?' He shrugged. 'She'd just laugh it off.'

Blake found it hard to understand. It took a lot of bravado (and, he would normally have said, stupidity) to ignore a death threat altogether. 'All the same, I understand from DS Marshall that you were worried,' he said. 'You suggested she should tell someone else. But as far as you're aware you're the only one she confided in?'

Cooper stuck his hands in his jeans pockets, smiled and strutted over to the tall window. 'Reckon it was just me,' he said. For a moment he peered down onto Trinity Street below. 'We hit it off.' He turned to face them again and folded his arms, accentuating his biceps. 'She used to talk to me about the academics sometimes. I don't think she found them anything to write home about. Sometimes she'd say it was only we two who made things happen here.'

'Sounds as though you were close,' Blake said.

Cooper nodded, jutting his chin out. 'I'd say so.'

'So if you were so concerned for her,' he moved a step closer to the man, 'why the hell didn't you step in? Tell someone what you'd seen, and that you were worried? Surely it was your responsibility to bring it up with the institute's head, or the administrator?' For a man in charge of security he seemed to take his duties pretty lightly.

Cooper's eyes narrowed at his raised voice. 'She was an independent woman,' he said. 'She knew what she was doing. No way would she have wanted any interference.'

'But if you cared about her?' Emma said quietly.

There was a long pause and Blake noticed Cooper had bunched his fists. 'I cared enough to respect her right to privacy.' The man glanced over Blake's shoulder towards Samantha Seabrook's office door. 'The institute's a small place. One careless word and everyone knows your business.'

'You sound as though you're speaking from experience,' Blake said.

Cooper rolled his eyes. 'Me? I'm beyond taking any notice of what people say,' he drew himself up, 'but I have to look out for the staff I support.'

There was a pause.

'You must be crucial to the management of this place,' Emma said.

Blake kept his face neutral. He couldn't have faced buttering Cooper up himself, but it was in a good cause.

'People don't always see it that way,' the supervisor said, his shoulders starting to relax again, 'but you're right. And Samantha understood that. She never saw me as second class to the academics. And she and I, we kept similar hours. I get in around six in the morning as a rule, and it wasn't uncommon to find her here too. And then I'll normally be around until eight or so in the evening.'

'And the professor stayed late as well?' Blake said.

There was a fond light in Cooper's eye. 'Not always. She had a life outside too, but she had plenty of drive. When she was working at something she'd go for it day and night. Rather different from some of her colleagues.' He gave them a meaningful look. 'You don't see the institute head, Professor da Souza, in here before ten o'clock, even on a good day. As for Samantha, I don't reckon she needed much sleep. She had a lot of waking hours, and she devoted them to work or play, whatever met her needs at any particular time.'

Needs was an interesting word to choose. Blake watched Cooper's expression. 'Did you socialise outside work at all?'

He laughed at that but there was something slightly forced about it. 'I need more sleep than she did. No. Anyway, when she was taking time out from her work, I'd still be doing my long hours here.' He paused. 'No rest for the wicked.'

Cooper was no longer meeting Blake's eye. Maybe he'd made up to Samantha Seabrook and never got anywhere. If so, he probably didn't want anyone digging in that direction; he was the sort who'd hate to lose face. But, alternatively, he might be lying about how personal their relationship had become. 'Do you know what she did in her spare time?' Blake asked. 'Did she have any particular hobbies, for instance? Music maybe, or sport?'

But Cooper just shrugged. 'Spending time with friends, as far as I know.'

'Speaking of which, is there anyone here you think Professor Seabrook was close to?' Blake took a deep breath. 'Apart from you, that is?' He was trying, but the flattery Emma used refused to trip off his tongue. He could hear the light dusting of sarcasm in his voice.

Cooper's eyes narrowed as he shook his head. 'No one in particular. Who she socialised with depended on what was happening at the time.'

Once he'd left the room, Emma looked at Blake. 'Seems as though Cooper and Seabrook had some kind of "special relationship", whether or not it extended beyond work. Maybe she was the only one here who made him feel valued.'

Blake nodded. 'Maybe. And if that's the case, I wonder what he might have done if she'd let him down?' He closed his eyes for a moment. 'Do you reckon he could climb a high wall?'

Emma nodded. 'He certainly looks young enough and fit enough to manage it. He must have to be strong and agile to do his job if he's in charge of the maintenance here.'

Blake had been thinking the same thing. 'I watched him when I asked whether the professor had liked sport. I couldn't tell if he was covering up, but could you check with Kelsey Kerridge sports centre? See if he or the professor were registered to climb there? Better check the rest of the staff here and at St Francis's College too.' The local sports hall's facilities might be a bit tame compared with the wall at St Bede's, but it was worth a try.

'Will do.'

'Thanks.' Blake frowned. 'Whether I could see him sewing handmade dolls is another matter.'

Emma raised an eyebrow. 'I don't know. I mean, a needle would look tiny in his hand, but he's bound to be dextrous if he does any kind of building maintenance, or wiring. That's pretty fiddly.'

And that was a fair point. 'Interesting what he said about Samantha Seabrook despising her colleagues. Whatever she said in private though, you can bet your life she made herself pleasant to people in public.' His mother always bemoaned the need to be charming to her colleagues, whether she liked them or not.

'Maybe she was the sort who managed to be all things to all people,' Emma said.

'Quite possibly.' Blake remembered Cooper's last words, about her social relationships being governed by what was happening at the time. 'I suppose we'll find out more about her personality when we look round her flat.' Other members of the team were already over at the exclusive penthouse where Professor Seabrook had lived. He and Emma were due to join them later so they could oversee developments. 'Then again, if she was as much of a workaholic as Cooper says, we might get just as many hints from this place.'

As usual, they looked at the big picture first, each scanning the office as a whole. It was too easy to home in on the details and miss something obvious.

In this case, the smell of the room had been the first thing to strike Blake, whilst they'd been talking to Jim Cooper. The over-riding scent was a cloying mix of flowers – there were some roses in a vase on the professor's window sill, already dropping their petals – and some kind of perfume.

'Rive Gauche,' said Emma, seeing him sniff. 'Classic and classy.'

'Thanks. I'm so glad I didn't have to put my own opinion into words. That and the flowers are doing a good job of masking it, but I can smell cigarette too.'

Emma nodded. He half expected her to tell him which brand, but she didn't. 'So you think the professor was a rule breaker, at least in a small way?' She glanced up at the smoke alarm on the ceiling. 'Maybe she stuck her head out of the window to avoid getting found out.'

He nodded. 'Sounds about right.' He walked over to the roses and peered amongst their stems but there was no card attached. 'Would you see if the receptionist knows who sent these? I presume no one buys themselves a dozen.'

Emma nodded. 'I'll get on to it. And did you notice the wall planner?'

Blake looked. There were various dates noted on it. Large-scale stuff – lines running over several weeks indicating the run of a lecture series, and a couple of deadlines for funding applications. One 'Application deadline – Social Impacts of Poverty' had been crossed out in an extravagant way: done with a flourish.

Blake raised his eyebrows and photographed it for the record.

They seemed to have reached the end of the obvious stuff. 'Let's look more deeply now,' he said. 'You take the desk and the in-tray. I'll tackle the filing cabinet.'

Emma nodded and went to work.

Blake opened the top drawer and found it was devoted to Samantha Seabrook's research interests. The big project she'd been working on most recently had focused on social relationships of children born into poverty. It probably ought to be mandatory police reading, Blake thought. Perhaps it would be in future, assuming someone finished the research. The drawer underneath held papers relating to previous projects, as well as lecture and seminar plans. All interesting, but it was the third drawer that shed more light on the professor's relationships within the institute. He found a file devoted to Chiara Laurito, Samantha Seabrook's current PhD student. He took it over to a chair and settled down to read.

'Blimey,' he felt compelled to say, after he'd glanced at the first couple of papers in the file.

Emma looked up from the desk drawer she was gutting, her curly blonde hair falling over her eyes. 'Boss?'

'Looking at Samantha Seabrook's comments on her PhD student's papers reinforces what Jim Cooper said about her low opinion of her workmates.' He held out the one he'd just been reading for Emma to see.

His DS looked down. '"Only an individual with a genuine and complete lack of imagination would be able to draw such a pedestrian conclusion from this data".' Emma winced.

'And that's just the tip of the iceberg if you look further down the page.' Blake sat back in the chair.

Emma read on. 'I see what you mean,' she said after a moment. 'Samantha *shared* this feedback with her student? Well, this Chiara Laurito's just leapt up the list of possible suspects.'

'Joking aside, Samantha Seabrook certainly didn't take any prisoners. That kind of criticism must have been pretty hard to stomach.'

'No arguments there.'

And it wasn't just that the professor had been harsh. There'd been a sort of exuberant relish in the way she'd styled her comments; as though she'd enjoyed composing them. She'd clearly wanted to make damn sure anyone who didn't make the grade knew it. And presumably her verdict would have got back to the rest of the institute staff too. It reminded Blake of that cynical old maxim: 'It is not enough to succeed. Others must fail.' He'd always found it funny, but he was guessing Chiara Laurito hadn't enjoyed the joke quite so much.

Emma handed back Laurito's file and he replaced it. There were one or two more in the same drawer relating to PhD students past.

Some of her comments on their work had been just as dramatic, but in a positive way. Either she was fair but with a total lack of tact, or she'd really had it in for Chiara.

At last he crouched down to search the final cabinet drawer. He'd been wondering what it might contain. The top three seemed to span the various areas of institute work Samantha Seabrook would have been responsible for.

Now, looking at the bottom one, he classified it as dedicated to 'extracurricular interests'. It was all the more fascinating for that. In it he found a bottle of gin (two-thirds empty), a packet of condoms (ditto) and various items that would have aided the professor if she'd wanted to leave the office and head straight for a night out. Prada shoes, a make-up bag containing lipstick, eyeliner and mascara, and a box with three necklaces in it and two pairs of earrings. It all supported Jim Cooper's claim that she'd had a healthy social life outside work. One of the necklaces in particular caught his eye. It was quite a different style to the others: old-fashioned – heavy and ugly in his opinion – but valuable-looking. 'Emma?'

She looked up.

'Would you recognise rubies if you saw them?'

She glanced at the large red stones set into the gold chain he was holding. 'You're kidding, right? But seriously, I'd say those look special.'

'There's an engraving on the back of the setting for the largest stone. A monogram – S.F.S. Those aren't the professor's initials – her middle name was Bella, after her mother, I presume – but maybe it's a family heirloom, passed down by a senior Seabrook.'

'Sounds possible.' Emma peered at it more closely. 'I can't imagine she'd have worn it much. Not her style, if the other jewellery's anything to go by.'

He took some photos of the drawer's contents. Emma was poring over a book. 'What have you got there?' he asked.

'Her desk diary.'

'Thoughtful of her to have had one. It's nice not to be forced to wait until forensics have finished trawling through her Outlook calendar.' They'd already taken her laptop away.

'I'm right with her there,' Emma said, her head still buried in the diary. 'I like to see my week laid out in front of me on paper. Stops things sneaking up and giving me a fright.' She went quiet again. He watched her flick back and forth through the pages.

'Found something interesting?' he said, when he couldn't bring himself to wait any longer.

'Maybe. I mean, a lot of it's just the usual stuff. But look here.'

She pushed the pages down flat and showed him a period spanning the last week in July and the first in August. The word 'leave' was written across the top of each page.

'So it's summer and she went on holiday. Hold the front page.'

Emma gave him a look. 'Thanks for your support. But look at these other pages.' She flicked back to late March. It was another page marked 'leave'; just one this time. 'Leave – Paris'. 'And then this one.' Emma flicked back again. It was an academic diary running from October to September. She'd reached December. From 28 December to 4 January, the diary was marked 'Leave – Bern'.

'There are other instances too,' Emma said. 'The most recent is the only one where she didn't write where she was going.'

'Okay, I take it all back. Under the circumstances that's definitely worth investigating.'

He turned to sift through a collection of papers on top of the filing cabinet, but before he got started, movement caught his eye.

Outside, beyond the glass panel in Samantha Seabrook's office door, a man was passing. Or wanted them to think that he was. Blake wondered how long he'd been standing there watching them. As soon as their eyes met, the guy had walked on, touching his forehead with one finger in a mock salute – he knew he'd been sussed. He hadn't looked bothered though. There'd been a spark of challenge in his eyes that had instantly made Blake's hackles rise.

He carried on looking out for one more long moment at the space the guy had vacated. Never mind. He'd find out who he was soon enough.

CHAPTER EIGHT

Tara mostly preferred to be alone, especially when she was working. Her preliminary research on Samantha Seabrook was absorbing, but part of her was always listening, straining to hear any sound that might be a warning. She worked in the kitchen, the willow outside the window casting constant shadows into the room, making patterns on the floor. Each time the flickering movement caught her eye she was jolted back to her immediate surroundings. The creaking of the house was the other thing that disturbed her. Sounds that she'd normally write off as wood expanding in the summer heat now made her think of footsteps, creeping closer. Beyond her four walls she could hear the swifts, high in the summer sky, but no human noise at all.

She'd left her bedroom window ajar whilst she was at home to try to get some air in. When a sudden gust blew in, making the thin bathroom door slam, she jumped so hard she bit her tongue.

With an hour to go before she had to leave the house, she went upstairs to get ready for her interview with Professor da Souza, Head of the Institute for Social Studies. Up in her bedroom, she kept half an eye on the common as she looked through her wardrobe. At last she picked out one of her best dresses – a designer number that had been a present from her mother and stepfather. For ages she'd let it sit there unused – she couldn't be bought – but not wearing it today was childish. It had a matching jacket and its sea-green colour went with her eyes and set off her red-gold hair. She chose low heels that she knew she could run in. As for her hair, she was going to take the advice of the crime reduction officer and put it up. She got to work with some pins, and went for an artfully tousled style, leaving the odd strand hanging down. And then she started on her make-up. As she applied eyeliner she wondered about the task ahead. Would the person who'd sent her the doll watch her as she left the house? Might they follow her to the institute? Or perhaps they'd be one of the people she spoke to that day, biding their time, waiting for her to understand their motives and what they wanted of her.

How long would it be before they ran out of patience?

She put on a scarlet lipstick, pressing hard. Well, they'd better not touch her hair. If they made a grab for it as it was it would bring the whole arrangement down.

She put the tiny digital recorder she owned in her bag along with her camera, notepad and phone. Then she added the bottle of hairspray she'd put by her bed.

For two minutes she stood staring at the knife she'd held for self-defence the night before. She knew what could happen if things went wrong, even if you weren't armed. And she knew the law. It wasn't legal to carry anything you intended to use as a weapon. She'd even heard of a woman getting done for fighting her attacker back with a set of keys. The prosecution had made much of the fact that she'd had them out and ready.

At last, she picked up the knife and put it diagonally into the side pocket of her handbag, with some paper tissues stuffed in on top. *She* knew she wasn't going to use it unless it was a choice of her death or injuring her attacker. Surely that had to be enough.

She'd decided to take her bike. She could just about cycle in her dress and although the idea of locking herself in her car appealed she couldn't use it door to door. The bike meant she wouldn't have to enter one of the town's multistoreys, out of the public eye. She'd still have to cross the common, but she'd be quick. Someone else on two wheels might catch her there – but only if they were fast. She was fit enough to out-pedal most people. And once she was on the roads she'd be surrounded by the summer crowds.

As she exited her back garden all was quiet, and the meadow smelled sweet in the still, warm air. She looked around for movement, holding her breath, scanning the willows that dotted the grassland, where someone might hide. Then she pedalled hard, trying to combat the jellyish feeling in her legs. She must have reached the relative safety of Riverside with its closely packed houses within a minute, but it felt like longer. On the way into town she kept an eye on the traffic around her – both vehicles and pedestrians. Was the man running along the pavement anything to do with her? Could the woman in the Ford who'd come within inches of her be a threat?

She locked her bike to the railings outside the imposing stone façade of the Senate House, jamming it in amongst the others that were parked there, overlapping, their handlebars tangled. The cycle chaos contrasted with the serene neoclassical backdrop the old building provided. A moment later she entered the road where the institute was based. For a few seconds she forgot the crowds around her – the sea of voices, many languages mingling in the canyon of Trinity Street – and saw only the towering medieval buildings to her left and right. Stone gargoyles and grotesques looked down at her – strange animals snarling, their teeth barred, a malevolent devil laughing. She'd read somewhere that the stonemasons made them like that to ward off evil. Demons to deter demons. It made the buildings forbidding to outsiders, but maybe the evil at the institute had come from within.

Samantha Seabrook had known the person she'd met the previous night well enough to trust them. And she'd gone with them to one of the university's colleges. Surely her killer had to be an insider – and probably someone she saw day-in, day-out – most likely in the very building she was about to enter.

Well, if so, she'd be in pole position to identify them, and stop them from making her their next victim.

She took a deep breath and turned to her right to walk under a shadowy archway to the entrance she needed. It was an oak door, rounded at the top, solid and dark. She pressed a buzzer and after a pause an unseen male voice told her he'd released the door. As she stepped inside she left the cacophony of street noise behind. Closing it behind her made her feel cut off. After a moment she heard the male voice again from behind the front desk – the receptionist, who must be on the phone. Without that hint of life she'd have thought the place was deserted. Everything was quiet and still. Then, as she waited, she heard a door creak, somewhere way off down the shady corridor, but no one came. The DS who'd been at her house earlier had said DI Blake would be at the institute for most of the day. She wondered if he was there now. It didn't feel as though there was any outside presence in the place.

At last the man who'd been on the phone came to the hatch. As soon as she'd explained who she was he called Professor da Souza.

The institute head appeared a minute or two later. Tara watched him as he approached down the long corridor. He was a tall, strongly built man – around sixty at a guess, and aging well. He had tanned skin and wore dark trousers and a crisp white shirt. As he came closer she could see that its buttons strained a little across his middle; he was solid – powerful rather than plump. Overall he looked comfortable – as though he'd lived well and had always had just slightly more of everything than was advisable. But today, his expression was drawn.

All the same, his grip was firm when he shook her hand. 'My rooms are at the very top of the building,' he said, after they'd introduced themselves. She knew from her research that he was originally from Brazil, but his accent hinted at an expensive private education in the UK. 'We might as well go straight up. Normally

I'd be able to introduce you to many more people who knew Samantha' – she noticed a slight catch in his voice as he said her name – 'but this place is deathly quiet in August.' There was an awkward silence. 'A lot of the staff take their holidays now, before the start of Michaelmas term.'

'Michaelmas term' to the university insiders; 'autumn term' to everyone else. Their footsteps sounded loud as they made their way along the empty corridor and up the stairs. It was a few minutes' walk to their destination, but da Souza didn't make small talk. Drawing alongside him, she saw his jaw was tense, and he brought his right hand up to rub his forehead more than once.

As they entered the professor's suite of rooms (one at the front for the absent institute secretary, and a palatial one at the back for him) she took in the rooftop views. Through a window to her right she could see the upper part of the university church, Great St Mary's, and ahead of her, another window showed the awnings in the market square. She and the professor were very high up and the crowds below looked tiny. It was difficult not to think of how isolated they were. She watched da Souza's strong arms as he put a capsule into his coffee machine and reached for a jug of milk from a small fridge.

'It's a beautiful office.'

'Thank you. What about you yourself? Do you work at your magazine's premises?'

She shook her head. 'I go in for meetings, but I'm mostly based at home. I'm by the river, so it's nice and peaceful.'

He nodded, and motioned for her to take a seat – there was a trio of plush velvet chairs in front of his desk, next to a coffee table. After a moment she had a coffee in front of her and permission to use her recorder. She hid it behind the milk jug in the hope that he'd forget all about it.

'As you can imagine,' he said, 'we're all still in a state of shock at the moment, but I'm glad that *Not Now* magazine has decided to cover Samantha's life. She was always ready to push the cause of the institute and you'll be introducing the topics she cared about to a new audience. Half the battle for us is to publicise our findings, to change the way people think.'

He spoke as though he was reading from a script, but she didn't believe for a moment that he was really that detached. He might be keeping himself in check for now, but she'd seen the emotion simmering just below the surface on their way upstairs. Her mission was to get under his skin so she could see what was hidden there and find out what he'd really thought of Samantha. Tara needed to see her through the eyes of the people she'd left behind. It was the closest she'd get to the truth.

And beyond that lay the possibility that da Souza had been the professor's killer… if she looked into his eyes and asked the right questions, would he be able to keep his secrets hidden?

A thrill of fear ran through her, though she fought to stifle it. If she tricked him into giving himself away, he'd see the realisation in her eyes. He'd know she was an immediate danger to him. She was walking the thinnest of tightropes.

But she owed it to Samantha to use everything she'd got to try to find out the truth.

She relaxed her shoulders, leant forward and swallowed to moisten her dry mouth. She'd need to measure each word she spoke, but the groundwork was the same as ever. She had to get him to relax before she started to dig for the answers she really wanted. 'It must be extraordinarily difficult for you,' she said, 'having to hold everyone else together as well as coping yourself. The circumstances are awful, but I'm glad we'll have the chance to help further Professor Seabrook's cause. Please – tell me what you'd like our readers to know about it.'

Da Souza relaxed back in his chair at that. It was a good start. Interviewing was like tennis: you had to know when to keep a nice gentle rally going and when to employ the drop shot that would catch your opponent out. There was nothing more addictive than playing that game.

She sipped her coffee and listened. Every so often she cut in to ask him for more detail and each time she did, da Souza's answer came more readily. Before long he forgot his script and they were conversing more naturally.

'It sounds as though Samantha was excellent at holding her own,' Tara said, after da Souza had told her about a run-in she'd had with a politician at a public meeting.

'Oh she was,' the institute head said. 'Even as a child.' He was smiling, but she could see tears in his eyes now, too.

Tara held her breath. She needed to react to that little revelation in the right way. Maybe it wasn't a big deal, but all the same, she didn't want to make him clam up by seeming overly interested. Bluffing would be best. 'I think someone mentioned you'd known her for years,' she said, frowning as though with the effort of trying to remember who. 'You were family friends then?'

Da Souza sighed. 'Someone told you, did they? People often mention it.' His tone was resentful. 'Yes, that's right. Her father and I were at Charterhouse together.'

That they'd attended the same exclusive school didn't come as a surprise, but the fact that they'd been contemporaries threw her off. 'I'm sorry – I had no idea. To be honest I wouldn't have said you looked remotely old enough.' Hell. He'd feel she was buttering him up; in fact, the words had just slipped out. She knew from her research that Professor Seabrook's father was seventy-five. She was relieved when the faintest smile flickered across da Souza's face. 'He was several years my senior, but we were in the same house.'

'I see. I wonder if you could give me your opinion on something I've been wondering about then?'

Da Souza's eyes were friendly as they met hers. 'Of course.'

She was about to stray further into the more personal territory she needed to write about, to hook her readers. She was betting she could keep him on side though, if she was careful.

'I noticed Professor Seabrook's PhD thesis was on cash-rich, time-poor parents. I couldn't help wondering if her choice of subject related to her own childhood? I know parents can have a tough time of it if they have to balance work and family life. Sir Brian and Bella Seabrook's careers were so impressive – they must have been fantastic role models – but perhaps they weren't around as much as Samantha would have liked?' She gave him a hesitant smile. 'But I might be putting two and two together and making five.' She paused for a moment. 'As a matter of fact, my mother's an actress, just as Bella Seabrook was. I didn't see much of her as a child, and my father wasn't around.'

The professor leant forward and there was no pause before he answered. 'That must have been hard on you.' His eyes were sympathetic and then he sighed. 'And your point's probably fair. Brian was certainly away a lot. They had a home help who came in though. And when he was there he'd do anything for Samantha – that was never in doubt. And Bella' – now he did hesitate for a moment – 'Bella did what she could, until she died.'

Tara nodded. 'I'm sure.' That pause before he spoke about Samantha's mother had been interesting. 'I gather Bella Seabrook was killed in some kind of accident?' she said.

Da Souza stiffened suddenly. 'That's correct,' he said.

Tara took a breath. She'd have to pull back again if she didn't want to lose him. 'I'm sorry,' she said, 'I shouldn't have brought it up. It must have been awful.'

His expression was sad but the shuttered look on his face was receding again. 'It's all right.'

She tried a different tack. 'I wondered if Samantha's ambition to work in the field of childhood inequality dated back as far as her own childhood?'

Professor da Souza picked up his coffee cup again. His pupils were large, and his gaze distant, as though he was remembering. 'It did; she told me so. Brian got interested in socialism at university and never let that go. He sent Samantha to the local school instead of getting her to board as he had.' He shook his head. 'It meant she saw children from all walks of life. She was aware of her privileged background and wanted to give something back. It mattered so much to her; she was certainly passionate about her work.' He held his drink tightly, his knuckles white. 'In fact, that word summed up her entire personality.'

His voice was quiet, and unsteady. She noticed too that his eyes were no longer on hers. Why? Because he didn't want her to see his tears? Or because he had something to hide? Tara took a slow sip of her coffee and paused whilst she mastered the flutter of nerves in her stomach. She needed to focus. There was more going on than just da Souza's attachment to Samantha Seabrook. She'd been able to tell from his tone that he thought her father's insistence on a local school had been an oddity. It was unexpected from a man who oversaw projects on inequality. Maybe he believed certain things in principle but not so much when they impinged on him or his friends. It meant she knew how to aim her next comment, anyway. 'It seems surprising in a way that they opted against a boarding school,' she said, 'if her parents were so tied up with work.'

Da Souza leant forward. His gaze was intense. 'Exactly what I said at the time! But it was no-go. Brian's principles won out.'

It was interesting that Professor da Souza had been involved enough to make suggestions about Samantha's schooling to Sir Brian. And if he knew the family that well, how had the others working at the institute felt when she'd suddenly landed a plum job there – to say nothing of her almost immediate promotion? There seemed no doubt that Samantha had been a top scholar, but all the same…

'Would you like to talk to Brian, to find out more about Samantha's family life for your article?' da Souza asked, dragging her out of her thoughts.

'That would be very useful.'

He nodded. 'I'm sure he'll want to help. There's almost nothing that will be of any consolation, but I know he'd like to pay tribute to her. I'll give him your contact details, shall I? Then he can get in touch.'

'That would be very kind – thank you. Do most people choose this field for the same reason Professor Seabrook did?' she went on. 'To give something back when they themselves have been so lucky?'

Da Souza put his head on one side. 'Her case certainly isn't uncommon amongst the staff here. I'd say it's a fairly even split between those with privileged backgrounds and those who've experienced the harsher side of life. The former want to improve the lives of those less fortunate than themselves, and the latter strive to give future generations better chances than they had.' His expression was earnest. 'We're all keenly aware that people who fall into that category have overcome horrendous odds to get where they are today. It's tremendously beneficial to have staff here from all kinds of backgrounds. It means we understand the people we're trying to help, but also those in power who might change lives by adopting new policies.'

It made sense, but categorising people like that sounded divisive and patronising. Even if da Souza only made the distinction in his head it had to affect the way he dealt with people. 'It must take a lot of skill to get everyone working smoothly together,' she said. 'Is that difficult?'

'It can be,' da Souza said, with a wry smile. 'Those who've been through troubles themselves tend to feel they're best equipped to find solutions, so disagreements can become quite passionate at times.'

How passionate? That was the question. Maybe her talk with Simon Askey, the other academic da Souza had put her on to, would

shed some light on relationships at the institute. Da Souza had
mentioned on the phone that morning that Askey and Samantha
Seabrook had been working on a joint funding bid. He'd be a good
person to talk to. His schedule meant she'd have to follow him back
to the college he was attached to. He had afternoon meetings there.

As she thanked the professor she took his hand one more time.

'It's a pleasure,' he said, shaking his head. 'It's been good to talk
about Samantha – cathartic in a way I hadn't imagined. If you think
of any more questions, please come and see me again.'

His words gave her a buzz. There was nothing better than
knowing she'd got an interview right. But it didn't alter the relief
she felt at rounding things off; she wanted to be out of his bolthole
and back in neutral territory.

As she moved quickly towards his office door, she noticed a tin
on a shelf next to some coat hooks. It had the St Bede's College crest
on it – a bird of prey depicted in scarlet, its head turned side-on.
He must have seen the direction of her gaze.

'St Bede's is my college,' he explained. 'I hosted a small drinks
party for the institute staff, just a month ago, in the garden where
Samantha was killed. She said at the time that it was enchanting,
and that she'd like to go back.'

The catch was back in his voice. Tara heard him take a breath,
as though he was about to add something, but when she turned
to look at him over her shoulder, his mouth was shut. He seemed
to have changed his mind.

Just because he was Brian Seabrook's contemporary didn't mean
he hadn't been in love with Samantha. The thought played in her
head as she walked down through the building, conscious of the
professor's heavy tread just behind her. And just because he was sad
about her death, didn't mean he hadn't killed her. She didn't know
what had happened the previous night in the college garden – only
that Samantha Seabrook had been drowned. Professor da Souza

certainly looked strong enough to have done that. She thought again of his well-toned arms. He was still in good shape too…

They moved on past deserted rooms, and down the echoing stairwell. By the time Tara finally saw the oak door that would release her back into the sunshine she had the urge to run.

CHAPTER NINE

Blake already had a lot of questions for Mary Mayhew, the institute administrator, but on the way to her office they passed the building's library and he added one more to the list. Emma noticed the plaque next to its double doors too and raised an eyebrow.

Dr Mayhew's quarters were in the basement of the institute. The whole place was dark and her room reminded him of a burrow. It had a window but it was small, and only the top part of it stretched above ground level. Every so often he could spot the feet of passers-by. Each of the office's walls was lined with bookshelves. It was as though Dr Mayhew had had to hollow out her own small space in the middle of it all. She looked distracted and her desk was covered in papers, notebooks and an assortment of personal stuff – a packet of paracetamol, a photograph of a dog and a box of tissues. The place smelled of furniture polish and cough drops.

'I understand it's you we have to thank for the phone call we received from Jim Cooper this morning?' Blake said. 'He explained that you'd encouraged him to ring us. Were you surprised to see him in Professor Seabrook's room?'

Mary Mayhew looked uncomfortable. 'I was,' she said at last. 'I'd given one of your officers Samantha's key and let everyone know the room was out of bounds. I knew Jim Cooper had keys for the whole building of course, but I didn't think he'd use them. And in my head he's security staff himself – just as much in charge of our safety as you are.'

'He's very far from being official as far as we're concerned,' Blake said. If she imagined the university was a law unto itself she could think again.

Mary Mayhew glanced from him to Emma Marshall. She looked affronted. 'I can assure you he is completely trustworthy.'

'He's a civilian who's compromised a murder investigation. Whether he's trustworthy or not is immaterial.' He realised he was blaming her for the trouble Max Dimity had got into with the DCI – but it was worth driving the point home.

'In any case,' Mary Mayhew said, 'I wouldn't read too much into Jim's actions. He's very conscious of his role; he's effectively the keeper of the institute. I manage him, but he's the one who gets his hands dirty. On reflection, he wouldn't see my instructions as referring to him.'

A man who thought he was above the rules. Great. It fitted with the earlier impression he'd got of Cooper.

'We understand that he and Samantha Seabrook were close,' Emma said after a moment.

There was a long pause. 'I don't think Samantha would have said so,' Mary Mayhew answered at last. She looked away for a moment. She was talking to them like a politician, doing her best to protect the institute's staff and its reputation. Surely she could see that a murder enquiry trumped her need to keep up appearances? Her attitude frustrated him; there was clearly more she could say. Why not just be honest, given what was at stake? He had to admit she'd put his back up from the moment he'd walked in to her office. There was something prissy about her that annoyed him. He was glad Emma couldn't read his mind; she'd tell him to stop being so prejudiced.

'Well,' he said at last, 'Jim Cooper claims to have had an affinity with her. Were you aware that they talked about things Professor Seabrook otherwise kept private?'

'No,' Mary Mayhew said, 'I wasn't.' She frowned. 'Samantha had the ability to make people feel special,' she added at last. 'Maybe Jim just imagines that that was the case.'

'As far as we're aware Professor Seabrook didn't tell anyone but Jim Cooper about the doll.'

She was silent and he decided to change the subject. 'What do you know about the professor's hobbies?'

She raised an eyebrow at that. The fact that Samantha Seabrook appeared to have climbed her way into St Bede's fellows' garden hadn't been made public, so Blake didn't explain. 'I've heard she was keen on climbing. Were you aware of that?'

Dr Mayhew frowned and hesitated. 'I believe I might have heard it mentioned.'

It was a pretty guarded reply. 'Who told you? And who went with her?'

Her hesitation was shorter this time. 'I'm afraid I can't remember.' After a moment she added, 'But no one else was mentioned.'

Blake wasn't appreciating her half-truths and edited highlights. 'Do you know if she used a local sports facility?'

'I'm not sure.' She sounded firmer now she'd got used to his line of questioning.

'Never mind. We'll ask around.' He made it sound like a threat and saw annoyance flit across her face. 'Speaking of leisure time,' he went on, 'we noticed the professor had some leave marked in her diary a few weeks before she died. Do you know where she went?'

Mary Mayhew sat back in her chair and relaxed her shoulders. 'No.'

He believed her this time. 'Would she normally share her plans with her colleagues?'

The administrator pulled a face, though within a fraction of a second she'd altered her expression back to neutral. 'It very much depended with Samantha. Sometimes she'd be full of her plans and we'd all be very well aware of what she was up to. At others she enjoyed keeping us in suspense.' She gave a smile now, but it was a wintery one.

Next, he moved on to the guy he'd seen loitering outside Samantha Seabrook's room.

'That must have been one of our senior lecturers, Dr Simon Askey,' Mary Mayhew said. Her tone told him she had mixed feelings about the man; feelings that Blake sensed he was going to share. 'He'll have headed off for the day now.'

Blake glanced at his watch. It was a bit early to call it home time.

Mary Mayhew was watching him. 'He's gone back to his college.' Her tone was tart. 'He's speaking to a journalist about Samantha and then he has a series of meetings.'

Bully for him. 'Did Dr Askey work closely with Professor Seabrook?' He was quite keen to know why he'd been so interested in his and Emma's activities.

'Their fields had a lot of crossover.'

Which didn't quite answer his question.

'Has Dr Askey been at the institute long?'

'About a year longer than Professor Seabrook was. He was appointed as a senior lecturer here at the university after leaving a lectureship at Manchester.'

Interesting that he hadn't progressed in the same way Samantha Seabrook had. 'Were he and Professor Seabrook ever in competition for a promotion?'

Mary Mayhew gave him an unfriendly look and he took pleasure in smiling back at her. 'That's not quite how it works,' she said stiffly.

'I'd still like to know.'

At last she relented. 'He did apply for promotion at the same time as she did. If he'd been successful he would have been promoted to Reader.'

Blake was familiar with the set-up, thanks to his mother. 'So he failed to move one rung up the ladder, whilst Samantha Seabrook skipped a grade and went straight to Professor?'

The frosty look was back in Mary Mayhew's eye. 'Inspector, do you have any idea how many pages of rules and regulations there are to ensure promotions are made on an objective and fair basis?'

'No.' His mother hadn't gone into that much detail.

'Forty-two, at the last count.' She nodded towards an enormous black hardback volume with 'Statutes and Ordinances' written on its spine in gold letters.

But rules could usually be circumvented. 'You're confident the process is fair?'

'As fair as anyone can possibly make it.'

Blake raised an eyebrow.

'When it comes down to it, life's unfair,' she said. 'That's the basis of all our work. If you get any kind of position here at the university – or indeed anywhere else – it's likely to be in part because you've had a decent education, which is, again, frequently down to your family background.'

All well and good, but he hadn't come here for a lecture on inequality. 'Is the promotion process perceived as fair by the staff?'

'Ah,' she said, sighing and slumping back in her chair. 'That's quite another matter.'

It was just the moment to bring up the library plaque. 'I suppose it must be all the more difficult to convince others that it's an even playing field if one of the candidates or their family have made a large donation to the institute? I notice this building is home to the Seabrook Library.' People didn't get things like that named after them for nothing.

Mary Mayhew turned an angry red. 'That bloody library donation!' she said. 'It's been nothing but trouble.' Then she blinked twice, quickly. 'I'm sorry. I shouldn't have said that. The funds for the library were donated by Samantha Seabrook's father, Sir Brian. That was a good five years before Samantha applied for her post here. And we have meticulous records to show exactly why she was the successful applicant then, and again when she got her professorship. She was by far and away the best-qualified candidate.' She sounded as though she'd made that speech before – and was sick of saying it.

'But I imagine that doesn't stop some people from drawing unfortunate conclusions.'

There was a pause. 'You imagine correctly.'

'Simon Askey included?'

'He's never said anything to me directly.'

'What about rumours via other people, snide remarks – that kind of thing?'

'There have been some. Not just from him.'

Blake could imagine.

'But in fact,' Mary Mayhew went on, 'there can't have been any significant disagreement between Simon Askey and Samantha Seabrook. They were just about to put in a joint multimillion-pound bid in response to a funding call. It would have involved them working closely together for three years. You don't sign up for that if you're at daggers drawn.'

'What was the funding call?' asked Blake.

'Social Impacts of Poverty. The deadline's in a week, and if they'd been successful they'd have been working together from next Easter.'

He noticed Emma sit up straighter at that. It rang bells with him too. His DS flicked open her notebook and angled it so he could see. It said: 'Social Impacts of Poverty – cancelled?' This was the funding call with the deadline that had been crossed out so emphatically on Samantha Seabrook's wall planner.

So it looked as though Mary Mayhew's information was out of date. And if Samantha Seabrook had thought better of putting in the joint bid with her colleague, what would Simon Askey's reaction

have been? Especially if its success had hinged on her cooperation…
Blake imagined he would have been angry. He'd be interested to
know how he might have vented his frustration. And what exactly
had made her pull out.

They were just about to leave Mary Mayhew's office when Blake
paused. He was behind Emma, halfway between the seat he'd
occupied and Dr Mayhew's office door.

'About Professor Seabrook's climbing,' he said. 'I'm well aware
you know more than you're telling me. I can't force you to be
frank, but this is a murder enquiry and your attitude's not helpful.
I don't know what you've got to hide, but if you seriously think the
institute's PR is more important than what happened to Samantha
Seabrook then go ahead and keep your mouth shut. I'll walk right
out of here knowing you're being deliberately obstructive.'

He kept his eyes on hers, hoping his expression betrayed every
ounce of frustration he was feeling.

She frowned and her eyes were angry, but he could see she was
about to agree.

'All right,' she said at last.

So he took his seat again, ready for her to explain.

When he and Emma left the room a short while later, after an
acrimonious but enlightening discussion, his DS gave him a look.

'I know what you're thinking,' he said.

'You do?'

'I'm a detective, remember. Since you are too, you probably
know what I'm thinking as well.'

'Mary Mayhew may not be your number one fan, but you can't
make an omelette without breaking eggs?'

'You're good. And we got our answer, didn't we?' He didn't much
care about anything else.

CHAPTER TEN

On King's Parade, people were spilling out of the cafés and eateries and wandering into Tara's path on the road. Tension had built up inside her at the institute and she was all but ready to boil over and shout at them. Giles calling her just as she'd left the building hadn't helped. She appreciated he wanted updates, but nagging her when she'd only just got started would simply hold her up.

She took a deep breath and channelled her energies into cycling fast towards St Francis's College, where Simon Askey was a fellow. It had been Samantha Seabrook's college too. At least she'd get the chance to see the professor's other base. Most academics had offices in their college as well as at their departments and institutes.

She turned right down a tiny side road to reach the place, which was close to King's College and next to the river. It was small and dated back to the early 1400s. She locked her bike to a lamp-post and entered a stone-lined tunnel to find the porters' lodge.

'Dr Askey?' A man in a white shirt and black waistcoat and trousers came out from behind the desk. 'I'll show you the way to his staircase.'

There was something in the man's eyes that increased the adrenaline already coursing round her body. His look was reserved, and he'd cooled a degree or two when she'd told him who she wanted to see. Askey wasn't well liked, she guessed. It didn't make him a murderer. But like everyone else she had to tackle, he was in the running. Part of her wanted to turn and rush back through the tunnel whilst she still could.

But she followed as the porter led her across a deserted court, its pristine grass a dark, lush green. All around her, the tall mullioned windows of the college rooms looked down to where she walked, too dark and distant for her to see if she was being watched. A couple amongst the many were open, and then suddenly, as she watched, someone pulled one closed, banging it against its frame. A crow that had been perched on a nearby stone ledge took off in fright, its strangled cry ringing out before it flapped its way over the high rooftop.

'Here,' the porter said, 'Staircase F.'

'Thanks.' She watched the man walk away, and felt her isolation.

There was a list of names and room numbers – white characters on a blackboard background – at the bottom of a stone spiral staircase. She found Askey's name amongst the others and made her way up, staring ahead of her to get a glimpse of what was coming.

What the hell was she doing? But there was no going back. Sticking her head in the sand meant relying on the police to catch her would-be killer – and she'd been let down before. If things went wrong, at least she had her knife.

At last she found the right door and knocked.

The man who opened up was blond, good-looking and with an air of confidence she could sense even before he spoke; it was there in his eyes and the set of his shoulders.

'Tara Thorpe? Great to meet you. I'm glad you've come to talk about Sam. She and I were – well, I guess you'd say sparring partners.'

From his voice she put him down as a native New Yorker. It was an accent she'd always found appealing, but that didn't stop her feeling wary. There was something in his tone that told her he might bring a very particular slant to Professor Seabrook's story.

He stood back to let her into his room. 'Coffee?'

'Please; that'd be great.'

'So,' he raised an eyebrow, 'what on earth are you doing working for *Not Now*?' His tone said it all. He probably thought he was the first interviewee she'd met who'd adopted a combative stance. How innocent of him.

She smiled, in spite of what she was feeling. 'So you don't count yourself as one of our fans?'

He shrugged, but smiled back as he set his kettle to boil. 'My wife reads the magazine – in between nappy changing and feeding duties. We've got a six-month-old.'

Tara nodded. 'An exhausting age.' Not that she'd know, really. 'Delighted we can provide some light relief.'

'She knew your name when I said I'd be talking to you. She tells me you're good – so that's why I wondered what you're doing working somewhere like that.'

It was her turn to shrug. She offset it with a grin. 'I'm biding my time. I'm not always one hundred per cent happy with our content, but I'm a realist. And they let me do what I want – the article on Samantha Seabrook won't go out unless I'm happy with it.' Tara had found Giles was generally too lazy to force an issue if she really dug her heels in.

Askey's eyes were on hers and a smile played round his lips. 'I can believe that.'

His intimate look made her want to step back and she was glad when he strode over to a worktop to put coffee into a cafetière. He made small talk as he worked.

As they chatted, she took the opportunity to put some distance between them. From the other side of the room, she made a show of admiring the view from his window. It faced over the court she'd crossed to get to him.

'Sam's room was just over there.'

She caught her breath. He'd managed to join her without making a sound.

Looking at where he pointed she saw a twin staircase to the one they were currently in, diagonally opposite them across the court.

'It's funny to think I'll never see her bound out of that doorway again,' he said. He sighed, but Tara knew bad acting when she saw it. She didn't think he was that upset. Interested, maybe, by the turn of events. Even nostalgic perhaps for some past times they'd spent together – but definitely, she reckoned, not unduly cut up.

He could be the professor's killer.

She had the urge to stay near the window; to make sure she could be seen from outside if anything happened…

Askey went back to the cafetière and pushed the plunger down. 'Milk? Sugar?'

'No thanks.'

'A woman after my own heart.' He came over to hand her the drink, holding onto it for just a little longer than was necessary after she'd taken hold of the saucer it rested on.

She was still by the window. Should she risk testing his reactions? She might get useful information – or more than she bargained for.

'I had a bit of a rough night last night, so the coffee is especially welcome.' She forced herself to smile, and watched his eyes. Did he know the background? Had he sent her the doll?

But Askey just smiled back, his left eyebrow slightly raised. She simply couldn't tell. And now he was motioning her to take a seat, back in the darkest part of the room, away from public view. It was an easy chair, next to a low coffee table. She felt anything but relaxed as she sank into it.

'So, how can I help?' he said.

He was probably keen to be featured alongside Samantha Seabrook in her article, and it would work well as far as Tara was concerned. The promise of puffing him up in *Not Now* was a good sweetener to introduce at the outset. Even if he had filed the magazine under 'gutter press', it was the publication of the moment. Appearing in its pages would give Askey his five minutes of fame. 'I'd like to focus on the areas where your and Professor Seabrook's work overlapped,' she said. 'It would be good to celebrate what Samantha achieved but also to give *Not Now*'s readers a glimpse of the work that you will take forward now that she's gone. If you don't mind, I could just set my recorder going. That way we can relax and I won't be scribbling away in my notepad the whole time. Would that be okay?'

'Sure. Go for it.' He leant back in his chair, his eyes on her as she moved to get her recording kit.

She found herself holding her breath as she put the machine down on the table and switched it on.

'So Professor da Souza mentioned you and Professor Seabrook were about to put in a joint funding bid?' Tara began. She mustn't lose focus.

He didn't instantly reply. Perhaps the process hadn't been plain sailing, in which case it was a promising avenue to explore.

'Will you go ahead with the application, now that she's dead?'

He nodded. 'For sure. It would be wrong to pull out. I'll just have to adjust the way the initiative will run. I'll ask for funding for a deputy.'

She was sure he would have been Samantha Seabrook's second-in-command on the project, if the professor had survived. 'Putting something like that together must involve a lot of concentrated effort and creativity. I can't imagine what it must be like to work that closely with someone.' She gave him a smile. 'I'm not great at that kind of give and take, to be honest.'

He laughed lightly. 'Whereas it's my forte.' He rolled his eyes. 'Yeah, well, I'm kidding. I guess you knew that?'

'I'd find it harder to understand someone who said they found it easy.'

He nodded. 'I completely agree. And when you're working on a bid like the one Sam and I were pursuing, the tension tends to build because the hours involved are so long.'

'That must be tricky too, when you've got a young family at home.'

'Right again. It tested my wife's patience. The thing is, research work is… unconventional, and she finds that hard to accept. You can just as easily be thrashing things out in the corner of a pub as in an office. It often helps, in fact, to move out of your normal environment to get the creative juices going.'

Tara imagined Askey arriving home at midnight smelling of beer, ready to tell his wife what a tough day he'd had. Her heart bled for him.

'You can't hold back in this job,' Askey went on. 'I'll say that for Sam, she certainly gave it her all.'

'So it was intense.' She leant forward. 'How did you pool your thoughts, then? What happened when you had opposing ideas for the direction of the funding bid, for instance? How did you decide whose to use?'

'Usually via a full-on row.' Askey gave her a look and she grinned. 'Let's just say she minded like hell about her work,' he went on. 'She and I had that in common – that and the fact that we were each always certain we were right. The thing is, I'm a high achiever too and I didn't like her questioning my judgement any more than she liked me doubting hers.'

His tone was light, but his fists were clenched. She saw him take a deep breath before he carried on. 'Of course, she came from the sort of family where people tended to indulge her, so she wasn't used to being challenged.' He pulled a face. 'And I come from the sort of family where no one indulged me, so I got used to being bloody-minded and refusing to take no for an answer.'

She sighed. 'Sounds tough.'

He gave her a half-smile. 'Ignore me; I got through it. It's just that I'm a sucker for a sympathetic listener. So, my dad was in prison for most of my childhood and my mum was a junkie. But hey, look at me now. And I'm not alone – Kit, the postdoctoral researcher on my project, had a shitty upbringing too. An alcoholic dad, a mother who died young and a sister who topped herself when he was just a kid.' He rolled his eyes. 'The people here at the institute really are a mixed bunch. Kit and I buck the trend though. There are precious few who weren't born to parents from middle- or upper-class families.'

'So really,' she went on, remembering what Professor da Souza had said, 'you could argue that people like you and your researcher are better placed to see what needs to be done? If you've both seen the problems people encounter first-hand.'

He shrugged, but she could tell the nonchalance was put on. 'I tend to feel that way. And my work's been getting some great reviews.'

'I expect you'll be next in line for a professorship, given all that.'

He grinned. 'Thought I might have got one before now, but people like me never rise as quickly as people like Sam.'

Tara knew he was older than Samantha Seabrook had been. 'She was outlandishly young to have risen so far.'

He nodded in agreement. 'She was. You're just saying what a lot of people thought but refused to put into words. It's refreshing to hear you come out with it.'

But Tara had simply meant Professor Seabrook had been an exceptionally high achiever; not that she'd had preferential treatment. Askey was leaping ahead, and clearly assumed she'd be on his side. Her careful approach must be working then. How far did his jealousy go?

'Off the record, did you think it was unfair?' she said. 'I mean, that she got promoted more quickly than you did, what with all your experience – both through your research and in life?' She wondered whether anyone had ever told him it's never off the record when you speak to a journalist.

He gave his characteristic shrug again. 'I don't want to be petty about it, but the promotions committees move in mysterious ways. Of course,' he went on, 'Sam was excellent at getting funding and that always makes an impact. She had a winning way with that pretty face of hers, and her influential connections.' Tara bit back anything she might have been tempted to say. She could contain herself if it meant learning what he really thought about Samantha. And keeping him sweet might save her skin, too. Askey leant back in his chair again, but she wasn't fooled. His shoulders were tense. 'Of course, I'm not saying she wasn't talented too. She certainly had a decent mind. But charm and knowing how to steer people can take you a long way.'

He did a fine line in passive aggression. He was keeping everything simmering, just below the surface. She knew herself how dangerous that could be.

For a second, she imagined him standing over Samantha Seabrook, her hair yanked taut in his hand, her head thrust beneath the water as she struggled for her life.

Shit. She mustn't let the conversation slide away. It was an effort to drag her focus back to the man across from her. 'So she was just as happy networking with decision makers as she was doing her research?'

He nodded. 'Oh yeah – she loved to socialise. She was the sort who needed constant stimulation and sought it wherever she could.' There was a long pause. 'She worked and played hard.'

As Tara watched, she saw Askey's fingers clench, his nails digging into his palms.

'Did she spend time socially with you and other people from the institute?'

'Sometimes. When she was in the mood for us. Never with her PhD student though, Chiara Laurito.'

Tara raised an eyebrow.

'Personality clash,' Askey explained. 'Have you met her yet?'

She shook her head.

'A treat in store. I suspect she'll be keen to give you her point of view, if you feel like asking her.'

'Thanks. I'll have to look her up after a billing like that.'

He touched his forehead with the forefinger of his right hand in a mock salute. 'Glad to be of service.'

She moved on to her next question. 'I know most people find it hard to be completely honest when someone's just died, but what did you think of Samantha's character, if you don't mind me asking?' She was guessing Askey would rise to the bait. He'd hate to be classed as 'most people'.

'Honestly?' He laughed, but it sounded forced. 'She could be a right royal…' he paused for a moment, 'pain in the ass.' He held up a hand. 'Don't put that in your article. Let's just say she was like a kid. Totally intense one minute, frivolous the next. And every so often she'd throw a tantrum worthy of a two-year-old.'

Tara arched her eyebrows. 'Difficult to predict then.'

'For sure. And she was mischievous too,' Askey went on. 'The day before she was killed we all knew she had an escapade planned for that evening. She kept dropping little hints. Oh boy,' he took a deep breath, 'she was desperate for someone to press her for information. She loved to keep us guessing. But even if anyone had asked she'd never have told. That was her all over.'

Tara felt a chill run through her. If the police were right and she knew who it was she was meeting that night, Samantha Seabrook's killer must have been awfully sure of her personality. They'd set up the meeting then gambled that she would enjoy withholding information about her night-time adventure from her friends and colleagues. Keeping their identity secret had depended on them being right. And they had been.

'Of course, the rumours going around now are that old man da Souza did her in,' Askey went on, 'what with him having known her outside work, and her body being found in his college gardens.' His eyes were amused.

This was uncomfortable territory – especially as Askey seemed to be treating it as a joke. 'He certainly didn't seem the sort, when I met him earlier.' It was easy to say; in reality she wasn't sure.

But Askey was nodding. 'I agree. He probably wouldn't have it in him.' His eyes met hers. 'But then who knows what anyone's capable of, given the right provocation?'

Was he giving her a message? Her skin was crawling again, and she fought to focus on the questions she needed to ask. 'You think she provoked people knowingly?'

His look was steady. 'I think it was one of her favourite hobbies.'

'You sound as though you're speaking from experience.'

He gave a slow, lazy smile. 'I must tell you about it some time. Off the record again. I could come and visit you. Didn't you say you lived by the river? That must be nice – though lonely perhaps. Do you ever find that? I'm always up for another drink if you fancy it.'

Tara felt a chill crawl up her spine. Was he coming on to her? Or was this a threat?

She spooled back through the small talk they'd exchanged as he'd made her coffee. Had she mentioned where she lived? She'd been nervous, her mind less focused than usual, but she didn't remember giving him that information...

She found herself wondering how many other people were in their rooms on that staircase. If she cried out, would anyone hear? It was the very quietest time of the academic year. So many people had decamped for the summer, leaving nothing behind but piles of dusty books.

'It's not as isolated as you might think,' she said at last. 'There are always children out on the common.' She hoped he believed her. Whether he was hitting on her or something worse, she didn't want him turning up on her doorstep. 'Young ones playing by day, and youths drinking by night.'

'Really?' he asked, stretching out his legs. His eyes never once left hers. 'Still, maybe you're missing a bit of *adult company*.'

With his gaze still on her she grabbed her recorder and pushed herself up out of her chair.

'I have to go,' she said. The knife she was carrying filled her mind.

He chuckled and got up from his seat too, moving between her and the door.

Her hand was over the side pocket of her bag, one finger slipping inside. But at that moment he laughed again and opened up the door to let her go. 'I'm sorry,' he said. 'I didn't mean to scare you off.'

But Tara suspected he'd enjoyed the experience. As she walked back down the spiral staircase, her legs shook.

Simon Askey had tried to hide it, but his feelings towards Samantha Seabrook had clearly been a maelstrom of mixed emotions. She'd seen admiration fighting with resentment. The time they'd spent together in Cambridge's pressure-cooker environment could have pushed his reactions to extremes.

And now, Askey seemed interested in her. Too interested. And for a moment she let fear get the better of her.

She rode home on autopilot, only noticing where she was as she pelted over Silver Street bridge. To her right she passed the gleaming white frontage of the Anchor pub. She could hear its clientele somewhere down below, chatting as they enjoyed their riverside drinks. But as she went beyond it, her way narrowed, and the dark university buildings pressed in close. The shallow pavements were solid with tourists and a large group spilled into her path. It was as the road curved round to the right that she realised she was going too fast. Another cyclist pulled out of the narrow entrance to Botolph Lane – emerging from behind overgrown trees in the neighbouring churchyard – and she swerved to avoid them. As they pedalled off, oblivious, she tried desperately to pull the bike back into balance, but she was hurtling inexorably closer to the hard tarmac. She'd lost all control. She knew the impact was coming but could do nothing to avoid the fall. She hit the road with a harsh jolt to her hip, her hand, arm and the side of her face making contact an instant later. Still in motion, she skidded several feet, the bike sliding with her. Dimly, she was aware of a car braking, people calling out and someone busy with a phone.

'I'm okay,' she said. 'I'm okay.'

She didn't want an ambulance; didn't want the attention. Just wanted to get home and lock the door. But as she watched, she realised the woman with the phone had stopped anyway, one finger hovering over the keypad. Her eyes were on an object a couple of feet away from Tara. The kitchen knife she'd been carrying. It had jolted out of her bag, along with the tissue she'd used to cover it, and was lying there in the road. Tara's eyes went from the knife to those of the woman who'd been about to call for help.

As she scrambled to her feet, blood dripping from her cheek, the woman's eyes were wary, and she backed away.

CHAPTER ELEVEN

Blake bit back the curse that had been his instant reaction on seeing Tara Thorpe. 'What happened to you?'

She hadn't called him before she left town, as she'd promised DS Wilkins when she'd spoken to him that morning. So Blake had turned up at her place unannounced, right after he'd finished looking round Samantha Seabrook's posh apartment on the north side of the city, where the CSIs were still busy.

All he could see through the crack in the still-chained door was one half of her face – a plaster on her cheek and bruising spreading beyond it. If she'd forgotten to get in touch he could see there might be reasons behind that. Slowly, she released the chain and pulled the door back. Her arm was taped with medical gauze around the elbow and her movements were stiff.

She pulled a face. 'I don't know why Samantha Seabrook's killer's even bothering. I managed to do this all on my own.'

He raised an eyebrow. 'Bike accident?'

'How did you guess?'

It was a relatively common Cambridge affliction. 'No one else involved at all? You're sure?'

She didn't hesitate. 'No one. I was forced off track by another cyclist but they weren't even looking in my direction. I wasn't targeted. I was just going too fast.'

Blake stepped into the square hallway, glancing over his shoulder for a second as he did so. Stourbridge Common was quiet. 'I gather DS Wilkins explained that I wanted another word? I'm guessing you got distracted.'

She closed the door behind him and put the chain back on. She clearly wasn't going to relax just because he was there. 'I did,' she said. 'But not because of coming off my bike. I was cycling too fast because I wanted to get away from Simon Askey, a colleague of Samantha Seabrook's.'

Him again. 'I've already come across the name. What happened?'

'He was angling for an invitation to visit me at home. He was pretty pushy about it, to be honest. He knows I live by the river too, and it freaked me out.' She frowned and then winced as though the movement must have hurt her injured face. 'I don't remember telling him that.'

That was worrying. Tara Thorpe didn't strike him as the forgetful sort. But then again, she was operating under a hell of a lot of pressure, and – he guessed – on almost no sleep.

She led the way to the kitchen and motioned for him to pull out one of the ladder-back chairs at the oak table. 'Can I get you a drink?'

He shook his head – too distracted to want to think about it, one way or the other. 'What exactly did Askey say?'

She explained how he'd offered to come and keep her company, and said how lonely it must be by the river. Blake could see it would have been intimidating – but whether Askey had been indulging in some heavy-handed flirting or whether he'd deliberately tried to frighten her was up for debate. Either way, Blake wanted Askey's version of events. 'I'll warn the rest of the team,' he said. 'And speak to Askey. I don't want him to know what you've told me, though.'

She nodded. She was over by the worktop and he noticed the cracked tiles on the wall behind her. Maybe she wasn't much interested in interior décor. Or perhaps there was another reason she hadn't made the place her own. She had the air of someone who might take off at any minute.

He stretched in his chair. The day had made him tense and his muscles ached. 'I haven't had the chance to eat yet. D'you mind if I order a pizza to have whilst we talk? Would you like some too?'

'That'd be good.'

They agreed on quattro stagioni and he put in an order to an independent on Mill Road.

'What did you want to talk to me about?' Tara said, removing a strand of hair that had got mixed up with the plaster on her cheek. She was wearing an updo but Blake noticed that around 40 per cent of it was now down. She still managed to look good.

'I want your help.'

She raised an eyebrow.

'You're talking to exactly the same people I'm interested in. And they're likely to say somewhat different things to you than they would to me – even if they don't mean to.'

The look she gave him was guarded.

'How do you record your interviews? Digitally?'

She nodded. 'Usually.'

'I want to ask you to share the files with me.' Her expression wasn't getting any more relaxed. He suppressed a sigh. He'd met journalists before who were cagey about their work. He'd thought she'd have more sense, given it might save her neck. The file he'd read on her past floated through his mind. Maybe it was that that was holding her back. He realised he was leaning towards her, letting his impatience show, and he made a conscious effort to relax in his chair. 'I understand you've had more than your fair share of experience with the police. And I get that you probably feel let down. I know you were stalked before, and we didn't catch the perpetrator.'

By contrast to him she folded her arms and sat up straighter; her mouth formed a firm line.

'What?'

'There was more to it than that – I would have understood if the officer in charge had been stumped. But no. He'd become obsessed with one man. He was convinced this guy was guilty, even though he never found enough evidence to charge him. It meant he missed the opportunity to look elsewhere. I did my best to make him see sense. In fact, I was so sure he was wrong that I walked past the man he suspected three times on the street as a test. He didn't even recognise me. There was no doubt. I told the lead officer, but he took no notice. Word was, the suspect said something at interview that really riled him and after that he couldn't see past it.' She put her head in her hands for a moment, then took a deep breath. 'The guy died in the end – the suspect who wasn't really guilty, I mean. Of natural causes. And the lead officer on the case rang me up to tell me, as though it would be a huge relief. Clearly the fact that I knew he wasn't the one hadn't sunk in at all.'

Great. Blake silently thanked the officer who'd queered his pitch. And he wondered who was right. He could imagine Tara Thorpe being just as dogmatic as the lead officer had been. 'Are you sure the suspect couldn't have just pretended not to recognise you?'

The look she gave him said it all. 'Certain. I managed to cross his path out of the blue, so he'd have had no chance to prepare. He didn't react at all; no discomfort and no flicker of recognition.'

It sounded convincing.

'Given all that, have you been wondering if there's any connection between your stalker back then and the person who sent you the doll?'

She shook her head. 'Of course I did wonder, but the person back then wanted me to suffer on a day-to-day basis, in an ongoing way. The stalking was the whole aim – they were already doing what they wanted, which was to calmly take my life apart, until I couldn't go on. The person this time seems more focused: to have got a purpose for me.'

The police psychologist Blake had managed to snatch a word with mid-afternoon had said much the same, though in fancier language. She'd also made an initial assessment of the killer, based on their level of planning and the use of the handmade dolls. It hadn't come as a surprise to learn they were looking for someone intelligent, single-minded and obsessive, but the psychologist had also added 'patient' to the list. And of course, it made sense. It must have taken time to plan such intricate operations, and to make the dolls too. But the profiler had pointed out that the patience might not last. Some people who kept tight control of their actions could lose it spectacularly when the pressure finally got too much.

There was a long pause.

'I know I have to give you the recordings of my interviews anyway,' Tara said. 'Whether I like it or not.'

It was true but he'd rather she did it willingly, and not only to avoid the red tape involved if he had to force her hand. He didn't just want to listen and draw his own conclusions. He wanted her input – to know how each interviewee had come across whilst they'd talked. Their body language. Whether or not they'd been sweating like Jim Cooper…

Tara got up and paced the room. 'It's not that I don't want help. But the fact remains, the last time I gave the police information they ignored it. The upshot was, they missed their chance to catch the person who tried to destroy me.' There was a long pause. 'My life would be very different if they hadn't failed.'

He wanted to ask her more about what had happened back then, but at that moment there was a knock on the door. He saw Tara Thorpe flinch but she controlled it in a fraction of a second and went to open up. It was just the pizza. He'd ordered Coke too. Sugar, more carbs and caffeine. After the day he'd had, he was famished, and the smell of the fresh basil, anchovies and pepperoni made his stomach rumble.

'Expenses will take care of this,' Blake said, reaching past her to hand over the cash.

Back in the kitchen they ate out of the box, lifting the ring pulls on their canned drinks, and for a moment there was silence.

'I've met a lot of journalists,' Blake said between mouthfuls.

'Goes with the territory, I imagine. They're a pain, but they help you too?' She was giving him a look, which he returned.

'Agreed.' He swigged his Coke. 'But one valuable lesson it's taught me is that they're not all the same. It's a profession made up of individuals – some principled and intelligent, some who're the boils on the backside of society.'

She rolled her eyes now. 'I've met quite a lot of police officers too. I grant you they might not all be like the one I dealt with years back.'

He nodded. 'Well, I single-handedly plan to revolutionise your opinion of the police by the end of this case.'

She eased another slice of pizza from the box in front of her, its mozzarella stretching and finally parting company with the topping on the slice next to it. 'Fine words, and if you fail, a side effect might be that I'm dead – in which case you'll be off the hook anyway.'

He put down his Coke can and raised an eyebrow. 'There's no need to be negative.'

She laughed, and he found himself joining in, but he knew he was about to ruin the mood. 'What about your more recent encounter with the police, after your run-in with that other journalist?'

Her expression hardened. 'They made me feel like a criminal.'

'Because of the assault thing?'

'Well, yeah.' Her head tilted to one side.

He held up a hand. 'Mitigating circumstances, what with your past. Plus the records make it quite clear the guy you decked was completely out of order.' He paused. 'But he could have still hauled you over the coals for it. It's a good job you didn't use a weapon.'

She'd put her pizza down. 'Tell me something I don't know.'

Blake remembered his promise to DCI Fleming, after some idiot at the briefing earlier had joked about Tara getting tooled up before she went out. Blake had said he'd talk to her about it; tackle it head-on in a way that soupy Pam, their crime reduction officer, wouldn't. Perhaps now was the moment. He looked her straight in the eye. 'I presume, given what you've just said, that you haven't resorted to carrying a weapon since you received the doll?'

Her eyes flicked to one side and in that split second – as he followed her glance towards her bag – he knew. *Hell.* He hadn't really thought she would. But then, under the circumstances, he wasn't sure why he'd come to that conclusion.

'I'm guessing it was a knife, if you managed to slip it in that bag.'

She didn't reply.

'But I take it that Askey's still in one piece, given you were pelting away from him?' He had a vision of DCI Fleming and soupy Pam, looming over his shoulder, appalled at his flippant words. But the ghost of a smile crossed Tara's lips, and he needed her on his side. That was becoming increasingly clear on many counts. The wrong approach could start the whole thing sliding out of control.

'I'm sorry,' he said, meeting her eyes. 'You've had a hell of a twenty-four hours, and I know I'm only guessing. You don't have to tell me. I just need you to know that knives don't make you safer. It's a statistical fact. And if you take a weapon to your would-be murderer, likely as not you'll just accelerate their plans.'

She rested her elbows on the table. Her head was back in her hands; he couldn't see her eyes. 'Yes,' she said. 'I know.'

CHAPTER TWELVE

They didn't try to talk through the rest of the pizza. Blake savoured the fishy taste of the anchovies; he was used to getting his calories under all circumstances. Being able to compartmentalise his stress kept him sane and well-fed. He noticed Tara Thorpe had left several pieces though. Maybe she'd microwave them up later, when he'd gone.

'What about those digital recordings then?' he said, handing her a USB stick.

She got up, took the machine out of her bag and ejected the memory card.

As she was copying off the files for him, via her laptop, his mobile rang. Patrick Wilkins. He got up from the table and stepped into the hallway.

'Got an update on the boyfriend, boss, Dieter Gartner – though it's not much of one.'

'Go ahead.'

'I found three academics of that name employed at German universities. Only one was working in the same field as Samantha Seabrook, but I checked them all anyway.'

'Good.'

'One's an emeritus professor who's in his eighties, doesn't travel and tells me he's never heard of Professor Seabrook. I haven't managed to get the second one yet – he's away on honeymoon.'

Which didn't totally rule him out, but made him less likely.

'And then there's the third,' Wilkins went on, 'the one who works in the same field Samantha Seabrook did.' Blake heard

Patrick's impatient sigh. *'His university says he's on leave but under the circumstances they found me his private mobile number. Only it's disconnected – must be out of date. I've left a message on his work one, but I guess he might not pick that up. His university's asking around to see if they can find someone who knows where he is or how to contact him.'*

Blake watched Tara Thorpe through the doorway as she removed his USB stick from her laptop. 'Okay. Thanks. Let me know when you've heard more.' It wasn't the best time of year to try to track down academics, of course. His own mother decamped to Florence every year whilst she was free of lectures. She always said she worked better there… go figure. Still, the fact that the man was currently completely uncontactable added one more question mark to a sheet full of them.

Before he went back to the kitchen he took out his private mobile and held it in his hand, looking at the time on its screen. Babette would be getting Kitty ready for bed.

Give K a kiss from me. Tell her I love her.

He sent the text then switched the phone off. He couldn't bear not to message, but getting in touch meant restarting the exchange with his wife, too.

Back in the kitchen, Tara Thorpe handed him the memory stick.

'So this is Professor da Souza and Simon Askey?'

She nodded.

'Thanks. I'll listen to them after I've left. But what were your impressions? Da Souza for instance; do you think he left things unsaid?'

She sat down at the table again and he followed suit.

'Yes,' she said at last, frowning. 'He was cagey about Samantha's mother. I tried to find out how she'd died. He didn't like that one bit and I had to backpedal.'

Blake could understand him clamming up about Bella Seabrook's death. He'd had to pull rank himself to get the information out of him. It wasn't the kind of story family and friends would want splashed all over the press. Sir Brian would never have managed to airbrush the details if the news had broken today; a whisper would have slipped into the fast-flowing currents created by social media and fed the gossip-hungry hordes for a week or so. But back when she'd died, he must have been able to pull strings in the print media, thanks to his background and the money he'd put into various news organisations.

Tara Thorpe was looking at him closely. 'You know what happened to her, don't you?'

He nodded but she didn't ask.

'Da Souza also mentioned that he'd held a drinks party in the garden where Samantha Seabrook was killed, just a month ago,' Tara added. 'There was a wistful look in his eye and he hesitated and opened his mouth as though he was about to say something else. But he clearly thought better of it.' She paused for a moment. 'Most of the conversation left me wondering exactly how far his and Samantha Seabrook's relationship had gone.'

It was a good question.

'And what about Askey?' Blake said. 'Any insights there?'

'Have you met him yet?'

He shook his head. 'Not to speak to. I've seen him in passing though.' He remembered again that cocksure look the academic had given him when Blake had caught him peering through Samantha Seabrook's office door.

Tara told him how Samantha's rooms in college had been opposite Askey's, across a court, and that he'd spoken about watching her from a distance. She also said how quiet he was on his feet, appearing at her shoulder without warning. Finally, she gave the overriding impression that he was a womaniser. It might be odd that he knew Tara's address, but other than that it was certainly possible to put his approaches to her down as a pushy form of flirting. The guy sounded every inch the creep that Blake had first judged him to be. 'Was he honest about what he thought of the professor?' he asked.

'Fairly, I'd say, but in a deliberately larger than life, I-say-what-I-think-I'm-so-forthright-and-unconventional kind of way.'

It was no wonder that just the sight of him had set Blake's teeth on edge. But even if he was obnoxious it didn't mean he was a killer.

'I didn't like him,' Tara said, 'not even at the outset. But I played along with him to get the most out of the interview. You'll probably hate me by the time you've finished listening to the recordings.' Her expression told him she didn't care.

'I'll be prepared.'

Tara traced a knot in the wood on her table with a forefinger, her eyes far away. 'His body language was interesting. He wanted to show me just how relaxed he was. He kept sitting back in his chair, opening his arms, and all of that. But his tone when he talked about the professor, and the tightness of his jaw, gave him away. He was telling me all about the joint funding bid they were working on. He says he'll still go ahead and put in the application.'

Interesting. Could it be that Askey hadn't known Samantha Seabrook was planning to pull out of the bid, and let him down flat? Or was he simply keeping the fact quiet to avoid admitting he was nursing a grudge? Either way, he obviously wasn't put off by going it alone.

As for Tara Thorpe's comments on Askey's body language – well, they were making Blake uncomfortable. She'd probably clocked his rising impatience, earlier in the evening.

'Anything else?'

'He's not the sort who likes being crossed, and I'll bet he holds on to his grudges. When he mentioned Samantha Seabrook's privileged background he had to take a breath to steady himself. So I guess he's resentful.'

'Though he might have good reason? If he was constantly reminded of Samantha Seabrook's wealth?'

She shrugged. It looked as though Askey wasn't the only one who objected to being crossed.

'He certainly feels his background has affected the way he's been treated. And he was quick enough to assume I'd take his side. I presume he's used to winning people over.'

He must be a poor judge of character then. Blake had been quite sure from the start that Tara Thorpe was no pushover. Then again, she said she'd played along… maybe her acting skills were as good as her mother's.

Much later that evening, after listening to Tara's recordings back at the station, and poring over the evidence one more time, Blake made it home. The place used to be a haven. Even the sight of a pink plastic bowl encrusted with dried baked-bean juice in the sink had been reassuring. It meant normality. Security. A contrast to his working life. The last hours of the day were always filled with the promise of seeing Kitty and Babette. Kitty's mere existence had put everything else into perspective; nothing was more important.

But all that had been an illusion. His ability to detect stuff in his day job had earned him a lot of praise over the last couple of years, but at home he'd managed to miss clues to some very fundamental truths.

And now the home had become simply a house – a hollow stage set, holding only his own props, which reflected his solitary existence back at him.

But despite all that he didn't want Babette back. Even though being apart from Kitty tore at his insides – a raw, physical pain. And even though Babette wanted to start all over again.

✴

It was past midnight when former DC Paul Kemp finally called Tara. The sound of his voice brought back a multitude of memories. She'd met him on her way out of the local police station as a seventeen-year-old. (He'd just resigned, and she was full of rage at the officer who was supposedly 'leading' her stalker case.) But that first impression was now overlaid with the years of contact they'd had since, from the sessions where he'd taught her self-defence to the last night they'd spent together – a year ago now.

'I guessed you wouldn't be asleep, under the circumstances.'

In the background she could hear laughter, followed by a shout and the sound of a glass breaking. 'You guessed right.'

He sighed. *'You're sure the person who's doing this isn't the same one from way back?'*

Tara only paused for a second. 'Sure. This is different. And it's definitely not just about me this time.'

'Fair point. I wish I could come and do some digging but I'm stuck on a job in Berlin.'

She smiled for a moment. It was probably just as well. He wasn't the subtlest of people; if he rocked up Blake would definitely notice. As would anyone else in a five-mile radius. 'I don't think the police would tolerate that kind of interference anyway, especially once they knew your background.' Kemp and the force hadn't parted friends.

He laughed then. Loud but not bitter. She reckoned he might have had a few drinks. *'No. You're right there. So, what have you got in place?'*

She told him about the Heath Robinson work she'd done at the house (she'd repeated it that evening), as well as what the crime reduction officer had advised and the work the police team had done on her security. She left out the knife she'd taken with her when she'd gone to interview da Souza and Askey.

'Sounds reasonable. Get one of those marker dye sprays too. The downside is, they don't hurt your attacker. The upside is that means

it's legal to carry them. They'd buy you time – no one reacts quickly when they've taken an explosion of dye to the face. And the stains are pretty hard to wash out, so anyone you get ought to be identifiable for a good while afterwards.'

She sat back against the headboard of her bed and shut her eyes for a moment. 'Yeah. Sounds good; I'll do that.'

Kemp's tone turned serious. *'You can handle this, right? I can chuck the job and come anyway if you want.'*

He'd be able to follow her round like hired muscle. But she was handy herself now, and she certainly wouldn't be able to do her job with him there. Besides, she hated being beholden to anyone. That was just another way of giving up.

'No, I'll be fine. I appreciate the offer though. You stick to duffing up bad guys in Berlin.'

He laughed again. *'All right. But keep me posted.'*

'I will.'

After she'd hung up she lay down and felt for the handle of the knife under her pillow. It was a long time before she slept.

CHAPTER THIRTEEN

Multiple thoughts ran through Tara's mind the following lunchtime as she waited for Samantha Seabrook's PhD student, Chiara Laurito. Half her focus was always on her surroundings. She was sitting on the low wall opposite the Mill Pond. The place was crowded with a mix of tourists and locals, enjoying take-outs from the Mill pub. Her eyes ran over the sea of faces, tensed for the possibility of meeting someone's gaze – someone whose eyes were deliberately on her, and for all the wrong reasons. She glanced over her shoulder frequently too. Behind her, Scudamore's were doing a roaring trade hiring punts to parties headed upriver, towards Grantchester. And ahead of her, beyond the path, on the grass, cattle explored the small gaps between groups lounging with their drinks.

But she had other preoccupations, as well as looking for any signs that she'd been followed. Bea had texted that morning. Bea – more like a mother to her than Lydia had ever been, and probably the only person in the world Tara felt properly close to. Tara imagined her, snatching a moment in the stuffy basement kitchen of the boarding house she ran, whizzing off a text as the bacon for her hungry guests sizzled in the heavy old pan she used. The message said:

How goes it? Fancy popping in for a G&T one evening?

Tara had flung off a reply before she had time to dwell on the secret she was keeping.

Would be lovely soon. Busy with report on St Bede's murder victim for a few days. Hope all well with you.

A few days… she wouldn't – couldn't – see Bea until after this was all over. Bea was the only person who could read her. She'd know something was wrong and Tara wouldn't allow her to get involved. She'd just have to hope it was all sorted out before her mother's cousin started to get suspicious. And that nothing would happen. If Tara was killed, and she hadn't confided, and Bea was unprepared… it didn't bear thinking about. Not that Tara would be around to cope with the consequences of course. Everything would be beyond her control.

And then her thoughts strayed to DI Blake's visit the evening before. God, she'd just been thinking no one could read her like Bea, but the detective had had a pretty good go. The accuracy of his guess about the weapon she'd been carrying was unnerving. He probably thought she was reckless and a loose cannon. She'd been considering him too, of course. She still hadn't decided how he'd measure up against the officers she'd dealt with in the past. All in all, he'd been occupying more of her headspace than she felt comfortable with these past twelve hours. Guilty until proven innocent, she reminded herself.

She sighed. He'd be watching her to see how she behaved. And Samantha Seabrook's killer must be spying on her too.

This is a warning.

It implied she had a chance to save herself if she behaved in the way they wanted. She was being manipulated. She wanted to investigate Samantha Seabrook's life to satisfy her own curiosity – but others wanted it too. Giles at *Not Now* planned to use a killing to make a killing. And the murderer presumably wanted her to delve into Samantha's life as well – for reasons she didn't yet understand. By doing her job, and what she loved best, she was pleasing at least two people she'd do almost anything to be free of. For a second she thought of Blake and the police. They were digging for information just as she was, to try to get justice for Samantha. And they had right on their side, whereas she had Giles breathing down her neck. Well, it couldn't be helped. She clenched her fists and her nails dug into the palm of each hand.

The current day ought to reveal much more about her subject. Sir Brian Seabrook had been in touch by email and arranged for a family friend, Pamela Grange, to show her round Samantha Seabrook's flat at seven that evening.

And, after the build-up Simon Askey had given her, Tara couldn't wait to meet Chiara. She'd emailed her just after DI Blake had left the previous evening, having got her details from the institute website. She'd also found her photograph there, so hopefully she'd recognise the woman when she appeared by the Mill Pond. In her email, Tara had asked if Chiara would be willing to show her the places she most associated with the professor. Hopefully she'd relax if she was focused on her task, rather than the questions Tara was slipping in. And then who knew what might come out?

Chiara had replied to her email within minutes, suggesting a time and promising to come back with a meeting place. It looked as though she was keen to pass on her views. Her message suggesting the Mill Pond as the rendezvous point had arrived whilst Tara's new back door was being fitted. She'd checked it over after the joiner had finished. Everything looked secure. She'd fixed extra locks to all her windows too, whilst he worked. It might be easier to get some sleep that night, which would make a change. Despite barricading herself into her room again the night before and sleeping with the knife under her pillow, it had been impossible to switch off. Sounds on the common carried. Outside, the occasional noise of a bike, braking before it went across the cattle grid and on to Riverside, had reached her through the house's ill-fitting windows. The weather was still hot during the day and uncomfortable at night, but she'd kept the sashes closed. What with the heat and the tension she'd only managed short snatches of dream-ridden sleep.

Her memories of the night before faded, and Tara looked around her again at the grass, the Mill Pond and the crowds. A man in a gingham shirt, blue knee-length shorts and deck shoes was stretched out on the nearest patch of grass to her. A cow approached and tried to nose its way into the crisp packet he was holding. He laughed, keeping his eyes on the woman he was with as he nudged it gently away with the palm of his free hand. The scene looked so easy and relaxed, but she doubted they were as carefree as they seemed. Life wasn't like that.

At that moment she became aware of someone standing still, a little way to her right, and looked up.

There was no mistaking Chiara Laurito. She'd come across people who were hard to identify from their work mugshots. They'd had them taken years back, or paid for a professional job that made them look like a screen idol. But Chiara was stunning enough to be a model in real life, just as she'd been in her institute photograph. She was wearing a beautifully cut sleeveless black dress and gold jewellery. Tara might have been able to match up – in clothes at least – if she'd still had the designer dress she'd worn the day before at her disposal. Unfortunately, coming off her bike had written it off – there was a long tear down the skirt now. And then there was the unsightly graze on her cheek and elbow.

Tara stood up, feeling stiff after her fall, and caught the woman's eye, moving forward through the crowd with her hand outstretched. 'Chiara? I'm Tara. Thanks for agreeing to meet me.'

The woman flashed a scarlet-lipstick smile that revealed straight, white teeth. 'I'm glad to be included.' Her Italian accent was just discernible. 'I was a little surprised that you contacted me. I didn't think Professor da Souza would put me forward as an interviewee.'

Presumably the institute head knew about the personality clash, then. 'Because you and Samantha didn't get on?'

Chiara looked wary. 'You're well informed.'

'I'm a journalist so I tend to stick my nose in. I want to hear about Samantha Seabrook from all sides, so I'm able to write the truth. If I can find people who're willing to be honest then I'm very keen to talk to them. I won't drop you in it, or name names when it's not required. I don't intend to present anyone as petty or vindictive.' *Well, not unless it's justified, anyway.*

Chiara's shoulders relaxed a little. 'That makes sense.' Her eyes met Tara's. 'And I'm happy to tell you what I know.'

'Then that's great. Thank you. It was actually Simon Askey who suggested that you would be a good person to talk to.'

Chiara looked surprised for a second. 'Did he really? That's nice of him.' Her eyes sparkled and Tara noticed a slight blush touch her cheeks. She also remembered Askey's sarcastic comments about Chiara the day before, when he'd told her that meeting Samantha Seabrook's PhD student would be a 'treat in store'.

'Can I get you a drink?' Tara asked, nodding behind her at the Mill.

But Chiara shook her head slowly. 'That's okay, thanks. I thought we could start our tour from here, but I've got another place to show you too.'

Walking the streets of Cambridge, with its attendant traffic noise and hubbub, meant recording the discussion might be tricky, but the trade-off ought to be worth it.

'Okay. Sounds good. So, what made you choose to begin at this spot?'

Chiara's gaze was far away. 'My colleagues from the institute come here for a drink after work sometimes. When you asked what place I most associated with Samantha, at first I could only think of her in her room at the institute, passing on her words of wisdom.' She closed her eyes for a second. 'But then I realised there are other fixed memories I have of her. One is the image of her here, lying back on the grass with Simon and Kit. Kit's Simon's research associate.' She sighed. 'I came across them unexpectedly. They must have waited for me to leave for the evening and then sneaked off here for a drink.' She gave Tara a look. 'I think Samantha was the ringleader. I believe she persuaded the others not to tell me they were planning to get together after work. When I arrived unexpectedly, both Simon and Kit leapt up. They were falling all over themselves to buy me a drink. And would I like crisps? And where would I like to sit?' She sighed. 'It wasn't really their fault, but I could see they felt guilty about it.'

It sounded hurtful, but of course, Tara didn't know Chiara yet, or why Samantha might have cut her out. 'And what did Professor Seabrook do?'

'She just lay back, exactly as she had been. She looked totally relaxed and she smiled at me, but with this look in her eyes. It said, "You haven't misread the situation. I left you out on purpose."' Suddenly she laughed. 'So, you're quite right, we didn't get on. I was surprised that Simon had suggested you talk to me; I suppose he knew the sorts of things I might say. It proves what I've always thought, that he's a fair person. And he saw through Samantha eventually, even though he might have been convinced by her in the past.'

Tara's radar was quivering. Had something happened to change Simon Askey's opinion of Samantha Seabrook? 'I did get the impression that he had reservations about her,' she said carefully, watching Chiara's face.

The student paused for a moment, but then nodded slowly. 'She had a very hard edge beneath that charismatic veneer. She convinced most people to start with. Da Souza was clearly a little bit in love with her, that's for sure.' She sounded bitter. 'Even Kit, who I like, came to study at the institute because of Samantha Seabrook and her reputation.'

'So, Simon fell out with her too then, just as you did?'

Chiara paused for a moment. 'I think the scales fell from his eyes.'

More and more interesting.

Chiara must have seen her expression and put a perfectly manicured hand up to her mouth. 'I don't mean anything serious by all this. Simon wouldn't have killed Samantha.'

Tara tried not to show the conclusions she was drawing from the woman's words. 'All the same, someone did. And once the truth is known, I presume it will come as a shock, whoever was responsible.'

Chiara's eyes widened. 'We all realise that. It's a horrible thought and although none of us can imagine it's anyone from the institute it has made us all very tense.' She looked down at the dusty path under her designer-sandalled feet. At last she shook her head. 'No. Of course Simon wouldn't have done it.'

'Don't worry,' Tara said. 'I'm just writing about the professor's life and what happened to her. It's not my job to try to work out who killed her. You can say what you like to me.'

And as she smiled, Chiara at last smiled back. 'As for mine and Samantha's relationship,' she said, 'I think we were just too alike in some ways.'

Tara raised an eyebrow.

'We both came from privileged backgrounds; both had parents who championed our causes – personal as well as professional.' She shook her head. 'I'm sorry. This isn't relevant. I wouldn't wish what happened to her on anyone. I never imagined—' She broke off suddenly. 'Would you like to follow me up Mill Lane? The other place I most associate with Samantha Seabrook is up on the New Museums Site.'

As they walked past the narrow entrance to Laundress Lane – named for the university's washerwomen, who had once used the river to complete their chores – Tara asked Chiara about Samantha Seabrook's standing at the institute.

'She had a marvellous academic reputation,' Chiara said. 'No one can take that away from her. And she was used to managing people: their expectations, their impressions of her and her projects.' As they reached the end of Mill Lane, she added: 'It's all necessary in a place like this.' She gestured ahead and to her right, towards the ancient walls of Pembroke College. Just one building, but Tara could see how it encapsulated the university as a whole: all that tradition and history, all the countless interconnections and relationships, and a rigid hierarchy.

As they crossed over into Pembroke Street, Chiara looked over her shoulder and met Tara's eye, her long, glossy hair twisting and gleaming in the sun. 'But Samantha wasn't just doing what was expedient. She actively enjoyed it. She liked to be... uppermost.'

'Uppermost? In people's minds you mean? Or in terms of success?'

'Both, naturally,' Chiara said. 'Occasionally we have important visitors to the institute. They make a great show of talking to all the staff, from the lowliest to the most exalted, but I bet you if, after they'd left, they'd have been asked who stuck most in their minds it would have been Samantha. And that would have been because she'd made it so. She'd have made sure she seemed the most fascinated by what they said, the most ready to ask them questions about themselves, that kind of thing. All carefully orchestrated; but I ought to have admired her for that. It's the same thing my father taught me. An important life skill.'

After a short walk, they came to the entrance to the New Museums Site, home to several of the university's science departments. The old Cavendish Laboratory, where Watson and Crick had discovered the structure of DNA, was one of the older buildings that stood there, but from where they were standing most of the constructions they could see were more modern and utilitarian.

'The site doesn't look like much, does it?' Chiara said, once again looking over her shoulder at Tara. 'Not the most beautiful part of Cambridge.'

Tara agreed, though one or two of the buildings stood out as exceptions to the rule, with their bold, modern architecture.

'Even though people don't often come here to sightsee,' Chiara said, 'the view from the top's magnificent.' She raised an eyebrow. 'Or at least, I assume it must be, to have made it worth Samantha's while to climb up there.'

Tara looked up at the dizzyingly high wall Chiara had brought them to. 'Seriously? She did that?'

Chiara nodded. 'Have you heard of the night climbers of Cambridge?'

Tara shrugged. 'Vaguely. I thought it was a group who scaled the city's buildings back in the 1930s or something. Isn't there a book about it?'

Chiara nodded. 'There is, but they're still active today. Google it and you'll find an article all about it in the Cambridge *Tab*.'

'I'll do that. So Professor Seabrook was part of the current group of night climbers?'

Chiara rolled her eyes. 'Nothing so official. Apparently, you have to answer a whole load of questions via some kind of secret email in order to be admitted. Samantha wouldn't have had any patience with that; she loathed jumping through other people's hoops.'

'So she came and climbed independently?' Tara remembered Simon Askey telling her how much Samantha Seabrook liked to regale her colleagues with her adventures. 'And then went and told everyone at the institute?'

'Absolutely,' said Chiara. 'That was the sort of thing she loved to share. Though she was a bit too full of her news. Mary Mayhew, the administrator, heard her talk about it and reacted rather badly. I don't think I've ever seen anyone so angry.' She paused for a moment. 'Almost never.' She met Tara's eyes. 'You can see why. A lot of students looked up to Samantha. Imagine if they'd copied her. What she was doing was both life-threatening and illegal. Someone emulating her without the right know-how could easily get themselves killed. It was Mary Mayhew's worst nightmare.'

It was just after she left Chiara Laurito that Tara heard the text from her colleague Matt come in.

Darling, The cops have announced that Samantha and her killer climbed into that garden. Can you believe it? I'm putting it up as breaking news now. Watch yourself, won't you? Another pub trip soon? x

Good old Matt; just like him to think of updating her so quickly. And the proposed pub trip sounded tempting, but she'd have to put him off for a while. She didn't want to tell him about her death threat – or for him to guess she was hiding something.

She made her way slowly back to where she'd parked her bike, down by the river, deep in thought. The story of Samantha Seabrook's route into the garden at St Bede's tied in with her hobbies all right. She wondered how many other details DI Blake was keeping from her. It seemed she was being treated just as any other member of public. It figured. But she'd hoped she might be entitled to something more, given she'd been lined up as the killer's next victim. She'd thought she and Blake had established some kind of working relationship the night before, but of course, he'd never trust her fully. She was a journalist, and he had his head screwed on.

It must be nice to be on the inside; able to get behind the closed doors that only a police badge could open.

CHAPTER FOURTEEN

Waiting in the foyer at the Institute for Social Studies, Blake checked his messages. The first was a round-up of the news (or lack of it) relating to the necklace found round Samantha Seabrook's neck. The team had done more checking but no one they'd asked had seen the professor wearing it before; what's more, they'd been incredulous at the thought of her even owning a crucifix. Certainly, nothing Blake had seen inside her flat hinted at religious leanings. Meanwhile, Max Dimity hadn't found any shops that sold that precise design of pendant, either. Blake could only assume it had been in the killer's possession for a while. In which case, he was sure the choice of design must be significant. There had been no prints on it, and no DNA other than the professor's. Blake wondered how the killer had persuaded her to put it on. Maybe they'd forced her to do it when they'd let her up for air. Hell. What kind of a mission had they been on?

The next message was from Emma Marshall. She'd found that the roses in Samantha Seabrook's office had been sent by her father, so not much to be learnt there, probably.

By the time he got to the third message, confirming that some CCTV footage taken on Queen's Road showed Samantha Seabrook approaching St Bede's College – alone – Blake was beginning to feel dispirited.

Tara Thorpe's tapes had been interesting though. Revealing and unnerving in equal measure. She could sure as hell turn on the charm when she wanted to. Only Blake knew how calculated it was; judging by their responses, her interviewees had lapped it up. But it had paid dividends – for him, as well as for her. The recordings had prompted him to dig for information on Askey's dad. Of course, the sins of the father shouldn't be visited on the child. In theory... He'd repeated the mantra to himself as he'd looked the guy up. The fact that Askey senior had done time for drug possession and armed robbery didn't make his son guilty of anything. Still, it must have affected his outlook on life.

At that moment, a man who wasn't Askey appeared in front of Blake. Young – mid-twenties at a guess, wearing jeans and a charcoal-grey open-necked shirt. He had wavy dark hair and blue eyes.

'DI Blake?' His accent was Liverpudlian.

Blake stood and nodded, taking the outstretched hand.

'I'm Kit Tyler, the research associate on Simon Askey's project. I'll show you up to our offices.'

So Askey had sent a deputy. It figured. Guilty or not, Blake would look for every opportunity to put the guy in his place. Without being childish, obviously...

The impulse was heightened when they reached the office Kit Tyler had mentioned only to find it empty. From the expression on the research associate's face, Blake guessed he hadn't expected this either. There was a note on the table nearest the door, scribbled on a carelessly torn bit of lined paper.

Apologies. Had to take a call. Back in ten.

Back in ten. Kit Tyler was watching him. Blake wasn't sure if he was embarrassed for his supervisor or not. He bloody well ought to be.

'It makes no odds,' Blake said. 'I wanted to talk to you as well, anyway.'

'Sure.' Kit motioned for him to take a seat at the table. As Blake drew out a chair he took in the scene outside the window. The room faced the opposite direction to Samantha Seabrook's office, down onto a cramped courtyard somewhere in the area bordered by Trinity Street and the market square. It made it rather dark.

'When did you first meet Samantha Seabrook?' Blake asked.

Kit pushed his hair out of his eyes. 'The day I started here. I wasn't working with her directly of course, but she was like that. She made a point of welcoming new staff.'

Blake remembered Mary Mayhew, the institute administrator, saying the professor had had the ability to make people feel special. He got the impression Kit had made the same assessment.

'I'll tell you now,' Kit glanced towards the door, then back towards Blake and laughed a little, 'I actually applied for this job at the institute because Samantha Seabrook was here. Simon knows that, but it's not the kind of thing he likes to be reminded of.'

Blake could imagine. 'So you hoped to work with her when you came?'

Kit shrugged. 'The role was with Simon and I was very happy with that. The project we're working on is fascinating – and the difference we might make keeps me going. But I also thought it would be good to be part of the same institute where Samantha was doing her work.'

Blake nodded. 'So what's your background then?'

'I started off just up the road, north of Ely in Peverton – but my dad moved us to Liverpool when I was small, after my mum died.' His gaze met Blake's. 'The seeds for my future career were sown all the way back then. Mum did piecework for a living; altering clothes for boys who went to the local fee-paying school. Even when she got ill she'd stay up until all hours, so we could make ends meet.' He stared down at the table between them and shook his head. But after a moment he looked up again and smiled. 'There are still way too many inequalities today, but I'm happy. I know I'm in the right place to bring about change. So, after school I went to Newcastle to do my first degree, and then back home again for my PhD. I stayed on in Liverpool for a bit, working as a researcher on a project there.' He shrugged. 'Then the opening came up here.'

'I see. And how much did you interact with Professor Seabrook generally?'

'A fair amount,' Kit Tyler said. 'We attended the same cross-institute meetings and events, and chatted in the coffee queue. Some of us would go off for a drink after work too.'

'A big gang of you?'

Kit shrugged. 'Quite often it was just her, me and Simon, in fact. I think she felt less constrained without some of the more senior staff around.'

'Professor da Souza and Mary Mayhew never joined you?'

Kit laughed now. 'No! Never. Mary Mayhew wasn't Samantha's number-one fan, to be honest. Sam was too much of a rule-breaker. And I think she found Hugo da Souza's paternal concern patronising. Besides, people were always talking about the family connection between them. The last thing she wanted was to encourage gossip.'

'And no Chiara Laurito?'

He watched Kit Tyler's expression.

'Not if Sam could help it.'

'They didn't get on?'

'That's something of an understatement.' He paused for a moment. 'It was odd, really. They had a lot in common, and their backgrounds were pretty similar, just as mine and Simon's are.'

'And you and he get on?'

Kit nodded. 'We don't socialise beyond after-work drinks, but our working relationship is fine.'

'Presumably Simon Askey and Samantha Seabrook hit it off all right too, if she didn't object to him joining the pub trips?'

He waited for Tyler to fill the silence.

'Samantha accepted him as an equal, I guess; someone she could tussle with.'

At that moment the man Blake recognised as Askey ambled into the room. He stood behind Blake's chair and to the right, holding out a hand. In his other was a fresh mug of coffee.

Good to know you haven't rushed back, then.

Blake got up to perform the formalities, even though he knew he was being played. Kit Tyler rose to his feet too.

'I might go for a coffee too,' he said. 'Can I bring one back for you?' He met Blake's eye.

'No thanks.' Blake sat down again and waited for Askey to realise he was going to have to follow suit. Either that or stand around looking like an idiot. At last he gave in, though he made his journey to the seat opposite Blake as slow as possible.

'So, I understand you and Samantha Seabrook were going to put in a joint funding bid,' Blake said without waiting for him to get settled. 'But she pulled out on you. That must have been annoying.' It might not have been that way, but going in hard ought to produce a reaction. It would give him some direction.

'Who told you that?'

So, he had known then. Blake didn't bother to answer and – satisfyingly – it took Askey a moment to revert to his laid-back, cool-guy posture.

When he did, he shrugged. 'Sam was a tricky character; you'll have gathered that already if you're any sort of detective. We disagreed over the approach to the research and instead of thrashing the matter out, she threw a tantrum.' He smiled for a moment. 'I think she was rather surprised when I made it clear I was going to put the bid in anyway, with or without her help. No one's indispensable.'

'You won't miss her now that she's dead, then?'

Askey made a sound that was probably meant to express shock. It came across as phoney. 'Oh, come on!' he said. 'That's not playing fair!'

Blake gave him a look. 'I'm not playing.'

Askey gave a heavy sigh. 'Look, she riled me, okay? But I'll miss her all right. She livened things up around here.' All the same, there was no mistaking the bitterness in his voice; emotion that he couldn't hide.

'What precisely did you disagree on, when it came to the funding bid?' Blake asked.

'Seriously?' Askey sat back in his chair, carefully choreographing his body language once again. It all tied in with what Tara Thorpe had said. He took a sip of his coffee. 'Surely you don't want to know all the technical details? No offence, but it won't mean anything to a layman anyway.'

'Indulge me.'

Askey sighed. 'Okay.' He took a moment to stare at the ceiling before meeting Blake's eye again. 'I'm just thinking how to explain so you'll understand. So, it was simply to do with how we were going to select the participants for our research.' He put his head on one side. 'Her approach would have skewed the results.'

Really? Blake made sure he didn't break eye contact. 'I'm surprised someone as experienced as Professor Seabrook would make that kind of error.'

'So was I,' Askey said. The muscles round his jaw were taut. Was he lying? Or just angry to hear Blake emphasise the professor's expertise?

'I gather you've spoken to a journalist who is writing about the professor – what do you know about her?' Blake watched the man try to find his mental footing again.

'How do you mean?'

Blake leant forward. 'I mean,' he took a deep breath, 'what do you know about the journalist who's writing about Samantha Seabrook?'

Askey looked pissed off. 'Suit yourself. I don't know what you're driving at but for what it's worth she's called Tara Thorpe and she works for a low-brow magazine called *Not Now*. I gather her mother's the actress, Lydia Thorpe.'

Blake waited. 'And?'

Askey shrugged. 'Easy on the eye, charming to talk to but no doubt trained to be that way. Jim Cooper mentioned she lives by the river. He goes past her house every day. I get the impression he enjoys the view. I can't say I blame him.'

Time for another deep breath. Blake forced himself to sit back in his seat before he spoke again. 'When did Cooper mention her?'

Askey frowned. There was curiosity in his eyes. 'Just after Mary Mayhew told us all that Tara would be visiting us. Cooper was clearly looking forward to it. Mary heard his comments on the subject and told him to put a sock in it.'

'So Mary Mayhew passed the news on to everyone? You were all in the room?'

Again signs of curiosity flitted across Askey's face. 'Yes. Everyone who's around at the moment, that is. About three-quarters of the staff are off sunning themselves before the students come back. Sorry – I mean to say, off pursuing their research interests until term starts.'

So Jim Cooper had definitely known about Tara Thorpe's riverside house when she'd been sent the doll. And soon after, Askey, Tyler, Laurito, Mayhew and da Souza learnt about it too. Had any of them also known all along, just like Cooper? That was the question.

'Do you like climbing, Dr Askey?'

There was anger in the man's eyes now. 'I saw the news report, so I can at least tell where you're coming from there. No, I don't. It's not something I've ever done as a hobby.'

'Thank you.' Blake liked that. A nice, flat-out denial. If he ever found so much as a sniff of evidence to the contrary he'd have caught Simon Askey out. He intended to check very thoroughly.

CHAPTER FIFTEEN

Tara had got permission to visit the institute library to research some of Samantha Seabrook's recent publications.

The librarian – a Jeremy Irons lookalike of around fifty – helped her find the journals and books she needed, and they stacked them at one end of a long, polished wooden table next to a tall window with leaded panes. Sunlight drifted in, catching the dust motes they'd stirred up with their activity. The place smelled of books and printing ink.

Tara got busy with the top journal and tried to focus.

'Do ask me anything you'd like today,' the librarian said, before she'd managed to zone in. 'The library will be closed next week. We have a shut-down during August. It makes sense for me to go on leave when the institute's so quiet.'

Tara nodded. 'I'll shout if I've got any questions about Professor Seabrook's work, but what about her as a person? It's always useful to have another viewpoint.'

She saw the librarian flinch, as though the thought of what had happened hurt him physically. 'She was fabulous,' he said at last. 'Tremendous fun. I really can't believe she's gone.' He gave a laugh that caught in his throat halfway through. 'I think it's fair to say the library wasn't her natural habitat. Quiet isn't an adjective I'd use to describe her. If ever I heard a guffaw or a sudden cry of outrage, I could be pretty certain she was responsible. I'd go and tell her off and she'd roar with laughter and say: "Well, go on then; throw me out! The sun's shining, so I won't really mind." I shall miss her.' He swallowed and looked away.

'I'm sorry.' Tara averted her gaze too, and focused on the article she'd just opened. 'I'll have a look at this now. Is there any background you can give me, so I understand it better?'

He seized on the lifeline she'd thrown him. 'Ah yes, I remember that study. Fascinating. It's reasonably self-explanatory. The sample of children she used came from one of the more deprived areas here in Cambridgeshire – close to where she was brought up, in fact.' There was a fondness in his tone again now. 'I remember her saying she wanted to "do something for the folks back home". It was a slightly tongue-in-cheek comment though. I dare say the village she grew up in was a world apart from the locations she used for that research.' He tapped the corner of the journal. 'Cambridgeshire is such a varied county. Like a lot of places, of course.'

After that he left her to it. The paper focused on the relationship between childhood poverty and truancy. The librarian was right, it *was* fascinating, and written in an accessible way, but within five minutes Tara had still lost concentration. The room was warm, and lack of sleep was catching up with her, tugging at the edges of her mind and pulling her towards a dream-like state. She tried to snap out of it, but Professor Seabrook's work sent her thoughts off on the wrong train too. She'd said academics must avoid becoming blinkered. Even if a particular conclusion seemed obvious, they needed to look beyond it to test their findings. Without that they risked failing the young people they were trying to help. Her words made Tara think again of the police investigation into her previous stalker, and how the officer on her case had become so blind to any conclusion other than his own.

Her mind ran over her old tormentor's plan of campaign. The envelope full of dead bees had come first. It had arrived two days before her sixteenth birthday with a note on the outside in block capitals that said, 'NO PEEKING'. She'd assumed it was a present. She remembered squeezing the package; trying to guess what it might be. It felt soft, loose and a bit bumpy, and she'd been excited and curious for forty-eight hours. On her birthday morning she'd been staying with Bea, but her mother's cousin had slept in and Tara had gone downstairs first. She hadn't planned to open any of the presents on her own, but at last she'd given in to curiosity for that one packet. She'd ripped the seal and then leapt back, dropping the envelope when she'd realised what was inside. It had been stuffed full. As she'd thrown it away from her, handfuls of bees had scattered over the floor, spraying over her other presents. Bea had done her best to clear them up, but they kept finding them later. There'd been one mixed up with the bow on her present from Bea, and one had landed in the cup of hot chocolate she'd made herself.

The envelope had had a Cambridge postmark and was empty apart from the bees. Bees for her birthday at Bea's. Had that been deliberate? Now, each time she heard the name of the person she was closest to, she had to push away the feeling of horror. Mind games.

She and Bea had taken the packet to the police, but it hadn't led anywhere and six months later it seemed to have been a one-off. It had still preyed on Tara's mind, but she'd tucked the memory away as something horrible and inexplicable – but over.

And then the next delivery had come. It had arrived in a different kind of envelope that time: Tyvek branded – strong and waterproof.

She'd been at her mother's, out in the Fens, but the rest of the family were away. Her mother and stepfather had taken her two-year-old brother on holiday to the south of France. They'd invited her, but the idea of tagging along hadn't been appealing. And she'd seen the relief in her stepfather's eyes when she'd turned them down.

Although the envelope had been a different sort from the one containing the bees, the postmark was Cambridge again. And the feel of it had been odd. Something weighty had slid inside as she picked it up and she remembered feeling nervous. Instinct had made her hold off opening it at first. The feel of the packet set her hairs rising but a nagging voice kept telling her she was being ridiculous. At last she had opened just one corner, with a pair of scissors. The scissors had come back stained dark red. She'd got the blood on her fingers.

She'd called Bea with shaking hands and her mother's cousin had come, dropping whatever she'd been doing to reach her. Bea had had a closer look with a torch and then they'd taken the envelope to the police station in the nearby town of March. The packet had contained a pig's heart and some bits of chopped up intestine.

After that the deliveries got more frequent. Bird feathers. Maggots. But by then any unexplained package put her on high alert. Just the sight of a suspicious envelope was enough to throw her into full-blown panic, with sweats and palpitations. The police were receiving and opening the deliveries for her now, but she still ended up finding out what had been inside and sometimes she handled the envelopes. Each time her mind conjured up an image of what might be enclosed. It had been almost as bad as looking at the reality. There was no limit to the horrors the human mind could invent.

And her tormentor must have been watching her, because it wasn't long before they realised their little presents were being taken straight to the police.

That was when the bastard had killed her cat. Two days before, a plain letter had turned up for her with no indication that it was anything out of the ordinary. It contained a printed message: '*I don't like being ignored*'. And on the day that Dodger had been wiped out they'd posted a note through Bea's letterbox, addressed to Tara, telling her to look behind a wall in a nearby lane.

Tara had stopped wanting to go out. Stopped trusting new people that she'd met, but also stopped trusting her friends. She couldn't sleep at night. And then, all of a sudden, the deliveries had stopped. But the damage had been done, and she never knew if her tormentor was still out there somewhere, watching and waiting.

Why had they stopped when they did? It had been part of the reason the detective on her case was so certain that the dead guy had been guilty.

It was only Kemp who'd got her through, really. He'd reminded her of who she was, and that she could fight back.

'Are you all right?'

The librarian was staring at her and she realised her eyes were wet.

'Yes. I think it's the dust.'

'Well,' he smiled, 'don't let the cleaners hear you say that. They'd be most insulted.'

CHAPTER SIXTEEN

Blake had been feeling low all day. Babette had replied to the text he'd sent the previous evening, whilst he was at Tara's, by asking him again to take her back.

Kitty cried when I told her you loved her, she'd texted. *She said she wants you. Please, Garstin – think about it. We need to talk.*

He knew the ache he'd tried to quash inside was showing on his face – whenever he wasn't dealing directly with a suspect for Samantha Seabrook's murder, at least. When Babette had left him, she hadn't just been going around the corner. She'd bought one-way tickets for her and Kitty to Australia. She'd made the journey too. It had taken her two weeks to realise she'd made what she called 'the most dreadful mistake of my life'.

He was now conscious of DS Emma Marshall watching him from the passenger seat of his car. He focused on the road ahead, and their upcoming interview with Sir Brian, hoping she'd take the hint. He could guess what she was thinking. Officially, Emma was the only one at work who knew he'd had a bust-up with his wife. By choice he wouldn't have revealed anything, but she'd walked in on him during an acrimonious phone call. Blake had kept back the details though. Emma didn't know what Babette had been planning and why, and then why it had all fallen through. But she knew enough to guess he was hurting. The fact made him deeply uncomfortable.

After a second she said: 'You okay, boss?'

'I'm fine, thanks.' He overtook a tractor carrying bales of straw. Small fragments of the load blew in through the passenger window and Emma swatted them away. The smell of dried grain filled the warm air.

They were out in the wilds of Cambridgeshire under a baking sun, now passing flat fields where combine harvesters were still busy. Whichever way he looked he could see the horizon, occasionally interrupted by a farmhouse, and off to the east by Ely Cathedral. It was referred to as the 'Ship of the Fens' because of the way it rose above the flat landscape. The emptiness of their surroundings reminded him of how he felt inside.

There was an awkward silence.

'Nearly there,' Emma said at last, which they could both see (and indeed hear), thanks to the satnav.

Sir Brian Seabrook lived on the edge of the village of Great Sterringham. The houses there were lined up along one side of the road and looked out onto the countryside. They were detached and large with it – grand Queen Anne-style residences with plenty of space between them. But that didn't stop a neighbour giving them the once-over as they drew up in Sir Brian's spacious drive.

'I'm tempted to give her a wave,' Emma said.

'Best not.'

She sighed. 'No. You're right. Oh God. I'm not looking forward to this.'

He wasn't either, but needs must.

It was Sir Brian himself who answered the door. He looked marginally more together than when they'd seen him at Addenbrooke's mortuary. Just as pale, but more composed.

'Thank you for seeing us,' Blake said, stepping through the door as the man stood back. 'The more we can find out about Samantha, the quicker we can identify the person who did this and bring them to justice.' He fought to ignore the possibility that they'd never find the guilty party. Or that they'd identify them, but fail to get a conviction.

Sir Brian nodded and ushered them through to a shadowy drawing room where the heat of the day was less intense.

Before he'd even sat down, Blake's opening question had changed. He gestured at a photograph he'd spotted on Sir Brian's mantelpiece. It showed Samantha in climbing gear, sunlight gleaming off goggles that were pushed up on her forehead. She was hanging off some snow-encrusted outcrop of rock. There was a man next to her: tanned, with a smile that was as dazzling as the white backdrop. 'I understand Kirsty Crowther's explained how your daughter got into the college garden where she was found.'

The pain in Sir Brian's eyes made him want to look away. 'She has.' He put a hand over his face. 'I paid for climbing lessons for Sammy when she was in her teens. At the time...' he hesitated for a moment, 'at the time it seemed the perfect way to direct her energies. She loved excitement. But if she'd never learnt...'

'There's risk in everything,' Blake said. 'The only person to blame for what's happened is the one who attacked your daughter. If she hadn't climbed they'd have found another way.'

Sir Brian paused but then nodded.

'We've been wondering who she usually climbed with. Is the man in the photo a current contact?' The picture looked recent, judging by the professor's appearance.

Sir Brian nodded. 'That's Dieter Gartner.'

'Samantha's boyfriend?'

The professor's father looked at the carpet for a moment. 'I believe they were quite close at one point,' he said, 'as I explained to DC Crowther. But they wouldn't have been climbing together in Cambridge.' He paused. 'He visited the UK occasionally, but he's based in Germany, as you know. That photograph was taken in the Bavarian Alps.'

'I see. And he hasn't been around recently?'

'I don't think so. The last time Sammy mentioned him he was certainly in Germany, as usual.'

'Was it Samantha who brought the topic up?'

That look of discomfort again, coupled with a pause. 'No,' he said at last, 'I don't believe it was.' Interesting that he'd been asking, then.

'You were wondering about their relationship?' Emma asked. Her voice was gentle and she was clearly on the same page as Blake. 'My father tends to ask me similar questions.'

Sir Brian looked relieved. 'That's right. Parents can't help being concerned. And maybe it's old-fashioned but I liked the thought of her settling down, one day.'

Given the expression on his face Blake guessed there was more to it than that. What was he missing? 'How about fellow climbers closer to home?' he said. 'Do you know anyone else who shared her hobby?'

Sir Brian shook his head slowly. 'She never said.' There were tears in his eyes. 'I keep thinking how little I really knew about her life.'

Blake waited for a moment. 'I'm sorry, Sir Brian, but I have to ask: do you know of anyone who might have wanted to harm your daughter?'

He hadn't waited long enough. The tears came now. Sir Brian pulled a damp, monogrammed handkerchief from his trouser pocket and blew his nose. After a moment he said: 'No. No, I really don't. I believe she had her tussles at work. Things didn't always run smoothly. But nothing that could be related to such a heartless attack.'

'She mentioned trouble with her colleagues?' Blake asked.

Sir Brian shook his head. 'Not in general. But she did say she was having some difficulties with her PhD student, Chiara. The quality of her work was poor, but Sammy was trying to bring her up to scratch. I had the impression that Chiara didn't take criticism well.'

Blake remembered Samantha Seabrook's annotations on the PhD student's work.

'Did she ever talk about her other workmates?' Emma asked.

'I'm afraid she didn't,' Sir Brian said. 'I don't even know most of their names. Though of course we'd discuss Hugo. Hugo da Souza that is, the institute head. I still see Hugo fairly often, and we've spoken on the phone of course. Especially since – since this happened. But if I hadn't caught up with him in a while I'd ask Sammy for his news.'

'We understand you and he have been good friends since school.'

Sir Brian nodded. 'That's right.'

'And Mary Mayhew – the institute administrator – explained about your generous donation in aid of the institute library,' Blake said. 'What made you decide to support the place? I understand it was well before your daughter took up her post there.'

'It's always been a cause that's close to my heart. You might not expect it, but I'm a socialist, Inspector. Sammy went to the village school. I was aware that some of her classmates had very different home lives to ours.'

Blake could only imagine. Though the Seabrooks had had their own challenges. His mind ran to Sir Brian's dead wife, Bella.

'Sir Brian, as you'll understand, we had to look round Samantha's office at the institute, just as we've searched her flat. Every location she occupied might hold clues that will lead us to her killer.'

The man nodded. 'I appreciate that.'

'There was one personal item in Samantha's filing cabinet that I wondered about.' Blake saw Sir Brian's anxious expression. Was he guessing at the sort of things they'd seen – the spirits, and the condoms? He'd better put him out of his misery. 'It was a necklace.'

Sir Brian looked up.

'She had various items of jewellery and make-up, we imagine so that she could prepare for an evening out, straight from work. We understand she did long hours.'

He nodded. 'She was very dedicated.'

'It's what we're hearing from everyone,' Emma said.

'There were a number of necklaces in her drawer,' Blake went on, 'and one amongst them was very different in style to the others. It might have been a present, or handed-down perhaps? It looked old. But I want to rule out that it belonged to a friend we've yet to identify.' It was the one with the monogram. Probably not important, but after all, a strange necklace had also been round Samantha Seabrook's neck. It had been niggling at him.

Sir Brian frowned. 'If you describe it to me, perhaps I might recognise it.'

'In fact,' Blake leant towards him, 'I took a photograph of it when we were at the scene. Here.' He slipped his phone from his pocket and called up the image.

The effect on Sir Brian was instant. The veneer of composure he'd managed to maintain crumpled. Tears welled in his eyes and spilled over. 'Yes,' he said, 'I do recognise it. It belonged to my late mother. A family heirloom.'

Blake put the phone back in his pocket. 'I see. I'm sorry. Thank you for clarifying that.' He had the urge to do something for Sir Brian, but what could you do for a man being reminded of a lost past, and the promise of a future that would never be? Emma had leant forward and put a hand on the man's shoulder. At least she had that instinct. It deserted Blake, even at the best of times.

'We saw you sent Samantha some beautiful roses,' Emma said, gently moving her hand away again. 'She had them in pride of place in her office.'

Sir Brian nodded. He was using the now-sodden handkerchief again. It was a good while before he spoke. 'I liked to send her little presents every so often. She was so precious to me.'

Blake had the urge to offer the man something practical. Tea sprang to mind and he suggested it. For a second he was worried

Sir Brian might think he was suggesting tea could help compensate for the loss of his daughter, but in fact the man seized on the idea.

'Tea. Yes. I'll make it. I should have offered before.'

He wouldn't hear of them helping, so Blake asked if they could go and look at Samantha's childhood bedroom whilst he was in the kitchen.

'Of course,' Sir Brian said, looking down at the floor. 'Turn right at the top of the stairs and go through the door straight ahead of you.' He disappeared across the hall. It wasn't surprising that he needed a moment, but something about his reactions made Blake spool through everything he'd said once more.

The galleried landing above was shadowy and cavernous, lined with many doors, all of them shut. He felt an odd sense of something almost like fear as he approached the door on the end as directed.

The inside of Samantha Seabrook's room heightened his sense of unease. It was partly that it looked as though it had been frozen in time. There were copies of teen magazines still on the shelves – *Just Seventeen* with a photo of some nineties pop star on the cover, and posters dating back to a similar era on the walls. And then there was the décor. When he'd visited Samantha Seabrook's flat the previous day he'd been struck by its trendy minimalism. But here everything was floral and there was a hell of a lot of pink. Perhaps Sir Brian had chosen it? He thought again of the climbing lessons the man had paid for. A safe way to take some risks. And then he thought of Samantha's 'No tomorrow' tattoo. Could he have been nervous about the adult she was becoming? Worried that she was following in the footsteps of her mother, perhaps?

Emma caught his eye and nodded towards some more up-to-date magazines. A recent copy of *Good Housekeeping* and one of *Vogue*, sitting on a side table. And then his eyes slid towards the carpet and he noticed a pair of slippers sticking out from under the bed. They were embellished with gold flowers and leaves and looked pristine.

At that moment, he realised Sir Brian had appeared in the doorway. The man recoiled a fraction at the sight of them; the reality of two police detectives standing in his daughter's room.

'She came to stay here recently?' Blake said, indicating the magazines. 'We understand that she'd had some leave from the institute in July. She spent it here with you?'

Sir Brian sighed. 'Part of it at least.' He paused. 'I'm not sure what other plans she had.'

'Did she visit often?'

The pause was longer this time. 'Not really. But if she needed a proper break then she knew she could come here and get away from it all.'

He nodded. 'Was she particularly stressed, the most recent time she came to see you? Do you think she felt the need to escape?'

But Sir Brian shook his head firmly. 'I wouldn't say so. She seemed as ebullient as ever.'

'I see she left her slippers behind.' Blake nodded to where they lay, under the bed.

Sir Brian had picked up a hairbrush that had been resting on a chest of drawers. It was blue and inlaid with cream flowers. Blake watched as he stroked it with his thumb, his eyes damp. 'She was utterly focused when it came to work, but little things like that could slip her mind.'

Emma had wandered over to a shelf near Samantha Seabrook's bedroom window. She held a framed photograph in her hand. 'This is a familiar face,' she said in a low voice.

Blake recognised it too. There had been a photograph of the same woman on the wall in Professor Seabrook's flat, sitting next to the professor at some club or other. They'd been drinking and laughing. 'We wanted to ask you about friends of your daughter's outside work,' he said. 'Could you tell us please? Everyone who comes to mind.'

Sir Brian's brow furrowed. 'I know she had contacts in Cambridge that I wouldn't necessarily be aware of...'

'Perhaps you could make us a list though, of every name or nickname you can recall? If you give us as much detail as possible, we can take it from there.'

He nodded.

'And what about the girl there in the photo?' She must be a long-standing friend. In the snapshot here, she looked young. She was a good twenty years older in the one in the flat.

'One of Sammy's old school friends,' Sir Brian said. 'Damned if I can remember her name though.'

Blake found that hard to believe. Sir Brian didn't come across as the forgetful sort. 'Please put it on your list when it comes back to you,' he said, holding the man's gaze. 'It could be important.'

CHAPTER SEVENTEEN

Tara had locked her bike to a lamp-post and was walking towards Samantha Seabrook's apartment block. She made her approach along a wide, leafy pavement, the sun slanting down towards her before she entered the shadow created by the grand building. She wanted to take some photos inside, but Pamela Grange, the friend of Sir Brian Seabrook's who'd agreed to show her round, had insisted they meet at 7 p.m. Tara glanced at the sky. Samantha had owned one of the penthouse flats. It had floor-to-ceiling windows, but she'd still have to work fast to catch the light.

And it would certainly be dark by the time she made her way home.

She remembered the patronising face of the crime reduction officer as she'd told Tara she *obviously* shouldn't stay out after sunset. But curfews and working as a reporter didn't mix. The moment she'd been offered the chance to see inside Samantha Seabrook's flat, accepting had become non-negotiable as far as she was concerned. Seeing a person's natural habitat revealed all sorts of information you couldn't get any other way. Maybe Sir Brian wanted the world to see the material signs of his daughter's success. Though the £2.5 million penthouse (Tara had checked) couldn't have been purchased on the back of her professor's salary alone. Perhaps family money had swelled her coffers.

There was no doubt that the flat would have been carefully 'prepared' ahead of Tara's arrival – Pamela and the family would want to ensure it told the story they had in mind. But it wouldn't be a blank canvas. The smallest things could be telling. It ought to be a valuable visit.

As Tara stood outside the complex's huge glass doors, the fitted green dress she'd chosen felt more or less suitable, even though she'd got it in a sale. It was too warm for a jacket. Shame she was encrusted with scabs from her bicycle accident. Her movements still felt stiff and uncomfortable.

Ahead of Tara, a woman entered the building clad in designer gear, a phone held to her ear. Just behind her there was a guy, also looking as though he'd come straight from work – he was carrying leather document cases and wearing a tailored suit.

Tara buzzed the entry phone for Apartment 4 and announced herself.

'Please come in.' The disembodied voice was clipped and precise, prim almost. It made Tara wonder what Pamela Grange would be like to deal with.

She heard a small click and pushed on the door, allowing her access to the cavernous glass atrium ahead. As she made the transition from outside the temperature plummeted. Someone had seriously overdone the air con. So much for being too warm for a jacket.

To her left and right were expansive corridors, bathed in natural light from the vast glass entrance halls to the front and rear of the building. It was upmarket in the extreme, but she couldn't imagine wanting to live anywhere that self-advertising. And the shared entrance would enforce some kind of social interaction with the neighbours. Thank God for her tumbledown house on the common.

She heard soft footsteps from somewhere ahead of her and glanced up to see a woman making her way down a sweeping central staircase.

'Tara Thorpe?'

Tara nodded and walked over to shake Pamela Grange's slender outstretched hand.

The woman was presentable. The tweed skirt and white blouse made her look like a young Queen Elizabeth in country gear, ready to walk the corgis at Sandringham. Her smile was reserved.

'Thank you for agreeing to show me round,' Tara said. 'I can only imagine the sort of pressure you and Professor Seabrook's family must be under at the moment.'

The woman inclined her head. 'It's certainly not an easy time.' She paused. 'Poor Brian. But he was keen for you to see the place.' Her eyes met Tara's for a moment. 'He was very proud of his daughter.' She hesitated again, then added: 'Well, naturally he was. It's only proper, for a father.' She sounded as though she was reminding herself of the fact. Perhaps she'd said it when Samantha had been alive too, like a mantra. Tara wondered how Pamela Grange fitted into the Seabrook set-up. When she'd got Sir Brian's email she'd bought his description of Pamela as a family friend. But now, something about her tone hinted she might be more than that. Ms Grange was looking at her. She seemed to be expecting some kind of comment.

'It's an impressive place,' Tara said.

'It certainly is,' the woman replied. 'Of course, a professor's salary isn't enormous, but Samantha had savings.'

Tara wondered if her mother had left her money, when she'd died. And of course Sir Brian might have contributed too; he certainly had the means. But as Samantha had pointed out in her PhD thesis, generosity with cash couldn't replace a parent's attention. All the same, solvency did make life a lot easier...

Pamela Grange turned and retraced her steps, back up the staircase. 'I hope you don't mind,' she said. 'I can't abide lifts, and besides, it does us all good to use our legs.'

Samantha's apartment was on the third floor. There were only four flats up there; each one must be vast.

'I have a key card,' Pamela said. 'Brian's, of course – not mine. Let me show you in.'

If she'd just been a family friend, there would have been no need to clarify that. Tara was beginning to suspect that Pamela and Sir Brian were lovers. She wasn't the sort Tara would have expected Papa Seabrook to go for – given his first wife had been a glamorous actress. Perhaps his tastes had changed as he'd got older.

Pamela Grange took out the key card and released the door lock. She opened up to reveal a hallway so wide that the stylish sofa in it looked small. Plush seating purely to aid the comfortable removal of footwear was serious luxury. On the wall there was a large abstract painting in reds and blues. An original, though Tara didn't recognise the name of the artist.

She ran her eyes over the rest of the room. It was an interesting mix of classic and modern, but it worked. A mahogany coat stand stood in one corner. Next to it, a mirror with a shelf below in the same wood accommodated a tortoiseshell comb, as well as a Christian Dior lipstick and matching blusher compact. Then there were several pairs of shoes on a whitewashed shelf near the floor. They were mostly designer – Jimmy Choos and the like – though there were some Dr Martens boots too, and a pair of Converse. Samantha Seabrook had clearly switched between different guises. Which had been the real her? That was the question. Or maybe she was a true chameleon, ever changing, not wanting to be pinned down.

Pamela Grange had moved to the other end of the hall and opened a heavy-looking white door. It moved silently on its hinges. 'And here's the flat's main room,' she said.

It was vast. To their right were two large outside walls, with the floor-to-ceiling windows Tara had seen from down below. The space was filled with the evening light, but the room set Tara on edge. There were no curtains. Tara imagined Samantha standing here in her ivory tower, looking down onto the communal gardens below. They were accessible to the public. Had her tormentor lurked down there, watching the object of their obsession?

Why the hell hadn't she told anyone official about the doll? Had she thought she had everything under control? Or maybe she reckoned she knew who'd sent it, and that they weren't a serious threat…

'I don't imagine many thirty-five-year-olds get to live like this,' Pamela Grange said, breaking into her thoughts. Then after a pause she added: 'Though of course Samantha had a tough upbringing. With her mother dying young, I mean. So, it was good that her life took a turn for the better when she reached adulthood.' She paused for a moment and closed her eyes, no doubt reflecting on the irony of that statement, given recent events.

Again, Tara had the impression that Pamela Grange was voicing something she'd told herself before. She longed to ask her what she'd really thought of the professor, but she knew the direct route wouldn't work. Apart from anything else, this wasn't an interview, only a guided tour. Tara would just have to chat and see what came out.

She took out her camera; she needed to get cracking before the sun went any lower. Already it was filtering through the mature trees in the rear grounds of the complex. And besides, removing the direct focus from Pamela Grange might create a better atmosphere for eliciting confidences. 'I'll take a few shots, if I may?'

'Of course. Brian explained that you would want to.' Her hostess walked to the opposite end of the room, where there was a kitchen area with units that looked handmade. She opened the door of a cavernous fridge. 'The milk in here is still in date. Can I make you a cup of tea? I feel rather dry. It's the wretched air conditioning.'

'Thank you. That would be lovely.' But the thought of drinking the milk Samantha Seabrook had bought just before she died made Tara shiver. She'd been alive and well so recently. The whole apartment still felt full of her presence. There was a faint smell of perfume and cigarettes, and a lingering hint of furniture polish.

The air seemed alive with the memory of the drowned woman. Samantha Seabrook's appearance was well known to Tara now; she even knew her facial expressions and the intonation of her voice thanks to YouTube. Images of the professor wandering to and fro in her flat came unbidden: making herself coffee, working at her desk, applying her designer make-up with a confident smile, ready to go out and paint the town red.

Tara turned her attention back to the photographs she needed to take. Viewing the room through a lens, from different angles, made her focus on small details. An exotic ashtray on a mantelpiece told her that the professor had probably travelled, or had friends who had. She walked closer for a moment. The tray still held a dusting of ash, and there was a lighter nearby. Next to the ashtray was a card with a beautiful lino-cut print on the front. Tara glanced up but Pamela Grange was pouring out the freshly boiled water. She edged closer and managed to glimpse the wording inside: *My darling, I'm so proud of you. Your work will change the way people think about childhood. Your contribution humbles me. Your loving Papa xxx* Sir Brian might not have been around for her as a child, but it looked as though he had been trying to make up for it since.

Above the mantelpiece and to one side there was a montage of photos. Tara's eye was drawn to one of Samantha herself. She was clearly overseas – Thailand perhaps? There was a guy next to her: good-looking, with thick, dark hair. Another of the photos showed Samantha with a woman. They were in some dark bar, each in party gear, cocktails in front of them, their arms flung out wide and their mouths open as though they'd been singing and laughing at the same time. A third photo showed an elegant woman in a shot-silk dress standing outside a shop or gallery front. There were vases and other ceramics in the window in the photo, as well as jewellery. The woman had her head on one side, a wry grin on her face. Tara wondered if it had been taken in Cambridge; the scene looked faintly familiar, but the name of the business wasn't visible. The fourth and final picture was of a greying man in a perfectly cut suit outside Buckingham Palace. Although he was clearly the focus of the photograph there were tens of people – all dolled up to the nines – milling around behind him.

She paused for a moment. Pamela Grange was approaching with a tray containing tea in an Emma Bridgewater pot with matching mugs and a milk jug.

'I'm sorry,' she said. 'No cups – Samantha thought they were a waste of time – and no sugar either. She didn't take it herself.'

'I don't either,' Tara said. And she preferred her drinks in large vessels too. All the same, Pamela's statement told her Samantha Seabrook hadn't been the accommodating kind. She was getting the impression of someone with a 'like me or lump it' mentality. Tara preferred that sort; you knew where you were with them, and the fact that they usually had thick skin meant they were difficult to offend. But few people would be tough enough to shrug off the gift of the doll.

'These are lovely photographs,' Tara said, as Pamela poured the tea.

Her hostess looked up. 'Ah yes. That's Brian there, on the day he received his knighthood.' Tara had guessed as much. Pamela's tone was wistful. 'I didn't go myself. He and Samantha treated the occasion as a father–daughter outing. He said he thought she might receive an honour in her own right one day.' She busied herself with the milk.

The comment seemed to confirm Tara's suspicions about Pamela Grange and Brian Seabrook's relationship. Why would she feel cut out if she wasn't romantically involved with him?

'And did you spend much time with Samantha?' Tara hoped the question sounded casual.

A small, rather sad smile touched the woman's lips for a moment. 'Brian would always try to get me over for drinks or dinner if Samantha was staying with him. But that wasn't often; she was so busy.' Then a frown crossed her brow. 'Fortunately, he did see something of her last month; she spent a few days with him in Great Sterringham.'

Tara sipped her tea. 'How did she seem to you then?'

But Pamela Grange shook her head. 'I didn't see her on that occasion in fact.' She paused. 'I – well, I think they were having some private father–daughter time.'

Tara wondered why.

'I presume the other pictures are of Samantha's friends?' Tara said, turning back to the photographs on the wall. 'It could be useful to talk to some of them if you think they might be willing.'

She watched as Pamela Grange's eyes went from sad to wary. 'The man is Dieter Gartner. He works in the same field that Samantha did.'

The picture showed the couple leaning in close and there was a light in the professor's eye. Had they been more than colleagues? Of course, if they were together the police would already know about him. Being able to demand private details as your right had to be a huge bonus.

'And are the women in the pictures work colleagues too?' Tara asked.

Pamela Grange's face twitched, as though the suggestion were laughable. 'I understand the girl in the nightclub is a friend who dates back to Samantha's schooldays: Patsy, I think her name is. I'm afraid I don't have her number.' She sounded relieved. 'And I don't know who the person in the fourth photo is.'

Her tone shut the topic down. All the same, Tara had found out the names of the schools Samantha Seabrook had attended. She'd be able to discover more about the woman in the nightclub.

After they'd drunk their tea, Pamela went to wash the mugs and pot, giving Tara one last chance to look round. Standing in the entrance to the room and glancing back into the hallway she could see what must have been Samantha Seabrook's bedroom;

the door was ajar. The bed looked queen-sized and had a red satin dressing-gown slung over it. There was a packet of Gauloises on the bedside table. The other doors off the corridor were closed. One of them probably led to a study; Tara felt the missed opportunity as she walked back into the open-plan living space.

She was only just inside the room when something that jarred caught her eye. On a side table, that was mainly home to papers, a pile of post and some stationery, was another lipstick. It was nestling in a box that contained a pen with a floral decoration and a set of matching pencils. It was an odd place to keep make-up, but it was also the brand that caught her attention. Rimmel. Its lid was battered and brittle-looking.

In the background, she was conscious of Pamela Grange saying something about plans to clear the flat, but Tara's mind was overtaken by memories. She'd been pretty much brand-loyal to Rimmel as a teenager – preferring it over the expensive makes her mother had tried to persuade her to use. She could afford it herself and that was what counted. Rimmel hadn't gone upmarket since and Samantha Seabrook would have thought the make well short of the mark if the Dior items in the hallway were anything to go by. Which begged the question, what the heck was it doing there? Had someone who'd stayed with her left it behind? And if so, had she been planning to return it next time they came? Otherwise why keep it?

Pamela Grange was drying up the mugs they'd used and putting them back into a cupboard in the kitchen.

Tara went to the massive window again, her mind still on the make-up. The sun was right down now, and the grounds were in near darkness. The moon gave a faint, silvery light to small areas of grass, but the towering trees with their broad branches and thick leaves put most of the lawn into deep shadow.

She turned and saw that Pamela Grange was making her way back towards the entrance hall.

'If you've seen enough I should like to begin my journey home now,' she said.

'Of course.'

They walked back through the apartments' shared upper landing, down the stairs and back to the ice-cold atrium. It must be past the time when most people returned from work. The building was very quiet now, and the entrance was deserted.

They stood for a moment, each searching for their keys. Pamela's had a BMW fob; Tara's own were for her bike. Once again, she'd gone for an option that took her door to door.

The pool of startling halogen light inside made the contrast with the grounds – now in total darkness – all the more intense. But the paths to the road were lit periodically with lamps, set into the ground, providing a gentle atmospheric glow. There were three walkways, fanning out in different directions.

Pamela Grange opened the main door and ushered Tara out. She heard the entrance click closed and lock again behind them.

'Where are you parked?' Tara asked.

'Just a little way along the road there.' Pamela Grange gestured in the opposite direction to where Tara had secured her bike.

'I'm just over here,' Tara said pointing. 'Thank you very much for showing me round.'

Pamela Grange nodded and took the hand she held out as they said goodbye. 'Brian and I shall be interested to read your article.'

Tara was glad she wouldn't be watching them when they did. She wouldn't know in advance if she was passing on truths that would be news to them.

As she turned to take the path she needed she glanced around her. Apart from herself and Pamela Grange, there was just one other person out there: a tall figure in a long coat. The ground-level lights were disconcerting. The figure's trouser legs and boots

– lace-ups – were illuminated, but the rest of him (*was it a him?*) faded into shadow. His face was cast down.

There was no reason to suppose he had anything to do with her.

All the same, she started walking quickly, an unreasonable shiver of fear darting through her core.

She was almost running when she reached the pavement and found the lamp-post where she'd locked her bike. As she fumbled with the key, she glanced over her shoulder. The tall figure was nowhere to be seen. She took a deep breath and tried to steady her breathing. He must have headed off without giving her a second thought. But had he looked like a resident? Had his clothes been smart enough? Hell. She really *was* on edge.

She put her lock in her basket, slung her bag crossways over her body and mounted her bike before pedalling off. Her hands shook slightly on the handlebars, and she tightened her grip.

The street was quiet. It was the same with all the most exclusive roads in Cambridge: the houses or apartments were at the end of long driveways and once evening set in, the pavements could feel deserted. But she was on her way. *Perfectly all right.*

And then, behind her, she heard a faint sound. The subtlest of noises, an almost imperceptible squeak of rubber on metal.

Bicycle brakes.

She caught her breath. She had thought she was alone on the road.

For a split second she had the urge to look round, but instead, she stared ahead and pedalled faster. Yet still she could hear the other bike behind, gaining on her. Whoever it was, they were fast.

But it could be anyone. Fear was making her irrational. They'd probably overtake her in a minute and then she could have a good laugh.

So at last she looked over her shoulder. But the person behind her was no ordinary cyclist, she was sure of that now.

On that hot summer's evening, they wore a black balaclava, hiding their face.

CHAPTER EIGHTEEN

Tara cycled harder then she'd ever done before. Her lungs burned, her legs felt like jelly. It was akin to nightmares she'd had. She knew escape was crucial, but her body wasn't functioning the way it should.

She didn't look over her shoulder again. She could hear enough to know her pursuer was still there. Instead she pelted around a corner, out from the lane of exclusive new properties. *Where was she?* Back amongst Cambridge's terraces now, at least, but the road was still dark and deserted.

She mustn't crash again. Though surely if the other cyclist caught her now, people would come out of their houses?

But maybe not. Several of the homes were in darkness.

And then suddenly she saw salvation: a main road ahead, and to her left a pub.

She threw her bike down on the pavement as she leapt off – not bothering to lock it – and hurled herself through the door to the Punter.

She was dimly aware of the clientele inside, looking up from their drinks and meals as she almost fell, but her sole focus was on making her way further inside, away from the person who'd chased her.

One of the pub's waitresses was at her elbow. 'Are you all right?' Her look of concern almost made Tara lose control. She could feel tears welling up behind her eyes and swallowed hard before she nodded.

'I'll come and order a drink in a moment,' she said. 'I just need to make a call first.'

'Of course.' The waitress's eyes held a mixture of curiosity and unease.

Tara auto-dialled Blake, her fingers still trembling. She'd only given him her location and the briefest details before he broke off to issue instructions to unseen officers. He must be at the station. Patrol cars were being despatched. It was true that a cyclist in a balaclava was distinctive, but surely her pursuer would have taken it off the moment they were out of her sight?

'Did you tell anyone where you were tonight?' Blake said, speaking to her again.

'Only colleagues at *Not Now*.'

'Right. Stay where you are.' She could hear he was on the move too. His voice changed, becoming more echoey. *'Wait inside the pub. One of my team will drive you home and get more details from you. You've met Patrick Wilkins, haven't you? It'll be him, so you'll know his face.'*

For once, Tara was in no mood to argue.

✷

Some hours later, Blake arrived back at his house in Fen Ditton. He was intending to snatch some sleep, but his mind was still buzzing. The team had gone door to door on Samantha Seabrook's old road, as well as to the other flats in her apartment block. No one had seen anyone wearing a balaclava, and only one person said they'd noticed a stranger – a tall guy in a long coat. It sounded like the man Tara had described, but whether he'd been the one on the bike was another matter. No one had seen him out on the road, only in the apartment block grounds. Of Samantha Seabrook's other former neighbours, no fewer than three had been watching *The Great British Bake Off* at the relevant time, and one had been having a bath. The whole planet could probably have been taken over by aliens without anyone noticing. He despaired of the human race.

Checking CCTV coverage would come next. If the cyclist had been captured removing their balaclava… but how likely was that?

He went to the pine cupboard in the corner of the kitchen and took out a bottle of whisky and a tumbler. He poured himself the sort of measure that was only reasonable after a day hunting a murderer and sat down at the round oak table. None of his furniture matched, but each piece meant something. The table had been his grandmother's. When he was younger, he'd mistrusted people who had everything new, just for the sake of being up with the latest trend. But now he wished he could change the items that reminded him of Babette. Maybe the other people he'd noticed, whose houses looked like show homes, were simply trying to erase bad memories.

He took out his phone. It was getting late, but he needed to call Tara Thorpe. Sir Brian Seabrook had been at home that evening when Emma had called to check, just as he ought to have been. And he'd confirmed – assuming he was telling the truth – that he hadn't told anyone about Tara's appointment with Pamela Grange. Ms Grange herself had said the same, as had Tara's colleagues. She'd given Wilkins their numbers so they could follow up. So Blake was pretty certain she must have been followed.

He called Tara's number.

'*Yes?*'

She hadn't been sleeping, that much he could tell from the speed at which she answered. Not that he'd have expected otherwise. She must be drained by now. That damned knife he suspected she'd been carrying… had she had it with her that evening? If she was running on empty she was all the more likely to do something stupid with it.

'You all right?'

'*Dandy.*'

Her answer brought a smile to his lips for the first time that evening. 'Look on the bright side. You could get quite a scoop out of this.'

'Yeah. Thanks.'

He imagined her rolling her eyes. On conjuring up the image, he realised he'd noticed they were a rather beautiful green.

'So, what's the news?' she asked.

Back to business. He relayed the latest updates – or lack of them.

'I wanted to ask you about the people you've seen today. Where were you immediately before your meeting with Pamela Grange?'

'I went to Gardies for a bite to eat. Before that I'd been at the institute library and it didn't seem worth going home.'

Gardies: the Gardenia restaurant on Rose Crescent and probably the closest place to the institute to eat. Any of the staff could have followed her there – or spotted her on their way home. He sighed.

'Then earlier on I was with Chiara Laurito, Samantha Seabrook's PhD student, wandering the streets of Cambridge,' Tara finished.

Blake took a large swig of whisky. 'How was the interview with Chiara? Enlightening?'

'It was. But there's no recording this time I'm afraid.'

There was a moment's pause. He could see it wouldn't have been easy if they'd been on the move, but had she arranged it that way? To make sure she still had some command over the information she was gathering? Surely she must want to share, if it would help keep her safe? But there were other things at play here too. Tara Thorpe had probably spent a lot of her life fighting for control. Her stalker would account for that, and people like the rival journalist who'd tried to put one over on her. She'd got her own back on him, of course, when she'd decked him one. Still, she might not see things as other people would.

'I've written up some notes I can give you,' she said at last.

'That'd be good. Could you email them over?'

'*One moment.*' She went off the line for a second. '*They're on their way to the address on your card.*'

'Thanks.' But it wasn't quite the same. 'And what about insights? Anything that struck you?'

Another pause.

'*Simon Askey was right about Chiara and Samantha Seabrook not getting on. Chiara was surprised I'd come to her for an interview, and*' – there was a sound that told Blake Tara was having a drink too, and he guessed it wouldn't be cocoa – '*she seemed pleased that it was Askey who'd put her forward. She blushed a bit. Whereas I got the impression Askey has mixed feelings about her.*'

'I see.' He dragged himself up from his seat and carried the phone over to the sideboard, trying to ease the drawer open there. He knew there was an unopened packet of cashews somewhere. 'What else?'

It suddenly came to him that his questions were coming out rather abruptly – because he was ravenous and tired and not quite sure where he was with her. She didn't seem to care though.

'*You'll see from the notes that she reckoned Askey and Samantha got on at first, but she said he'd seen through her in the end. And then she caught the look in my eye and said: "But Simon Askey wouldn't have killed Samantha." Or words to that effect.*'

Blake whistled as he removed the nuts from the drawer.

'*I know. I'd never implied he might have, so I'd say the thought's crossed her mind independently, even if she's dismissed it.*'

There was something in her tone. 'You don't think she has though?'

'*I'd say she was trying to convince herself as much as she was me.*'

'That's very interesting.' Tara Thorpe sounded wired, in spite of everything she was going through. She was getting that rush from the information, just as he did. Journalists and police shared some things.

He was glad. It meant she'd be tempted to share her hoard of information so someone else could admire it. He was just the same. 'Anything more?' He'd sat back down again and jammed the phone between his shoulder and his ear, so he could rip the cashew packet open.

'A couple of things. One was that she kept saying how alike she and Samantha were.'

'Clear-sighted of her.'

'Yes. And the other was that – even though she and the professor hadn't got on – she made a point of saying she'd never wish that fate on anyone. Standard stuff, but in the same breath, she said: "I never imagined…" and just let the sentence hang. That made me think.'

He swallowed the cashews he'd been chewing. 'I'll bet. I wonder what she meant by it? That she'd had some inkling that Professor Seabrook was headed for trouble, but she'd "never imagined" anything of this magnitude?'

'That's what it sounded like. So why was she doing any imagining on that score in the first place? Was it just that she thought Professor Seabrook had it coming, and daydreamt about her getting her comeuppance?'

Blake frowned and swigged more whisky. 'Or did she have some specific reason for believing that she was under threat?'

'Quite.'

'And after you'd finished with her you went to the institute library?'

'That's right. The reading I did was interesting…' She paused for a moment and he wondered what she was thinking. *'But I also found someone other than Professor da Souza who seems to have genuinely liked Professor Seabrook.'*

That was news. 'The librarian?' he guessed.

'Yup. He clearly had quite an indulgent view of her high spirits, even when they disturbed his peace and quiet.'

Blake wondered if everyone at the institute had been in Samantha Seabrook's thrall. Whether they'd loved or hated her they all seemed to have been affected. 'Anything else of interest from him?'

'Not really.'

'What about the visit to the flat then? And your conversation with Pamela Grange.'

He heard her sigh. *'Again, not recorded as it wasn't an official interview.'*

He wasn't going to let her use that as an excuse to clam up. 'I don't believe you'd have let that get in your way. You owe me, Tara. We're covering your back and I need to know what you know.'

The sound of the breath she took transmitted a mixture of impatience and resignation. *'Okay. Well, there were some interesting photos on the wall – which you'll have seen when you visited, I guess. Of course, you'll already know all about Dieter Gartner.'*

'The absentee boyfriend? Yes.' The moment he said it he realised he'd fallen into her trap. Had she even known Gartner and Samantha Seabrook had been in a relationship? He'd slipped up, but it was too late now. 'There was another photograph in there that I was interested in,' he said. 'Of a woman sitting next to Samantha Seabrook in a bar – looking rowdy.' He bit back the information that the same woman also featured in a photo in the professor's childhood bedroom, and that Sir Brian Seabrook claimed not to remember her name.

'Oh yes.' She waited a moment. *'Pamela Grange was vague about her. Someone from Samantha's past, I think.'*

'I see.' He paused. 'Tara, I need to let you know that Sir Brian and Pamela Grange deny telling anyone else about your visit to the professor's apartment this evening. Your colleagues at *Not Now* say the same.'

He heard her swallow. *'Okay.'*

'I think it's fair to assume that wherever you are, Samantha Seabrook's killer won't be far away. If you ever feel annoyed about sharing information with us, you might want to consider that.'

CHAPTER NINETEEN

Blake sat at his kitchen table. The house was so damned quiet. If Babette hadn't left, she'd probably have been in bed by now. Kitty certainly would have been. But the signs of their presence would have been there: the lingering smell of a supper Babette had cooked; the creak of a floorboard as she shifted in their bed; a half-cry from Kitty, caught in a dream. He might find a toy kicked under the sideboard, ready for him to pick up and put on Kitty's chair, knowing how pleased she'd be to find it in the morning.

He pushed the thoughts away and drained the last of his drink. He'd have to watch out for Tara Thorpe. He'd been talking to her like a colleague that evening. Probably tiredness and the whisky that had done it. And the fact was, he'd been enjoying himself. For a moment, in the heat of the investigation and sharing opinions about Chiara Laurito, he'd forgotten everyday life. But he needed to remember that although Tara portrayed herself as a straight talker she was anything but. She was measuring everything as she said it; much more than he had been that evening.

At last he dragged himself from his chair and up the steep cottage stairs. He switched on the light in the empty bedroom and walked to his bedside table. The only one that had stuff left on it. He put his phone on to charge, removed his jacket and slung it on a chair. After that he lay down on the bed without bothering to get out of the rest of his clothes.

Thoughts of the day mingled uncomfortably in his head, refusing to coalesce into anything useful. Simon Askey's arrogant grin,

Kit Tyler's speculative look, Sir Brian and his reticence when it came to discussing his daughter's friends. His caginess about her relationship with Dieter Gartner.

He needed to switch it all off; for now at least. Sleep on it for a few hours and something might slide into place. But when he tried to avoid thoughts about the case, his brain shifted to his private life. Knowing it was the wrong thing to do, he reached out and lifted his phone from the bedside table, pulling it towards him so that its charging wire was taut. Once again he found himself staring at the message Babette had sent earlier.

Please, Garstin. Let's meet.

It was a follow-up to the one she'd sent when she'd told him about Kitty crying.

How could she? How *could* she?

Mustn't go down that spiral. He could feel his anger building up, his heart rate increasing. He took a deep breath and closed his eyes.

✱

Being escorted home by DS Patrick Wilkins had added to the tension that had built up in Tara that evening. She hadn't liked the detective sergeant when she'd first met him and being chaperoned by him hadn't changed her mind. ('Well done. You did the right thing to call us.' Yes, she knew that. But being stalked by a killer didn't mean she wanted to be treated like a five-year-old. *Oh congratulations. You were being followed by the person who sent you a death threat and you worked out you should phone the police.*)

Talking to DI Blake had been better but his final words still rang in her head.

For a second she felt a pang of guilt. Maybe she should have admitted she'd discovered the first name of the raucous woman in the photo in Samantha Seabrook's flat. But this Patsy person was a friend from the professor's teenage years. What relevance could she have to a case that so clearly revolved around Samantha Seabrook's academic life? If Tara could talk to her first she'd get her fresh; not after she'd already polished whatever story she wanted to tell. That would make the material for her article a whole lot better.

And then she thought again of DI Blake's take-home message.

Where was the killer now? Were they watching her house? Noting which of her windows was still lit? She'd leave lights on when she went up to bed, but tonight she'd have to sleep. She was trying to work but her head was spinning with fatigue. She'd allowed herself a shot of vodka to steady her nerves but it had made her feel queasy.

For now, she sat at the back of the house in the kitchen, the curtain drawn across the window that faced towards Fen Ditton. She'd left the door to the hall open, and she was right next to the back door, which was more secure now than it had been. She wanted to keep her eyes on the main entry points to the house. It wasn't logical. An intruder would be more likely to try one of the windows.

She tried to distract herself from the thought of the empty common outside her cottage. She'd seen some useful things that day. And DI Blake knew it. Once again it was as though he could read her mind. Respect for that. She wasn't used to it; she was able to fool most people. Still, she'd got one over on him, too. She smiled. She bet he was kicking himself for giving her that information about Dieter Gartner. Boyfriend confirmed. And the way he'd said 'absentee' made her think they were having trouble tracking him down. That latter detail wasn't anything she'd give to Matt at *Not Now* as breaking news, though. She'd only be able to quote it as a rumour, anyway, and even then she couldn't be certain that that was what DI Blake had meant. It didn't make sense to take risks with her career at the moment. Besides, it would be pretty shitty to drop Blake in it like that. It might have been different if it had been DS Wilkins who'd said it…

She was putting off going to bed. Sleep was dragging at her, pulling her limbs and making them weak, but she opened a web browser as one last delaying tactic. Once she admitted it was well and truly night she'd feel even more vulnerable.

She sat there idly googling, entering various combinations of words and phrases into the search box at once. 'Night climbers'; 'Cambridge'; 'Samantha Seabrook'; 'Unofficial'; 'Pembroke College'; 'Scandal'; 'Institute for Social Studies'.

Blearily, she scanned the results with the précis of each page's contents. The article in the *Tab* that Chiara Laurito had mentioned came up, as well as the book she'd remembered on the topic. And then, five pages of links in, she spotted something that made her catch her breath.

An anonymous blog by someone who indulged in the sport of night climbing themselves. The précis referred to 'a certain Cambridge professor' and the words 'recent rumours' and 'scandal' were used.

She clicked through. This blogger had clearly heard about the rumpus Samantha had caused at the institute. All the references to her were veiled, but there was no doubt. Female. Unusually youthful for her senior academic role. Employed at one of the city's institutes. Much admired by many male students and colleagues (and some female ones too). It looked as though the official night-climbing community had mixed feelings about her. Maybe they were irritated that she hadn't felt the need to be part of their gang.

And then Tara saw a sentence that made the hairs rise on the back of her neck.

'It is believed that the good professor might be responsible for this anonymous but public Instagram account.'

Tara clicked through and felt her mouth go dry. The most recent photograph was of dark trees, lit only by moonlight. Behind them was a brick wall. And in front, a fountain, its water gleaming palely in the night.

Her eyes ran rapidly to the next picture. It was taken from a height, looking across a green expanse towards a main road in the distance, lit by street lights. Queen's Road, she was sure of it. This was Samantha Seabrook's secret Instagram all right; and these pictures had been taken the night she'd died.

And then she saw the next image. A dark shadow stretched across it. She clicked to enlarge it, unable to tell what she was looking at.

The photo had been artfully taken. It showed a figure clad in black, down to black gloves on their hands. They were sitting astride a wall. The wall to St Bede's fellows' garden – there was no doubt. They'd reached the top and paused. The image showed them from the neck down.

And then Tara clicked on the photo before, but that had quite clearly been taken on a different night and showed a view from one of the ancient colleges.

She sat tense in her chair. Her skin crawled. This had been part of the killer's game. They'd known Samantha would delight in tantalising her followers. She'd have been pleased at the idea of taunting them. And the killer had been too. They'd wanted this.

Would the police already know? If they had her mobile then presumably they would… but if it had been stolen by the killer they might not realise yet.

Except… She kept scrolling. There were comments on the most recent photo from that day. If anyone knew Samantha Seabrook was responsible for that account they'd have surely alerted the police?

Several of her followers had put generic things like: 'You rock!' or 'Very cool, as always'. But further down she found one posted the previous day. It said: 'What goes around, comes around.'

She looked around for her phone to call DI Blake, then realised she'd left it in her bag in the hall. It was only as she got up, breaking the spell that had focused all her attention on her laptop, that she heard the noise.

The sound of footsteps on the gravel outside the sitting room window. Heavy. Almost as though someone wanted her to hear; to know they were there.

The queasiness she'd felt earlier intensified and her breath shortened. She stood perfectly still, listening. A soft thud. Not a knock, but as though a solid mass had leant against the door suddenly.

The camera. The police had put in a camera to transmit photos of anyone who approached the house straight to the station. And she had the alarm they'd left her. She'd left it on the kitchen dresser. In a second she'd pressed the button to alert them. But of course it made no sound, there in the house. The police hadn't wanted to frighten off their quarry.

And now Tara wondered if the whole system was working properly at all. The photos had to transmit. The alarm had to sound at the station. And then there had to be officers close by to come to her aid. And any one of those things could fail.

She needed to look herself. If the cameras didn't work properly she'd be the only one who could tell the police who it was who'd been outside. But she didn't want to be seen.

She went through to the sitting room, just as she'd done when DI Blake first came to see her.

She entered the dark room quietly, moving towards the bay window. The moonlight shone through the threadbare chintz curtains. Once she was closer she'd be able to ease one of them back to get a glimpse of the figure outside.

She was only a couple of feet from the window when the sound of footsteps on the gravel came again. Whoever it was, they were on the move. And then, as she stood within reach of the curtains, leaning forward, a dark shadow fell across the window. The silhouette of one hand raised up and pressed on the glass.

CHAPTER TWENTY

Blake was glad he'd stuck to one whisky. Even as it was, that – coupled with the fifteen minutes' sleep he'd managed before the call from the station – weren't conducive to a sharp mind. He hated a cat nap; it was worse than no sleep at all.

Now, he was making his way behind a row of shops on Chesterton High Street. A single lamp gave the route a sickly glow. The narrow alleyway led between a newsagent and a burger joint, and was daubed with unimaginative graffiti: the black spray-painted initials of the person who'd been responsible. He'd walked through scraps of rubbish, including what looked like the remains of one of the burger meals – ribbons of onion, a handful of squashed chips – bursting over the tarmac, and some suspicious-looking meat. The smell of it mingled with the odour of urine.

Round the back he had found iron stairs leading to the door of the flat that he wanted. Now he was standing in front of it, looking at its peeling paintwork. He'd knocked three times (loudly) and waited four minutes before he heard any sound from inside. When he did, it was a crash, as though someone had knocked something over. After that there was a thump as (he guessed) someone fell against the other side of the door he'd been pummelling.

'Police! Open up!' he shouted once again. He'd already run out of patience – it had deserted him somewhere around the Milton Road junction of the A14. He was glad he hadn't had to speak to DCI Fleming before he'd driven to Chesterton. He could imagine her now, asking why he wasn't organising a voluntary interview, so everything could be recorded officially, but Blake had a feeling he'd be turned down. Even if he wasn't, he'd lose the chance of using surprise to get an unguarded response. Waiting for a solicitor to arrive was hardly going to give Blake the advantage. He wanted to see where this approach got him first. If he needed to make it official he could pick up the pieces later.

At last the door opened and Blake took in a mix of rippling muscles, vest top, skinny jeans and buzz cut. The ruddy face that looked back at him was scowling.

Time to find out what Jim Cooper had been doing loitering outside Tara Thorpe's cottage. The fact that he'd left without doing anything before the police arrived was a relief all round but it raised plenty of questions.

'I'd like an account of your movements this evening please,' Blake said, making it clear that 'please' was just a figure of speech. 'Start from when you left the institute. I want to know where you've been and who you've seen.'

Cooper pulled back slightly, blinking and frowning. 'Why d'you want to know? What's happened?'

'That's not something you get to ask. But I can promise that if I'm happy with your answers I'll let you go to bed and sleep it off. I'd like to get to bed too.'

'If you can tell I need to sleep it off, then I'm guessing you already know where I've been.'

'The smell suggests a boozer, but a bit more detail would be helpful.'

Cooper's fists bunched for a moment, but then he leant sideways against the doorframe. 'Feels like I'm always the first port of call when someone's got a problem. Have I got trouble written on my forehead or something?' He looked too drunk and too knackered to reach the level of anger he might have managed otherwise. Just as well. Blake would have had trouble dealing with a man of his bulk if he'd got aggressive. 'All right then,' Cooper said at last, through a yawn. 'Have it your way. I was at the Mitre.'

'That's more like it.'

He looked aggrieved. 'Can't you keep your voice down?'

'Surely you're not worried what the neighbours think?

He gave Blake a look. 'I've already had the odd complaint.' He lowered his gravelly voice. 'Nothing to do with me – there's a fussy woman next door. She complains if she hears my ironing board creak. I don't want to get booted out.'

Finding anywhere affordable to live in Cambridge was a challenge; Blake recognised that well enough. He was dog-tired but he made an effort to speak more quietly. 'I could come inside if you want to tell me all about it?'

'I don't.' The man was leaning forward again now; he had the shoulders of a wrestler.

'But the sooner you do, the sooner I'll be out of your hair. Then you can get your beauty sleep.'

He could see Cooper was tempted by the path of least resistance. At last he sighed, his breath damp and heavy with alcohol. 'All right then.' He stood back to let Blake in, but even then, it was a squeeze to get past him.

Cooper's hallway was narrow, with just three doors opening off it. He led Blake through one that opened onto a living space: an oblong room with a sofa that looked ready to sink into the floor, a kitchenette and a small, square table. The table had an overflowing saucer-cum-ashtray on it, and there was a calendar featuring topless models on the wall. Other than that, the place was pretty bare, and also tidy. Cooper took the chair at the table. Blake didn't fancy the sofa; he'd be way lower than the building supervisor if he sat there, not well placed if he needed to take any physical action. He leant against the wall instead.

'You went straight from the institute to the Mitre?'

Cooper took a packet of fags from his pocket then rummaged again and dragged out a lighter. 'S'right.'

Blake nodded. 'Anyone go with you?'

Cooper lit up, taking a moment to get his lighter's flame to meet the end of his cigarette, then shrugged. 'Askey. Kit Tyler. Rick – the guy who does reception part-time.'

'Were they all there the whole while you were?'

Cooper took a long drag on his cigarette. 'Rick was. The others left a little while earlier. Glad to see the back of them if I'm honest.' He was flicking the thumbnail on his left hand back and forth against the nail of his middle finger. And there was a muscle going in his jaw.

'They pissed you off?'

The flicking stopped. 'There's just a bit of "us and them". You know, between staff and the institute's academics.' He stared at the ceiling for a moment. 'Normally, when you talk about the "staff" at a place you mean everyone who works there, don't you?'

'Agreed.'

'But it's not like that at the institute. When they say "staff" it's in the old sense.' He brought his head down again and met Blake's eye. 'Like the servants. That's how we're viewed.'

Blake wondered where that left Mary Mayhew, the administrator. Staff, but with a PhD to her name. He was guessing she drank on her own if she ever went to the pub. But she didn't look the sort anyway. 'So, you and Rick the receptionist left the Mitre together,' he said. 'What time was this?

'Round about closing. They stay open till midnight on Thursdays and Rick likes a drink. As for me, well, I wasn't in the mood to go home yet.'

'What had you and the others been talking about?'

Cooper put his head in his hands for a moment. 'We were reminiscing about Samantha, and that made me want to drink until I couldn't think any more.' For a second Blake caught sight of a tear in the corner of the custodian's eye. His face was flushed.

'And then what?'

'Rick went off one way, and I went off the other.'

'You cycled?'

Cooper shook his head slowly. There was a centimetre of ash on the end of his cigarette. The smell was making Blake feel ill. He didn't mind it normally, but the whole flat was full of it too – stale and all pervading. 'Needed to walk it off a bit.' He stifled a hiccough.

'Which route did you take?'

He frowned for a long moment, his eyes unfocused. 'I can't— No, wait, I've got it. I went down Portugal Place.'

Blake imagined Cooper weaving his way along the narrow, vehicle-free lane, and pitied the residents. It was one of the most picturesque streets in Cambridge, but given its position – so close to the bustling pubs and restaurants on Bridge Street – it couldn't be the quietest place to live. Thank God for his village bolthole. 'And then?'

'Across Jesus Green, of course, and all the way along the river until I got to the Green Dragon bridge.'

The wrought-iron footbridge that crossed the River Cam.

'You went straight home?'

'It was late.' He looked pointedly at his digital watch. 'I *have* got work in the morning.'

'Right.' He waited until Cooper looked up at him and met his eye. The ash had fallen from his cigarette onto the table. 'So, what were you doing peering through Tara Thorpe's windows then?'

Cooper sat forward in his chair, his shoulders tense. 'She reported me?'

'No. You were seen. It tends to look pretty suspicious when someone's prowling round an isolated house very late at night. Especially when they don't knock. What were you doing?'

He sighed. 'I wanted to speak to her.' His head nodded forward for a moment, but at last he straightened up again. 'I mean it's all just like I was saying. People of my sort, we don't count. I knew Samantha Seabrook better than anyone else at the institute and this Tara Thorpe's writing about her, but has anyone told her she needs to interview me?' He took a deep drag of his cigarette. It looked tiny in his hand. 'Course they bloody haven't. What on earth could I have to say that's remotely interesting? How would I presume to know anything about one of the professors? Shit.' Blake could hear the emotion in his voice. He ground the cigarette out on the edge of the full saucer, tipping it up, and spilling half its contents on to the table.

'How did you know where she lives?'

He slumped back in his chair. 'At work, after Samantha died, Mary, my boss, told me to expect a journalist called Tara Thorpe. Explained she was writing a tribute of some kind in the magazine she works for. I'm in charge of security, so if a stranger's going to be walking the institute corridors I need to be informed.' There was a note of pride in his voice now. 'And we're getting a lot of calls from all and sundry about the murder at the moment. Mary doesn't want just anybody blagging their way in. She showed me and Rick on reception Tara Thorpe's photo, to make sure we'd know whether anyone giving that name was genuine.'

He smiled suddenly, and Blake didn't like the look in his eyes.

'But to me, she's not a stranger,' Cooper went on. 'I cycle past her cottage every day, and I've clocked her a few times. I saw her moving in. She had to cart her stuff across the meadow on trolleys.' That look again; a leer of sorts – he was too drunk to hide it. 'I watched her for a bit. Almost offered to go and help, but I didn't reckon she'd appreciate it.'

You're right on that score, Blake thought.

'Okay. So, you're telling me you went to talk to her, but although you hovered round her door and tried to see through her window you didn't knock?'

'I wasn't sure if she was still up. I was looking for a light inside the house. I knew it was late.'

'And what could you see?'

'There was a faint glow from the front.' His eyes closed for a moment. 'Then after I walked off I looked back and I could see light from round the curtain of one of the side windows. But by that stage I'd thought better of it. It was after one. I still want to talk to her though.' He pointed a chunky finger at Blake. 'I can tell her things no one else can.'

Blake took a large lungful of air once he'd left the flat. He'd spent a while longer trying to get Cooper to explain the private knowledge he claimed to have of Professor Seabrook. The custodian's answers hadn't been satisfactory; he'd just gone on about the way he 'understood' her, and wouldn't say any more.

Blake could still smell the inside of Cooper's flat on his clothes. He'd need to get his jacket cleaned. He pondered the man's reactions to his other questions. He'd been quick enough with his explanation for stopping at Tara Thorpe's cottage, and his hurt at being left off her list of interviewees sounded genuine too. But deciding to pay her a visit in the small hours was hardly normal. Had he been drunk enough, at the time, to feel it was acceptable? Or was the explanation more sinister? Even if he was desperate to talk to Tara Thorpe, it didn't mean he hadn't harmed Samantha Seabrook. In fact, his obsessive interest in her made it more likely.

He checked his phone and double-took. Jim Cooper's visit wasn't the only development of the evening. News of Samantha Seabrook's secret Instagram account had him pausing halfway across Chesterton High Street until a lone driver honked at him. The information came via DC Max Dimity, who'd followed uniform over to Tara's cottage when she'd pressed her alarm button earlier that night. Tara Thorpe had discovered the account before the team who'd been tracking down Samantha Seabrook's phone records.

He tried to imagine Jim Cooper deliberately engineering a carefully posed and incomplete photo of himself, ready for Samantha Seabrook to post as a tease to her followers. He was impetuous, at least when drunk – as shown by his actions that evening. Could he be equally controlled and full of guile when sober?

Blake frowned. His head felt as though it had a gang of miniature tap dancers practising in it. He glanced at his watch. Time for a couple of hours' sleep. And then he'd go to see Tara Thorpe on his way in to work.

At the last minute, before turning down the side road where he'd parked his car, he looked back towards Jim Cooper's flat. And there was the shadow of the building supervisor, looking down at him from the living room window. He was standing tall now – as though he must have sobered up quite a bit.

When Blake found his car and unlocked it, his mind was full of that last view of Cooper. It didn't do to take anything for granted.

CHAPTER TWENTY-ONE

Tara was watching DI Blake through the sitting room window as he made his way from Riverside towards her cottage. He'd texted to warn her he'd call in. She already knew it had been Jim Cooper outside the previous night – the detective constable who'd come to her from the station had told her that. Perhaps DI Blake had an update; he looked as though he might have been working all night. She had to admit, he wore the rough look well. She went to open up.

'DI Blake.'

'Just call me Blake. Everyone does.' The detective's eyes met hers and she tried to read his expression. He was probably marvelling at how awful she looked.

'I can imagine what you're thinking,' she said, standing back to let him in.

'On this occasion, I bet you can't.' There was a faint smile behind his eyes. 'I'm sorry if I look... informal,' he went on. 'I've avoided mirrors this morning.'

'Me too, but I'm going to have to sidle up to one soon. I'm due out in the sticks later – to interview Sir Brian. I'm assuming you'd like coffee?'

'Thanks.'

They walked through to the kitchen.

'So, have you spoken to Jim Cooper?' She turned to make the drinks.

'I have.'

And...? He paused long enough for her to glance back at him over her shoulder. *Surely he can give me more detail, under the circumstances?*

Perhaps he'd read her look. As she turned back towards the kettle, he sighed as though making up his mind and then spoke again.

'His explanation fits with what we know about him – and he was quick to come up with it, despite seeming quite drunk.'

He explained what the man had said about knowing where she lived, and having been shown her photo.

'I'll get Mary Mayhew to confirm his story, of course,' Blake added, 'but even if he's telling the truth, it doesn't mean he can be trusted. Maybe he's a good actor who can think on his feet. It was certainly an odd time to drop by for a chat.'

Tara nodded and put a mug of black coffee down in front of Blake. 'Well, if he claims he's got so much to tell me I'm definitely going to arrange to talk to him.' She read his look. 'Don't worry. I'll make it somewhere public. Besides, I'll have my knife.'

He opened his mouth.

'Kidding.' She didn't want him arresting her. But in truth she wasn't sure whether or not she was joking. She'd meant to leave the knife at home when she'd gone to meet Chiara Laurito, but at the last minute her nerve had failed her. Now she'd got the spray dye Kemp had recommended too, but when push came to shove, what if it wasn't enough?

'Tara, what are you going to do?'

She raised an eyebrow.

'To cope. I'm guessing we're both running on empty. I will eventually get some sleep, but what about you? What if tonight's like last night? And then the next night is too?'

He must be wondering what kind of a freak she was, to have no one she could stay with.

'I'm ahead of you,' she said, after a moment. 'At around two this morning, I booked myself a room for tonight at the Newmarket Road Travelodge. Not sustainable long-term, given the prices, but if I get my eight hours it ought to tide me over for the next few days. It's the institute summer garden party this evening and I've been invited along, so I'll go straight back to the hotel from there.'

The party was an annual tradition, apparently, marking the anniversary of the institute's inauguration. Under current circumstances, she'd thought Professor da Souza might have cancelled it, but he'd said he wanted a chance to bring everyone together at such a harrowing time. He was planning to use the occasion to pay public tribute to Samantha Seabrook. Tara rather wished she could skip it.

Blake nodded. 'Good move.' His eyes were on hers. 'I'll look forward to hearing any intel from that event.'

'Point taken.'

He sighed. 'And you don't need me to tell you this, but make sure no one follows you back. It's pretty easy to slip past the front desk at a Travelodge. And then all you have to do is follow someone with a key card and you're through to the rooms.'

And she knew he was right.

Before she left for Samantha Seabrook's childhood home, Tara emailed Jim Cooper. She wanted to hear what he had to say and besides, if he was going to start hanging around her house she'd prefer to head him off. She suggested meeting him at the Pickerel that afternoon. He might be ready for a hair of the dog by then, and the booze should loosen his tongue. She'd probably see him again at the institute garden party that evening, but she'd rather his colleagues didn't overhear their interview.

As she walked from her cottage towards Riverside, she kept an eye on the meadows around her. The noise of crickets filled the hot, dry air. The people she could see looked innocent: a dog walker, a man and a boy on bikes, an older man fishing by the side of the river. But round the perimeter of the common there were dense patches of trees. The startling sunlight made the shadows there all the more intense. Tara strained her eyes, removing her sunglasses for a moment when she thought she caught movement. She couldn't be sure. But someone had been watching her recently, just as Blake had said. She hoped they hadn't got access to a car if they were on her tail now. She'd left her Fiat where it was for days, but who knew how long they'd been spying on her. They might know exactly which car was hers, and where it was parked.

Tara found it hard to keep her eyes on the road ahead as she began her journey. Two cars had left the same network of backstreets at a similar time to her. She couldn't say for sure if either of them had stayed on her tail. They weren't immediately behind her on the A10, but the traffic was heavy and they could be hanging back. The distraction meant she didn't feel ready for her interview when she arrived in Great Sterringham. She sighed and closed her eyes for a moment. She was going over stale territory anyway, given Blake had already visited. She realised she'd been hoping she'd spot something he'd missed. She knew it was childish – and pointless. How would she know, anyway, when he hadn't shared his conclusions with her?

Sir Brian let her in, insisted on making her coffee and began to talk before she'd got going on her questions. They sat downstairs in an elegant drawing room for the interview and she recorded the lot. Blake would be pleased… but it was Sir Brian's demeanour that interested Tara the most. On the face of it he seemed like a kind man, knocked sideways by grief, but she recognised his type. In spite of what life had thrown at him – the loss of his wife at a young age and now his daughter too – he had that air of being entirely secure in his own sphere. Awful things had befallen him, he was no stranger to tragedy, and yet nothing had shaken his self-belief, or his sense of where he stood in the world.

After they'd talked they went to look at Samantha Seabrook's bedroom. Tara had angled for this. She'd said how helpful it would be to see the professor's own space. She'd muttered something hackneyed about understanding Samantha in the round, from the girl she'd been to the woman she'd grown into. And when they got up there she was glad she'd talked him into it – there were several things that made her wonder. And then she saw the photograph on the wall. It was of the same woman who featured in the drunken shot in Samantha Seabrook's flat – the one Blake had asked her about. Thanks to some googling – using the first name Pamela Grange had supplied, and the school Professor Seabrook had attended – Tara now had a surname for her too. It was interesting – clearly Blake hadn't managed to get Sir Brian to hand that information over.

'Oh,' she said, walking towards the picture, 'isn't that… yes, it really is! Patsy Wentworth!' She watched his face as she said it and saw it fall. In fact, it plummeted.

'You've met?' he asked.

'I haven't seen her in a long time, but she's hard to forget.' Which judging by his reaction she must be. She decided to go for it. 'I'm sorry to ask, but you don't by any chance have her up-to-date address, do you? She sent me the details, but it was on a phone of mine that got pinched.'

Sir Brian was standing there, clasping and unclasping his hands.

'Perhaps you could call to check she doesn't mind, if that would help?' She was taking a risk, but she was willing to bet he wouldn't. His expression told her he wanted to keep his distance.

'I only know it myself because she came to stay here whilst I was away,' he said at last. 'Sammy decided she wanted to throw a house party in the country. There wasn't enough room at her apartment in Cambridge, and not much private outdoor space. When I got back I found various belongings that her guests had left behind, including a scarf of Patsy's. I offered to post it back, because Sammy had already gone home.'

He turned and walked out of the room and she followed him, slowing her pace to match his sad, heavy tread as he descended the stairs. There was a small thinning patch of hair on the back of his head, only visible now that she was above him, and a couple of fine grey hairs rested on the shoulder of his jacket.

In the hall he took a green leather book from a table and leafed through it to the section for W.

The pause gave her one last chance to glance around, peering through doorways into rooms they hadn't visited.

'Here.' Her attention snapped back to him. He held up the book for her and she copied the London location into her iPhone.

He'd got her email address too – that was unexpected but handy.

Sir Brian followed her eyes and shook his head. 'She never acknowledged receiving the scarf I sent, I'm afraid. I asked Sammy for her email address so I could contact her to check it had arrived.'

'Thank you. It'll be good to get back in touch.'

All of a sudden, he put his free hand out and touched her arm. 'Don't read too much into anything she might say about Sammy,' he said. 'Patsy was always wild; not a good influence. Sammy tended to show a rather different side when they were together.'

Suddenly, Tara's tiredness washed over her. 'Of course,' she said, summoning up her last ounce of energy. 'I understand. And I know what Patsy's like.'

As she walked from the house, down the long drive, she thought about just how much of her life was a sham. She took a deep breath and told herself it was all in a good cause. But suddenly, she wasn't sure she believed it.

Out on the pavement she looked back at what had been Samantha Seabrook's family home. The place was large and square, built from soft red brick with tall chimneys. Two of the three family members were dead. Sir Brian must rattle around in it, assuming he really was living there alone...

As she'd stood in the hall, her view into the kitchen had revealed a packing case, sitting on the wooden table. She'd been able to see some of the contents: cups and other crockery. And in the hall, next to a stand full of what looked like Sir Brian's footwear, were some women's lace-up walking shoes, as well as some boots. No space on the rack for them, making Tara think Sir Brian's collection of Oxfords and Derbies had expanded to fill the space available, before there was any competition.

Tara thought of Pamela Grange. Might the shoes belong to her? They looked like her style: sensible and classic. When they'd met, Tara had wondered if she was more than just a family friend...

And if she was moving in, why now exactly? Just because she wanted to be on hand to support Sir Brian in his hour of need? Or because she and Samantha Seabrook hadn't got on, and the way was now clear for her and Sir Brian to make their move?

It seemed likely that Samantha Seabrook had had just as much power over her father as everyone else.

As Tara got into her car, ready to tackle the drive home, she checked her phone for emails. Jim Cooper had replied. She clicked to open the message.

Sorry for last night. I'd had a few beers and thought you might be up and about still. I've heard journalists work long hours. Although I was keen to talk to you about Sam, it was the drink that made me think I had something important to say. I'll only be telling you what you've already heard from others so I won't come along this afternoon. Thanks all the same.

Tara clenched her fists and rubbed them into her eyes. She was so tired she knew she was only just fit to drive. She'd stop for more coffee on the way back.

She looked again at the email. It was Jim bloody Cooper who'd frightened her the evening before, and his fault she was wrung dry. And now, suddenly, he didn't want to talk.

She wasn't going to let him off the hook that bloody easily.

There was no auto signature on his email, so she went back to the institute website, found his direct line and dialled.

CHAPTER TWENTY-TWO

Blake was sitting in the office of Samantha Seabrook's agent, opposite the man who'd been overseeing her book publishing career and who'd got her one appearance on a chat show where she'd had the chance to put her work in front of a wider audience.

The man – Guy Fitzpatrick – was in his early thirties, Blake guessed, and wore a suit that aimed to be as classy as Blake's. He knew his fashion designer sister would say it had missed the mark.

They'd got drinks in front of them. Fitzpatrick's was a short macchiato – apparently. The woman who'd asked for their orders had seemed startled when Blake had requested a black coffee. She'd echoed his choice back to him, having translated it to 'an Americano'.

'I saw Samantha was dead on the news,' Guy Fitzpatrick said. 'It was tacked on at the end – not being London and not really a national affair – but they couldn't resist slipping it in. The tragedy of it, and the setting. Samantha always was TV-friendly and in death nothing changed.'

Blake frowned. 'I saw the recording of her appearance on *Tomorrow Today* on YouTube, but I didn't know she'd done more TV on top of that.'

Guy Fitzpatrick's floppy fringe quivered as he shook his head. 'Really? Is that back up again? It's infringing copyright.' He made a note on the pristine pad in front of him with an expensive-looking pen.

Blake made another bid for his full attention. 'She'd done other television then?' he said.

Fitzpatrick shook his head. 'No. Unfortunately I wasn't able to persuade her, though she had plenty of offers.' He took up his cup, sipped and then pulled a face. 'It was a failure from my point of view. I can normally talk clients round. It would have been a lucrative avenue for both of us.'

At least he was honest. 'But that didn't tempt her?' Blake thought of her apartment. She hadn't needed the cash, if that was anything to go by.

Fitzpatrick shook his head. 'And if her mind was made up, there was no changing it.'

'What put her off? Did she have a bad experience on *Tomorrow Today*?'

The man laughed. 'Far from it. She had a whale of a time whilst it was all going on. Though she got a bit bored in make-up. She wasn't used to waiting around. No.' His eyes were far away for a moment. 'Just after that show she was keen to do it all again. She wanted prime-time viewers to understand more about poverty, and how far-reaching its effects are. But after the programme aired there was some argy-bargy on Twitter.'

Blake hadn't got wind of that. 'How come?'

'One or two people took offence at a privileged Cambridge professor talking about people in poverty as though she could really understand what life was like for them.'

'Were any of the messages threatening? Or especially aggressive?'

Fitzpatrick shook his head. 'Not by Twitter's standards. Nothing we complained about or asked to have taken down. Just a lot of the "who do you think you are?" sort.'

'So that was what put her off?' It wasn't uncommon for complaints to come in to the police from people who'd been harassed and threatened on social media. And even tweets containing general insults could destroy someone's quality of life – especially if there were hundreds of them.

But Fitzpatrick smiled. 'God no – not that in itself. Samantha's skin was like rhino's hide. No. She realised – bright as she was – that the offers of TV work only really took off after that spate of tweets. She became aware that the companies wanted her as a controversial figure – not because of the quality of work she was doing and the way she was influencing political thinking.'

'And her objection to that was important enough for her to give up her aim of spreading her message?'

'Well, that and a chance comment she overheard after the first appearance. One of the producers was talking to a colleague, saying what great tits Samantha had. And how that, coupled with her being such a looker, would really bring the viewers in.'

'Okay. I'm definitely seeing it her way.'

But Fitzpatrick still looked irritated. 'After that she said not to bother calling her unless the production company had a commission from BBC Four. I would have been able to set that up, in time, I'm sure, but the pay wouldn't have been as good.'

Blake had a tedious drive back to Cambridge, along a log-jammed M11. It gave him plenty of time to think about the case. And about the text Babette had sent the day before, too…

Please, Garstin. Let's meet.

The anger he'd felt the previous night rushed through him again. But then he thought of Kitty. Suddenly, he realised the traffic in front of him was slowing yet again. The brake lights of an expensive-looking Audi were only a couple of feet away when he pulled to a halt. He needed to focus.

Back at his desk, he took out his private mobile.

Whatever happened, he and Babette would have to talk. Going on like this was unbearable and he needed to tell her so: set out some boundaries, and a proper routine, for Kitty's sake. And – he had to admit – for his own. He couldn't wait to see her.

You're right, he texted. *We should clear the air. My place, Saturday 6pm?*

He'd be working all weekend, given the gravity of the case, but he ought to be home by then. He sent the message and then tried to block the whole thing from his mind. He wanted to search for the tweets about Samantha Seabrook that Guy Fitzpatrick had mentioned.

There were a lot to go through but even the handful he saw were worrying. Some of them made reference to her family home, as well as her exclusive flat. It all felt very invasive, but of course Samantha Seabrook had shrugged off a death threat that had been delivered into her hands, so Guy Fitzpatrick's story about her nonchalant response to the tweets was believable.

Emma Marshall appeared at his side. 'Are you ready for us?'

Patrick Wilkins was just behind her and Blake nodded. They went to get coffees from the vending machine and then shut themselves in one of the meeting rooms.

'So, tell me,' Blake said. 'What news? Start with Dieter Gartner, Patrick.'

His DS took out a notebook. 'The university managed to get us an up-to-date private mobile number from the emergency contact on his HR files. I've now left three messages on that line, and similarly on his work mobile, which has been switched off. The emergency contact – a friend rather than a family member – said they believe he's travelling, possibly in the UK.'

They all looked at each other.

'I've searched online for his social media,' Patrick said. 'There's nothing relevant that I can view on Facebook but he tweeted a photo of Arthur's Seat in Edinburgh yesterday morning. I've been in touch with our counterparts up there to see if they can track him down. Find out where he is now. And more importantly, when he arrived and where from.'

'Good.' Why the hell wasn't he answering his phone or returning their messages?

He turned to Emma. 'What about the background checks on Samantha Seabrook's contacts?' He'd got her digging into all the professor's connections – both private and professional. She'd been looking for various key triggers.

'Okay,' Emma said, flipping open her own notebook. 'First, anyone with religious connections.'

This was off the back of the crucifix, found round Samantha Seabrook's neck.

'I have a candidate for you. Wait for it…' She gave Blake a look. 'Peter Mackintosh, the librarian at the institute.'

'Really?' Blake raised an eyebrow. He remembered Tara mentioning the guy, and how he seemed to have liked Samantha Seabrook.

Emma nodded. 'He's the churchwarden in the village where he lives.'

'Ah.'

'I know. Pillar of the community, I imagine. Beyond him, I have another suspect for you. Mary Mayhew.'

'Go on then. Shock me with your details.'

'She's a regular attendee at the Catholic church on the corner of Lensfield Road.' She grinned. 'I know, I know. So far, so normal. But she's certainly keen. I found a blog post she'd written, talking about a retreat she'd been on in a religious community. The post was on their website as a way of attracting others in, I suppose.' She sighed. 'And that's the best I can do. For everyone else, it's just the occasional attendance at run-of-the-mill services. Sir Brian Seabrook's not religious. There are various interviews he's given in the past that reveal that, as well as his generally left-wing views.'

'Hmm. Interesting.' He looked at them both. 'Now, tell me some good news. You've also found that either Peter Mackintosh or Mary Mayhew are expert climbers?'

'No can do, I'm afraid,' Emma said.

Patrick flipped over to the next page of his notebook. 'A woman with rooms on Professor Seabrook's staircase at St Francis's College was registered to use the climbing wall at Kelsey Kerridge, but she only came to Cambridge from Harvard at the start of last term and there's no indication she and the professor were more than nodding acquaintances. The other people we found registered have even less of a connection.'

'But of course, we know Dieter Gartner climbs,' Emma said.

'We do.'

At that moment, there was a knock at the door.

'Yes?' Blake called, glancing over his shoulder.

It was Detective Constable Max Dimity. Since Max's young wife had died a few short weeks ago, his features – formerly lit by wry humour – had become shuttered and wooden. For the first time since the fatal car crash that had shattered the DC's world, there was a spark in his eye.

'Sorry to interrupt, boss, but there's some interesting news on the dolls that were sent to Samantha Seabrook and Tara Thorpe.'

Blake caught his breath. Could it be a breakthrough? He'd been trying to keep his tone positive, for the sake of his team, but they desperately needed something. 'Go ahead, Max.'

'Apparently they're old.'

'Old?'

He nodded. 'That's right. Or more precisely, the cotton they were sewn with is on the point of perishing, and the material is similarly dated. If they were made recently then they were made with cotton that's been hanging around in a sewing basket for a long time. But it seems that's not likely. The report said anyone trying to use the thread in the last few years would have had a frustrating experience; the cotton would have snapped each time they put the slightest strain on it.'

It took a moment for Blake to speak. 'Do we have any idea how old?'

Dimity nodded. 'Around thirty years. The team used carbon dating on the cotton.'

Around five years younger than the professor… Blake glanced at Emma, and then at Patrick. They looked as perplexed as he felt. Two dolls, pretty much identical and both old?

How did that make any sense?

But it would. Sooner or later it would. 'Thanks, Max,' he said. 'If you've got any thoughts at all on where this takes us, please let me know.'

Max ducked his head in a nod, and the flicker of the DC he'd first recruited showed in his face before he turned and left the room again.

Tara Thorpe had texted to say that she and Jim Cooper were going drinking in the Pickerel shortly. Maybe she'd finally taken on board the value of sharing.

What started as a positive thought turned on its head and made him uneasy; it was such an unequal relationship. What would she say if she heard Max Dimity's news about the dolls? He knew he couldn't share the information, but withholding it felt wrong. Knowing more could only make her safer.

He glanced at his watch. He was due with Professor da Souza in twenty minutes, to interview him for a second time. After reading Tara's notes on her talk with Chiara Laurito, he wanted to know more about the woman's relationship with Samantha Seabrook.

As he drove across town, air con on, the sun bouncing dazzlingly off his car bonnet, his mind went back to the institute's librarian,

Peter Mackintosh. You could hardly presume someone who acted as a church warden had outlandishly strong religious views. But the guy was in charge of a library that had been funded by Samantha Seabrook's father. Did that extra connection mean anything? And then there was the institute administrator, Mary Mayhew. She was another unlikely candidate for murderer on the face of it. And yet she'd clearly disliked the professor. Could something have pushed that dislike far enough for her to kill? She was certainly meticulously organised – and so, most certainly, was their perpetrator.

But what connection could either of them – or anyone else they were in contact with – have with two old rag dolls?

CHAPTER TWENTY-THREE

Tara had chosen to meet Jim Cooper in the Pickerel in the hope that it wouldn't be too crowded by mid-afternoon. As with Chiara, she'd found his mugshot on the institute website, so she knew who she was looking for. Inside the pub, she waited for a moment as her eyes got used to the light levels. The building dated back to the 1500s, and its low ceilings and the placing of its windows left it shadowy, even on hot August days. You couldn't beat it for atmosphere and history though. It had a chequered past, having been a brothel and an undertaker's before it became a pub. It had been C. S. Lewis's favourite watering hole and even had its own ghost – a former landlady who'd drowned in the river nearby. Not that Tara believed in any of that, but she bet it helped draw in the punters. She ran her eyes over the clientele now, walking round to get a view of the more tucked-away spaces Jim Cooper might have chosen to sit in. It seemed she'd arrived first, so she went to the bar and scanned the beers available. In the end she ordered a small bottle of something called a Bitburger Drive. Low alcohol for a clear head. She asked them to put it in a large glass though, to make it look like she'd already drunk half. She wanted Cooper to think she was as relaxed and well-oiled as he was. The drink was welcome; she was parched after cycling up the river full-pelt. She'd grabbed a sandwich at home after her sticky drive back from Great Sterringham, then come straight out again. She was longing for a shower. She glanced at her watch and wondered if she'd manage one before the institute garden party.

The seats near the pub's front windows were all taken, so she went into its darker interior and bagged a spot there. It would be nice and intimate for a quiet chat. She'd probably have been able to get a decent recording if she dared to suggest it, but she wouldn't. Not after Cooper had almost pulled out on her. She craned round so that she could see the pub door, but after five minutes there was still no sign of him.

She picked up a beer mat and tapped it absently against the table. Maybe he'd changed his mind again. She'd spent a fair while coaxing him into reinstating the planned meet-up. And all the while she'd been wondering what he had to hide. Why go from being so keen to talk, to pulling out? But she'd kept her tone casual. ('Your views matter,' she'd said, 'and at the very least it'll be nice to stop for a beer. The weather's so hot and I don't know about you, but I've been hard at it all day.' He'd hesitated when she'd come up with that line. And then she'd said: 'I'd heard that the professor was close to you, in fact.' She was careful about which way round she put it. 'It was only time pressure that stopped me from getting in touch sooner.' That tipped the scales. 'Someone mentioned that, did they?' he'd said. She'd assured him they had, only she couldn't quite remember who.) The ends justified the means. In Cooper's case, she didn't question her methods. He might be the man who wanted to kill her.

She was just starting to get seriously fidgety when a tall man, bulked up with muscle, strode in. Cooper's portrait on the institute website hadn't given away what he'd be like as a physical presence. Under the pub's ancient wooden beams, he looked like a giant. His shaved head and large shoulders told her he wanted to be seen as a force to be reckoned with. She could imagine he had to read the riot act to umpteen students who broke the institute's rules, but she was sure he wouldn't have developed his look just for them.

She stood up and put out a hand. 'Jim Cooper? I'm Tara Thorpe.'

His expression wasn't altogether friendly as he nodded. He took her hand though, and shook it, his grip firm and rough, his palm warm.

Tara indicated her pint. 'I'm all sorted, but what can I get you?'

His face relaxed one degree. 'I can't lie, I could do with one,' he said. 'I've been running late all day and the heat's getting to me.'

Along with a hangover, if Blake's account of their interview the previous night was anything to go by. They went to the bar and Cooper opted for a pint of Foster's.

Back at the table Tara said: 'I'm sorry about all the mayhem last night. I gather someone reported an intruder outside my house but it was you all along, and you just wanted to talk to me about Samantha Seabrook. Sounds as though you had a whole load of hassle in return for trying to track me down. Pretty ironic, given that I wanted to talk to you anyway.'

He sighed, and nodded. 'Right enough. Not your fault though. I just happened to be passing but I didn't want to disturb you if you'd already gone to bed. I was trying to see if you had a light on.' He took a long swig of his beer.

'I am a bit of a night owl, but interviews work best during the day when I'm fresher.' She didn't want him dropping by in the small hours again.

He took a longer draught of his drink this time. 'Who have you spoken to already?' he asked.

He was leaning towards her now and his shoulders still looked tense. Could he be the person she'd seen in Samantha Seabrook's secret Instagram photo? The picture had cut across their body so you couldn't judge the breadth of their shoulders. That and the fact that it was night, and the trees in the background below the figure were distant, meant it had been hard to judge their stature.

For just a second, Tara's nerves were set on edge. The table was small, and Cooper was within inches of her. She could feel the warmth of him; his knee almost brushing hers. She dug her nails into the palm of her hand. Focus, and she could get what she wanted.

'I'm sorry?'

'I was just wondering who you'd spoken to before me.'

Maybe he hadn't bought her story about wanting to talk to him all along. 'Let's see, Professor da Souza was first, of course. I couldn't really speak to anyone before him. It' – she rolled her eyes – 'well, it wouldn't have gone down well.'

After a second Cooper put his shoulders back a little. 'No. Well, I can see that.'

'And then I spoke to Simon Askey because Professor da Souza had set that up for me on the same day.' She controlled her features as she mentioned the doctor's name, but Cooper's expression told her he wasn't a fan either. It would give them some common ground, so she allowed her feelings to show as she finished her sentence.

'You didn't like him?' he asked.

She looked down deliberately into her low-alcohol beer. 'I shouldn't have let it show.'

Cooper grunted. 'You don't have to worry about it front of me. The guy's an A1 shit.'

Tara allowed herself a smile that wasn't entirely put on. 'I got the impression he and Professor Seabrook didn't get on either.'

'You're right.'

'Is that why you don't like him?'

Cooper let out a long breath. 'Partly.'

She sipped her drink. 'When DI Blake came round this morning to explain what all the fuss was about last night, he mentioned you were on your way home from a pub session with Askey and some of the others.'

Cooper put his pint down suddenly. 'He was really taking the piss at the Mitre. That was part of the reason I—' He stopped abruptly.

'Part of the reason you stopped by at my place?' Her mind was racing. Had Askey egged Cooper on somehow, knowing she'd be scared?

Cooper looked at her from under his thick eyebrows and nodded. 'He was riling me about Sam,' he said at last. 'But what he said was wrong. I know that. And what you've told me proves it. Shit – multiple people know how much she valued my friendship.'

'I knew Askey wasn't honest when I talked to him,' Tara said, leaning forward. 'Whatever he said to you, I wouldn't trust it at all.' She peered at him over her glass as she took another sip of her drink. Cooper's eyes met hers. 'It sounds as though he upset you,' she went on. 'He upset me too, to be honest. What did he say? You might feel better if you get it off your chest.' She'd feel better, anyway.

He nodded slowly. 'I'd been talking about Sam. I was getting a bit upset, if I'm honest. I was tired – end of the day and all that. I should probably have gone straight home rather than out drinking. Anyway, I suppose he got sick of me reminiscing over old times. He suddenly turned round and told me Sam had, well' – he paused – 'sort of bad-mouthed me behind my back.'

Tara widened her eyes. 'Doesn't sound likely, from what I've heard.'

'Exactly.' Cooper's shoulders were still tense but she could tell it was the thought of Askey that was keeping them that way now.

'Maybe Askey was jealous of you,' Tara said.

Cooper raised an eyebrow.

'Maybe he didn't like Samantha because he knew Samantha didn't like him. If he realised you two were close, he might have resented you for it. He'd be dying to put you down and make himself feel better.'

Cooper didn't look like the kind of guy who'd want to show emotion in front of any other human being, but his eyes were moist, and his grip on his pint had tightened. He took another long swig of his drink, so that the glass was three-quarters empty. 'You think?'

Tara decided to press ahead, given she was getting a reaction. 'Seems like the kind of mind games he'd play, if my experience is anything to go by.'

Cooper nodded. 'He is like that.'

'But you know better, don't you? I mean, I got the impression you and Professor Seabrook were as thick as thieves. I'm sorry.' She met his eyes. 'This must be a terrible time for you.'

'Thanks.'

'Would you feel able to tell me some of the ways you thought she was special?'

After a moment, he nodded. 'It was just that she always stuck by me. And if there was ever any trouble, she'd just laugh it off.' He laughed himself, just for a moment, but it was a hollow sound. 'The institute can be a poisonous place to work sometimes,' he said. 'So many people, all wanting recognition, all wanting things run their way. And then a load of students, full of confidence because they haven't lived life yet. Don't know what it's like when things go wrong. Basically,' he necked more of his pint, 'there's always someone who's ready to do you down, or make your life tricky. Either to bolster themselves up, or just for a lark.'

'You've had trouble with the students?' Tara took a long drink of her own soft beer.

Cooper nodded. 'And one time, it all revolved around Sam. They'd noticed we were close, I guess, and then, well…'

'They started rumours about the two of you?'

'And "funny" posts on Facebook. You can imagine.'

'Charming.'

'Right. I was embarrassed, but Sam just laughed it all off. Said she was flattered by the attention.' He finished his beer. 'Not shamed by it, like Askey said.'

She paused and then, not looking at him, she asked: 'Did Askey ever taunt you about Professor Seabrook when she was still alive?'

Jim Cooper's eyes remained damp, but the light in them sharpened. 'No,' he said. 'He didn't.'

He'd seen the conclusions she might draw, depending on his answer. He was quick; and maybe he had reason to be on his guard, too.

'I guess you've talked about her more since she died, and he's seen his chance to get at you.' It was the best follow-up she could manage, and Jim Cooper's eyes were still suspicious.

'Maybe,' he said, finishing his pint.

God, she needed the night in the Travelodge. She wasn't firing on all cylinders and given it was her life that was on the line, that wasn't an acceptable risk.

CHAPTER TWENTY-FOUR

As he sat in Professor da Souza's eyrie with a coffee in front of him, Blake wished the chairs weren't so low and that they didn't recline so far. He wanted the man to understand the urgency of his questions. These seats were only fit for discussing the weather.

He decided to ask about Dieter Gartner first, and showed the professor the photograph he had with him.

Da Souza took it and held it tight between thumb and fingers, bending it. 'Yes. Yes, I've met Dieter. Samantha never said anything telling about him, but I did get the impression they had some kind of dalliance.'

Dalliance? 'Dr Gartner's not married, is he?'

'No, no.' Da Souza's lips were tight. Whatever the background, he clearly didn't approve.

'Were you worried about the way he treated Professor Seabrook?'

There was a long pause where Blake got the impression the institute head would have liked to pin some kind of criticism on the man, but couldn't. At last he said: 'Take no notice of me, Inspector. I'm old-fashioned, that's all.'

Fair enough. If that really was all. Blake remembered that both Tara and Chiara had wondered if da Souza had been in love with Samantha Seabrook himself.

'I'd like to know more about Samantha Seabrook's relations with other members of staff here, too,' Blake said. Specifically those with an interest in religion, however tenuous. 'What about Mary Mayhew, for instance?'

Professor da Souza shrugged. 'Mary's not the most effusive of individuals. She works very long hours, and the pressure can be immense sometimes. But what she lacks in warmth she makes up for in professionalism.'

'She must have been frustrated by the professor's hobby of climbing all over university property.'

Da Souza sipped his coffee and put his cup on its saucer before he answered. 'She dealt with it sensibly.'

'Did the professor ever talk to you about it?'

Da Souza smiled for a moment. 'She said she'd had her hand slapped. And then she giggled.'

'She wasn't too bothered about losing Dr Mayhew's good opinion then?'

'Samantha wasn't the sort to worry about things like that. She saw it as wholly unimportant. She was focused on research that could change the lives of millions of people. I think she felt that if Mary had decided instead to devote her life to dusty rule books and keeping up appearances then that was her own affair.'

Blake could only imagine what institute socials must have been like. Professor da Souza would need to be a dab hand at breaking up spats and keeping the small talk going. He was betting they got through a lot of booze, to try to foster some level of bonhomie.

'And what about Peter Mackintosh in the library?' he asked. 'What was his attitude to Professor Seabrook, and vice versa?'

Da Souza relaxed back in his chair. 'Warm,' he said, 'in both directions. They weren't a bit alike, but they found each other refreshing. Perhaps it's because Peter's rather separate. His work runs parallel to ours but he's not tussling over the same end goals.'

It confirmed what Tara had said. Da Souza looked calm now, but Blake had just the thing to jolt him out of it. 'And what you can you tell me about relations between Professor Seabrook and her

PhD student, Chiara Laurito?' He leant forward as best he could in the ridiculous chair.

Da Souza's eyes were wary for a second, but then reverted back to their 'earnest and keen to help' expression. 'They weren't close.'

'I saw some of the comments the professor wrote on Chiara's work,' Blake said. 'I can't imagine the atmosphere between them was easy, given Professor Seabrook's blunt way of delivering her criticisms.'

Da Souza sipped his coffee and shook his head. 'Samantha always was one to say what she thought.' He met Blake's eye. 'Personally, I admired her for it. But it's true that some of her younger colleagues found it harder to take in the spirit in which it was meant.'

Having read the words, Blake thought Chiara Laurito had probably taken it in exactly the spirit it had been intended. 'I hear the professor also tried to cut Chiara out of informal social gatherings.'

Da Souza frowned. 'It's very easy for a sensitive person like Chiara to mistake a chance happening for a deliberate slight.'

'So the professor wouldn't have left her out deliberately?' Blake's eyes were on the institute head.

The man hesitated. 'I wasn't aware of it if she did. And I *am* aware that Chiara Laurito is' – he stretched out a hand as though hoping to clutch the right words from the air – 'highly strung.'

'And what's your evidence for saying that?' Blake was up on the edge of his chair now, feeling triumphant at having finally got vertical.

Da Souza sighed. 'I don't want to muddy the waters of your investigation with irrelevant tittle-tattle,' he said. 'Apart from anything else, it would be wrong to colour your views of either Samantha or Chiara unfairly.'

'Just give me the facts, as you know them; there's nothing unfair about those.'

The man waited for a moment, but then gave a sharp sigh. 'All right. All right. Chiara Laurito had put in a formal complaint against Samantha. Only to us here at the institute; it hadn't been escalated.'

'And what triggered it?'

'She felt she'd been singled out for unfair criticism; she went so far as to allege that Samantha was trying to drive her out.' Da Souza's tone was irritable. 'We took action. It's my duty, and I wouldn't shirk it just because the accusation involved a personal connection. Chiara's work was sent for an outside, objective review, and Mary Mayhew made enquiries about Samantha's attitude to Chiara more generally.'

'And?'

Da Souza looked at him. 'Some of Mary's findings tie in with your assertions. Yes, there were occasions when several people had gone to the pub without Chiara. Yes, some people felt in a general way that Samantha didn't enjoy her student's company. But there was no evidence of any whispering campaign or deliberately cruel behaviour.'

And there was no law to say you had to invite people you didn't like out on social occasions. But Samantha Seabrook had been Chiara's manager, with a duty of care towards her. And her repeated rejection must have stung… enough to make Chiara kill, or aid a killer? And what about Mary Mayhew? She must have been frustrated to have to deal with yet another scandal caused by the professor. 'What about Chiara Laurito's work?'

'The external reviewer found that Samantha's comments had been justified.'

Blake caught the slight hesitation before he'd uttered his final word and raised an eyebrow.

Da Souza looked up at the ceiling for a moment. 'They did suggest she could have phrased her criticisms more tactfully.'

'But in the end, her complaint was found to be an overreaction? And that led you to conclude she's over-sensitive?'

'That's correct. She involved her father, who has been requesting updates from me almost daily. He's been in touch since Samantha's death; he wants to know who will supervise his daughter now. And he's demanding to vet them.'

'I see.' That did sound over the top, but he could readily understand why Chiara had been upset. The professor's comments had been brutal; he wouldn't forget them in a hurry.

'It wasn't like that in my day,' da Souza went on. 'We were expected to fight our own battles. And – as we've delved this far – I can say that I don't believe Samantha Seabrook is the only person Chiara's fallen out with since her arrival here.'

'No?' He waited for da Souza to prove how unreasonable Chiara Laurito was in comparison to Samantha.

'I happened to be walking past Simon Askey's office and heard raised voices. I could only hear him, as a matter of fact. He sounded furious; I'm afraid he has a short temper. I was three-quarters of the way down the corridor when I heard his door open. I glanced over my shoulder for a second and saw Chiara Laurito come out. She'd clearly upset him too.'

Interesting. 'When was this?'

Da Souza was brought up short. 'Goodness, I don't know. Sometime last month maybe? Not that long ago.'

From Tara's notes, Chiara had been *pleased* that it had been Simon Askey who'd put her forward as an interviewee for the article in *Not Now* magazine. Tara mentioned she'd blushed. Perhaps she'd taken the news as a sign that Askey had got past their disagreement? Maybe he'd flared up on the spur of the moment. There were plenty of people who could be ferocious one minute and fine the next. But then he remembered Tara thought Askey still had a gripe with Chiara…

So maybe he hadn't forgiven her then, for whatever it was she'd said. He'd probably just offered her up for Tara's entertainment. But that blush Tara had mentioned… did Chiara fancy Askey maybe? He quelled a shudder. There was no accounting for taste.

Blake frowned. How the hell did this all fit together? Sleep might help him think but he'd have to wait a while for that. He rubbed his eyes and tried to focus. 'Did you catch what Askey said to Chiara that day?'

Da Souza stared at the coffee table, his brow furrowed. At last he looked up and said: 'Something about how it wasn't always best to tell the truth. Maybe she'd put him in an awkward situation through a lack of tact.' He put his empty coffee cup down. 'She and Samantha were both apt to voice their thoughts without considering the consequences.'

It worried Blake that being honest at the institute might lead to being yelled at. Had it also led to Professor Seabrook's death?

Blake told da Souza not to bother seeing him downstairs. He knew the way, and besides, he wanted to take his time. He walked the length of each corridor, alternating the staircases he used to descend, which lay at opposite ends of the building. A lot of the rooms were empty. Shut up with notes on the doors, explaining how to contact the absent occupant. Conducting research in New Orleans; gathering material in Sicily for a new book. Both academics back in September before the start of Michaelmas term.

What had Simon Askey been talking about when he'd advised Chiara Laurito against telling the truth? And why had da Souza been so against Samantha Seabrook's relationship with Dieter Gartner? Had he really just disapproved of the love affair because it had been casual? And then there was Chiara Laurito, in Askey's thrall perhaps, and deeply hurt by Samantha Seabrook's personal attacks. And Mary Mayhew, whose ordered world had been repeatedly thrown into chaos because of the professor's hot-headedness. And in the middle of it all sat da Souza, treating the memory of his star employee as beyond reproach.

At that moment his mobile rang. He picked up as he was exiting the building, through the heavy wooden door and out under the archway, into the sunshine. 'Blake.'

'Boss.' It was Wilkins.

'Go ahead.'

'We've got a student in.' A pause. *'Jeremy Patten. He's a member of Pembroke College and attends a couple of lecture courses at the institute. He wanted to talk to us about Jim Cooper.'*

'Yes?'

'Says he saw photos of Samantha Seabrook in Cooper's drawer at the institute. He'd gone in there to report a fault with one of the printers. Cooper had to reach into the drawer for some kind of smart card and this Jeremy Pattern was looking over his shoulder.'

'Is he still with you now?'

'He is.'

'Right,' said Blake. 'I'm on my way.'

CHAPTER TWENTY-FIVE

Going to the institute late-summer garden party was the last thing Tara felt like. It made her realise she was at rock bottom. If ever there was an occasion that ought to be an eye opener it was this one. She had the promise of seeing how all the staff interacted with each other; and how they dealt with the gaping hole left by as big a personality as Samantha Seabrook. She needed that information. She needed to be there. But back at her cottage, seated at her kitchen table, she stared into space. When she managed to check the time she realised she'd been there, sitting absolutely still, for half an hour.

At last, she dragged herself up out of her chair and went to prepare. A cool shower that lasted under two minutes. A tailored dress, and make-up to hide the shadows under her eyes. After that she grabbed a rucksack from her wardrobe and stuffed overnight gear into it. Then she picked up her handbag. Each time she lifted it she tried to ignore the extra weight; tried to block out the knife she'd put in there two days earlier, before she'd gone to interview Professor da Souza and Simon Askey. But the thought was there. She should leave it behind. She looked out of her bedroom window, down at the common. She wouldn't have to cross it that night.

But two minutes later, when she left the room, the knife was still there in the bag's side pocket, knocking lightly against her hip through the soft leather.

She cycled to the Travelodge, checked in and dumped her rucksack on her bed. She was so tempted to lie there for a moment, listening to the traffic rumble by on the main road, but she turned away, went back down to reception and out of the building. Within fifteen minutes she'd arrived at some cycle racks just beyond the door to the Institute for Social Studies, locked up her bike, and walked under the stone archway towards the grassy courtyard that lay to the rear of the building. A small crowd was already assembled. She noticed Simon Askey first; his voice carried as he was facing in her direction, and she recognised his New York accent. He looked up over the shoulder of Chiara Laurito, who he'd been talking to, and caught her glance. She could see the derisive amusement in his eyes. Chiara must have sensed she'd lost his attention too. She glanced behind her for a moment, her chiffon dress shifting slightly in the light breeze. Her eyes refocused on Tara and her expression was a lot cooler than it had been when they'd first met. Of the others, she recognised the librarian, Peter Mackintosh, Professor da Souza of course – and then, there was Jim Cooper. Even though she had known he was likely to be there, she could have done without a second encounter with him that day.

Da Souza came over, accompanied by a middle-aged woman in a skirt and short-sleeved jacket. 'Good evening,' he said. 'It's lovely to see you again, Tara. May I introduce Dr Mary Mayhew, our administrator?'

Mary Mayhew nodded.

Tara was about to ask her about Samantha Seabrook, but da Souza opened his mouth to speak again, forestalling her.

'We're just going to say a few words about Samantha. We want to pay tribute to her, and for people to know it's all right to talk about what's happened. Everyone needs the chance to air their feelings.'

His eyes were anxious and eager, but Mary Mayhew's expression, she noticed, was grim. The pair went to stand on the grass next to the drinks table, where da Souza picked up a glass and tapped it with a fork. It took Mary Mayhew to call order though. Her sharp voice cut across the chatter.

It was interesting to watch the faces in the crowd as da Souza spoke. Simon Askey was unsmiling, but hardly sad. He downed his drink within seconds, Tara noticed, after which his eyes kept drifting towards the open bottles on the table. Chiara tapped the fingers of her right hand on her left arm. Her eyes were on Askey's face. Peter Mackintosh's attention seemed entirely concentrated on da Souza's words. He nodded at several points, a smile on his lips, his eyes damp. Jim Cooper's features were contorted, his fists clenched. As she watched him, Tara suddenly realised the custodian was trying to contain his emotions. Mary Mayhew was poker-faced.

Da Souza finished by encouraging them all to use the occasion to remember Samantha.

Tara suddenly found herself with no one to talk to, and awkwardly near to Simon Askey and Chiara Laurito, whose heads were close together. Chiara looked petulant and Askey dogmatic, his jaw clenched.

Askey hadn't acknowledged her but now, without warning, he manoeuvred so that she formed part of his and Chiara's circle. 'Speaking of people who get a helping hand from their parents,' he said, drinking his glass of fizz in one go, 'I heard a little rumour about Tara Thorpe here, and her mother.'

His voice was unnecessarily loud, and several other guests turned their heads to look. Tara felt her chest tighten. She could guess what was coming – and that Askey was going to make the most of it.

'What's that?' Chiara said. 'You're always in the know, Simon.' She leant towards him, smiling. He returned the smile, though when she turned away his look was cold.

'Well, as I'm sure we all know, Tara Thorpe here has a famous ma. One Lydia Thorpe.'

'Lydia Thorpe the actress?' Peter Mackintosh, the librarian said. 'No! I didn't know. I've always been a great admirer of her work.' He smiled at Tara, who bit hard into the side of her cheek.

'You, Peter, and of course so many others,' Askey said. 'Well, I can tell you that a couple of short years ago, *Not Now* magazine – the publication Tara works for – was at rock bottom. Not selling, not admired, and certainly not the fashion accessory it is today.'

Professor da Souza had moved closer to Askey, as though he knew he was out to make trouble but couldn't work out how to prevent it.

'That was until Lydia Thorpe was photographed holding a copy of the magazine under her arm. Suddenly that niche publication became the magazine of choice for everyone who's anyone. And Tara here – who up until that point was working for them freelance, and fairly infrequently, as far as I can make out – got taken on as a staff writer and promoted to the top of the tree.'

His eyes met Tara's and he smiled. He reminded her of a lizard, comfortable with the sun on its back but watchful and cold-blooded at heart.

'So you see,' he continued, 'one more example of how people who come from a privileged background have it easy compared with those who don't.'

Professor da Souza patted Askey on the shoulder. 'But Simon, it's only natural for parents to try to look after their children. And it's not the fault of those children if they end up benefiting. It's simply that we need to change the system so everyone's on an equal footing.'

'Don't worry.' Peter the librarian had joined her. 'Everyone knows about your reputation as a journalist. You won an award, didn't you? I remember reading you could get truths out of people that no one else could uncover.'

Tara could see Jim Cooper had picked up on Peter's words. He gave her a sulky glare. And, of course, she hadn't managed to get to the bottom of *his* story. If Simon Askey was already taunting him about the professor before she'd been killed it was only natural that he'd deny it. If he'd known she was laughing about him behind his back it would make him a plausible suspect. Could he have formulated such an elaborate plan to make her pay? If he had, maybe he'd regretted it afterwards. His love and remorse might have prompted him to come to Tara, wanting to pay tribute to the murdered object of his obsession. It would explain the way he'd blown hot and cold about wanting to share his memories.

She took a large swig of her wine.

'Have you met Kit?' Peter asked. A man of about her age stepped forward. He had dark wavy hair and deep blue eyes.

'I'm the research associate on Simon Askey's project,' he said. He had an attractive northern accent. 'I knew Samantha quite well too, of course, if there's anything you want to ask.' He looked around the assembled group, Chiara pouting, da Souza looking lost, Cooper gritting his teeth and Askey rolling his eyes. 'Though if you've already had it up to here with the lot of us, I will perfectly understand.' A smile crossed his lips.

She took a sip of her drink and responded in kind. It was nice to find someone who could see the institute staff with an unbiased eye, despite being one of them. 'Not at all. I want to find out all there is to know. Did you like her?'

He raised an eyebrow. 'I thought you'd want to ask my opinion on her work.'

'The verdict on that seems to be unanimous – unless you're about to surprise me?'

The smile was back. 'Fair point. And no, I'm not. All right then. I suppose I saw Samantha in the round. I could understand why she attracted such polarised views. People either loved or hated her. I even wondered if some people did both.' He paused, his eyes on the middle distance. 'I guess it was a dangerous combination, though I'm sure she never realised it. She was very focused on whatever her passion was at the time. She never noticed anything peripheral, which could be frustrating. Some people saw it as a by-product of her genius, but some people reckoned she was too bound up with herself.'

Very analytical. It probably stemmed from his work. It was useful, but she wanted his personal opinion too. 'What did *you* think?'

He shrugged. 'I came to Cambridge specifically because I wanted to work alongside her and I've never regretted it. Nothing she's done has changed my mind about her.' He pulled a face. 'But, to be fair, her style did make for an intense atmosphere.'

Tara raised her eyebrows.

'Too many forceful personalities in a small space.'

Right on cue, Chiara's voice rose. She sounded more than halfway to being drunk. 'You see, Professor da Souza realises it's only natural! And it's exactly what Samantha's father did for her too. He smoothed her path all the way. Her situation and mine were so alike, yet she could never see it. Her reaction to my parents' concern for me was pure hypocrisy. She was spoiled, of course.'

There was an awkward silence. Peter Mackintosh looked as though he was about to say something, but then shut his mouth. Kit caught Tara's eye and da Souza stared at the ground. Maybe he felt he couldn't say much without having it thrown back in his face, given the library donation by Samantha Seabrook's father, and his own closeness to her whole family.

Askey was the one who spoke, his dry drawl loud in the hush. 'I can't deny your point, but your timing's dreadful as usual, Chiara.' He met her eye. 'You really must learn to keep your mouth shut.' He turned and walked away.

Tara saw the PhD student's eyes widen with shock. Askey had made it impossible for her to retort without chasing after him.

Cooper put down his empty glass and picked up another. He held it so tightly Tara was surprised the delicate flute didn't break in his hand.

'You'll be glad to know these dos normally wind up by around 8 p.m.,' Kit Tyler said, his lips quirking. His smile was infectious. 'Can I get you another drink?'

All in all, she was more than glad of his presence. His dry humour made the evening slightly more bearable than it might have been.

Tara excused herself when Professor da Souza left. By that stage, Chiara was going over slightly on one ankle in her high heels, and definitely slurring. She must have had it out with Askey after he'd put her down so publicly. She was back at his side now. He kept removing her hand from his arm but then having to hold on to her to stop her wobbling over. He looked properly irritated. Mary Mayhew was standing to one side, drinking orange juice and pursing her lips. Peter the librarian and Kit were helping Jim Cooper clear some of the glasses.

As she turned to leave, Kit caught her eye and raised his free hand. The sun was already well down. Just the odd last streak of light stained the sky as she walked out under the stone archway to where she'd left her bike. She glanced to her left and then over her shoulder as the noises of the party receded.

She turned the key in her bike lock and went to put the chain in her basket – her usual way of transporting it whilst she cycled. It was only then that she saw the envelope someone had put there, hard up against the wickerwork, tucked in so she hadn't seen it before.

Her name was printed on the front.

Her hands shook as she eased open the seal. There was just one printed sheet of paper inside.

I'm looking forward to reading your article. I only hope you've found the real scoop. Journalism's a cut-throat business. Second-rate professionals might find themselves in trouble.

CHAPTER TWENTY-SIX

Blake sat opposite Tara. He had her latest letter, slipped inside an evidence bag, in his hands. She had a vodka and tonic in hers. She picked up her glass and the ice in it chinked against the side. They were sitting in the Champion of the Thames. The pub was tiny, and still very warm after another hot day. Someone had propped the front door open and Blake watched a moth fly in. Outside, the streetlights had come on.

When Tara had called him, he'd sent a car to follow her journey from the institute to the pub, where they'd arranged to meet. He wanted to know everything that had happened that day – especially at the garden party. As before, he'd checked immediately on the whereabouts of Samantha Seabrook's father, and on Pamela Grange. They'd been safely at Seabrook's home in Great Sterringham; he'd spoken to them both. Barring an unknown outsider, the institute staff were the main suspects for having sent Tara the message. Wilkins was checking with the editor of *Not Now*, and another staff reporter who'd known where Tara would be, but the main focus was on Professor da Souza's merry gang. Unfortunately, nothing allowed him to narrow things down further. Tara had talked to most of them in turn, but hadn't noticed when they came and went.

And it sounded as though they'd all known in advance that she'd be at the party; it had been mentioned at a staff meeting. They'd have had plenty of time to prepare the typed message.

Askey, Chiara Laurito, Mary Mayhew, Kit Tyler, Peter Mackintosh, da Souza, Jim Cooper... the list went on.

Had it been someone who'd loathed the professor or someone who'd adored her? The thin line between love and hate was a harsh reality. He only had to think of Babette to know that.

'I wish I knew what was on the bastard's mind,' Tara said, breaking into his thoughts. Her long, red-gold hair kept catching his eye as it gleamed in the lights that shone above the bar. 'He's set me a test and so far, I don't understand the rules.'

Her eyes were dry, her jaw set.

'It might not be a he,' Blake said. 'You – we – need to watch everyone.'

She swigged her drink. After a moment, she nodded.

'What else happened today?' he asked.

'I went to interview Jim Cooper just before the garden party.' She gave him a look. 'No recording of that one. I couldn't risk asking; it would have frightened him off.' She explained how he'd tried to back out of the arrangement. 'I don't know what he's afraid of. There's something about him that makes me uneasy, but it could just be that he doesn't want to get involved.'

'I'd appreciate your notes then, when you've done them.' She'd probably been going to send them anyway, but he couldn't bring himself to leave it unsaid.

She just nodded again, but then after a moment she sighed, as though she was giving in, and told him how Simon Askey had been taunting Cooper. The fact that he'd been casting doubt on the supposedly close relationship he'd had with Professor Seabrook must have led to an acrimonious encounter between the two men. 'I'm still not clear on when the taunting started,' she said, 'before she died or afterwards.'

Their eyes met for a long moment. 'Thanks for that,' Blake said. 'I'll make enquiries.'

'And Cooper mentioned that some of the students have had fun at his expense too – putting it about that he and the professor were having an affair.'

Blake thought of the student who'd seen photos of Samantha Seabrook in Cooper's drawer. When they'd gone to investigate, it turned out they'd just been press cuttings. Cooper had shared them readily enough, but they still made the custodian look obsessive.

'And what about your visit to Sir Brian?' he asked.

She told him about her journey up the A10, glancing up at him for a second, her green eyes meeting his over the rim of her almost-empty glass. 'I did wonder if someone was on my tail. There were a couple of cars that left Garlic Row at the same time as me.'

'But you didn't see them when you arrived in Great Sterringham?'

She shook her head. 'I came to the conclusion I'd succumbed to paranoia.'

He put Tara's bagged note in his jacket pocket and drained his Coke, wishing it was something stronger.

Her glass was empty now too. Part of him didn't want to suggest another. A sober potential murder victim was more likely to see another day than a drunk one.

'Another?' Tara said, as though reading his mind. She got up from her chair, scraping it backwards on the floor, and picked up her glass.

He got up too, glancing sideways at her. He wasn't sure if she'd been drinking at the garden party too, though she looked steady. 'I'll have to watch myself,' he said at last. 'Too many Cokes on duty and all that.'

She gave him a sidelong glance. 'Is that your way of telling me I should watch myself too?'

He sighed. 'Do you make a habit of reading people's minds?'

She smiled. 'You've been doing it to me too, recently, or hadn't you noticed?'

But he couldn't tell what she was thinking right that minute. 'I suppose we both spend a lot of time trying to see the truth behind what people tell us,' he said at last. 'We get a certain amount of practice.'

But he hadn't seen through Babette's lies. When she'd faced him with the truth it had come as a complete shock. The thought made him catch his breath. If he'd missed *that* – something so huge – then he could miss anything.

Tara ordered another vodka and tonic and he asked for his Coke. 'Don't worry,' she said, without catching his eye. 'I'm careful. I'm never out of control.'

Apart from when she'd decked that journalist of course. Though maybe she counted that as being in control, in fact.

'What did you think of Sir Brian?' he asked, when they were back at their table.

'A weird combination. It was as though he'd been knocked sideways, yet he hadn't lost his sense of self, if you know what I mean.'

He'd felt the same.

'You'll be pleased to learn I recorded the interview with him,' she said. 'My kit's back at the Travelodge but I can send the file across to you.'

'Please.'

Her voice had a tone he recognised now; it was the same as she'd had the previous night when she'd told him what she'd got out of Chiara Laurito. And there was a spark in her eyes too, despite all the shock and exhaustion. Whatever it was she'd found out he could see she was longing to share, to show off her spoils.

'What?' he said. He found himself smiling.

Her own smile was in her eyes. She ran her forefinger absently round the rim of her glass. 'I saw a couple of interesting things.'

'Come on then; don't keep me in suspense.'

'I managed to get Sir Brian to show me Professor Seabrook's old room.'

'I'm impressed.'

She put her head on one side. 'Thank you. So, the slippers intrigued me.'

He remembered noticing them; glamorous and in good condition.

'They were this season's,' Tara said. 'I saw them in the window of Harvey Nichols last time I was in London; £150, no less.'

'You can spend that much on a pair of slippers?'

'Yup. Or at least, if you're Samantha Seabrook you can. Or indeed, if you're Sir Brian.'

'You think it was he who bought them, not her?'

'I did wonder. They're gorgeous – and I suppose if the professor had chosen them herself she'd have probably taken them with her. She hasn't struck me as the disorganised sort. Nor the sort to make frequent stays back at the family home and leave them there for convenience.' She sipped her drink.

'No,' he said at last, wondering why he hadn't got that far with his thinking. 'You have a point.'

'And then there's the matter of the magazines that were in her room.'

He vaguely remembered those too.

'*Vogue*, yes,' Tara said. 'Having snooped round Samantha Seabrook's apartment I could imagine her buying that for herself, but *Good Housekeeping*? It's a quality glossy, but I'd have said it would be more Pamela Grange's scene.'

'The sort of thing Sir Brian might have bought for his daughter, not having made a thorough study of the women's magazine market?'

'Exactly that sort of thing.'

'Interesting. So if you're right' – her look told him she wasn't suffering from self-doubt – 'then Sir Brian was making a special effort for his daughter's most recent stay.'

'I'd definitely say so,' Tara said. She frowned and took another sip of her drink. 'I mean, I could imagine him buying the magazines when he knew she was coming. Or putting some flowers in her room maybe. But the slippers seem to go beyond that. He was really looking after her. I wondered if she'd been ill, and had gone home to recuperate?' Her eyes suddenly lit up. 'In fact, that would fit with something Pamela Grange said too.'

'Really?'

She bit her lip. 'Hell, yes. Sorry – I think it slipped my mind when I reported back on my meeting with her, what with being chased on my way home and everything.'

Or had she just been holding back? Still, she sounded genuine. He waited.

'Pamela said Samantha had been to stay in Great Sterringham quite recently. And she mentioned that would normally be a cue for Sir Brian to invite her over too, but on this occasion, that didn't happen.'

'That does sound interesting.' Samantha having been ill was a good theory. Blake made a mental note to look into it. 'I know you hate us all,' he said, 'but you could have a second career as a copper, if you ever fancy switching jobs.'

She gave him a look. 'Yeah, right.'

CHAPTER TWENTY-SEVEN

As she cycled back to the Travelodge, Tara realised Blake was on her tail in his car. The traffic was as heavy as usual, and she could slip through the gaps, so their progress was finely balanced. In fact, she was about to lose him. She turned to check over her shoulder, moved into the right-hand lane to make the U-turn to reach the Travelodge, and gave him an ironic wave as she went. Her route meant she had to double back and the streetlight shone in through Blake's windscreen. She tried to catch his expression, but his face was still in shadow, down to his chin.

She pulled up in front of the Travelodge and secured her bike outside. She didn't hate all police. She was just selective – God, she was with all people; life had taught her that trust wasn't something to hand over lightly. Blake was all right. Probably. If nothing else, the suggestion about her training to be a police officer showed off his excellent sense of humour. She found herself smiling just for a second – at the same time as shaking her head.

There was no one on the reception desk as she walked past. She took her hotel key card out and let herself through the door to the sleeping accommodation. On the other side there was a deserted corridor full of anonymous doors, as well as a route off that led to a stairwell and the lifts. It was oddly quiet. She chose the stairs to reach her floor. Avoiding situations where she might get cornered was instinctive; she hadn't needed the crime reduction officer's advice. And Kemp had drummed it into her when she'd learnt self-defence too. At the top of the flight, she went through another fire door and on to the corridor where her room was located. As she entered it, she heard another door close quietly. Who'd just disappeared from her line of sight? She listened for the sound of someone talking. To know she was next door to a family, or a couple, would have been reassuring. But everything was quiet and still. She touched her key card to the card reader. The light went red and the door didn't open.

She tried it again. The same.

And then the third time, the light went green. She took a deep breath.

Inside, her room was just as she'd left it. She went into the bathroom. Nothing was out of place. Back in the main room, she went to draw the curtains shut. Instinctively she pulled at them from an angle, standing well back from the glass. If Samantha Seabrook's killer was out there watching, she wasn't going to give them the satisfaction.

After the second shower of the day – a scalding hot one this time, that lasted for ten minutes, not two – she sank down onto the bed.

She had long enough to worry that she wouldn't sleep. Her heart was racing. Probably the result of the day, and the note. And possibly the vodka on top of the garden-party Prosecco. But after that she must have gone out like a light.

Sometime in the early morning she got up to go to the bathroom. The palest hint of first light was creeping in behind the curtains. Newmarket Road wasn't the quietest place to stay. Outside she could hear an emergency vehicle screaming its way past. She was instantly relieved it wasn't anything to do with her, but someone was in trouble. It just wasn't her turn.

She felt strange when she woke again at nine thirty in the morning – almost as though she'd been drugged. The unfamiliar effects of a really good night's sleep. She wondered if Blake had managed to catch up too. Though after all that Coke at the pub he'd have been lucky; he must have been wired. Slowly, she began to gather her things together. A quick check of the emails on her phone revealed several she would definitely ignore – either until later or altogether. One such was from Giles, *Not Now*'s editor. The message was flagged as important. He was disappointed in her for not drip-feeding him more breaking news ahead of filing her feature. Sod that. If she told him her latest it would steal her thunder and she wouldn't get any of the credit. For a moment she thought back to Blake's joke the night before, about her retraining as a police officer. It had to be said, she didn't much like being beholden to someone like Giles, and the ideals he stood for.

At last she saw that there was one email of interest. Patsy Wentworth, the childhood friend of Samantha Seabrook's who featured in the drunken photo in the professor's flat, had answered the email she'd sent. Patsy would talk to Tara that afternoon, if Tara could be bothered to get herself to Camden Town in London. Tara emailed back to say that she could be bothered and would see her later. She felt another passing stab of guilt at not having told Blake that she'd found the woman. But she had to have some things for herself. An old mate from school might tell her more about what had really made Samantha Seabrook tick. She put it out of her head and made up her mind not to look at anything else to do with work until she was back at home.

She went down to the reception desk and picked up a breakfast box thing with a muffin in it, and yoghurt, amongst other stuff. Then she holed up in her room to eat it. The last thing she wanted was to sit in the café with the world going by, watching her.

She wanted to keep her mind blank; wanted to stay there tucked away from reality. But she needed to look life in the face. If she dug hard enough she might work out what Samantha Seabrook's killer had been after. And if she managed that, she might identify them.

Within ten minutes, Tara was cycling down River Lane towards Riverside, past Victorian terraces on her left and new-builds on her right. You could tell it was Saturday without looking at the calendar. Several of the houses she passed still had their ground-floor curtains closed and the man and woman she saw walking along the pavement were moving at a leisurely pace. She was gesticulating, he was nodding. And then he laughed.

It was only when she reached the end of the lane and cast her eyes right, down Riverside towards Stourbridge Common, that she realised something was wrong.

Police. A lot of them.

The iron gate that normally barred the entrance to the common had been opened and in the distance, in the meadows on the way to Fen Ditton, she could see more than one police van. Just beyond the vehicles, a tent had been erected and an area of common cordoned off.

The hair stood up on Tara's arms.

In front of the scene, white-suited figures moved purposefully to and fro.

She'd carried on cycling at a snail's pace along Riverside, slowing to process what she was seeing. Now she stopped. Her legs were quivering, shivers running through them and up through her stomach. She tried to catch her breath.

'They've only just started letting people on to the common again,' a voice near her right ear said.

She started and looked round. A man she vaguely recognised, wearing shirt, trousers, socks and sandals, had wandered across the way to talk to her. She thought he lived in one of the houses along there.

'They were crawling all over the cattle grid and the pedestrian gate up until half an hour ago.' He nodded towards her house. 'You didn't hear anything?'

He clearly recognised her then. Knew where she lived. She'd made herself conspicuous. The weird woman who'd made her home in the middle of nowhere.

'No,' she said at last. 'I was away last night.'

The man gave her a look from over his brown tortoiseshell glasses. 'Just as well, by the look of things.'

'Do you know what…?' She let the sentence hang.

'No one knows what or who,' the man said. 'They won't tell us anything. They've sent the press away.'

Tara's phone started to ring. She didn't bother to look at it.

'Right.'

She set off again. Her legs didn't feel as though they'd got the strength to propel her but she kept going through the motions. She didn't stop at her house, but ploughed on, towards the police cordon, bumping over the tufty grass, the smell of the cattle all around her.

A uniformed officer was waving at her. 'You can't come any closer,' the woman said. 'Are you a journalist?'

Best not to answer that one. 'Is DI Blake here?'

A momentary frown crossed the officer's face and for a split second she glanced behind her. A few of the white overall-clad figures had clearly caught sight of their exchange. They were looking in Tara's direction. And then one figure broke away from the rest and strode over to the cordon where Tara and the officer were standing.

As the figure got closer she realised the eyes visible under the hood and above the mask were Blake's. He turned to the uniformed officer. 'This is Tara Thorpe.'

Understanding sparked in the woman's eyes and she walked away, just enough to give them some space.

Tara looked at Blake and waited. She felt sick.

'This is for your ears only,' he said, 'because of your involvement. If any of this goes public it'll be my head on the block as well as yours. We want some time to get initial questions in before it all goes public.' He was deathly pale and there were dark rings under his eyes.

She nodded. 'Understood.'

'Chiara Laurito.' He nodded over his shoulder, towards the tent. 'We'll be moving her body in just a moment.'

She could hear the emotion in his voice and felt her chest tighten. Had he had any idea that Chiara might be a target? Or had his attention been focused solely on her?

Blake turned to her again, his eyes haunted.

CHAPTER TWENTY-EIGHT

Blake had only spent a second longer talking to Tara. He'd said he or one of the team would be in touch to talk to her again later. They would let her know if what had happened to Chiara gave them any more clues about the killer, and the way their mind was working. His words had been professional and controlled, but she could see from his eyes the effect that Chiara's death had had. Visions of Samantha Seabrook's glamorous PhD student filled Tara's head as she stood near the window of her sitting room, staring out across the meadow towards the tent and the river. Why had Chiara been killed? Was it because she'd been outside Tara's home? Perhaps it was somehow her fault that Chiara was dead.

In her hand she held a note she'd found on the doormat when she'd let herself in. It was from her mother's cousin, Bea.

Darling – don't think me an old fusspot, but I've started to worry. You've been a bit elusive recently and I popped round on the off-chance I might catch you in. I imagine you're out on the town. I hope you're having a lovely time. Don't be a stranger. Bea xxx

The note tugged at Tara's insides. Bea couldn't help worrying; it had been just the same when she'd looked after Tara as a child. And in trying to keep her out of what had been happening, to protect her, Tara had made her more anxious. What would she think when she saw the news of Chiara's death?

And when had she dropped the note round? When Tara had been at the garden party? Whilst she'd sat in the pub with Blake? Or later, when Chiara and her killer had been out on the common? It didn't bear thinking about.

She had to wait some minutes to control her reactions – pacing round the house to get rid of the wobble she could feel in her legs – but at last she sat down to call Bea. It was better she heard Tara's version of events now, rather than reading about the murder outside her house and rushing over again in a panic.

But she still wouldn't mention the frightening dance she was performing, to the tune of someone who'd now killed two women.

✱

Blake and Emma Marshall stood outside a small but beautifully kept terrace in the Kite – a pricey area of Cambridge, close to the centre of town. Unusually, it had a driveway (which probably added fifty grand or so to the value of the place). On it was parked a Mini, finished in racing green. All the signs of a secure and comfortable life. He took a deep breath. He was still trying to assimilate the fact that Chiara Laurito was dead. Nothing had flagged her as a potential victim. He'd failed her and everyone who'd loved her. *What had he missed?* Even if the killer had lashed out this time, instead of employing the same meticulous planning they had previously, there would be a reason they'd targeted Chiara. And if there was a reason, he should have been able to predict what would happen. He closed his eyes for a moment, trying to take a step back from his guilt and think. Samantha Seabrook and Chiara had been at daggers drawn, by all accounts. Who was it who'd had reason to kill them both?

'What's her name again?' Blake asked. His mind had gone blank.

'Mandy. Mandy Holden.'

They looked at each other and then at the house Chiara Laurito had shared with her flatmate.

'Better get it over with,' Blake said, and they walked up the drive, along the narrow path.

'Ms Holden?' Blake said, to the woman who opened the door. She was tall and willowy with spiky blonde hair.

She nodded and looked from one of them to the other, a frown tracing its way across her face. 'What's wrong?'

'We're here because of your housemate, Chiara.'

She was chewing her lip now. 'Why? What's this about?'

He pulled out his warrant card. 'Do you mind if we come in?'

The woman took them down a hallway that was barely wide enough to accommodate the coats and shoe racks it housed as well as the incoming visitors. Blake wasn't massively tall, but his shoulders were broad and he turned sideways to follow her into a compact front room. In it everything was designer, expensive and plush in rich colours. The armchair and sofa were covered in purple velvet. But each item was also in miniature. It had to be in a house that size. All the same, Blake knew for a fact that places round there went for four or five hundred thousand. He wondered what Mandy Holden did for a living. She didn't have the look of a high earner, with her tie-dye crop top.

'I'm afraid we have some bad news for you, Ms Holden,' Blake said, as the woman motioned them to take a seat.

She blinked quickly, and her frown deepened. 'What do you mean?'

He paused for a moment, then took a deep breath. 'I'm very sorry to have to tell you that Chiara Laurito's body was found on Stourbridge Common this morning.'

Mandy Holden stood up suddenly. 'It's not possible,' she said, moving towards the door. Within seconds she was striding up the steep staircase to the upper floor. They heard a door open, and then a half-shouted curse that turned partway through into a sob.

'Hell,' Emma whispered. 'She didn't even know she wasn't upstairs in bed?'

'Looks that way.' If he'd realised he'd have tried to break the news differently.

Mandy Holden came back into the room, her face pink, her eyes red. She clutched at her short hair, her fingers knotted. 'What happened?' she said, slumping down in the armchair.

'I'm afraid she was attacked.' Blake paused whilst she took it in.

'Raped, you mean, before she died?'

He shook his head. 'The pathologist will be checking everything but on first appearances we don't think so.' He paused for a long moment. 'She was strangled.'

Mandy Holden's head was in her hands now, her eyes closed tight. 'Shit. Shit. I didn't even know anything was wrong.' She leapt up out of her chair again and paced the room, up towards the windows and then abruptly back again. 'I can't believe it. I just assumed she was in her room, sleeping it off. Why the hell didn't I realise?'

Emma stood too. 'If you thought she was in her room you wouldn't have known there was any reason to check. Please could you tell us what happened yesterday evening? We know Chiara was out at a garden party.'

Mandy Holden rolled her eyes. 'Oh yes. The institute late-summer garden party. I *knew* that would be trouble from the moment I saw the invitation arrive.' She sighed. 'Chiara didn't find the institute all that easy, socially. She usually coped by getting tanked up at their events. But that just made her more outspoken than usual, which led to fresh problems.'

Blake nodded. 'So, what were you up to last night? You're not associated with the institute yourself?'

She shook her head. 'Chiara and I are both attached to the same college. I'm researching for a PhD in psychology.'

Blake nodded, and couldn't help but glance around the room. 'It's a lovely place you've got here.'

Mandy Holden put her head in her hands for a moment. 'Chiara's parents bought it for her. Said there was no point being fleeced for an outrageous level of rent when they could buy a place for her outright.'

Outright. Okay.

'Going back to last night,' he said, 'did you see Chiara after the garden party?'

She nodded. 'I was here when she returned, getting ready to go out with my girlfriend.' She gave a quick sigh. 'I'd been held up at work, so I was running late and it was a special occasion – her birthday – so I was already on edge. Then Chiara came in, drunk as usual – though I presume she must have sobered up a bit on her way home. She was upset, but I didn't want to listen to another long ramble about the institute gang.' She rubbed her eyes with the back of her hand. 'I told her to make herself a cup of coffee and that she'd be able to cope a lot better with everything if she could stay sober for once.' Her blue eyes were huge and full of tears. 'I wasn't very sympathetic.'

'You couldn't know what was going to happen,' Emma said. 'Sounds like sensible advice on the face of it.'

Mandy Holden shook her head.

'So, you left and went to keep your appointment?' Blake said. 'What time was that?'

The woman frowned for a second. 'Our table was booked for nine at the restaurant. My girlfriend didn't finish work until eight, so it was a late-ish dinner. I arrived five minutes behind schedule, so I guess I left here around eight fifty?'

'And you didn't hear anything further from Chiara during the evening?' Emma said. 'She didn't call or text?'

Mandy Holden shook her head. 'She'd no reason to. Sadie – that's my girlfriend – and I went out clubbing after our meal and then back to her place for a bit.' She looked down. 'I would have stayed over, but she'd got to work this morning, so I came back here after that. I must have been home by around four.'

Blake nodded. Emma was taking notes.

'There was no sign of Chiara of course, but I could see she'd had her coffee.' Mandy looked up and winced. 'And then some brandy after that. She'd left a mess in that way people do when they've had too much to drink. The cafetière was in the kitchen sink, unwashed. There was a glass out on the coffee table here,' she indicated it with her hand, 'with a depleted bottle of Courvoisier next to it.'

A tear trickled down her cheek. 'I assumed she'd just crawled up to bed at that point. I never thought for a minute she'd have gone out again.'

If only he could have guessed the woman was in danger. The pain in her flatmate's eyes was hard to witness. 'There were no signs that she'd entertained anyone round here last night?'

Mandy Holden shook her head. 'Just the one glass, and nothing obvious that had been left behind by anyone else.'

Blake certainly hadn't got the impression that there'd been any kind of drama in the house recently. All the same, the CSIs would need to have a look round. He told Mandy Holden to expect them.

'Was it usual for Chiara to go out on her own in the evening?' he asked. Mandy Holden clearly hadn't worried about returning home in the small hours. It would still have been dark at four that morning.

'No. She wasn't…' Holden paused for a moment, 'well, she wasn't a very self-sufficient person, to be honest. Even the idea of her going for a stroll round the block doesn't ring true. There's no way she'd have gone onto one of the commons alone, however drunk she was.' She gave Blake and Emma a look. 'We're all of us aware there are places you just don't go on your own, late at night.'

Emma nodded.

So presumably someone had come knocking at the door then, to persuade her out, or had arranged a meet-up close by. Chiara's mobile had been on her body and was being checked as they spoke. They'd need to review all the likely CCTV cameras too. If they were lucky they might pick up some useful images.

He caught Emma's eye. His DS was shaking her head. She was probably going through the same thought processes and having the same fears: that the killer they were dealing with would have thought about CCTV. But there were cameras all over the place. They'd just have to hope.

'Can you think of anyone who would have wanted to harm Chiara?' Blake asked.

Mandy Holden let out a long breath. 'Hell. Not to the extent that they'd kill her for it.' But Blake notice her eyes were worried, as though she was debating something inwardly.

'Sometimes small things can escalate,' Emma said, pushing her blonde curls out of her eyes. 'If you've got anything that might help us, we'd be glad to hear about it. You needn't worry. We always try to be discreet, and if you give us information we'll check the facts carefully before we draw conclusions.'

Mandy Holden nodded. 'I understand that. I was only thinking that Chiara did tend to rub people up the wrong way. If Professor Seabrook hadn't been murdered I'd have said she was the person with the strongest reason to dislike Chiara.'

Blake raised an eyebrow and waited for her version of the relationship breakdown between the two women.

'Samantha Seabrook was very down on Chiara's work. I'm no expert I'm afraid,' Mandy Holden said, 'so I don't know how justified it was, but Chiara took it very personally. She upped the ante by getting her father involved, and the more she protested, the more vigorous the professor got in her criticisms.' She flopped back in her armchair. 'Truth to tell I got a bit fed up with the constant stream of vitriol from Chiara, and the blow-by-blow accounts of their interactions.' There were tears in her eyes again. 'Then one day there was a glimmer of hope. Chiara came home all upbeat. She'd talked to another of the academics at the institute – Dr Simon Askey.' Holden's tone changed as she mentioned him, as though she was naming the star of a blockbuster movie. She gave them a sidelong look. 'She had a bit of a crush on him, to be honest. Anyway, Askey had listened to her problems, and sympathised, and promised to raise the matter with Professor Seabrook.'

All very interesting. 'And what happened?'

'I'm afraid it was a false dawn,' Mandy said. 'For whatever reason he didn't make any headway – if he kept his promise. I guess Chiara felt let down, but – unusually for her – she didn't offload so much on me after that. Clammed up, in fact, so I'm not too sure of the details.'

Blake remembered da Souza's description of the row he'd overheard between Askey and Laurito. What was it that had happened that Chiara hadn't wanted to share with Mandy Holden? And then he remembered the words that da Souza had thought he'd overheard. Askey reminding Chiara Laurito that it wasn't always best to tell the truth.

CHAPTER TWENTY-NINE

Tara considered texting Kemp to let him know about Chiara's murder, but eventually she decided against it. She didn't want him abandoning the job he was doing in Berlin and muscling in. After a moment she messaged Matt at *Not Now*, telling him there'd been some kind of incident on the common. She didn't give him any details, though. It was a big story, but she wouldn't break Blake's confidence, and it would feel totally wrong anyway. Her mind was constantly on Chiara and the horrors she must have endured the night before. At last it was time to leave for London, and she made an effort to switch her focus to the interview with Professor Seabrook's old school friend, Patsy Wentworth.

Tara had never liked the Underground. Now, she found herself standing with her back against the station wall as she waited for a train from King's Cross. The platform was heaving. She ran her eyes quickly over the sea of faces around her. No one she recognised.

Only when the Tube had pulled right into the station did she move forward, ready to enter the train. Inside, there was one seat, deep down in the carriage, but she stayed standing. She didn't want to get hemmed in.

When she emerged from the Underground at Camden Town, she found it was raining properly for the first time in weeks. The London dust and dirt mingled with the large raindrops that hit the hot pavement at her feet, making marks the size of ten pence pieces.

The smell of car exhaust and diesel from a passing bus mingled with that of coffee wafting out from a branch of Costa. She checked the map on her phone and scanned the road signs until she reached the right back street. The place was full of large, Victorian townhouses, with basements and attic windows; once grand, now tatty. The on-street parking displayed a fair share of motorbikes, as well as dilapidated old cars, and the pavements contained a scattering of wheelie bins. Through one of the windows, she could see a tree of life wall hanging, and another one had a chain of crystals, hanging down from the catch of its sash.

Patsy was at 4a. She found number 4, its front door painted black, with a faded sticker saying 'no junk mail' attached to it. The buzzers went from a to d; rain had managed to seep its way inside the casing of the labels, and the ink had run.

The woman who came to answer the door was tall – around six foot, Tara guessed – and thin. She wore long, black, baggy trousers and a sleeveless black vest top. Her hair was long too, reaching well past her shoulders, and her make-up was dramatic.

'Patsy?' she said.

The woman nodded, a slow grin spreading across her wide mouth. Tara was quite sure she was being judged, and that Patsy had decided she wasn't a force to be reckoned with. The professor's old friend clearly fancied herself a rebel.

'Come on in,' Patsy said, leaning for a moment against the door frame. When she spoke, Tara noticed her tongue was pierced.

Their route took them along a dark hall and down some stairs. It seemed natural, somehow, that she should occupy the basement. A bright, airy ground-floor flat wouldn't have suited her aesthetic.

The place smelled of joss sticks, hash and petunia oil. She couldn't detect any trace of food, which – combined with the woman's thinness – made her wonder if Patsy was the sort of person who barely bothered with proper meals. A piece of toast here, maybe, a cup of coffee there. She was very pale.

Patsy motioned her to a low sofa. Or in fact, was it a sofa at all? Something long and flat, covered with a cotton throw. Tara had a feeling she was meant to feel diminished once she'd sat down. She gave Patsy Wentworth a look to tell her she'd have to try harder than that.

'Mind if I record our interview?'

'Do what you want,' the woman said, rolling her eyes.

Tara went through the formalities of expressing her sympathy over Patsy's friend's death – mainly because she was curious to see if she'd bother to fake a reaction. She certainly didn't look emotional.

'So, Pa Seabrook gave you my contact details?' she said, in a gravelly voice. Tara was guessing at forty a day. There was a look of amusement in her eyes. 'I'm kind of surprised.'

'He was a bit cagey about you at first.' With the police too, apparently – though she wasn't going to tell her that.

'I was never his favourite individual. It was unfortunate for him that mine and Samantha's friendship was the one that lasted. The most outrageous of all her classmates.' She drew herself up a little higher. 'All the Sophies and Tiffanys went by the wayside.'

'Are Patsys different then?' Tara couldn't help herself, even though she knew she was spoiling for a row.

Patsy's eyes narrowed. 'This one is. Samantha was too. That was why we got along.'

'How do you mean, different?'

Patsy took out a packet of Camel cigarettes from one of her baggy pockets and lit up. No filter, Tara noticed. Not on the cigarettes anyway. The woman was certainly applying one to the impression she wanted to give Tara, but it was transparent. 'We were both poor little rich girls. Every financial advantage but with crap parents.'

'I didn't think Sir Brian seemed so especially crap.'

'Oh "Sir" Brian, is it?' Patsy let out a laugh as hard and sharp as a whip crack and then coughed. 'I hadn't heard. But of course, I assume he got the "Sir" for spending his whole time thinking about things other than his daughter.'

'I understand he had a difficult time. I heard about his wife...' But not enough, obviously. Did Patsy know the truth about what had happened?

'The tragic Bella? Yes, he spent a lot of time running around after her.'

She couldn't bring herself to admit she didn't know what had happened to Sir Brian's wife. Hopefully Patsy would let something slip, but she wasn't going to go begging for it. She'd find out on her own terms or not at all.

'So, you and Samantha sympathised with each other?' she said. 'You had a bad time with your parents too?'

'Never mind about my parents. Let's just say we haven't spoken in a long time now. As for sympathising; we weren't the sort of girls to sit around snivelling into silk handkerchiefs.'

'What did you do?'

'Fun and games, Tara.' She leant back in her chair. 'Fun and games.'

She was enjoying being the one with the information Tara wanted. She must know her knowledge was all that was preventing Tara from standing up and walking out.

Patsy's cigarette had a centimetre of ash on it now. There was an ashtray on a bookshelf across the room from her, but she'd never reach it without losing what she'd already got to the carpet. Looking down, it was clear it wouldn't be the first time. Patsy drew the packet out of her trouser pocket again and flicked it open. 'Have one,' she said.

Tara shook her head. 'No thanks.'

Still Patsy held out the packet. 'I said have one. Have one, and I'll tell you what Samantha was like when she was at school.'

This was crazy; like bullying. Normally, it would have been the worst possible tactic to take with Tara. But how much did she want to know the truth? She ought to be able to override her desire to stay in absolute control if it meant getting what she wanted. Her heart was racing; anger was a powerful emotion.

'Here.' Patsy pushed the packet towards her and Tara waited for a second.

'All right,' she said at last. 'If going along with your screwed-up games is going to pay dividends, then sure.' She took the cigarette and put it in her mouth before Patsy asked her to. She didn't want to have to follow any more orders.

The moment the cigarette was between her lips, Patsy pulled out her lighter. 'Now,' she said. 'If you smoke that, like a grown-up girl, I'll tell you exactly what you need to know.'

Just for a second, Tara thought she was going to lose control. Heat and fury flew through her like fire across a petrol spill. She fought to calm down.

'Go on then,' she said at last, and her voice was steady. 'I'm delighted if I'm relieving the tedium of your life by doing this, but I haven't got all day. What was Samantha like at school?'

For a second the look in Patsy's eyes made Tara wonder if she'd blown it; taken the fag for nothing. But then, without warning, the woman laughed. The laugh turned into a cough again. 'That's what I'm showing you, you thick bitch. Why are you smoking now?'

'Simply because you've got something I want, and it seems that unless I do what you say, you're not willing to let me have it.'

'Quite right, so take a good big lungful right now.' She watched. 'Very good. And that's just what Samantha did.'

Tara exhaled into Patsy's face but the woman seemed oblivious. 'I'm sorry?'

'She had what a lot of the kids at school wanted: beauty, lots of money, a wicked sense of humour, intelligence of a high order—'

She broke off to cough again. 'Charisma. I suppose that was it. She was the girl everyone was desperate to be in with. The cool one. And because she had what everyone else wanted, she could make people do whatever she wanted too. Simply to be closer to her.'

'What about you?'

'Hah! I got them to do what I wanted too, but I did it by being bigger and stronger than they were. Whereas charm's more insidious, more deceptive. If I got a child to do something that got them into trouble, there tended to be blood and bruises and tall Patsy standing there looking guilty. When it was Samantha, there was this sweet, beautiful, clever child, with the obviously difficult home life.'

'But you had the difficult home life too.'

'Not in such an attractive and tragic way as Samantha did. It was largely because of that that she never got the blame. People used to assume she'd got in with a bad lot. They never realised she *was* the bad lot.'

It certainly put a different spin on the Samantha–Patsy relationship from the one Sir Brian had created.

Patsy let her ash fall on to the rug at her feet again. 'She was a ringleader; a classic tearaway. Not that I blame her. She did have a lot to cope with.'

'What type of things did she get involved in? Drugs?'

'In a small way. Only hash; Great Sterringham wasn't exactly awash with dealers. No, it was mainly other stuff: thieving, vandalism, boys…' She paused at this, her eyes far away. 'God yes, there were lots of boys.'

Tara could imagine. 'What kind of thieving?'

Patsy waved the hand with the cigarette. 'All sorts. Shoplifting, money and knick-knacks from family and friends, you know the sort of thing. I think it was her way of trying to get her dad to focus on her for a change.'

'Did it work?'

Patsy let out a long breath. 'Not really. Pa Seabrook had to put quite a lot of time and effort into smoothing ruffled feathers, compensating the local branch of Boots in return for not prosecuting her, mysteriously "finding" items she'd pinched from their acquaintances after they'd been to stay. But he only did the necessary. As soon as the latest crisis was over his focus was straight back to Bella again.'

She stretched her long legs out in front of her. 'It's funny,' she said, after a moment, 'I don't think Samantha was ever able to stop looking for his approval and his love. For me, I chucked all that in a long time ago. If my parents couldn't see things my way, I'd rather we just parted company, but for Samantha, not so. She'd never have admitted it though, even to herself.'

'You think that's why she went into the area of research she chose? Because it was her father's pet cause?'

She got up and flicked some ash into the tray this time. 'For sure.'

'And had she settled down, by that stage, in other ways?'

Again, that crackling laugh. 'I don't know about that. We didn't see so much of each other once she moved to Cambridge, but old habits die hard, so who knows? When it came to the stealing it almost seemed like a compulsion. And she was shameless.'

Patsy shuffled over to a side cupboard, painted sea green. She opened one of its doors and reached down for something. When she turned back to Tara she had a small photo album in her hand. 'Here,' she said, flipping it open clumsily, still busy with her cigarette. 'Look at this.'

Tara recognised Samantha Seabrook in the photo. She looked radiant and the laughter was clear in the set of her mouth and her eyes. Around her neck was an ornate necklace with large red stones set into a gold chain. The thing looked antique.

'Yes, those *are* rubies, in case you're wondering,' Patsy said. 'Huge, aren't they? That necklace belonged to her grandmother before she lifted it. Her father knew she must have it really, but she hid it well, and apparently he could never bring himself to raise the matter. She said he used to make veiled comments about it, but I suppose he thought sticking his head in the sand was less painful. Never ask a question unless you're prepared to hear the answer.'

As Tara walked back to the Tube station she thought of Blake. She should have told him she'd identified the woman in Samantha Seabrook's photograph as Patsy Wentworth. She was going to have to confess that she'd been dishonest. Nothing about the professor's life was insignificant. She hadn't been that sort of a person.

CHAPTER THIRTY

Blake and Emma were on their way to Simon Askey's house off Mill Road, just south of the police station. Blake was hoping they'd get the chance to break the news about Chiara. He wanted to see Askey's face, to judge whether any show of surprise was genuine.

He kept his eyes on the road but could feel his DS watching him.

'You think he could be the killer?' she said after a moment.

He shrugged as they drove over the railway bridge, past its colourful mural featuring a mishmash of international flags. It marked the crossing into the southern section of Mill Road, an area popular with students, and crowded with lively independent shops and world food outlets.

'We know he and Chiara Laurito argued about something,' he said. 'And he certainly didn't have any time for Professor Seabrook. Plus I think he's a shit.'

'That'll stand up in court.'

He signalled to turn left. 'It just adds to the picture.'

'No note or doll sent to the victim this time,' Emma said, 'as far as we know at least.'

Blake pulled off the main road. 'No. And from what Professor da Souza said about her character, I couldn't see her keeping something like that to herself.' There was a pause and he turned off the side road into a modern development of smart townhouses. If all of the accommodation off Mill Road went this way, it would be even harder to afford than it was now. 'Maybe there were only ever two dolls made, way back whenever that was. But why two in the first place?'

He wiped a hand across his brow. It *must* mean something. 'Or, on the other hand, if the murderer has a whole stack of old dolls, maybe he or she didn't threaten Chiara Laurito with one because they had to act quickly for some reason. Perhaps Chiara knew something that could implicate them, or' – he pulled up on the kerbside and engaged the handbrake – 'if they intended Chiara as a victim from the start, along with Professor Seabrook and Tara, then maybe something's testing their self-control, and their planning's starting to slip.'

'If the killer has had them all in their sights from the outset, then Samantha, Chiara and Tara must share something. What on earth do they have in common?'

Blake unfastened his seatbelt. 'Good question. Professor Seabrook and Tara both have or had actor mothers. Chiara and the professor both come from privileged backgrounds. I suppose they all do really. Tara's mother can't be short of a bob or two – though that might not always have been the case. I read somewhere that she had Tara when she was very young.'

Emma grabbed her bag and opened the passenger door. 'Either way, maybe it means they're more likely to have made a mistake this time.'

'I bloody well hope so.' But the thought that the killer might be getting impatient and lashing out made his chest contract when he thought of Tara. She'd be striding around in her bloody-minded way, brave but terrified, living on the edge of her nerves and likely to strike out herself. One way and another he was spending a lot of time thinking about her at the moment.

They walked up to the door of number two – panelled and painted a pristine white – and knocked.

A woman half-opened the door and peered round. She was still in her night things – a creased, striped pair of pyjamas, the top two buttons undone – and held a baby over one shoulder.

She furrowed her brow and looked at them through eyes that were three-quarters closed against the morning light. The baby was crying. 'Yes?' Blake had the feeling she'd already had enough of her Saturday.

'Is Dr Askey in?' he asked. But at that moment Askey appeared behind her, approaching slowly, a cup of steaming coffee in his hand and a newspaper under his arm. He was dressed in jeans and a navy V-necked jumper, a white T-shirt showing underneath.

He gave Blake a look he was getting used to. Bored eyes and a contemptuous smile. 'I didn't expect visitors on a Saturday.'

Which was just as Blake had been hoping. 'Can we come in?'

Askey motioned them into the hall and the woman with the baby moved into the interior too.

'Why don't you head back upstairs?' he said, meeting his wife's eye and then nodding over his shoulder towards the landing. Blake imagined he'd rather she didn't overhear their conversation.

Askey led them through to a spacious living room with cream sofas. Blake wondered how that would work once the baby was on its feet, with its roving sticky fingers.

'Smart house,' he said.

'Thanks.' Askey raised an ironic eyebrow. 'It's a step up from the sort of environment I was raised in.' In truth, Blake disliked show homes where no one could relax.

They all took seats on the sofas. Askey caught Emma's eye and gave her one of his deliberately charming smiles. She was smiling back. Blake hoped it was a tactic, though he didn't know how she could bear to play along.

'You've no doubt heard that Chiara Laurito's been found murdered,' he said, without giving Askey the chance to take control of the situation. He gave the man 100 per cent of his attention as he said it.

The shock looked genuine. But then, if he knew what was coming he'd have had time to prepare; a chance to work out how to arrange his features to best effect.

'I can't believe it.' He flopped back in the sofa he occupied and stared for a moment at the ceiling.

'Sorry we didn't break the news more gently,' Emma said. 'We thought it would have spread.'

Askey sat forward again. 'If it had been a working day I'm sure it would have. But we've just been here at home, chilling out with the papers.'

Blake bet Askey was speaking solely for himself. Upstairs he could hear the baby crying again. 'And were you also here last night?' he asked. 'Did you come straight home from the institute garden party?'

Askey nodded. 'Those dos always wear me out. What happened to Chiara? How did she die?'

Blake ignored the question. 'Can your wife vouch for you?' he said instead. 'I presume she was here too.'

Askey frowned. 'She was, but she'd gone to bed early. She gets very tired, what with all the broken nights. I often find she's gone into Davey's room and fallen asleep in there, next to his cot. It's where the spare bed is.'

'So she won't be able to vouch for you? That's what you're saying?'

'I don't much like your tone, Inspector,' Askey said.

Blake smiled. 'But is that what you're saying?'

'Sandra came back to bed at some stage. I don't know when it was. You'd have to ask her.'

'We will.' Blake relaxed back in his seat. 'I understand you and Chiara Laurito had become quite close.'

Askey's frown deepened. 'I don't know what you mean.'

'Chiara's flatmate, Mandy, says you offered to mediate between Chiara and Samantha Seabrook. I presume you must have felt sorry for her. You thought Professor Seabrook had treated her unfairly?'

Askey pulled his hands through his blond hair and gritted his teeth for a moment. 'The pair of them, honest to God. I wouldn't wish either of them dead but they were enough to drive the rest of us to distraction.' He took a deep breath. 'Okay. So Sam didn't mince her words when it came to criticising Chiara, and at first I hadn't had time to look into whether her criticisms were justified or not. Either way, I thought she was overdoing it, so yes, when Chiara came to me I did offer to try to build some bridges between them.'

'But you didn't come through with the goods, from what Chiara's flatmate says.'

Askey's eyes darkened. 'Sam showed me some of Chiara's work and defended her stand. I could see she had a point. It was more complicated than I'd originally thought. I ended up figuring that Chiara needed to learn to take Sam's comments on the chin.'

'Because they were justified?'

'That's what Sam had me believe.' He paused for a second. 'But then maybe she only showed me Chiara's worst work. She was good at pulling the wool over people's eyes and only telling the truth when she felt like it.'

Blake noticed his knuckles were white as he gripped his coffee.

'So Chiara must have felt let down by you.' Blake paused. 'Is that why you argued?'

'Excuse me?'

'The entire institute heard you by the sound of it,' Blake said. 'A couple of weeks or so before Samantha Seabrook died. Chiara was in your office and there was a whole load of shouting.'

'Jesus!' Askey put his mug down on a coffee table. 'That place is like a goldfish bowl. The same fish swimming round the same scummy water, watching each other.' He took a deep breath. 'Anyway, it sounds like a case of wild exaggeration to me. I'm trying to think back.' He paused for a moment and closed his eyes. *Buying himself time?* Blake and Emma exchanged a glance. She was thinking the same, he could tell. 'Yes, I remember now. It was to do with the funding bid I was putting in with Sam; the one she pulled out of. She'd suggested yet another ridiculous change to the methodology and it got my goat. She was always mucking things around just as we'd got them sorted.'

'In that case,' Blake said, 'I wonder why you were overheard telling Chiara it wasn't always best to tell the truth. Was that because being honest about someone's change of heart over research methodology could lead to discord?' He gave the man his most innocent smile.

Askey was clenching his fist. After a long pause he said: 'No. I remember exactly what I said now. I didn't tell her she shouldn't tell the truth. I said: "you can be too honest". It was because she was passing on what Sam had said about my own methods, word for word. It wasn't complimentary.'

Blake turned to Emma, who leant forward. 'One final thing,' she said. 'We wanted to ask you about Jim Cooper.'

'Jim?' Askey's shoulders relaxed a little.

Emma nodded. 'We understand he feels that he and Samantha Seabrook were pretty close, but in fact it's possible the professor didn't feel the same way.'

Askey let out a short, humourless laugh. 'She didn't. She spent quite a lot of time taking the piss out of him behind his back. Says a lot about both of them.'

'We wondered, did you ever tell Jim Cooper what Samantha really thought of him?' Emma asked.

Askey gave her a look. 'I'm not a complete bastard. But I did try to make him see that she was taking him for a fool. I didn't spell it out exactly, but I gave him some pretty heavy hints. I suppose I probably did make it fairly clear.'

So he was a complete bastard then. But a bastard that wanted people to think the best of him.

'And was that before or after she'd been killed?'

Askey took a deep breath. 'A bit of both. In fact, if I were you, that's where I'd be looking for the killer.'

Blake raised an eyebrow.

'Someone who obsessed over Sam whilst she was alive, killed her in a passion, and then got rid of Chiara when they heard her bad-mouthing her. She was telling everyone exactly what she thought of Sam at the institute garden party last night. If the killer felt proprietorial over Sam, maybe they didn't like that.' His angry eyes were on Blake's. 'So I suggest you take yourselves off and focus on someone who might have actually committed a double murder, rather than bothering me.'

Annoyingly, of course, he could be right. The thought had already crossed Blake's mind. If it proved to be true, Askey would forever think he'd been the one to spot the possibility. Just another one of life's frustrations.

Before they left they spoke to Sandra Askey, who confirmed what her husband had said. She'd been asleep when he'd returned home. She'd woken at some stage, when the baby had, had given him a feed and then gone back to their shared bed. She'd got no idea what time it had been. After dark, before dawn. Time meant nothing these days. She felt like the living dead.

As they drove back to Parkside, Emma said: 'I should think Sandra Askey might be tempted to turn violent towards her husband if only she had the energy.'

'You could be right. What did you reckon to his reactions?'

'He did look gobsmacked about Chiara, but he might just be a good actor.'

'I thought the same.'

'And his response when you questioned him about the row was interesting.'

'Yes. He looked as though he was playing for time.'

'He did. But when he finally explained, he sounded genuine.'

It had struck Blake that way too. But if that was the case, then why hadn't he told them straight off? And why had he looked so uncomfortable when he realised just how much of their conversation had been overheard?

CHAPTER THIRTY-ONE

On her journey back from London to Cambridge, Tara had sent off her email to Blake, telling him that she'd found the woman in Samantha Seabrook's drunken snapshot and interviewed her too. There wasn't a good way to explain the fact that she'd misled him, so she didn't bother. He'd only think she was gutless and mealy-mouthed as well as dishonest. At least she had a recording of the interview she could send him.

After that she'd considered what line of enquiry to pursue next. Samantha Seabrook's childhood had become more and more fascinating. It might not help solve her murder, but gossip about her upbringing would bring Tara's article to life.

With that in mind, she'd decided at last to call her mother. It was just possible she'd have inside knowledge: she and Bella Seabrook had worked in the same industry, after all. So, whilst staring out of the train window at the farmland that flitted across her line of sight, she'd made the call. The sun had put in an occasional appearance, casting patterns over the fields.

Her mother had sounded surprised (and slightly put out) at the request to come and visit her as soon as possible. To be fair, Tara hated having things sprung on her too. It probably ran in the family. Tara could hear Lydia gradually recovering her poise and modifying her tone. By the end of the conversation it was as though her mother had invited her. Tara wasn't looking forward to driving across the Fens to keep the appointment, but she couldn't let the threat she was under control her life. She wouldn't be the only one on the road, even though they'd agreed she could visit the following day, on a Sunday.

She'd arrived back in Cambridge and was on her bike, just nearing her cottage on Stourbridge Common, when her phone rang.

As she picked up she looked over to where the tent and police cordon still stood and thought again of Chiara.

Her heart was already sinking. And then it was Giles on the phone. Didn't he know it was Saturday? Not that journalists got the same perks as other people when it came to hours, but there ought to be some respite – especially from bosses.

'Yes?' She knew she sounded short-tempered.

'Delightful to speak to you too.' He was drawling. He did it knowingly, for effect, which made it all the more annoying.

'I've been down in London all day working on the story.'

'Very commendable. It's the story I wanted to talk to you about, as a matter of fact.'

There now.

'I'm in town. Come and meet me at the Copper Kettle? You must need refreshments if you've been out all day. And there are some pretty major developments relating to Samantha Seabrook's murder, wouldn't you say? I'm surprised you haven't been in touch.'

Tara looked longingly at her cottage. 'Giles, you said I would be writing a feature about Samantha Seabrook and her work. You said *Not Now* would be covering her even if she'd died at home in her bed. I wasn't aware I was meant to be writing about the police case.'

Giles laughed. *'Please don't play the innocent with me, Tara. I know you can put on many guises but that one's especially hard to swallow. I'll wait for you at the café.'*

Tara could have told him to go to hell, of course, but there was something about his tone that stopped her. Her heart pumped faster now. She was spoiling for a fight; better to have it face to face.

The Copper Kettle was crowded, but Giles had managed to bag a table by the window. He didn't bother to stand when she arrived. In fairness, she hadn't put herself out either. It was too hot to rush. London, followed by the train journey, then a bike ride into town and a café full of people who happened to include Giles, had made her feel fractious. She pulled out the chair opposite him and sat down.

'So,' he said. 'I gather you've become chummy with the police.'

Tara looked at the menu. If Giles was going to force her to sit there he was bloody well going to buy her some tea. 'We've spoken a few times.'

'And this latest "incident", as you so vaguely described it when you emailed Matt this morning, took place right outside your house, yet you're telling me you didn't know it was another murder, and you weren't aware the victim was connected to Samantha Seabrook?'

Did he really think his desire to make cash out of other people's misery was the most important thing here? 'I told Matt everything I could at the time.'

'Everything you *could*? Everything you wanted to tell him, more like. You're buggering things up for me, Tara. You came across a scoop that would have sent our hit rates soaring and you kept it to yourself. Are you crazy?'

'I was asked not to pass on the news because it would affect the police investigation.'

'By this policeman you've been seeing, I assume?'

Tara raised an eyebrow.

'Gav and Shona were in the Champion of the Thames the other night. Interesting that you didn't notice them. They reckoned you and the detective were looking very cosy. He's a bit of a looker, Shona said. Haute couture and rugged stubble.'

So much for loyalty amongst colleagues.

'As for his request that you should keep things quiet, you ought to have found a way round that. You could have gone straight to Chiara Laurito's house and asked if she'd returned home last night. Then we could at least have reported her missing, along with the news that a body had been found. People would have made the leap.'

'Giles—' Tara caught the eye of a passing waiter. 'An iced tea, please,' she said to him. 'Giles, had it occurred to you that we have a duty not to muck up the police's operation? Because so far two innocent people are dead, and it might be nice if they could catch the killer before the number goes up?'

Giles sat back in his chair, his arms folded. 'That's what all this is about, isn't it?'

'Excuse me?'

He nodded. 'Self-interest.'

'You've lost me.'

'You want the killer caught to protect yourself. I've heard a rumour that you've been threatened.'

Tara wasn't quite sure if it was the relish in his voice, the assumption that she didn't care about anyone else, or the pure fact of him knowing her business that was worse. What the hell was she doing, working for this man? She didn't want anything to do with him. He was seeing her fear, and the threat against her, as another potential news story, just as she'd known he would.

'Well,' Giles sipped his coffee as the waiter arrived to deliver Tara's tea. 'I can see from your face that the gossip's true then. Very interesting. And it's another thing you could have told me if you were genuinely onside. Christ, Tara; a true journalist wouldn't have held back for personal reasons. They'd have seen this for the gold that it is.'

'Gee, thanks.'

But Giles wasn't joking.

'How did you find out, anyway?'

But he sat back in his chair and folded his arms. 'I told you before, my dear: I've got eyes and ears everywhere. Where I got it from isn't the point. I need team players at *Not Now*. People who share my vision for the magazine. I felt I owed you something, given the publicity your mum got us when she was photographed carrying the magazine. But you're far from indispensable. And with your record I doubt other publications would queue up to employ you.'

'I haven't got a record. Nothing official as far as the police are concerned.'

He smiled. 'My dear girl, if your record's known to me I can make it travel – and fast. Official or not. So, here's the deal.' He stretched in his seat now. 'You give *Not Now* a full and frank inter-view explaining exactly what's happened since you got your death threat. I want fear, I want speculation and I want your past. The lot on a plate. Daughter of famous actor Lydia Thorpe terrorised a second time. Will she be the killer's next victim? That will make it worth keeping you on the payroll.'

She knew she had a temper on occasion, but she'd rarely known such fury. She opened her mouth, but he held up a hand. 'Don't be too hasty. Can you afford to pay the mortgage for that dump you call home if you turn me down? I guess your mother would sub you, but I imagine you wouldn't want that.' Then he laughed. 'I know,' he said. 'It's horrible being beaten, isn't it? All journalists hate it. Perhaps you are one of us after all.'

She got up and walked out without finishing her tea.

Outside, she was still smarting – big time. She knew she'd yanked the café door open in such a way that had made her conspicuous. She'd felt the eyes of the clientele fix on her, drawn by her anger.

She hoped they were all staring at Giles now, and thinking of him as the shit he most certainly was.

Unseeingly, she turned up King's Parade towards the market square; she'd had to park her bike outside Great St Mary's as the nearest racks were full. But then suddenly she saw a face that she knew. It was Kit, the researcher she'd been introduced to at the institute garden party. He'd been about to go into one of the shops but she could see that he'd spotted her. He paused to smile, then waited until she reached him.

'Tara! I can't believe we're both enduring central Cambridge on a Saturday. What are you doing here?'

She suddenly realised, looking at his face, that he mustn't have heard about Chiara yet. Blake had said they wanted to control the release of the news, of course. Her secret knowledge meant it was hard to react normally. 'I had to meet a work contact, otherwise nothing would have dragged me in.' She did her best to keep her smile natural.

He was looking at her closely, as though he could tell something was up. 'Well, take care, okay?' he said, his blue eyes on hers. 'It's good to bump into you. Maybe…' He paused. 'Well, maybe we'll bump into each other again.' Then he gave her a smaller smile, almost shy, coupled with a wave, and walked off up the street.

Tara kept thinking of the latest lot of harrowing news that Kit would have to cope with in the coming hours. The encounter had given her a moment to calm down and put Giles into perspective. She could see the world around her again. The Saturday crowds on King's Parade filled her view. Guides holding flags on poles strode through the human traffic. The tourists milled after them, their cameras held high on selfie sticks; their screens flashing in the sunlight. People on bikes tried to weave their way through the gaggles of shoppers that had flooded out into the road; she saw one shout a sharp word at a man with a pushchair.

Now she'd got some feeling of normality back, she realised there were things she needed from Boots. She turned right down St Mary's Passage, watching the tea-time picnickers in the grounds of the university church to her left, sitting on tartan rugs, eating ice creams and cupcakes.

Then she cut through the market square, where she could smell the freshly squeezed orange juice from the juice and smoothie stall, as well as a waft of cooking from the ostrich burger stand. They were still busy, despite it being so late in the day.

At last she reached the open walkway of Petty Cury, passing a guy selling tiny, colourful helicopter toys that he propelled into the air with rubber bands. He'd attracted a huddle of children, all staring upwards.

And then she turned left into Boots and headed towards the No. 7 section. She needed to restock her supplies. If life was intent on leaving her pale and mostly sleepless, then make-up was all the more essential to ensure she looked human.

It was after she'd grabbed some foundation that she caught sight of the Rimmel section. She thought of the battered lipstick she'd seen in Samantha Seabrook's Dior-filled apartment. Instinctively, she went closer to the Rimmel stand and stood looking at the lipsticks there. The prices were still good – just as they'd been when she was a teenager – but the packaging had changed a lot. Appearance-wise, there wasn't a lot to choose between the smarter brands and the ones on the rack in front of her.

And then she thought back to the cheap-looking, battered object in the apartment and suddenly it came to her. She'd assumed it had looked like that because it had been knocking around in the bottom of someone's bag. But of course, that wasn't it.

The reason it had looked brittle and trashed was because it was old.

CHAPTER THIRTY-TWO

Blake re-scanned the email he'd got from Tara as he sat in his car around the corner from Kit Tyler's flat. She'd identified the woman in Samantha Seabrook's photograph as Patsy Wentworth, tracked her down and been to interview her. *Right.* He might have known she'd kept something from him. She was a journalist after all, even if he'd almost let himself think of her as a partner in this. He thought about emailing back to tell her exactly what he thought of her sense of priorities, but he was quite sure she already knew.

Blake skimmed the details of the interview that Tara had sent through. He'd listen to the full recording later, but there was nothing of fundamental importance as far as he could see – though a few more incidental pieces of the jigsaw slotted into place. Annoyingly, Tara had got Patsy's address from Old Man Seabrook himself, whereas he'd told Blake he couldn't even remember her name. Tara was better at sweet-talking people than he was. Or better at manipulation and deception. It all depended how you looked at it.

Too many people were lying to him at the moment.

'What is it, boss?' Emma asked.

'Information. Do you remember the ruby necklace we found in Samantha Seabrook's filing cabinet at the institute, that first day we looked round?'

She nodded, her hair bouncing.

'Sounds as though we were right about it being a family heirloom. Apparently, it belonged to her grandmother, and if her school friend's telling the truth then she stole it. Stole from her own family. The word is her father knew she must have taken it but couldn't bring himself to confront her. No wonder he went to pieces when we asked him about it. We were confirming his worst fears, and at the worst possible time too.'

'Death has a horrible habit of revealing things,' Emma said.

He nodded. 'I've had another update too – from Patrick. Simon Askey's in good company. Jim Cooper also has no reliable alibi for the time when Chiara Laurito was killed. In fact, so far, no one from the institute seems to. They're loners, or keep odd hours and don't interact in the way the rest of us do.'

But then he thought of his own empty cottage in Fen Ditton. How would he prove where he'd been overnight, if anyone wanted to know?

They got out of the car and walked round to Kit Tyler's flat. It was above a Greek restaurant and the door had peeling paint, but because it was in town, not Chesterton like Jim Cooper's place, Blake reckoned it would still be setting the researcher back a fair bit.

Emma pressed the bell.

When Kit answered it was clear he'd already heard the news. 'You've come about Chiara?' he said, stepping back to let them in.

Blake nodded and introduced Emma. 'Who told you?'

'I came back from town to a round-robin email from Mary Mayhew.' He spoke slowly. Blake wondered if he was still assimilating what had happened. He still felt that way himself, despite his head start.

It was Patrick Wilkins who had informed Mary Mayhew, but Blake knew he'd told her the police wanted to break the news themselves.

'She was keen to let us all know before we got doorstepped by the press.'

Blake suppressed an exasperated sigh. That figured. As before, she'd clearly decided the institute's reputation was paramount. Unless she had her own reasons for managing the news. He thought again of her interest in religion and the cross that had been on Samantha Seabrook's body. Gut instinct told him the killer was male, but he might be wrong. Mary Mayhew looked fit enough and she'd struck him as callous.

'She didn't give us any details,' Kit added, as though sensing Blake's frustration. He led them through a small hallway lined with books on one side and coat hooks on the other.

'We haven't made them public yet,' Emma said.

Kit nodded. 'Can I get you a drink?' He motioned for them to take a seat. They'd entered a rectangular living room which contained everything from a kitchenette at one end to a sofa bed at the other. Emma sat on the sofa bed and Blake took an upright chair that had been tucked under a small table.

'A glass of water would be great,' Emma said. Blake asked for the same. The room faced south, and it was stifling. Kit had opened the hopper window but the large main pane was fixed.

It was a far cry from Chiara's place, though it was clean and uncluttered, apart from some neat piles of papers and books. They were stacked next to shelves that were already overflowing. There were some other homely touches too: a framed photo of a young girl with long, dark hair, standing next to an older woman, sat on a narrow side table. There was a blue pot next to it, decorated with silver birds.

Kit Tyler passed them a glass each. One reminded Blake of the sort they used to get given at school, and had a chip in it. The other looked as though it might have once lived in a pub.

Kit caught his eye and gave a half-smile. 'They came with the flat. Landlord really pushes the boat out.'

'Doesn't alter how grateful I am for a cool drink,' Emma said, and took a swig.

'So how can I help?' Kit asked, perching on the sofa bed next to her.

'We're talking to everyone who saw Chiara at the institute garden party yesterday evening,' Blake said. 'As a matter of course, we want to know what time everyone left, where they went after that and if anyone can vouch for them.' He looked around Kit's one-bed pad. He was guessing he'd be another one with no alibi.

'I left around eight,' Kit said. 'Chiara wasn't in a great state by then to be honest. She'd had too much to drink. Not to the extent that I was worried about her getting home, but she was pretty far gone for that time in the evening.'

'Did you see her again that night?' Blake watched Kit Tyler's eyes.

'No.' He frowned and then shook his head. 'I should have hung around. Made sure she got back to her house. Or at least called her flatmate to check she'd made it home. We could have been out looking for her if only we'd known.'

Unless he was bluffing, he didn't realise she'd spent time back at her house, before she'd gone out to meet her killer. But then again, bluffing wasn't impossible. And someone was.

'You know her flatmate then?' Emma asked.

Kit pulled a face. 'I'm afraid it isn't the first time Chiara's got hammered at an institute do. We've called Mandy in before to come and get her. She probably got a bit fed up with it, in fact.'

Blake nodded. 'Can you think of anyone who might have wanted to harm Chiara? Or anyone who'd been acting oddly around her recently?'

Kit frowned and paused for longer than Blake thought was natural. At last, he said, 'I suppose Chiara worked in very close proximity to Samantha. Maybe she knew something that threatened her killer.'

'If you suspect someone, it would be better to tell us.'

But Kit shook his head and his tone was firm now. 'I don't.'

'So, to pick up on the events of last night,' Blake said. 'Where did you go after you left the party? Did you come straight back here?'

The man nodded.

'And did anyone see you come in?' Not that it would prove he hadn't gone out again.

'I'm afraid not,' Kit Tyler said. 'Or at least, not as far as I know.'

Blake closed his eyes for a moment. It felt as though they were going nowhere.

As he and Emma descended the stairs from Tyler's flat, Blake pulled his phone from his pocket to check for messages. One made the hairs on the back of his neck rise. A clue. It had to be. But where did it take them?

Emma had caught his change of mood and raised a questioning eyebrow.

'Here.' He passed her his phone, with Tara's message about the lipstick she'd seen in Samantha Seabrook's flat. Her new theory was interesting.

'Old?' Emma said. 'Like the dolls?'

He nodded. 'Exactly. I want the lipstick picked up, so we can test Tara's idea: find out when that lipstick was in production.'

'I'll organise it,' Emma said. 'I wasn't out at the crime scene in the night. Remember what Fleming said.'

The DCI had called him between his interviews with Askey and Tyler to tell him to go and get some sleep before he carried on. She knew he was running on empty; the last thing she wanted was him making mistakes. 'Delegate' had been the last word she'd said to him.

'Yes. I remember.' He shrugged. As though he was going to be able to sleep at a time like this. All the same, he knew deep down that his boss was right. 'Old dolls and an old lipstick. What does it mean? Do they date back to Samantha Seabrook's teenage years?' He rubbed his chin. It felt even rougher than usual. 'Da Souza knew her back then. And she lost her mother. Life was tough on Sir Brian.' He suddenly wondered if Pamela Grange had been a family friend back then too.

But he was too tired. He couldn't string it all together. Maybe a couple of hours' rest would let things slide into place.

As Blake neared Fen Ditton he found it hard to focus on the road. He thought of DCI Fleming's words on the phone: 'You're no good to me unless you're firing on all cylinders.' Two women dead, and he was being put down for a nap, like a baby. He jumped when his phone rang, making him realise how close he'd been to dozing at the wheel.

He answered hands-free without registering who was on the line.

'Garstin? It's me. I'm at the house.'

Babette. Hell. He'd said six on Saturday. Since then he'd forgotten both the day and the time.

'I'm around the corner.'

Blake had spent the first ten minutes of Babette and Kitty's visit with Kitty on his lap, trying to hold it together. They were in the sitting room at his cottage, with Babette looking on. There were tears in her eyes. Kitty was showing him her colouring book, and for some reason the elaborate, enthusiastic scribbles brought tears to his own eyes – a symbol of her and her exuberance, he supposed. And then suddenly she stopped turning the pages, cast the book down on the floor and just hugged him, wriggling further into his arms.

But after a while she clambered off his lap and announced her intention to go to the playroom.

It was after that that Babette and Blake discussed the real reason she'd tried to emigrate with Kitty.

'I'd gone under, Garstin – I was overtaken by guilt and the thought of what was best for Kitty.'

Yes, he knew. And there was a reason for it too. 'You tried to make me feel that same guilt,' he said. 'You used it to force me to let you both go.'

He hadn't told anyone the full background. Maybe he should – it ate at him from the inside – but he wasn't ready yet.

'I know,' she said. 'It was unforgivable.' And as she said it, the realisation seemed to overtake her. She looked tiny and defeated, slumped there in the armchair. Her blue eyes were huge and full of tears as she raised her head to look at him. 'Oh God,' she said. 'It really *was* unforgivable, wasn't it? Literally. You won't ever be able to give me another chance.' He could see the shock on her face. 'Of course you won't. I'm sorry. I'm so sorry.' The last words came out in a whisper and Blake felt his chest tense. He wanted her to be wrong, but deep inside, he knew she wasn't.

He got up and hesitated. For a second, he almost went over to kneel on the floor in front of her chair. He had the urge to take her in his arms, to try to ease both their pain. But at last he turned and walked away. Inside, a voice said: *This is up to you. You could forgive her. Deep down you want to hurt her. You want revenge.* He pushed the thoughts away, left the room and closed the door behind him.

Upstairs he could hear Kitty stomping around. Of course – no stairgates any more. But she'd got up there in one piece; it was all right. And he could hear her giggling. She hadn't witnessed Babette's upset. He went up to the floor above, taking the stairs two at a time, swallowing down his emotion.

Kitty was in her old room. He'd have thought it might upset her – it looked so bare now – but she'd found something to play with. As he entered she turned her solid, cuddly body, clad in its deep-blue dress, covered in daisies, and saw him.

'Daddy!' She ran to him and clung to his legs. 'Look!' She held up the toy, her eyes dancing, a wide smile on her face.

'You've found Small Bear!' he said, bending down and sweeping her up in his arms. 'Where was he?'

'There.' She pointed at the blue and yellow bookcase.

'Behind it you mean?'

Her head nodded emphatically. 'But he was sticking out.'

Blake smiled. 'He must be glad to be back with you.'

Kitty nodded again, but Small Bear was somewhere behind his back now. Kitty was clinging to him again, snuggling her silky head into his shoulder.

Your choice.

Blake paused for a long moment. Kitty's hair smelled of Johnson's baby shampoo.

'Shall we go down and show Mummy?' he said at last, still not knowing his plan.

Kitty nodded her head against him, not lifting it up as he carried her downstairs.

He opened the door to the sitting room slowly, talking to Kitty to give Babette some warning of their approach.

He entered the room with Kitty still on his hip. Babette lifted her head to look at them. She'd managed to wipe away her tears, though her eyes were still red.

They met his, questioningly, over Kitty's head, as he held the child tight.

That night, he dreamt of Samantha Seabrook and Chiara Laurito. He saw them in turn, dead where they'd been found, but in both cases he knew there was someone else there too – a man, he thought, but he couldn't see who. He woke with a start and saw that a message had popped up on his phone. It was still glowing. Perhaps the vibration had woken him. Tara.

Meant to mention, I think someone your end's leaking info. My boss knows about my death threat. He wants an exclusive from me, so readers can gloat.

CHAPTER THIRTY-THREE

As Tara got ready to drive to her mother's the following day, she wondered how long Giles would give her to make up her mind about her job. Not that she needed any extra time; there was no way she was going to give him the needy exclusive he wanted. No, she'd made up her mind all right. She was just putting off making it official because the prospect of paying the next mortgage bill would instantly become more frightening.

She'd have to sell her feature as a freelance instead. If she had to she'd include some of the details Giles had been so keen to have, to make it more attractive. But it would be under her own terms and she'd be denying him, which would count for something.

If only she had more savings. Shame she'd had to splash out on the new back door.

As usual she was wary as she crossed the common. Swifts swooped overhead and the church bells from St Andrew's in Chesterton rang out across the river. A gaggle of children was feeding the ducks. It was the most innocent scene you could imagine, but over in the distance the tent that had covered Chiara Laurito's body was still there, in her mind's eye.

Tara was glad of her dark glasses as she drove towards her mother's; the sun bouncing off the flooded land to her left was dazzling. To her right there was a vast channel of water too, and behind her the road stretched back, turning corners to navigate its way around the

near-saturated land, but never dipping out of sight. So much sky.
So much dark soil. She could see one car behind her; none ahead.
It was just another driver, headed towards one of the villages located
in that watery landscape. Of course it was. But Tara didn't like the
fact that there was only one other vehicle in view. What if it was the
killer? They'd clearly been keeping tabs on her. If she broke down
out there she wouldn't have a chance. It was such a lonely place.

She tried to focus on the road ahead and waited for the car to
turn off. By the law of averages it ought to, sooner or later.

But it was only when she made the turn towards her mother's
house, on the outskirts of the moneyed hamlet where she and
Tara's stepfather lived, that Tara finally lost the small green car. The
day was hot and sticky, but that didn't stop the goosebumps that
crawled their way over her flesh.

Tara's Fiat bumped up the rutted drive. It wasn't lack of funds
that stopped Lydia from having it tarmacked – the house was a
family home and her mother liked its rural character. Tara was always
worried the bumps would knock her exhaust off, but her mother
and stepfather had a Land Rover Discovery, so it didn't bother them.
In the height of her career, Lydia Thorpe had hardly ever occupied
the place. She'd had a pied-à-terre in London, which suited her
acting and modelling work. But now Lydia was in residence more
often than not. If she went away it was for a chunk of time to do a
dedicated job. Other than that she would 'retreat' to her rural idyll.

The house was huge and square: a former rectory that had been
built in the mid-eighteenth century. Vicars in those days seemed to
have done all right. It was surrounded on all sides by immaculate,
lush green lawns, with a tennis court and a maze round at the
back. And then there was a separate garage block and some stables
– though no one used them.

As well as the Land Rover, Tara saw there was a taxi waiting on
her mother's driveway and instantly wondered if either Benedict

or her half-brother, Harry, had decided to make an emergency getaway, ahead of her arrival.

Tara walked up to the front door and knocked.

It was her stepfather, Benedict, who answered. He planted a firm, it's-my-duty kiss on each cheek. 'Tara, darling. I'm so glad I caught you. I'm having to dash to catch a train, but I was hoping you might make it over here before I left. Are you well?' He picked up a briefcase and trolley suitcase and stepped outside.

'I am thanks. And you?'

He nodded. 'Yes, thank you.' He sounded relieved to have got the formalities out of the way. Tara was too. 'Well, I must away to London. We're about to close a deal on a new luxury development in Dubai, so I have a plane to catch.' He peered back into the house. 'I believe Lydia's in the kitchen.'

Tara went on into the hall, with its artwork, sofa and Farrow-and-Ball blue walls, leaving him to sort himself out. 'Mum?'

She listened for a second and heard her mother's voice from the next room. She was giving someone instructions that seemed to relate to floral decorations for an event. Tara assumed she must be on the phone; she couldn't hear anyone answer.

'Be with you in a second, darling,' Lydia called through, followed by: 'No, no, red won't do. They have to be the palest pink, with the trailing greenery and white ribbons. Silk. Yes, that's right. Good.'

A second later she appeared, and kissed Tara on the cheek. She was wearing a figure-hugging sleeveless dress made from shot silk. As she turned, its colour seemed to alter from sapphire to sea green. Her mid-brown hair was shampoo-advertisement shiny and neatly arranged into a French pleat.

'So, this is a lovely surprise.' Her mother's voice still had that faint hint of accusation to it. Tara made a mental note to give her at least a week's notice in future. 'Such a shame you've missed Harry. He's visiting a friend today, but he said to say hello.'

Tara suspected her mother had invented the message to promote family harmony. The wanted-child had probably made good his escape the moment he knew she'd be descending on them.

Lydia put her head on one side. 'You look lovely,' she said at last, and if it hadn't been for the pause, Tara might have believed her.

'So do you. Beautiful dress.'

She gave a little shrug. 'Birthday present from Benedict. Let's go out into the garden. This weather's too good to miss, and it's so peaceful there.' She took the mobile she'd been holding and left it on the hall table. 'I've got some refreshments ready for us in the kitchen. I managed to get them from the village just before the shop closed – once I knew you were coming.'

Tara followed her through and saw she'd laid out pastries on a plate underneath a lace dome. She took the protective cover off and transferred the plate to a tray that also held a couple of glasses and some side plates.

'Will you bring the bottle of elderflower pressé? It's in the fridge.'

Tara fetched it and they walked out of the back door that led off the kitchen and into the garden. Near the house it was a riot of colour, with roses, delphiniums and sweet williams against a backdrop of leafy trees, gnarled with age. Sweet scents from the flowers reached her as a soft breeze stirred the air.

Tara's mother followed her eyes. 'The rain in April and now the warmth seems to have done its stuff,' she said.

'It's all looking very well kept.' Tara knew gardening wasn't one of her mother's passions, even though she enjoyed the end results.

'New gardener,' her mother said. 'Benedict found the last one asleep in a deckchair when he was meant to be pruning.' She walked over to the marble-topped table they'd had since Tara was a child, with its decorative iron stand. It was sitting in the shade of a willow.

'It's lovely to have the chance to catch up,' her mother said. 'What brings you over here?'

If her mother had been one of her interviewees she'd have spun her a line at that point; not to mention preparing the ground more patiently. But blood relations deserved honesty, and her mother would see through her anyway.

'The desire for showbiz gossip.'

Lydia raised an eyebrow and the ghost of a smile crossed her face. 'Really? Related to Bella Seabrook, I suppose, given that you're writing about her daughter.' Tara had explained that much on the phone. 'Don't you think it's a bit seedy to dig up the past like that?'

Tara shrugged. 'I don't feel I can write a balanced story if I don't know those sorts of facts.'

Her mother gave her a look, but Tara didn't react. Lydia could take the explanation at face value, or leave it.

'The more I find out about Samantha Seabrook the more I want to know. Her childhood's not what anyone would expect as far as I can see. She was clearly a rebel, with a doting father who was never around and a mother who – well, that's where I'm stuck. Lots of hints, an air of tragedy, people saying less than they know.'

'So you hoped I might be able to fill in the gaps?'

'I thought you might know someone who knew someone, even if you didn't know the whole story yourself.'

Lydia poured them their drinks and motioned for Tara to take a pastry. 'I went to their parties sometimes,' she said. 'And we crossed over at various award dinners and that kind of thing.'

'Do you know how she died?'

Lydia frowned. 'An accident. That's what everyone said. I got the impression the details were hushed up.'

Tara began to eat the apricot and almond filled pastry she'd taken, enjoying the sweetness of the fruit. 'Did you like them?'

'I never got to know them well. Brian Seabrook did his best to keep up appearances, but everyone could tell there was something wrong with Bella. There was gossip about her among the casting directors. She was up and coming when I started out – already getting parts in big films. I thought she'd made it, but she started to get unreliable; that was what I heard.' She pulled a face. 'Drink and drugs, I'd guess, thinking back to some of the photos that appeared in the popular press. It happens. You either have to pick yourself up, get yourself clean and convince people to put their money on you again, or else it's over.'

'How long did that carry on for?'

Her mother sighed. 'A few years. Her parts got smaller and the rumours increased. And then I heard she'd died. I wasn't really surprised, even though it was a shame.' She pushed her chair back from the iron table and stood up. 'Just one moment,' she said.

She returned with a photograph album. 'There are quite a few shots from the old days in this one.' She pushed the pastries to one end of the table and put the tome down. She began flicking through the pages.

'Here.' She turned the album so Tara could see the rear view of the very house she'd visited a couple of days earlier. 'This would have been around a year before she died.' A woman wearing diamonds at her throat and wrist, with gleaming platinum-blonde hair, stood in a strappy silver dress, one hand on a much younger Sir Brian Seabrook's arm. She looked as though she needed him for support. Although she was smiling in the photo, there was a haunted look in her eyes, and pain in his. Tara took in the wider picture. Samantha Seabrook was nowhere to be seen, though she would have been grown-up enough to have attended parties by then – around fourteen years old. The sort of age when Lydia had 'let' Tara hand round canapés at the events she had hosted. Tara didn't blame Samantha for having made herself scarce.

Her eyes ran over the other guests. They were a glamorous lot, and most were posing, as though they'd been conscious of the cameras.

Except for one man. Tara had been thinking he looked vaguely familiar and suddenly she realised. This was a slimmer, younger

version of Professor da Souza, the head of the institute. And instead
of aiming half an eye at the camera, he was looking at Sir Brian and
Bella Seabrook. The look in his eyes echoed Sir Brian's.

'Did you ever talk to this guy?' Tara asked, pointing out da Souza.

Her mother frowned. 'Goodness, Tara – it's such a long time
ago. I might have.' She leant forward. 'Oh. I can see why you're
interested though. That's an interesting little cameo, isn't it?' She
sketched a finger round da Souza, Sir Brian and Bella Seabrook.
'I recognise *that* look. A spurned lover of Bella Seabrook's, do you
think? I gather she had quite a few.'

And Tara was sure she was right. Maybe that fondness she'd seen
da Souza display for Samantha hadn't been because he'd fancied *her*.
It looked as though he'd had a soft spot for her mother. After all,
if he'd been at school with Sir Brian he must have been connected
with him when he'd taken up with Bella Seabrook. Perhaps da
Souza wished it had been him she'd settled on.

A blackbird was singing on a branch in the apple tree.

'Mum, do you know anyone who might know more – either
about that situation,' she indicated the photo, 'or about what really
happened to Bella Seabrook?'

Her mother gave her a look. 'No one who'd tell me if I admitted
I was asking on behalf of my ambitious journalist daughter.'

'I don't suppose you'd consider being economical with the truth?'

Her mother sat back in her chair. 'Leave it with me,' she said
after a moment, and closed her eyes for a second against the sun.

Tara knew Lydia felt guilty about her upbringing, and that it
affected what she was prepared to do. It was against Tara's principles to
take advantage of that, but once again, the ends justified the means.

Of course, if she had been working for the police, like Blake,
she'd have found out the truth right after Samantha Seabrook had
been killed, without having to resort to subterfuge. Once again,
the thought frustrated her.

CHAPTER THIRTY-FOUR

Blake's mind had still been on his meeting with Babette the evening before as he'd entered the station that morning. *Have I made the right decision?* Doubt was still gnawing at his gut.

But all that had been pushed from his mind shortly after his arrival. He ought to have felt pleased that DS Patrick Wilkins had found Dieter Gartner. But oh boy, he'd really gone on about it. DCI Fleming had duly dealt out the required praise for the glorified admin job. Blake tried to look appreciative too, but now he and Patrick were sitting opposite Dr Gartner at the station, and Blake was feeling all the more irritable.

'Of course, I would love to stay for the memorial service,' Dr Gartner said. 'Samantha meant a lot to me. But I have commitments at home I cannot alter.' As far as he was concerned he'd already put himself out for them by travelling down to Cambridge and arranging to fly home from Stansted, rather than Scotland. Just like Patrick, Dieter had waited for them to make all the right appreciative noises.

Sir Brian had arranged the memorial service for the following day. Blake would be attending. 'You sound like a very busy man,' he said, trying to un-grit his teeth.

Gartner read his tone and – annoyingly – smiled. 'I understand about keeping up appearances, Inspector, but it's too late for me to make a difference to Samantha now.'

Fair point, though Sir Brian might have appreciated a final show of affection.

'So, you've been attending a job interview in Edinburgh, and that's why you've been incommunicado?' They'd already checked this out and it held water. Blake just wanted to make Gartner squirm for the time and effort he'd taken up.

'Well, yes, I was attending the interview. I got the professorship,' he said.

'Congratulations.'

'Thank you. But I was chiefly out of contact because of a problematic' – he paused for a moment – *'friend* of mine, who has been calling me repeatedly. She leaves a lot of messages and she is very demanding. I had to focus on the recruitment process, so I switched off my phones until it was all over, hence the delay in getting your messages.'

Patrick Wilkins leant forward. 'This female friend who won't leave you alone, she's a girlfriend, is she?'

'She's a woman,' Gartner said, smiling. 'She does not want me to move to Edinburgh.'

'Were you still in a relationship with Samantha Seabrook when she died?' Blake asked.

'We had a relationship, Inspector, and I guess it would have continued. We were occasional lovers. We enjoyed each other's company. We certainly weren't exclusive, if that's what you mean.'

All fascinating – or Wilkins looked fascinated, anyway. But also irrelevant, given that Gartner couldn't be the killer.

Blake sipped the tea in front of him and felt tired.

After they'd finished with Gartner, Blake went to find DCI Fleming, who was putting in overtime, just like the rest of them. He bumped into her in the corridor by the coffee machine.

His boss looked at him and raised an eyebrow, reading his expression. 'My office?'

He nodded, followed her in and closed the door behind them. 'Tara Thorpe messaged me. Apparently her editor has got wind of the death threat she's received. She thinks someone at the station's leaking information, and I'm inclined to agree with her. It's not the first time it's happened.'

Fleming nodded, her jaw tightening. He knew how angry the lack of loyalty made her. For him, it was the thought of someone putting their own agenda before the needs of the people they were trying to help.

'I'll have a word at the next briefing,' she said, and shook her head. 'We're just going to have to keep our eyes and ears open.'

But they'd been doing that for months. Unless he bugged his officers it wasn't likely to do much good. Not for the first time, Blake contemplated feeding false information to selected members of staff to see if any of it reached the press…

It was half an hour later that Jan, one of the computer forensics experts, dashed into his office. He could see she was high on overtime: her eyes gleamed like someone who'd taken something illegal – or stayed up all night.

'I've found something interesting,' she said, sliding into the chair opposite him and slapping a laptop down on his desk.

Suddenly his own tiredness fell away. You didn't get someone looking like she did unless the news was important.

'Tell me, for God's sake. We really need a break here.'

'It's a location search in Professor Seabrook's history.' She flipped open her laptop lid and spun it round to face him.

Google Maps showed a spot pinpointed with the standard red balloon marker, just north of Newmarket. He raised an eyebrow.

'The address belongs to a clinic. An abortion clinic.'

That made him sit up. 'When did she do the search?'

'Around a month before she died.'

'Right. Right.' He paused for a moment, his mind on overdrive. 'Excellent work. Thanks, Jan. Better let DCI Fleming know if you haven't already.'

She nodded and he was pleased she'd told him first.

'Anything else in her history related to that? Emails?'

Jan shook her head. 'Afraid not.'

'Doesn't matter.' Because this certainly looked like a breakthrough.

Twenty minutes later, he and Emma were sitting over takeaway coffees on a bench on Parker's Piece, the large, square green opposite the police station. The smell of his drink blended with the aroma of the recently cut grass at their feet. In front of him it felt as though half of Cambridge was out, enjoying the summer heat. Tourists lounged with bottled water and books, and parents watched as toddlers clad in sunhats stumbled to and fro. It made him think of Kitty. It felt odd to sit down to talk about a murder case with such an innocent scene in front of them.

Wilkins had gone for a break and Blake couldn't help being glad.

'So, let's go through it again,' he said to Emma. 'Tara Thorpe pointed out that the slippers and magazines in Samantha Seabrook's old room made it look as though her father had been taking special care of her.'

'And we now guess that that was because she was recovering after an abortion.'

'It seems quite possible. The wheels are in motion to get confirmation from the clinic, but once the red tape's out of the way we'll know for sure. It also fits with the way she left the holiday unexplained in her work diary.'

Emma nodded. 'No glamorous location noted there, nor any boasting to her colleagues, because her sojourn was just outside Newmarket.'

Blake frowned. 'I keep thinking of the crucifix. Could we be dealing with a religious extremist who disapproved of what she'd done?'

'We need to find out if Chiara had ever undergone a similar procedure.'

He nodded. 'Put in the requests for that, would you?'

'Will do.'

'And I'd now like to know when Dieter Gartner last slept with the professor. Shame he's just left for the railway station. I wonder if he'll answer his mobile this time.'

'If not we can get someone to intercept him.'

'And I'd also like a word with Sir Brian bloody Seabrook. I'm guessing he knew exactly what his daughter was going through, yet he didn't think we needed that information.'

'I suppose you can see why he wouldn't want it spread around.'

Blake gave a look.

'Sorry, boss. It's no excuse, obviously.'

Blake stood up, turned away and shoved his hands into his trouser pockets so hard it would have made his fashion-designer sister wince.

CHAPTER THIRTY-FIVE

The following day, Tara was walking along St Edward's Passage, past the Haunted Bookshop, when her mum called. The place was named for the ghostly lady, swathed in white, who was said to prowl its dusty rooms. Tara carried on, past its red-framed windows, crammed with second-hand volumes, and picked up. 'Mum?'

A sigh was the first sound she heard. Lydia had found something out about Sir Brian or Bella Seabrook, Tara guessed, and passing it on went against her better judgement.

'A close friend of mine, Simon Pace, knew the Seabrooks much better than I did,' she said, without bothering to say hello. She was getting it over with. *'He's always had a soft spot for me, so I thought it was worth calling to see what he remembered about the old days.'*

Tara thought again of the photograph she'd seen: the sadness in da Souza's eyes as he'd looked on at the actress and her publishing-tycoon husband. 'Thanks, Mum.' She hovered outside the church – St Edward King and Martyr – as a throng of book enthusiasts walked past, clutching parcels. They were probably heading straight from the Haunted Bookshop to another second-hand dealer, David's, just the other side of the church.

There was a pause. *'Yes, well, anyway, we got it wrong you and I, I think. We were both imagining that chap looking on was a discarded lover of Bella's. But if Simon's right it was* Brian *that the onlooker was gazing at. Simon said that the man – Hugo da Souza apparently – had been smitten with Brian Seabrook for years. There was never anything*

*in it; Brian was straight. But he and da Souza were terrific friends
and even though Simon thinks Brian must have known how da Souza
felt, the friendship was as strong as ever.'*

Any passing thought Tara had had that da Souza might have
killed Samantha Seabrook in some kind of crime of passion was
gone now. He'd minded about her all right, but she wasn't some
love child to be kept secret, and not a lover either. It was da Souza's
love for her father that had ensured his regard for her and the
protectiveness she'd seen him show.

'Are you still there?' her mother asked.

'Sorry, Mum. Yes, I'm still here. Thank you.'

*'I didn't see it could do too much harm to share it with you. It's not
something you'd put in your article is it?'*

Giles's greedy face flashed into her mind for a moment. 'No.
No, it isn't. Mum, this friend of yours, Simon. Does he know how
Bella Seabrook died?'

'Urm, no,' she said.

Yeah, right. Tara knew what that meant. For 'urm, no', read,
'yes, but that bit I'm not going to tell you'.

'If you change your mind about confiding in me, just give me
a call,' Tara said before she hung up.

Two minutes later, Tara was in the Tourist Information Centre,
showing them a blown-up image of the craft shop in the photo she'd
seen at Samantha Seabrook's apartment. The smart-looking woman
standing in front of the window full of ceramics and jewellery had
become somewhat pixelated thanks to her treatment of the picture,
but the shop itself wasn't too bad.

'I'm trying to locate the business,' she said to the guy behind the
counter. 'I'm pretty sure it's here in Cambridge, but I can't place it.'
She wanted to speak to the woman in the photo and was hoping
she might be the proprietor. She had that look about her: one
eye towards the window displays and pride in her eyes. If she was

based in Cambridge she might be the one thing Tara was lacking: a personal friend of Samantha Seabrook's from recent times.

The guy behind the desk frowned. 'I'm not sure,' he said, and glanced over to a second assistant who walked forward to join them.

She scanned the photo now. 'Green Street,' she said immediately. 'Pomphrey's.' She met Tara's eye and smiled. 'And in fact I think that's Adele Pomphrey in the photograph. I'm afraid I'm a bit of a Pomphrey's addict. It's pretty expensive but once in a while I crack. I go there for presents for close family.'

'Perfect. I'd heard it was good,' Tara lied. 'Thank you.'

'Glad we could help.'

An old-fashioned shop bell jangled as Tara opened the door of Pomphrey's and walked in. Her eye was caught by an enormous verdigris bowl on sale for three thousand pounds. Inside, the walls were stark white, all the better to display an array of artwork. If she hadn't been under imminent threat of either death or the sack she'd have looked at the price tags for the smaller ones, just in case. They might have made her house feel more like home.

A woman who wasn't Adele Pomphrey walked over to greet her. 'Good morning,' she said. 'Do feel free to browse, but I'm right here if you need any help.'

'Actually, I was wondering if Adele was around?'

'Ah,' the woman smiled, 'I believe she was on the phone a short while ago, but I'll just check.' Always good to have a get-out clause. 'What name shall I give?'

'Tara Thorpe. I'm writing about Samantha Seabrook's life and I understand Adele and the professor knew each other well.'

The woman nodded. She looked more uncertain now and disappeared through a door at the rear of the shop. Tara firmly expected to be told the proprietor's phone call was still in progress, and would be for some time.

But a moment later Ms Pomphrey herself appeared. Her eyes were sad, but not unfriendly. 'You're writing about Samantha, I understand? What publication do you work for?'

Tara gave her a business card. She wondered if the proprietor might not like the idea of talking to someone from *Not Now*, but her expression didn't change as she read Tara's details.

'I'm free now if you'd like to talk?' she said. 'I was just about to have a lemonade. It's not the fizzy sort. Would you like some?'

'Thank you.' Tara followed Adele Pomphrey to a small kitchenette where she removed a bottle with a swing-top stopper from a fridge and poured them each tall glasses of the sharp-smelling drink.

After that she led them through to her office, which was as stylish as her shop. The chairs were upholstered in green and yellow silk. Tara watched as Ms Pomphrey dabbed her eyes quickly with a tissue.

'I'm sorry,' she said. 'I'm still trying to get used to the idea of Samantha's death. If ever there was a person who seemed invincible, it was her. Larger than life, pumped-up with energy. The thought of her in any other state is unbearable. And your visit's rather unexpected.'

'I'm sorry to take you by surprise,' Tara said. 'I was in town and I thought maybe dropping in would be better than emailing. When something awful like this has happened being hands-off feels worse, somehow.'

Ms Pomphrey nodded. 'I know what you mean. I'm the same. I like to bite the bullet if I have to deal with an awkward situation.'

And, of course, it was slightly harder to ignore someone if they fetched up on your doorstep instead of sending you a timid message, asking to be seen. Harsh but true, as Tara knew all too well. Even now, she'd have to tread carefully. She decided not to ask to record the interview in this instance. She'd take notes instead.

'Do you mind telling me how you and Samantha Seabrook met?' she asked, taking a pad and pen from her bag.

'It was very soon after she first came to Cambridge,' Adele Pomphrey said. 'She popped in for a present for a colleague, in fact; the woman was getting married, I seem to remember.' She toyed with a glass paperweight on her desk that looked modern and elegant enough to have been designed by one of her craftspeople. 'I well remember it. It had been worryingly quiet all morning, and then suddenly the door opened, and in came a whole throng of people, with Samantha leading them. She caught my attention straight away; she was talking to them, not to me, but she had that kind of clear, ringing voice that carries.' She paused to smile. 'As well as buying the present, she ended up buying a ring for herself too, and then a couple of the others bought as well. I remember thinking she'd be great to have along to a private view. I could envisage her as a trend-setter.'

'And did you see each other often after that?' Tara said, sitting back in her chair.

'Not straight away. After a month or two, I had a private view featuring new work from the woman who'd designed the ring she'd bought. I invited her along to that, and she bought some more items. It was after that that we got chatting, and then we began to meet up socially.'

'Did she talk to you much about her family? Or life at the institute?'

'Her family, never. I only knew about her parents, in all honesty, because one day I got curious and looked them up on the net. It started to seem odd that she never mentioned them, even when I confided in her about mine. Occasionally I'd probe, just very gently, but the shutters always came down. I got the impression that she was – or maybe had learnt to be – fiercely independent.'

Tara hesitated. Was it too soon to try to draw Adele Pomphrey out? 'I had that impression too. It seemed she had a very active social life, for instance, but that she'd never felt the urge to settle down with anyone.' It was a leap, but pretending to know more than you did often reaped dividends. Besides, she'd seen the professor's party shoes in her flat, and of course she knew she'd gone out and done her night climbing too. She hadn't been a shrinking violet, that was for sure. And then there was the absentee boyfriend Blake had accidentally mentioned...

'Oh no, that's right,' Adele Pomphrey said. 'She wouldn't have wanted to be one half of a unit. I admired her for that. She'd occasionally let slip something about the man of the moment, but never with any proper details; just enough to give a flavour and a sniff of some gossip.' She sighed. 'I've wondered since she died what it must be like for the man she'd been seeing most recently.'

Tara's pen was poised over her pad but she let her hand relax. 'Dieter Gartner?'

Adele Pomphrey frowned for a second. 'Dieter? Ah, I met him once. They certainly had some kind of ongoing romance. But it wasn't him.' She gave a shrug of her elegant shoulders. 'No, all I know is that Samantha's latest was from the US.' The tears were back in her eyes again. 'I can see her now. We were sitting opposite each other in the Eagle. She was laughing and she told me her new man was someone she'd never considered previously as lover material. But he was actually very attractive, with a voice just like Robert Downey Junior's.'

Tara caught her breath and resisted the urge to stand up there and then and walk out of the room. It was time to cut the interview short.

CHAPTER THIRTY-SIX

Blake cut the call with Tara Thorpe and looked at Emma. 'When she died, or just before, Samantha Seabrook was seeing a man with a New York accent. Remind you of anyone?'

Emma blinked for a second. 'Wait. Simon Askey?'

'Damn right.' He rubbed his forehead with the back of his hand and closed his eyes for a moment. How would it have worked? 'We've got Chiara Laurito going to Simon Askey for support over the harsh way she's been treated by Samantha Seabrook. According to Chiara's housemate, Askey promises to help, but fails to follow through. According to Askey himself, Samantha Seabrook talked him round to her way of thinking. What if, during the course of winning him over, she turned on the charm and he found he liked it? They became lovers, and Chiara – who looks as though she had a crush on Askey – was left out in the cold. She must have felt very let down.'

'So Askey could have been the father of the baby that Samantha Seabrook aborted?'

'He could have been, if I'm right.'

'D'you think he knew about the termination?'

'In advance?' Blake let out a long breath. 'Hard to tell. But I do have a theory.'

'Go on.'

'We know that Chiara Laurito and Simon Askey had a humdinger of a row at the institute. Professor da Souza heard them at it, and Askey's words were audible outside his room.'

'That's right,' Emma said, glancing at her notes. 'Askey says he told her she could be too honest. And he claims that was in response to her repeating back something insulting Samantha Seabrook had said about him. What?' She looked at him. 'You reckon maybe she was telling him about the abortion?'

Blake looked steadily back at her. 'I'd say it's possible. If she'd somehow found out – and she was working in the same room as Professor Seabrook – then it probably seemed the ideal way to drive a big, fat wedge between Askey and her supervisor. If she fancied Askey herself, and was furious with the pair of them, then I could imagine her doing that.'

Emma nodded. 'It would fit. Then Askey doesn't let Samantha Seabrook know the secret's out. Instead, he arranges a clandestine midnight outing and drowns her in revenge. So he'd have to have been angry about her arranging the termination.'

Blake nodded. 'But not necessarily because he wanted her to go through with the pregnancy. He might just have been furious that she'd made the decision without consulting him.'

She nodded slowly. 'Could be... and then what about Chiara?'

'Tara Thorpe says she was snuggling up to Askey at the institute garden party. Maybe something she said made him think she'd guessed he was Samantha Seabrook's murderer.'

'So he killed her to keep her quiet?'

Blake nodded. 'It certainly sounds as though she'd have been happy to meet him wherever he suggested. Tara said she looked smitten, whereas he appeared to be irritated by her.'

He paused for a moment, trying to read the expression in Emma's eyes. She looked almost amused, despite the topic of their conversation. 'What is it?'

She shook her head. 'No, sorry. It's nothing.'

'Emma?'

She bit her lip, but the smile was still there in her eyes. 'Just that you refer to what Tara says a lot, that's all.'

Blake was brought up short. Maybe he did… but then, she'd made a lot of useful contributions, one way and another.

'Not that I'm feeling put out or anything,' Emma said. 'Her insights do sound well worth considering.'

'Nothing to yours, Emma, obviously.'

Her smile was broader now. 'Of course not.'

'So anyway,' he said. 'There were no relevant messages or numbers on Chiara's phone from the night she died, but Simon Askey could have arranged to meet with her at the party; or slipped out and called on her after her flatmate had left for her date. One thing's for certain: his wife's got no idea exactly when he came and went that night.'

'True,' Emma said.

'Time to invite Askey in for a voluntary interview,' Blake said. 'Think he'll come?'

'I suggest we make the request in front of his wife. He'll probably come with us if he thinks the alternative is a no-holds-barred chat in front of her.'

Askey sat in the interview room trying to look bored, but failing. Blake smiled. No amount of staring at the ceiling, leaning back in his chair or picking at his nails could hide the anger in Askey's eyes. But there was no fear as far has he could see, only defiance. Still, give it time. Blake hadn't got started yet.

'Why didn't you tell us you and Samantha Seabrook were having an affair before she died?'

There were probably dozens of people from New York currently in Cambridge, but one look at Askey's eyes told Blake he'd hit the bullseye.

But it only took a moment for the man to recover. 'I wouldn't have called it an affair. Hell, we only had sex a couple of times. Given that I'm married, and I knew it didn't have a bearing on Sam's death, I kept quiet.'

'The fact that she aborted your baby without your knowledge provides a pretty good motive for murder though, wouldn't you say?' Another gamble. There was shock in Askey's eyes now, and confusion.

'You shouldn't shout so loudly at work,' Blake said, smiling again.

'Chiara wasn't shouting,' Askey said, giving himself away nicely. She'd been the one to break the news then.

'Your response was enough for us to guess what she'd told you.'

Anger cracked its way across Askey's features as he realised he'd confirmed what had only been a suspicion.

'How did Chiara find out?'

Askey rolled his eyes. 'She first got wind that something was up when she walked back into their research room whilst Sam was on a call, so she said. She took Sam by surprise – she'd only just left to take her lunch break, but she came back because she'd forgotten her purse. Chiara only heard her say a date, and then something about recovery time, but it made her curious.' He pulled a face. 'She realised the date Sam had mentioned was the first date she'd booked off as leave and wondered what treatment she might be getting that was so secret.'

'And then what?'

'Sam was careless. She'd left her mobile in her office whilst she went to interview a visiting scholar in da Souza's room. Chiara heard her phone buzz. She claimed she was in Sam's inner office to look for a paper she needed to reference. I'm not so sure. Anyway, she "glanced at the phone", saw one of those automated appointment reminder texts had come in and that was that. She matched it with the clinic and understood the truth.'

'Must have been humiliating to find out Samantha's PhD student knew your business better than you did yourself.'

'For sure,' Askey sounded resigned, 'but as you can imagine, not humiliating enough for me to want to murder her. And what other reason could I have?'

'We can think of several,' Emma said. 'And although we hear Chiara was all over you the night she died, we understand you weren't her biggest fan.'

Askey took a deep breath; his eyes were fiery.

Blake felt another adrenaline rush and leant forward. 'What did you do when you found out about Professor Seabrook's abortion?'

'I told her what I thought of her; made it clear I never wanted to work with her again. Then she pulled out of our joint funding bid.'

'Passionate stuff. Are you seriously telling me you left it at that?'

Askey leant forward himself now, his shoulders hunched, fists clenched. 'If you think the row I had with Chiara was noisy, you should have heard the one I had with Sam. We were in her room at our college. Some nosy shit will probably be able to fill you in. But as for killing her for what she'd done, why would I? I've got one brat at home, I sure as hell wouldn't want another. I was just angry that she hadn't talked to me before going ahead, that's all. It wasn't her sole decision to make. That said, I'd have backed her up if she *had* come to me. And I'm not the sort to turn to violence over a matter of principle.'

Suddenly, Blake wondered if Samantha Seabrook had assumed Simon Askey had sent her the rag doll, to spook her after their argument. She might have thought he was just being dramatic, and that she wasn't in danger.

But had he been the one to send it to her? That was the question.

Blake terminated the interview and left the room for a moment, with Emma at his heels.

'We haven't got enough to charge him,' DCI Fleming said, coming to join them. She'd been watching from the observation suite. She put a hand on Blake's shoulder and he fought the urge to shake it off. 'This is excellent work but we're not home and dry yet. We need to do more digging. If he did it then the evidence will be there. Max is still trawling through CCTV between Chiara

Laurito's house and Stourbridge Common and we'll add a door-
to-door on Askey's street to the one we're conducting on hers, too:
see if anyone saw any comings and goings on the relevant nights.
And we can try to find someone who overheard the row Askey
mentioned at St Francis's College.'

Blake took a deep breath and felt both Fleming and Emma's
eyes on him.

'Okay,' he said. 'Okay.'

At that moment, Patrick Wilkins appeared at his side. 'Call from
Sir Brian Seabrook,' he said. 'He's been sent a note.'

All eyes were on Patrick now, which was just as he liked it. His
dramatic pause almost pushed Blake over the edge. 'What did it
say?' he asked, resisting the urge to shake the man.

Patrick looked down at his notebook. '"Death comes equally
to us all, and makes us all equal when it comes."'

'John Donne,' DCI Fleming said. 'How very Cambridge.'

Blake left Fleming and Wilkins to feel pleased with themselves.
He was due with Sir Brian that afternoon anyway, for Professor
Seabrook's memorial service. And now he had a long list of ques-
tions for the man too.

CHAPTER THIRTY-SEVEN

'Well, Tara?' Giles's confident voice poured from her phone like oil. *'When can we talk about your exposé?'* The news about her death threat had already been hinted at on *Not Now*'s website, with promises of more juicy details to follow. *'I don't think you should write the piece yourself. Come in for an interview. Shona would make a good job of it.'*

The bitch who'd told Giles she'd been in the Champion of the Thames, chatting with Blake. Or 'looking very cosy' as she'd put it.

'I don't think so, Giles,' she said.

'All right. You write it and we can jazz it up afterwards.'

'You've misunderstood my point. You're not getting your story. About me or about Professor Seabrook. I resign.'

Giles was silent for a moment. *'Tara, you're out of your depth. I can make sure you never work as a journalist again.'*

She laughed at that. 'Seriously, Giles? I think you're exaggerating your influence in the business.'

'Four years ago, you decked a fellow journalist and only just escaped prosecution. In the last week you've gone behind my back and kept stories from me that could have quadrupled our hit rate. Even the other staff here have gone off you. That's a lot of enemies to have.'

She wondered about Matt, her one friend at *Not Now*. She'd be sorry to lose him. And put like that maybe her prospects for future employment did look a bit chancy. But if her stories were good she could still get work as a freelancer. One thing was certain, she was going to finish her work on Samantha Seabrook's story; she wouldn't stop until she'd got to the truth. She was confident she'd be able to place it somewhere.

'Bugger off, Giles,' she said. 'It's an utter pleasure to leave your foul rag.'

Adrenaline flooded through her as she got changed, ready to drive north to Samantha Seabrook's memorial service. At first she felt elated, but by the time she applied her make-up the practicalities of the situation were edging their way into her consciousness. Her stomach was tense.

Something made her want to share her news. She emailed Kemp.

Just resigned before I got the sack, she wrote. *But hey, DI Blake, the detective working on my case, reckons I could have a second career as a cop, so all is not lost. How d'you think I'd look in uniform? My future is assured.*

She was joking of course, just as Blake had been.

As for her future, it had been hanging on a very thin thread ever since she'd got the death threat anyway. She moved her lips together to even her out her lipstick and then looked out at the common. When would the police catch the killer? Surely with two women dead some crucial evidence would come to light. But then she'd been interviewing Samantha Seabrook's key contacts too, and she hadn't worked out who'd done it...

She took out her phone and looked back at her photos, including the one of the doll she'd been sent in its plain blue skirt and white blouse.

Someone had worked hard to make it. Although neatly finished, the doll wasn't quite perfect, she now noted: one leg was very slightly longer than the other. She looked again at the way it had been dressed. *Almost like a uniform.* Did it mean anything? She closed her eyes for a moment. She was getting too close to all this; couldn't see the wood for the trees. All the same, she texted Blake to share her thoughts. It wasn't worth a call.

CHAPTER THIRTY-EIGHT

Blake was sitting opposite Sir Brian Seabrook in his sitting room. He had the note the man had received in his hand. The paper and print appeared to match the message Tara had found in her bicycle basket.

Sir Brian was dressed in a black suit and tie, ready for the memorial service, and his face was pinched. 'Do you think it's a warning?' he asked, nodding at the note.

'The content is different,' Blake said, 'so I'd guess the motivation for sending it is too. But we can't take that for granted.'

'I wonder just how long it will be before you track down this madman,' Sir Brian said. 'How many more people will have to die before you make any progress?'

Blake took a deep breath. Chiara Laurito's death weighed heavily on his conscience. He'd been so unprepared for that development. But Sir Brian had some explaining to do, too. 'We are making progress,' he said. 'But we need all Samantha's connections to be honest with us. Yourself included.'

Sir Brian shifted in his chair. 'What's that supposed to mean?'

'You pretended not to remember Patsy Wentworth's name and address, yet you passed it on to a journalist quite happily.'

A look of confusion crossed the man's face and Blake wondered what story Tara had spun in order to get the information.

'Patsy Wentworth was a childhood friend of Sammy's. Not one I approved of, and not one who had anything to do with her day-to-day life as an adult. I didn't tell you about her because I knew she was irrelevant.'

'With respect,' yeah, right, 'that's for us to decide as the investigating team. Everything helps us build up a picture. And you also hid the fact of your daughter's recent abortion. I find that inexplicable.'

Sir Brian turned a shade paler than he already was. 'Dieter Gartner is based in Germany, Inspector. I knew he couldn't have killed Samantha because of the abortion, so again, why would I mention it? It was a purely personal matter.'

'Did your daughter tell you Dieter was the father?'

A shadow crossed Sir Brian's face. Blake reckoned it really hadn't occurred to him that Samantha might have had more than one lover. In spite of his frustration he felt a wave of sympathy for the man.

'You should have told us, sir,' Blake said, quietly. 'It might have made a difference.' But it might not have. Either way, he'd failed: his lack of progress meant a second innocent woman had died.

He left Sir Brian to compose himself, ready for the service. As he left, a woman in a smart, conventional black suit and lace-up shoes flitted across the hall. Could this be Pamela Grange, the supportive family friend? Her look told him she laid most of their current problems at the police's door. Not unusual but hard to take all the same.

Sir Brian wasn't having people back to the house, Blake understood. There would be refreshments at the church for those that wanted to stay and chat – and then a proper, private funeral and wake for close family and friends later.

He went out to his car, got in and sat with the windows down as he waited for the appointed hour. A bus passed him, filling the car with diesel fumes. He opened the door for a moment to try to change the air, but it was so hot and still that it didn't help much.

He wondered about Askey. The guy was up to his neck in this business, but Blake had a creeping feeling that he wasn't their man. The note to Tara Thorpe didn't fit. The journey to Great Sterringham and the 'chat' with Sir Brian had given everything more time to settle in his mind. Whoever had threatened Tara Thorpe had chosen her because she was a relentless journalist who wouldn't rest until she knew all the facts. They wanted her to find out something about Professor Seabrook and splash it all over the press – for whatever reason. And try as Blake might, he couldn't make that fit Askey. The guy had been having an extramarital affair – and with a woman who'd been promoted above him, at that. There was no way he'd want that shared publicly: it would damage everything from his ego to his domestic life.

And the note Sir Brian had received made him wonder too. It didn't sound like a threat; it was more as though the sender was making a point… but they were making it to Samantha's *father*, as though they felt they'd taught him a lesson. Blake wondered whether the whole business had more to do with Professor Seabrook's family life than he'd originally thought.

And then there was the old lipstick in the professor's apartment and the dolls made from the perished cotton and aging cloth. What was the connection with the past?

At that moment he remembered Tara's text and frowned as he opened it up again. He reread her thought on the outfits the rag dolls wore. *Like a uniform.*

He was missing something.

CHAPTER THIRTY-NINE

The church car park was already full when Tara arrived at Samantha Seabrook's memorial service. She overshot the entrance and found a spot where the lane widened slightly, before narrowing again thanks to a russet brick wall that presumably bordered some grand country home. She glanced over her shoulder, wondering if someone driving past might clip her wing mirror. But she was short of time now and she reckoned she'd be okay. She slung her bag over her shoulder, locked up and jogged back towards the church, as quickly as her heels would allow.

Sir Brian Seabrook was standing at the church door, with the vicar next to him. They'd just turned to head inside.

Tara slipped in behind them and found a space in one of the rear pews on the right-hand side. It took her a moment to realise she was next door but one to Blake. He leant across the blonde woman who sat between them. 'Thanks for the text,' he said, as the organ music played.

'Just a thought. It suddenly occurred to me that most rag dolls are dressed more colourfully than my one was.' She thought again of her photo. 'Whoever made it certainly did a professional job; the stitching was very neat. The shape of the doll's legs was slightly uneven, but I don't think that can be significant. I didn't even notice it at first, it was so subtle.'

He nodded and she thought how good he looked in black. 'I think the clothes mean something. Especially as both dolls were dressed in exactly the same way.'

At that moment the music started, and the congregation stood up. Tara looked around her for familiar faces.

After a second she picked out Patsy Wentworth, squashed between a man and woman who were both in beige. Her parents? Tara could see why she'd rebelled.

And there was da Souza, standing erect, head held high, but she could see his knuckles were white where he gripped the rear of the pew in front of him.

Mary Mayhew, the institute administrator, was present too, and Peter Mackintosh, the librarian. Kit, Simon Askey's PhD student, stood between Mackintosh and Jim Cooper, whose head was bowed.

Across and to the right of them she spotted Adele Pomphrey.

Simon Askey seemed to be absent though. She scanned and rescanned, row by row, but there was no sign of him. She'd thought he would turn up for appearances' sake, even though he and Samantha Seabrook hadn't got on.

She guessed that the rest of the congregation was a mix of family friends, acting and publishing contacts of Sir Brian's, and academics too. There were no spare seats. Glancing behind her she could see a handful of people standing next to an arrangement of lilies by the door.

Her eyes drifted back to Blake, on his feet now, holding a hymn book. As she focused, she realised there was a circle of paler skin on the ring finger of his left hand. It made her pause. She hadn't noticed it before. What was the story there? He must have been married. And if it was over, then it was only recently. The sun hadn't filled in the pale circle.

It wasn't any of her business of course, but she hadn't thought of Blake as being involved with someone.

As the vicar spoke between hymns, more and more handkerchiefs came out. Pamela Grange was looking up at Sir Brian, her hand slightly raised, as though she wanted to touch his arm. Da Souza was watching him too, with pain in his eyes. It must be so difficult to witness the man he loved suffer in such an extreme way, yet have to maintain a level of distance.

Tara noticed Mary Mayhew cross herself when the vicar prayed for Samantha Seabrook's soul. She hadn't seen anyone do that in an Anglican church before.

At last the service was over. Refreshments on trays had been put on a table at the rear of the church but the late afternoon sun was still warm, and most people were helping themselves and then moving outside, into the churchyard. A woman with a walking frame approached and eyed the glasses of sherry. She'd find it difficult to follow the others outside holding a drink.

Pamela Grange frowned and Tara guessed she was thinking the same thing. 'Let's take the drinks into the churchyard,' she said. 'It will make it easier.'

Tara put her bag down to help and picked up one of the large trays as Peter Mackintosh took a second. Da Souza was unfolding an iron table he had dragged outside. It had chipped blue paint, and probably got used for church jumble sales, but once Pamela Grange had reinstated its white lacy cloth it looked all right.

Tara was standing by the drinks table herself, pouring an orange juice, when she spotted Kit Tyler coming outside. He nodded in her direction.

'Good to see you again, despite the awful circumstances.' He hesitated. 'Maybe one day we could go for a drink, when things are less pressured?'

'Sounds good.' And it did; though she found it hard to think beyond what was happening at the moment.

Kit nodded again, smiled and then turned to pick up a glass of sherry as Blake appeared at her elbow.

'I'd like to talk more,' the DI said, 'but I've got to get back once I've said goodbye to Sir Brian. One of Chiara Laurito's neighbours thinks they saw her with a man on the night she died. It could be a proper breakthrough. They're working on a photo-fit. Maybe we can catch up later when you're free? I want to go through all the facts again; every single thing you've seen that's struck you as odd.'

She nodded. 'All right. Call me.' He sounded as though he was onto something. A new theory? She hoped he'd share more information when they did talk. His request made her start to mentally trawl through the facts again, to try to grasp at the thin threads he was attempting to weave together.

But at that moment Peter Mackintosh came over. He wanted to know how her article was going, and when it would be published: the latter part of the question was tricky to answer, given her conversation with Giles earlier. She had to give up on trying to guess at Blake's train of thought and focus on some fast talking.

Gradually the crowds began to drift away until there was just a handful of people still present, including Sir Brian, Pamela Grange, the vicar, Peter Mackintosh and da Souza.

Ms Grange was talking to another woman of a similar age on the opposite side of the churchyard to Sir Brian. Tara overheard snatches of what she said. ('Of course, what she did was admirable.' 'Brian always tried to get us together when she visited.' 'We were never quite on the same wavelength, that was the trouble.' 'Too set in my ways, I suppose… I never meant to imply that I disapproved.' And 'Things were so different when we were young, weren't they?')

'Do you need a lift, Tara?' Peter asked, breaking into her thoughts.

She held up a hand. 'I'm fine thanks. I've got my car parked up the road. I'll just fetch my bag.'

She went to pick it up.

'Thank you for coming,' Sir Brian said, but his tone was cool; a contrast to how he'd been when she'd visited him last.

Feeling uncomfortable, she shook his hand, then Pamela Grange's, after which she exchanged a word with the vicar and said her other goodbyes. At last she was free to walk back along the edge of the country lane towards where she'd left her car.

As she rounded the bend in the road, she realised she hadn't been the only person who'd needed a parking space outside the church. A green car was now tucked in just behind her Fiat.

Even from this distance it looked oddly close to hers. She dashed forward. *Had they blocked her in?* She increased her pace and felt for the keys in her bag.

Her fingers scrabbled around – and found nothing.

It was true. The green car was back to back with hers, its rear bumper hard up against her Fiat's. And a couple of inches in front of her car's bonnet was the high russet brick wall.

Tara felt a chill crawling up her spine. Dimly, she remembered the green car she'd noticed on her tail as she'd driven over to see her mother. But even without that, she knew she was in trouble. Gut instinct told her.

She stopped trying to find her keys and reached in the outer pocket of her bag for her knife.

It wasn't there.

And nor was her phone.

'I found your knife when I went to take your mobile,' a voice said behind her. 'What kind of a person brings a weapon to a funeral? Still, I'm very glad you did. It'll come in handy.'

CHAPTER FORTY

Blake was driving past field after flat field. Ahead of him he could see a heat haze rising off the road. His window was right down, and he was driving fast, but the flow of air wasn't enough to make things comfortable.

Why *had* the dolls Samantha Seabrook and Tara received been dressed so plainly? And who the hell had made them, back in the 1980s? Why more than one? What was the significance of the crucifix around the professor's neck?

What was the link with the past? He thought about the people they knew with connections to Samantha Seabrook back then: Hugo da Souza, Patsy Wentworth, and, he now knew, after a quick bit of probing at the funeral, Pamela Grange too. She'd lived in the village all her life, apparently.

What had that note to Sir Brian meant? *Death comes equally to us all, and makes us all equal when it comes.* It related to Samantha Seabrook's job. Did the killer resent the professor – and maybe her family – for their comfortable lifestyle?

He remembered Samantha Seabrook's agent saying there'd been some kind of Twitter outcry to that effect after the professor's television appearance.

Chiara Laurito told Tara that she and Samantha Seabrook had been alike in many ways. And they had both come from money and had the support of parents who were used to getting their own way. Had Chiara really been killed because she could identify her professor's killer? Or was it their similarities that had made them both a target? And if so, where did that leave Tara, child of a famous mother, whose family home was a mansion in the same deserted fenland through which he was now travelling?

Blake's mind snapped back to the road. He was fast approaching a farm vehicle. There wasn't enough room to overtake – and wouldn't be for a while – but he was coming up to a turning off left. He took it. His satnav would reroute him.

His mind ran back to Samantha, Chiara and Tara. Sir Brian had donated money to the institute where his daughter worked, albeit before she landed her job there. Chiara Laurito's father had waded in to support her when her academic work had been criticised. And he'd heard – on the grapevine – that Tara's mother had helped put *Not Now* magazine on the map…

He was forgetting to pay attention to the directions. He looked up at the signpost at the junction he'd just come to. The satnav was telling him to take a right towards somewhere called Peverton, and he made the turn.

For some reason the name sounded familiar. The realisation sent a wave of fear through him, which he couldn't pin down.

Peverton. Peverton. Where the hell had he heard that name before?

CHAPTER FORTY-ONE

'You'll drive my Honda,' Kit Tyler said.

Tara's throat felt so tight she could hardly breathe. She backed up against his car's green paintwork as he came closer with the knife. Her knife. 'How did you know where I was parked?'

He laughed, and the sound was harsh and cold. Gone was the smile of earlier. It sent a thrill of fear through her, to think of how she'd taken him at face value.

'It wasn't difficult,' he said. 'I know your Fiat. I've been keeping an eye on you for weeks. When I saw the church car park was full and your car wasn't in it, I knew you'd be close by. But I didn't box you in when I first arrived for the service. It was only when I heard DI Blake talking to you over drinks that I knew today had to be the day. I left early, drove round and found your car in minutes.'

Through a fug of fear, Tara tried to focus on what Blake had said to her; the words Kit must have overheard. *Of course.* Someone was creating a photo-fit of a suspect for the second murder. 'They've found a witness who saw you with Chiara?' Her voice shook as she spoke.

'It sounds like it. I might be in custody by tomorrow. I can't let that happen before I've made my point. I wanted *you* to make it for me; I thought it would have plenty of impact that way. I wanted you to see Samantha for what she'd been – to uncover the harm she'd caused as a teenager. How she'd robbed others of their childhoods, then got an international reputation as some kind of saviour. But you failed. You weren't even looking in the right direction. Even in this day and age, people are blinded by wealth and class. They hardly ever see beyond the unfair advantages they bring.' His expression was fierce. 'But if you'd succeeded, I'd still have ended up in jail. I knew that. Once you'd unearthed the truth, I'd be the obvious suspect for Samantha Seabrook's murder. That was a sacrifice I was willing to make: to get the word out there. It would have made the story you were meant to tell all the more dramatic. People across the world would have seen Samantha and her class for what they are. Views would change, action would be taken, and my loss of freedom would be a small price to pay, in memory of my sister.'

His sister? Tara was still trying to work it out. Her mind felt frozen. She had to lean against his car to stop herself from sinking to the ground. Through the haze that had engulfed her, Askey's words about Kit started to filter back into her mind. Askey had said he'd had a tough childhood, just as deprived as Askey's had been. Kit's mother had died when he was young, and his sister had killed herself. But how did that fit with what Samantha Seabrook had done as a teenager? What was the connection?

'What are you going to do now?'

Kit threw her his car keys with his free hand. 'I'm going to get the publicity I wanted another way; before it's too late. And you're going to play a starring role.' For a second a smile crossed his lips, but it was a far cry from the one she'd witnessed before. The cold hatred was clear in his eyes. 'Open the door and slide across into the driver's seat.' He never took his eyes off her. He was only inches away, her knife in his hand, her back to the car. She'd got no room for manoeuvre, no chance to run.

As she turned to unlock the driver-side door she looked up the road, but there was no one. They were around the corner from the church now, and in the opposite direction from the village. For a second she thought of the crime reduction officer Blake had sent round to her house. *Shit.* Her legs shook; they felt like liquid. She'd let her guard slip. But she'd been on her way to a bloody memorial service, for God's sake.

A memorial service for a murder victim. For a woman who'd been drowned by the man standing behind her now, holding her knife.

There was no central locking and she had trouble turning the keys to open the door. She would have given almost anything not to reveal her fear like this. Other keys on the fob rattled against the car's green paintwork as she tried to let herself in. Her hand was visibly shaking. Bastard.

At last she managed it. Just for a second she wondered about making a sudden turn. She could hold the sharpest of the keys outward, ready to lash out. But she'd never overpower him. Keys versus a kitchen knife was no match. As she manoeuvred over to the driver's seat she wished to goodness she'd left her weapon back at the cottage. It was only down to weakness that she'd carried it in the first place.

'Drive,' Kit said, sliding into the car too. He pulled the passenger door shut with his left hand, his eyes never straying from her. 'Take the first right. We're not going past the church again. And don't bother doing anything stupid. I always knew I'd end up in prison anyway, and if I have to stab you where you sit I will.'

As she turned the key in the ignition, she caught sight of his eyes. Her stomach turned over. Once again she saw pure loathing, ice cold, sharp and resolved. She didn't doubt his words for one moment.

A few metres down the road she made the turn he'd asked for. Away from civilisation. Towards open fenland. The blink-inducing sun and the hot blue sky were relentless. The fields around them had never looked so stark. They went through a village, past a house with a thatched roof, hard up at the roadside, and a pub. But it was still only late afternoon; too early for anyone to be outside, drinking. No one would spot them.

After that they went back to the deserted lanes again and she saw water on her right. She tried to orientate herself. She was born and bred here, but it didn't look familiar. She fought to claw herself back from panic, her breathing so short she felt faint.

Kit spoke: 'Some people find this landscape beautiful, but it always made me feel trapped. There was no one to help me and my sister here.'

'You were brought up in the Fens?' Tara tried to remember. She hadn't heard that, had she? He had a strong Liverpool accent.

'We only moved north when I was seven,' Kit said. 'I even told your policeman friend, DI Blake, that, but he didn't put two and two together. He hasn't been looking in the right direction either.'

CHAPTER FORTY-TWO

Blake had only been in Peverton for two minutes when he'd remembered. Kit Tyler. Tyler had told him he'd been born 'up the road' from Cambridge, in Peverton, but he'd moved to Liverpool when he was a small child. The name had meant nothing to him, but he'd held it in his head somewhere.

The place was a far cry from Samantha Seabrook's home village. It was just a few short miles away, but it was down-at-heel and shouted poverty. Three of the five shops in the centre of the village were boarded up, and a row of houses he drove past told the same story. The front garden of one was full of rubbish – a rusty washing machine and a child's bike with one wheel missing.

He didn't see any school.

His mind ran on again. Kit Tyler would have spent almost all of his schooldays up in Liverpool anyway, but what was it that Simon Askey had said about his researcher, when Tara had interviewed him? He tried to recall the recording. Hadn't he mentioned Tyler's sister had committed suicide? And that his mother had died? Had that been before the move to Liverpool?

Suddenly he felt all the hairs rise on his arms. No school here in Peverton, but Samantha Seabrook had attended one in her home village. Just the local, thanks to Sir Brian's socialist principles. Might the Peverton kids bus in to attend school in Great Sterringham?

Kit Tyler had been born bloody close to where Samantha Seabrook grew up. It was too much of coincidence. There had to be a link. What if Kit's sister had been older than him?

What if she'd been Samantha Seabrook's contemporary?

Suddenly he thought of the recording Tara had sent him of the Patsy Wentworth interview. Patsy had pointed out that Samantha had had a tough home life. Her childhood had been a mix of glamour and tragedy. Because of that she'd never got the blame, according to her school friend. 'People used to assume she'd got in with a bad lot,' she'd said. 'They never realised she *was* the bad lot.'

And then, suddenly, Tara's words at the funeral came back to him. Whoever had made the dolls had done 'a professional job'. Professional. And what had Kit told him his mother had done for a living? *Altering clothes for boys who went to the local fee-paying school.* She'd been a seamstress before she'd died, leaving Kit to be brought up by his alcoholic dad. Had she made the dolls? But why two? And if it was Kit who'd sent his mother's home-made toy to Samantha, then had he meant her to recognise it? If she and his sister had been contemporaries might she have seen it before? Had he sent her some message that, after the passing of time, she'd failed to see?

Blake pulled the car into a U-turn, back towards Great Sterringham. He needed to speak to someone from the school, but of course it was bloody August. Bang in the middle of the holidays. And if he managed to track down any of the staff, would they remember the Tyler family? It had to be twenty-odd years since they'd left the area.

But he wasn't going to wait for confirmation.

He dialled Tara's mobile. She and Tyler had both been at the memorial service. What if he was the one? What if he decided to make good his threat against Tara, out there in the middle of nowhere?

The phone rang and rang, then went to voicemail.

He'd got no proof that his theories were right, but at that moment he just knew, in his bones, that he'd hit on the answer.

He put his foot down harder and called Emma at the station. 'I need to find Kit Tyler,' he said. 'I want him brought in. Now.

We can use his mobile: triangulation or GPS. Try Tara Thorpe's phone too. They might be together.' But then he thought of how far flung all the base stations would be, out there in the sticks. Fear flared up again inside him. He pushed the worst thoughts from his mind. 'Their last known location was Great Sterringham. Put a call out. Talk to Tyler's friends and relatives. Turns out he lived in a neighbouring village when he was small. Find any place that might have had special significance for him.' How slim were their chances? Blake swore. 'Try everything, Emma – and get everyone on it.'

CHAPTER FORTY-THREE

Tara had glanced at Kit Tyler's face when she'd heard her phone ring. She'd seen his expression, just before he'd chucked the instrument out of the window. As she'd watched it bounce on the road behind them in the rear-view mirror, he'd told her to drive faster.

They were navigating one of the banks, alongside a massive drain below. All around them the land was criss-crossed with channels of water: fenland stretching as far as the eye could see.

For the most part, Tara was holding her breath, staring at the way ahead, and trying to plan without knowing what would happen next. Every so often random, disparate thoughts came to her. Now the sudden appearance of Kit outside the Copper Kettle when she'd stormed out from her meeting with Giles flashed up in her head. Why hadn't she seen through him? He'd been on his way into one of the shops on King's Parade when she'd spotted him – supposedly. But that had all been a bluff; she realised it now. He'd been following her and for once she'd taken him by surprise when she'd burst onto the street so quickly. And what had he done when they'd exchanged their pleasantries? Walked off up the road. It hadn't occurred to her at the time, but thinking back, he'd never gone into the shop at all.

'Tell me about your childhood, Tara,' Kit said, breaking into her thoughts.

He made it sounds like a challenge. She felt a cold sweat trickle down her back. 'Pretty mixed really. Like most people's.' Her teeth were chattering, though the sun was beating down outside.

'And yet,' he replied, 'you've come through it fine, haven't you?'

She thought for a second of her parents' rejection and the effect a stalker had had on her, but her mouth was too dry and her brain too muddled to articulate what was going through her head.

'I mean, you're self-sufficient. You managed to get a decent education and a good job.'

'I resigned earlier today, on principle.' Her voice shook.

'There you are,' he said. 'Would you have felt able to do that, if you'd known real hardship?'

She didn't answer. She felt numb; she knew whatever she said it wouldn't make any difference. And maybe he was right about that one, small thing.

'We analyse all this as part of our research,' Kit went on. 'People have to deal with all sorts of awful things, but nine times out of ten, that isn't what makes the difference. It's their background that wins through.' His voice was calm now, almost detached. 'There are exceptions of course. Like me. Like Simon. We've got where we are despite our heritage, but we're the tiny minority. And even when we make it through, the people we have to deal with can't see us as equals.'

He paused for a moment and she glanced at him. His eyes were on her still, her knife held ready.

'I know a lot about all this, and for the most part,' he said, 'I'd argue that your future's set in stone, thanks to the circumstances you were born into. Think of the head start you've got if your family's got money and education. Your parent dies – okay, that's hell. But if you have relations who can step in, fund you through your childhood and fight your corner, just think how much more secure you are than someone in the same situation without that backing.

'Even if your relations suddenly lose all *their* wealth, if you come from the right background, you'll likely have books in the house, nice things around you, and people who speak in a way that makes those in authority take them seriously. Once again, you're streets ahead of people who've suffered long-term deprivation.'

Tara's hands were clammy on the steering wheel. 'What you're saying makes sense. I don't see how it's given you the excuse to kill two innocent women though.'

'Innocent?' Kit's voice was like ice in the sultry air. 'None of you are innocent. Samantha Seabrook talked so much about childhood inequality, but most of the kids she claimed she wanted to help haven't had anything like a "childhood". They're in the harsh adult world from the word go.' He passed his hand over his brow. 'I had to sit there, watching her on that television programme, *Tomorrow Today*, saying how few people really understand what their poorer contemporaries go through.' He thumped the dashboard suddenly with his free hand, making Tara jump. 'There never was such a hypocrite! Samantha Seabrook was responsible for my sister's death. Let me tell you about *that*.'

CHAPTER FORTY-FOUR

Blake sat opposite the head teacher of the high school in Great Sterringham. The woman looked to be around sixty. She had lines around her eyes, and streaks of grey in her hair. He'd found her via the caretaker, whose mobile number had been on the school sign. Thank God she'd got back from her holiday in Wales the day before. She'd invited him into her front room, and he'd already refused a cup of tea.

'I'll actually be back in school again from tomorrow,' she was saying, 'getting ready for the new term.' She gave him a look. 'People don't realise the amount of admin and preparation involved, along with our day-to-day tasks.'

Blake nodded and tried to suppress his impatience. 'I'm sure. Can you tell me,' he asked, 'did you work at the school twenty years ago?'

She nodded. 'I was just an ordinary teacher then, not head of the whole place.' She smiled. 'I didn't want to move areas, so I've stayed put. It's not uncommon.'

'Do you remember a family called the Tylers?' The woman's expression clouded immediately. The chills in Blake's stomach reached a new high. He'd been half hoping he was wrong.

'Hard to forget a family in those circumstances,' she said. 'Jane Tyler was a fifth former here when her mother died. She'd always been quiet and conscientious, but at that point she withdrew into herself. None of us felt we were managing to connect with her any more. Unfortunately, others succeeded where we failed. She got in with the wrong lot. And after that…' the headmistress sighed, 'well, after that she went off the rails.'

'When you say, "the wrong lot", do you remember who it was that Jane Tyler got in with?' Blake held his breath.

The woman took off her glasses, put them down on the coffee table in front of her and rubbed damp eyes. 'Yes,' she said quietly after a moment. 'Yes, I do. It was the girl who was killed recently, Samantha Seabrook.' She sat back in her seat. 'Jane Tyler hanged herself in the end, and it struck me at the time how similar the circumstances were that she and Samantha had had to endure, yet how different the outcome. But now they're both gone.'

'Could you tell me please, what happened?' Blake said.

'Samantha had already gone wild,' the woman said. 'Her mother – well, you perhaps already know the background there, the way she died?'

Blake nodded.

'Her father, when he was around, spent most of his time trying to cope with it. It was clear to us that Samantha played up in a bid for her share of attention. She was too young to understand what her father was going through, and of course she was suffering herself. For her it was boys, drugs and petty theft all the way. She pulled another girl, Patsy Wentworth, along in her wake.'

'And then Jane Tyler became rudderless?'

The headmistress nodded. 'Exactly. I think Samantha enjoyed scooping her up and including her. Jane had been such a mousy little thing. Certainly not part of the popular set, and when Samantha paid her attention she was so vulnerable. I could see the whole thing unfolding before my eyes, but I couldn't work out how to stop it. I tried talking to Jane, but by that stage it was no good.'

'What happened then?'

The headmistress bit her lip. 'Things came to a head when Samantha, Patsy and Jane were caught shoplifting in Wisbech.

Before that, they'd only taken things from the village store, and Sir Brian had found it reasonably easy to smooth things over, because he knew the owners personally.

'He stepped in again though, and saved the day, or so he thought. The school got involved but not the police. Sir Brian gave the Wisbech shopkeeper more than enough money to restock, plus a large donation to the man's favourite charity, and the matter blew over. That is, it did for Samantha. Sir Brian always felt guilty that he wasn't giving her the attention she needed. He drew her in closer after that incident. For a while at least.'

'But it was different for Patsy and Jane?'

'Patsy was more of a classic rebel. Her parents were cross, and she was grounded. You know the sort of thing.'

Blake nodded.

'But Jane Tyler's father was a vicious drunk. We all knew that. He ruled the household with a rod of iron. He'd been brought up by a strictly religious father himself, and he regarded what Jane had done as sinful. According to her suicide note, he'd told her it would have been better if she'd died, instead of her mum.'

She was crying openly now. 'I'm sorry,' she said, 'it's so long ago, but someone ought to have been able to prevent it. I ought to have been able to.' She blew her nose. 'I went to Jane's funeral and her father's face was so cold. I'll always remember Jane's young brother standing next to Mr Tyler, looking up at him. I often wondered what kind of future he might have, but I couldn't do anything for *him* either.' Her eyes were far away and still full of tears.

'At the crematorium they didn't have the money to buy a proper urn for the ashes, so I bought them one on behalf of the school: blue with silver birds on it.' She looked at Blake. 'That was the only thing I managed to do.'

Blake was in a hurry to leave. He got up and thanked the woman. As he strode to her front door, he remembered the ornate pot he'd admired on the shelf in Kit Tyler's flat: blue, with silver birds. It had been next to a photo of a woman and her daughter, of primary school age when the shot had been taken. In that moment the image came to him clearly, and he realised the girl had been wearing blue and white school uniform.

CHAPTER FORTY-FIVE

The story Kit had told her, about his sister and her suicide, still swam in Tara's head as she drove. She'd only started stealing after she'd palled up with Samantha Seabrook. At first it had been small things, like a pound from the handbag of a visitor. His father had put that coin on the mantelpiece at home where everyone could see it. Then he'd told each guest they had what Jane Tyler had done, and that they'd have to watch out for her. He'd made her stand in the corner with her back to the room as he recounted her wrongdoings so publicly. She knew what would happen if she stood up to him. Their father had been handy with a belt.

According to Kit, after that Jane had wanted to stop stealing, but at school she could only keep Samantha's good opinion if she carried on – and that mattered. Suddenly, Jane counted for something, in her friend's eyes at least – but only for as long as she idolised Samantha. Kit had presented it as coercion. Tara had pointed out that Samantha wouldn't have known the damage she was doing. It was then that Kit had shouted, making her swerve, almost sending them off the road. He said he remembered Jane crying: torn between displeasing her father and displeasing her 'friend'.

Samantha had upped the ante and taken Jane and Patsy to a chemist's shop in Wisbech. One of several things Jane had stolen was the Rimmel lipstick Tara had seen in the professor's flat. Kit had sent it to prick her conscience. Surely she'd remember, and understand why she was being targeted? But he said she'd never mentioned it. He doubted she'd worked it out.

'I need to make a call now,' Kit said suddenly, and she was back with him again. The decisive tone in his voice made her tremble. She couldn't imagine who he needed to contact, but she was sure it meant the worse for her.

'What do you mean?'

'We're nearly there, and I need to prepare the ground. I'm calling the press, you see. They're going to witness my last murder.' Tara felt his eyes on her. 'You'll be live on TV, Tara. And this is a far better way to get my message across. I'll have the world's eyes on me when I tell my story. I want everyone to know what Samantha Seabrook did – and why she and people like her, who sail through life without even seeing how lucky they are, shouldn't be in charge of shaping the future of children who need better chances.' For a second there was a catch in his voice.

And then he made the call. She wasn't sure who'd he'd chosen to contact – a press agency maybe, to make sure his message spread as quickly as possible? She tried to swallow. Her throat was so tight.

'The press will call the police,' she said, once he'd finished. 'They'll reach us first.'

But Kit's voice was calm. 'Sure, they'll call the police, but not – I think – all that quickly. They'll want their scoop. They'll probably be in their cars and on their way before they raise the alarm. And even if the police do reach us first, they won't dare approach.' He gave a bitter laugh. 'They'll see me as a madman; a loose cannon who could kill you at any second if they make the wrong move. I'll be in control of the situation.

'Turn left here,' he said suddenly. 'This is the place.'

Ahead of her the low-lying land sparkled as sunlight hit the water that wove its way through reeds and between higher patches of ground. To her right was a deep, wide, water-filled drain, and to her left two more channels of water, cutting them off from the land beyond.

Tara's body was shaking. Adrenaline. Once she was out of the car she'd be ready to run. But there was nowhere to run *to*. They were miles from anywhere.

Ahead of her she could see a cottage, but hope died as they drew closer. Its windows were broken, and the roof was falling in.

'Stop here,' Kit said. 'Park with the driver's door hard up against the wall. I want you to follow me out of the car on the passenger side.'

She did as she was told. The way he'd arranged it meant he was waiting for her as she slithered across the two seats, the knife held ready. But even if she'd been able to dodge past him she wouldn't have known where to turn. All around flat fields stretched, intersected by water-filled drains, ditches and marshy stretches of land.

CHAPTER FORTY-SIX

Blake didn't know where to turn. He didn't want to go back to Cambridge – there was no reason Kit Tyler would make for the city. Instead, he circled the roads around Peverton, waiting for news. He kept thinking of the things Tara didn't know – like where Kit Tyler had been brought up. If he'd shared everything with her, could she have foreseen the danger? She was every bit as sharp as he was.

It felt like forever before his phone rang. Emma. He answered hands-free. 'Blake.'

'No one knows where Tyler is. Da Souza was expecting him back at the institute but no sign, and he's not at his flat. His phone's switched off. But we've got a possible lead. Next of kin's an aunt, according to Mary Mayhew – Tyler's mother's sister. We called her and she used to live out in the Fens too. She's in a flat in Wisbech now. But years ago she and her husband had a smallholding. She says how Tyler's dad used to be handy with his fists, and when they could, she and her husband used to have Kit and his sister to stay, to keep them out of harm's way for a bit. They were out in the middle of nowhere – near a hamlet called Fen Reach. It might hold sentimental value for Tyler.'

She paused. Blake was already tapping the name into his satnav.

'We looked at the coordinates of the last location that showed up using Tara Thorpe's phone, when you rang it,' Emma went on. *'It would place them on the route from Great Sterringham to Fen Reach, assuming they're together.'*

It was slim, but it fitted. Everything Kit Tyler had done had harked back to his roots: the use of the crucifix, and the dolls in his sister's school uniform. Blake felt his pulse quicken. 'Great work, Emma. Send—'

But she cut across him. *'Backup's on its way.'*

Before her words were out Blake had accelerated away from the villages and out towards the Fens, the screech of his tyres breaking the silence of the marshland.

CHAPTER FORTY-SEVEN

'Samantha didn't see what was in front of her eyes,' Kit said. 'When I first arrived at the institute, I thought having a Tyler in the very building she worked would make her wonder. But she'd long since forgotten about Jane and what she had done to her.'

Tara was out of the car now, with Kit perilously close to her, still holding her knife. It glinted in the sun. Dare she try to reason with him? He'd already flown off the handle whilst they were in the car. She remembered her fear when he'd suddenly shouted at her. But she had to try. She edged back slightly in the hope he wouldn't catch her if he lashed out. Her palms were slick with sweat. 'Kit, this makes no sense.' She could hardly get the words out, her mouth was so dry. 'I found out a lot about Samantha Seabrook. True, I looked in the wrong places, but that was because it was clear someone from the institute was involved. And for the professor herself, yes, she made your sister's life a misery, what she did was horrendous – even if she didn't understand the full effect of her actions. But I'm guessing Jane wouldn't have killed herself if your father had treated her better.' She tried to make her tone as gentle as possible. 'What you're doing isn't justice.'

'Justice?' His eyes were fiery. 'There's no justice. I'm just evening the balance.'

She could see the fury in his face. She was desperate to calm him, or he'd do for her in a moment of passion instead of waiting for the press as he intended.

Her mind went blank for a second. At last she came up with a question. 'What about the necklace that was found on Professor Seabrook's body?' she said.

Kit paused for a moment. 'I had it with me, and I made her put it on when I let her up for air. I was stronger than she was. In every way. I had her by the hair, from behind, pinned against the fountain wall. I think she thought if she did what I said I might let her go.' He laughed. 'As if. The crucifix belonged to my sister. My father gave it to her at her confirmation. Samantha didn't recognise that either, even though Jane always wore it. But she knew the significance by the time she died. I explained everything bit by bit, each time I allowed her up from the water.'

Tara heard his voice slow as he reached the end of his sentence. She felt as though she could hardly breathe and again her mind went blank. She must think. 'What about Chiara?' she said after a moment.

'I wasn't going to kill her at first, but can you imagine what it was like? I had to listen to her day after day, criticising Samantha, when she came from exactly the same mould. She wasn't even a good academic, and yet there she was, sailing along, thanks to her rich papa throwing his weight around. I went and knocked on her door after the party. I thought I'd play it by ear, see how it went. By the time we were out on the common I couldn't wait to shut her up. I was evening up the balance again.'

'And I'm next on your list.' Tara was determined not to cry. She channelled all her determination into her voice.

'You are,' Kit said. 'Partly because you failed to find out the truth, and partly because you've been helped on your way, just as Samantha and Chiara were. But most of all, because you can help me get my message across.' His eyes had been hard – shuttered – but now they held some emotion. 'I'm glad I've come back here to do the job,' he said. 'It's the only place Jane was ever happy. I can remember her playing with me out in the garden of my aunt's cottage.' He nodded towards the derelict house. 'She used to laugh once.' His eyes met hers and she saw the determination in them. 'Her luck ran out. And so, as you can see, did my uncle and aunt's. None of this is a coincidence. I'm intervening now, so people pay attention to what happened to us all – to achieve change, so it's different for others in future. My work today will get far more attention than a lifetime's research at the institute. You've got until the press arrive, Tara. Once the cameras are rolling I'll use your knife to finish things. It won't be long now.'

He was right beside her, his free hand gripping her arm. She could feel his breath on her neck.

'Do you know what my sister did, just before she hanged herself?' he asked. 'She cleaned the whole house. She left it spotless. I can still remember the smell of bleach. My father noticed any mark we made – anything that was out of place. She must have wanted to avoid his disapproval, even when she was beyond his reach. Or maybe she just wanted to do that one last thing for us, before she took herself off. Can you imagine a childhood like that?'

Tara listened for emotion in his voice, but she could hear only iron. He'd gone beyond sorrow now; there was just an absolute determination to hit back at a world that had caused him so much pain.

'When I came home that day with my father he let me go ahead and find her body, even though he'd guessed what she'd done. And then he told me I ought to have guessed too. And that it was for the best. He was glad to be rid of such a sinful girl. He—'

He broke off suddenly. They'd both heard it. Very faint and distant. The sound of a siren. Kit knew how to handle the situation – even if the police reached them before the press – but it was clear he hadn't thought they actually would. And for that one instant, Tara knew his focus wasn't entirely on her.

CHAPTER FORTY-EIGHT

Tara had a split-second to react. Instinct took over and she jerked sideways. The knife's point grazed her arm as she yanked free of his grip. She didn't stop to fight. She knew her self-defence, but he was armed.

Instead she ran, kicking off her shoes as she went. She flung a look left and right as she fled, her eyes flying over the landscape. Her options were almost non-existent. The road was long and straight. There was no way of escape in sight. Could she outrun him? Who would fail first? He was fit. He'd climbed that college wall. Maybe he'd got into scrapes as a kid in Liverpool. He could probably handle himself...

She gasped for breath and stumbled on as her foot struck a sharp stone. Her heart was lurching, her chest aching.

Had the siren even been for them? Or had it been a coincidence? She snatched a glance over her shoulder. Kit was hard on her heels and her feet were being shredded by the tarmac. She couldn't see anyone ahead. He would easily outpace her if she carried on.

Her other choice was to run into the fields. But it wouldn't be long before she came to one of the deep, water-filled drains. She looked left and right, trying to see if there might be bridges to help her escape, but there were none. She was approaching one of the drains on her left, which sank below the level of the field next to it.

She only had a split second to decide. Her feet couldn't take the road. She stumbled off into the field, tripping between the crop stubble and furrows, kicking up the black, peaty soil. The cereal stalks, dry and cut short, stuck into her soles, hurting her as much as the tarmac had. Within a moment she was on the bank that bordered the drain, and then going over the edge, skidding down towards the dark water.

Just before she lost sight of the field she risked glancing over her shoulder for a fraction of a second.

Kit was horribly close.

She was faced with a narrow stretch of uneven mud and reeds to either side of her, running right next to the drain. If she took that route she'd probably fall into its watery depths before she made it very far. And the drain went on for miles: dead straight. Her only other option was to swim for it. The channel of water wasn't that wide, and she could already hear Kit behind her. She knew he could run and climb. She could only hope he wasn't great at swimming. There was no way she could escape him quickly enough if she tried to scramble back up the bank again.

She jumped into the drain.

The sun had been beating down all day, but nothing prepared her for how cold the water would be. She was gasping for breath, her arms and legs flailing as she tried to recover from the shock. Just as she managed to take a stroke, she heard a splash. Kit was in the water with her.

She took a great lungful of air, but it was hard to get the oxygen in: panic, the freezing temperature and the exertion were making her feel light-headed.

And then she felt a hand grip her ankle. She went under, the water swirling in her ears, reaching down her throat, blocking her nose. With every ounce of strength she had she kicked out, and felt the kick hit home. Her foot was free again, but she was spluttering, coughing up water. She took another stroke and ahead of her she could see the far bank: tufts of green grass and solid black mud.

But then the hand came again, firmer this time, grasping her leg.

CHAPTER FORTY-NINE

Blake drove like a maniac, but there were police cars ahead of him, blocking the way down the narrow lane surrounded by fenland.

He got out and ran, hurtling across the black fields, following the officers ahead of him. Someone had called an ambulance. It was stuck at a distance, still on the roadway. He could see some press, too, running with their cameras. And someone with a microphone? How the hell had they heard what was going on?

He reached the top of the bank and stared down into the drain. In front of him, an officer was in the water grappling with Kit Tyler. More were jumping in after him. He looked for Tara. She was nowhere to be seen. She had to be under the water.

He looked right and left. His gaze skittered feverishly back and forth over the surface of the dark depths. The scene was one of utter confusion, heads bobbing, arms flailing and the water swirling. At last he thought he caught a glimpse of Tara's hair; red-gold strands in the water like exotic seaweed.

'She's there!' he shouted, and in that moment, an officer turned and spotted her. Blake was in the water in half a second, ploughing towards the spot where he'd seen her body. He was fast, but the other guy was closer. Blake was just feet away when he saw the man heave her lifeless body up onto the far bank of the drain.

CHAPTER FIFTY

The following day in hospital, Tara was still unclear about exactly what had happened after Kit Tyler tried to drown her in the drain. Apparently she'd blacked out and had been given CPR at the scene – but by whom? She didn't remember anything after Kit had grabbed her leg that second time.

She'd already had a series of visitors, including Bea, who'd arrived first and fussed over her just as she had when she'd minded Tara as a child. Bea's husband, Greg, had come too, and been a calming influence. Her mother had also visited, causing a stir amongst the nursing staff, several of whom had asked for her autograph.

Tara hadn't been entirely honest with any of them about the threat she'd known she'd been under, and Bea had looked suspicious. Matt, her ex-partner in crime from *Not Now* magazine had also been in. He'd sworn he wasn't after an exclusive and that Giles didn't know he was there. The news had made the press though. Even Kemp had seen the reports of her narrow escape. *That was a close shave, mate*, he'd texted. *I would have come back if I'd realised you were dealing with such a nutter. Still, I might have known you had it covered.*

Hmm. The press had played up her attempted escape, making her sound as though she'd taken control quickly and decisively. She was glad her reputation was intact, but in no way had she 'had it covered'. It had been Blake and his team who'd saved the day. He'd found evidence Kit might be involved in the murders on his way back from Samantha Seabrook's memorial service. It had been Emma who'd got a lead on where Kit might have taken Tara, and then Blake had called in the cavalry. He'd arrived at the scene just as the posse of journalists Kit had rallied had turned up, but the police reinforcements he and Emma had summoned had beaten them all to it.

And then Blake had spotted her in the water. He had saved her life. He'd kept his promise about improving her opinion of the force.

He'd left her a message saying he'd see her soon, but so far it had only been other officers – the slimy Patrick Wilkins amongst them – who'd come to interview her.

CHAPTER FIFTY-ONE

Whilst Patrick Wilkins rushed around with various detective constables, gathering more evidence for the court case that would come, Blake and Emma were questioning Kit Tyler.

Tyler's grief for his sister and hatred for Samantha Seabrook had come across loud and clear – as had his motive for involving Tara: a desire for the world to know what had happened, and the underlying causes as he saw them. But the papers were telling a very different story today from the one he'd envisaged. The coverage was all focused on the dramatic chase across the Fens and Tara's escape. And when it came down to it, the history of what had happened back then was tragic, but not entirely of Professor Seabrook's making. Lots of kids went through wild times and egged each other on. Lots of kids came through the other side – more or less. The professor hadn't intended to make Jane Tyler's life hell.

He put this point to Tyler.

The man's eyes were a mixture of fire and ice. 'Samantha Seabrook was one of the brightest people I ever met. She might not have anticipated what would happen in advance, but what about when my sister committed suicide? The guilt from that ought to have hung around her neck like a millstone for life. But she threw it off. By the time I went to work at the institute, the name Tyler meant nothing. She didn't recognised the lipstick I sent her – which she bullied my sister into stealing – or the doll either.'

The doll. A minor matter in the grand scheme of things, but a mystery he wanted to clear up. 'What was the background to the dolls?'

Kit slumped forward suddenly, and put his head in his hands. 'My mother made them for Jane,' he said, his words muffled, his mouth half-covered by his upturned palms. 'They were meant to look like her – the same long, dark hair and her primary school uniform.' His voice shook – whether from sorrow or anger, Blake wasn't sure. 'I put a noose around the necks of the ones I sent to Samantha and Tara Thorpe, because that's how Jane killed herself. Yet still Samantha didn't make the connection.'

Blake remembered again the little girl with the older woman in the photo in Kit Tyler's flat.

'My mother made three dolls in total. She was a good seamstress, but she held herself to high standards. The first two weren't quite perfect.'

Blake thought of the uneven legs Tara had mentioned on the doll she'd been sent. He didn't recall any imperfection on the one sent to Professor Seabrook, but his rag doll standards weren't very exacting.

'She gave the best doll to my sister when she was small,' Tyler went on, 'but Jane still had it when she and Samantha palled up. Samantha would have seen it. Jane used to keep it on her bed.' Blake could hear the tears in his voice now. 'She'd still cuddle it at night, even though she was fifteen. She was heartbroken when our mum died, and the doll represented her love. It was only after Jane committed suicide that I got all three dolls.'

What a mess. So much tragedy, and more than one childhood spiralling out of control, moving towards disaster.

'You didn't give the third doll to Chiara Laurito.'

He shook his head, which was still down in his hands. 'Chiara was never part of the original plan. I just saw red when she was sounding off at the garden party about how reasonable it was that her father should smooth her way in life.' And now he looked up. His eyes – red and damp – met Blake's. 'But I'd never have given away the doll that was Jane's, anyway. It means too much to me.'

Blake nodded.

'Going back to the first murder, where did you learn how to climb?'

Kit sighed. 'Back in Liverpool, and in an unconventional way. I got into scrapes as a teenager, just like Samantha did. I never got caught, though. I became expert at running fast, and scaling anything that blocked my escape route when someone I'd wronged was on my tail. I never joined any clubs but I'd test myself each time I saw a climb that looked challenging.'

'And you discovered Samantha had the same passion?'

He nodded. 'I'd browsed the web, looking for good places to try, and found her secret Instagram account. There were various photos – as well as some gossip in the climbing community – that made me think it was hers. And it was her all over, anyway – attention-seeking and self-satisfied.' His fists were clenched tight. 'Ever since I'd arrived in Cambridge I'd been trying to work out how to make her see what she'd done to Jane. And suddenly here was a way. I'd heard about someone else managing to climb their way into the fellows' garden at St Bede's. They said how beautiful it was once they'd got inside, with its fountain in the moonlight. So I made my plan, and of course Samantha was all for it, and she *loved* the idea of making the whole adventure a secret. I knew she would. She thrived on attention and keeping everyone guessing ensured she had it.'

He stared into Blake's eyes. 'You can see what she was like, Inspector. The world needs to change. It shouldn't produce people like her.'

And then Blake remembered Kit's words, the very first time he'd interviewed him. He'd said he was 'in the right place to bring about change…' He could see what he'd meant now. He'd been close to Samantha Seabrook; ready to make his move when the time was right. Blake shivered.

'Tara Thorpe is just the same too,' Tyler went on. 'Her mother used her fame to make *Not Now* popular. Her product placement put Tara in the magazine's good books, and on the back of that she got her current job. It would have been fitting to have her help me get my message across.'

His tone was harsh; full of angry regret at a lost opportunity. Blake felt himself rise in his seat – in a move beyond his control – and then Emma's hand on his arm.

'We need to ask you about the times you followed Tara,' his DS said, as Blake sat back down.

Gradually they got the details. The night Tyler had tailed Tara by bike from Samantha Seabrook's old apartment had played out much as Blake had thought. Tara had stopped to eat close to the institute before heading off for the evening and Tyler had spotted her. He'd then followed her and hung around outside Samantha Seabrook's apartment until she reappeared. He'd had the balaclava in his panier. He wore it sometimes in winter, and had chucked it in there in case it proved useful. He'd spent a lot of time recently trying not to be seen.

Frightening her then, and when he'd left the note in her bike basket, had been his way of focusing her mind, he said. He wanted her to know she needed to get on with the job he'd given her.

'Why did you leave her in the dark?' Emma said. 'You could have told her where to look, if you wanted her to help publicise what went on between the professor and your sister.'

'That was the whole point,' Kit said, as though Emma was unforgivably stupid. 'It was a test. A test for Tara, as a representative of the press and society, to see if someone from the mainstream would look in the right direction. I wanted her to do it on her own: prove she could see beyond Samantha's glamour and her reputation to the little people she'd trodden underfoot before she got where she was.'

He'd admitted he'd been following Tara on other occasions too – and that she'd even caught him at it when she'd dashed out of the Copper Kettle on King's Parade unexpectedly on Saturday. He'd been wired after killing Chiara – unable to settle – so he'd hovered around all day, observing the crime scene from a distance. He'd been in amongst the trees on Stourbridge Common, near the cattle grid leading to Oyster Row, when he'd seen Tara approach her cottage, stop, answer her phone, then turn and cycle back towards town. He'd been curious and had cut round to Riverside to see if he could see where she was headed. After that he'd kept an eye on her until she'd caught him at it. He'd used the opportunity to chat her up. He knew that, sooner or later, he'd need to get her on her own if she failed in her task and he decided to kill her.

His tone had been matter-of-fact.

And then he'd gone back to his flat where, shortly afterwards, Blake and Emma had interviewed him. It made Blake full of pent-up anger to think how little they'd guessed at that point.

Tyler denied following Tara by car the day she'd visited her mother. It must have been someone else in a green car, on her tail by coincidence. And of course, she'd always said it might have just been paranoia…

CHAPTER FIFTY-TWO

Five days after her release from hospital, Tara was back in the Champion of Thames, opposite Blake himself. Now that the case was going to court, he'd shared more things with her, including what Kit Tyler had said at his interview.

He was off duty, and had a whisky in front of him as large as her vodka. She raised her glass and he followed suit, holding his to hers.

'So, thanks again for the small part you played in saving my life.' She gave him a look. 'You know, what with the clue solving and spotting me in the water and everything.'

'Teamwork.' He swigged his drink. 'We'd all been throwing bits of the jigsaw down onto the table, and then we saw the pattern. You commenting on how professionally the dolls were made, just before I drove through Kit Tyler's childhood village – where he'd lived with his seamstress mother – made something slot into place.'

'Bloody glad it did.' She hadn't known Mrs Tyler's profession.

'You and me both.'

She met his gaze.

'I keep replaying the clues Kit Tyler dangled in front of me,' Blake said. 'He told me he was born locally, before moving away. And that he came to the institute *specifically because* Samantha Seabrook worked there. He was clever – each time he fed me a titbit like that he was waiting to see if the penny dropped. I suppose he was testing me too. If I'd seen through him before he got to Chiara…'

She took a large slug of her drink. She could see the anguish in his eyes. 'It wasn't just you,' she said. 'He told me he came to Cambridge for the professor too. But the clues he left for us were pretty tenuous really. What happened in his life had consumed him for years, so the lipstick he sent Samantha Seabrook and his sister's old doll seemed like sirens to him. Absolutely un-ignorable. But to everyone else they were part of a cacophony of noise that life makes as it careers along.'

Blake looked at her for a long moment, but then he nodded. 'But I almost got blinkered too – just like the lead officer on your stalking case. I was convinced for a while that Askey was our man.'

Tara nodded. She'd thought the same.

'Have you heard the latest about him?' Blake asked.

'No. What?'

'His wife's expecting again. They had a minor scare, which meant a trip to Addenbrooke's. That's why he didn't show for Samantha Seabrook's memorial service. But apparently the scan showed all's well, according to Professor da Souza.'

Tara shook her head. 'And I expect if we ask after him this time next year he'll be Professor Askey, rather than doctor, too.'

Blake nodded and gave her a wry smile. 'Sadly, shit does tend to float.' But then his face became serious again. 'If I'd told you everything I knew, do you think you'd have worked out what Kit Tyler was up to before he abducted you?' His eyes were dark.

She'd thought about that a lot as they'd talked. She would have been better prepared if he'd at least tried to fill her in. There was a chance she might have seen the truth. But this wasn't the time to make him feel bad about it. She understood why he'd held back, and he *had* saved her life. It was just as well he was a good detective…

So she shook her head and changed the subject. 'I've quit my job, by the way.'

He raised an eyebrow.

'I couldn't stand my editor any more,' she said. 'But I'll try to sell the story to another outlet. I need the money, and it will be worth it just to annoy him, too.'

Blake gave her a half-smile. 'I like your style. Though I guess he might try to make things hard for you.'

'I suspect you're right, but let's not think about him.' She'd enjoy the challenge of beating Giles over the long term.

Blake nodded. 'Fair enough.'

Suddenly, she realised she envied him. He was still beating himself up – wishing he'd solved the case more quickly – but at least his conscience must be clear when it came to what he'd been aiming for. Whereas hers was always compromised because the desires of her media bosses were anything but pure. *Maybe if I worked for better publications…* But there were only so many of those jobs to go around.

Her mind drifted yet again to the privileged knowledge the police had access to. She'd never found out the truth about Bella Seabrook, Samantha's mother.

She mentioned it to Blake. 'Can you tell me, if I swear not to pass it on to anyone?'

He put his head on one side and paused for a long moment. 'If it was anyone else but you,' he said at last, and she felt something warm spark up inside her. 'All right then. Bella Seabrook had a drink problem and it wore the family down. Samantha in particular thought that her father's focus was always on Bella, and that no one cared about her. Eventually, she started to make her feelings felt. She'd pick fights with her mother, Sir Brian said.

'On the night Bella died, she and Samantha were up on the galleried landing at the family home. Samantha hurled abuse at her mother in response to what she saw as her bad behaviour. But it was a dangerous move. Sir Brian said Bella was completely out of control that night. She rushed at Samantha with an empty cut-glass decanter in her hand.

'Sir Brian said he arrived on the scene just as it happened. Samantha was standing with her back to the low bannisters, her mother running at her full tilt. He only had a moment to take stock of the situation. He pulled his daughter out of the way, to stop Bella knocking her over the railings onto the hall tiles below. But Bella was tall and unbalanced after all she'd drunk. She went straight over the bannister herself, and landed head-first on the floor below. It's clear Sir Brian feels he was responsible for his wife's death; but equally that if he hadn't acted, he might have lost his daughter.' Blake shook his head. 'I can only imagine Samantha must have carried that guilt with her, too.'

She'd wanted to know, ever since she'd first read the 'died in an accident' explanation, but now she wished she hadn't asked. Kit Tyler was right: the world was an unequal place, and action ought to be taken so that no one had to suffer like Jane had suffered. What she'd gone through was appalling. But he'd been wrong to allot so much of the responsibility to Samantha. She was a product of her background just as much as anyone else, and she'd had a horrible time too. It couldn't have been easy, growing up with an alcoholic mother, then watching her die as a result of a fight you'd chosen to pick. It had been a lot to deal with for a fifteen-year-old – that uneasy stage between child and adulthood. A time when you could make decisions that would affect your whole life, without having the maturity to fully understand your actions.

'You can see why Sir Brian wanted to avoid the publicity,' Blake said.

'You can.' She closed her eyes for a moment. 'Speaking of bad publicity, I suppose I won't be able to keep it quiet that Kit Tyler used my own knife to force me to drive into the Fens?'

Blake shook his head. 'Probably not. He had his own weapon too though. I guess using yours amused him. And yours was a bigger beast.'

Great.

They drank in silence, and Tara was aware of Blake's eyes on her again. It was evening time and he was wearing one of his well-cut jackets over a crisp white shirt, open at the neck, and dark trousers.

He leant towards her and she found herself responding in kind.

'There aren't many people like you around, Tara,' he said, and for a second his warm hand rested on her bare arm.

'Probably just as well.' She tried to laugh, but a shiver ran over her and she felt her heart rate increase.

'I…' he looked down at his half-empty glass for a moment and pulled back. 'I wanted to mention – well just to say…'

It wasn't like him to hesitate.

'I wanted to say, I've really enjoyed working with you on this case, and the time we've spent together.'

Blake was still only inches from her. She felt something flutter inside her chest and looked up at him.

But then suddenly, there was a new look in Blake's eyes. And for a second, his focus was on the table in front of them, rather than on her. 'My wife and I have been having difficulties,' he said. There was a long pause. 'But we're talking about giving it another go.' He looked as though he was asking something of her. *Understanding?* 'It's odd timing.'

She felt something sink inside her. 'What happened?' Why had she asked? It was none of her business, but she couldn't think what else to say.

'It's – well, it's complicated. A story for another day, perhaps.'

'Of course.' The story of Tara's life. Complicated.

She jacked up a smile and took in his eyes, and that dark stubble. He had the killer combination of scruffy and smart she had such a weakness for. 'I hope it works out,' she said, wondering if she'd managed to hide her feelings. Why the hell had she thought he was going to ask her out? It wasn't as though he'd ever done anything to suggest he might.

'Thanks.' He looked away for a moment, then turned back and downed the rest of his whisky. He got up from the stool he'd been sitting on and stood close to her chair. *Hell.* Even the lines around his eyes were attractive. 'I'll see you before the court case anyway.'

He put his hand on her shoulder for a moment. She had the urge to cover it with hers, but instead, she just nodded. A look passed between them and then she watched as he turned and walked over to the pub door, out into the sunshine.

Back at home Tara looked again at the reply Kemp had sent to her message, telling him she'd resigned from her job. He'd emailed it before the one in response to her near-death experience.

Your email made me laugh. The idea of you as a cop! You'd never wear being told what to do, or working in a team. Imagine it. You're too like me – a lone wolf. (I mean that in a good way, obviously. I don't regret leaving the force.) They'd benefit from your investigative skills though. Joking apart, it's just as well that's not the career change you want. I don't think you'd find it easy to get in, after what you did to that journalist. The circumstances have to be pretty exceptional for them to overlook that kind of history.

His message stung. If Tara put her mind to it she could do it. If she needed to fit in, she'd fit. She was disciplined. Hadn't Kemp realised that? She paced around the cottage's sitting room. She'd only sent the damned message to Kemp as a joke in the first place. What was his problem?

He doubted her, that was the truth.

But then she pulled herself up short and realisation swept over her. One short week ago she'd have agreed with Kemp 100 per cent. She had the wrong temperament for a job with the police, and she would never work for them anyway; not after the way they'd let her down.

But over the course of the Seabrook case she'd come to admire Blake and his methods. And at the same time, she'd had cause to re-examine her own work; to wonder how it might feel to use her investigative skills to a different end.

And then Blake had jokingly floated the idea of her switching careers… though she'd laughed pretty heartily at the time, the idea had started to take root.

For a second, her mind went back to what Blake had told her in the pub. Kit Tyler had confessed to following her on several occasions over the course of the case, but not when she'd driven to her mother's. Had the car she'd spotted on her tail gone the entire distance with her by coincidence? Or was there more to it?

Until the stalker from her teens was caught, she'd always live with bated breath; with that feeling that life was precarious. If she joined the police, she might even be able to access her old case files; see if she could succeed where the lead officer had failed…

Even as her heart rate increased at the prospect, her insides sank. Applying for a job that involved contact with Blake might not be the best idea. But anything she did would involve two years in uniform first, she knew that much. And there was no reason she had to be in Cambridge. She could let her cottage out. She needed a fresh start; she was finished with being used by people like Giles.

Ten minutes later, a large glass of red in her hand, she started to google entry rules for police officers. It looked as though they *might* let her in – even after her assault – if the circumstances had been exceptional. And they had been.

She made a note of who to contact.

Up yours, Kemp, she thought, smiling, as she closed her laptop lid an hour later. *We're not alike at all.*

A LETTER FROM CLARE

Thank you so much for reading *Murder on the Marshes*. I do hope you enjoyed it as much as I liked writing it. If you'd like to keep up to date with all of my latest releases, you can sign up at the following link. Your email address will never be shared, and you can unsubscribe at any time.

www.bookouture.com/clare-chase

My idea for this book came to me on a train journey to London; public transport is great for people watching (and it saves me from listening at keyholes…!). The interactions I overheard between parents and their offspring got me thinking about how childhood experiences can affect a person later, sometimes in unpredictable ways. After I'd finished worrying about the effect I might be having on my own kids, the idea for this story started to emerge. As ever, the seeds of the plot developed against a Cambridge backdrop. It's my home city and inspires me in all sorts of ways. In this case, its high-achieving, pressure-cooker atmosphere was important to elements of my story.

If you have time, I'd love it if you were able to write a review of *Murder on the Marshes*. Feedback is incredibly useful, and it also makes a huge difference in helping new readers discover my books for the first time.

Alternatively, if you'd like to contact me personally, you can reach me via my website, Facebook page, Twitter or Instagram. I love hearing from readers.

Again, thank you so much for deciding to spend some time reading *Murder on the Marshes*. I'm looking forward to sharing my next book with you very soon.

With all best wishes,
Clare x

 www.clarechase.com

 @ClareChaseAuthor

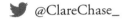 @ClareChase_

AUTHOR'S NOTE

Murder on the Marshes is set in Cambridge, and I've tried to remain generally true to the city's streets, architecture and open spaces. However, locals will notice I've taken a few liberties, in particular by adding a fictitious college or two, and giving Tara Thorpe a house on Stourbridge Common, where none exists. The villages outside Cambridge are entirely made up.

Although I have worked for the University of Cambridge – and one of its colleges – none of the characters in this book is based on any real person, living or dead. The people I met in the course of my job were some of the nicest I've known, and therefore unsuitable for inclusion in a murder mystery!

ACKNOWLEDGEMENTS

I'd like to begin with huge thanks as ever to my beloved family, Charlie, George and Ros, as well as to my wonderful parents, Penny and Mike – and also to Phil and Jenny, David and Pat, Helen, and my tremendously supportive wider family and friends. Special thanks too to my lovely colleagues at the RSC and to the Westfield gang, as well as to Andrea, Shelly, Mark, Hilary, Margaret and Ange.

I'd also like to say how much I appreciate the writer friends I've made both in real life and online – I really enjoy being part of such a friendly and supportive group. Most recently, I've been introduced to my fellow Bookouture authors, who are a fantastic bunch. I'm hugely grateful to them for making me feel so welcome.

Thanks as well to the wonderful book bloggers I've got to know, whose generosity, kindness and enthusiasm has been amazing.

I'm also hugely grateful to my readers. Getting messages via my website, Twitter and Facebook page is truly special.

And last, but definitely not least, I would like to thank everyone at Bookouture. I'm so grateful to my amazing editor Kathryn Taussig, whose ideas, advice and encouragement have been second to none, as well as to Maisie Lawrence, whose input has also been fantastic. I'd like to relay heartfelt thanks to Peta Nightingale for her encouragement when I first submitted work to Bookouture; it meant a lot. And massive thanks too, to the human dynamos, Kim Nash and Noelle Holten, who do the most incredible amount to promote our books! I also much appreciate the regular updates from Peta, and also Oliver Rhodes; it's great to feel so involved with Bookouture's plans and developments. This is my first book for the company, and I know there are many more people I've yet to connect with – I'd like to pass on thanks to them too.